DRAGON'S
FIRE

ANNE McCAFFREY
TODD McCAFFREY

DRAGON'S FIRE

A NEW NOVEL OF
PERN

BALLANTINE BOOKS • NEW YORK

2007 Del Rey Mass Market Edition

Copyright © 2006 by Anne McCaffrey and Todd J. McCaffrey
Excerpt from *Dragon Harper* copyright © 2007 by Anne McCaffrey and Todd J. McCaffrey

Published in the United States by Del Rey Books, an imprint of The Random House Publishing Group, a division of Random House, Inc., New York.

DEL REY is a registered trademark and the Del Rey colophon is a trademark of Random House, Inc.

Originally published in hardcover in the United States by Del Rey Books, an imprint of The Random House Publishing Group, a division of Random House, Inc., in 2006.

ISBN 978-0-345-48029-3

Printed in the United States of America

www.delreybooks.com

OPM 9 8 7 6 5 4 3 2 1

This book is lovingly dedicated to
David Gerrold.

Contents

Contents

Dramatis Personae

AT CAMP NATALON
Cristov, son of Tarik
Natalon, Masterminer
Tarik, Natalon's uncle, a miner
Kindan, son of Danil the wher-handler

AT THE HARPER HALL
Murenny, Masterharper
Zist, Masterharper
Cayla, Zist's wife
Pellar, adopted son of Zist and Cayla

AT CROM HOLD
Fenner, Lord Holder

CHILDREN OF THE SHUNNED
Halla, a young girl
Tenim, a young lad

AT HIGH REACHES WEYR
D'vin, wingleader, bronze Hurth
Sonia, daughter of the Weyr Healer

BOOK ONE

Pellar

Dragon's heart,
Dragon's fire,
Rider true,
Fly higher.

Prologue

HARPER HALL,
SECOND INTERVAL,
AFTER LANDING (AL) 483.7

"WHY DOES HE have to live in a cave?" Cayla muttered rebelliously as she and Zist waited impatiently outside.

"He was a dragonrider, perhaps it feels more home-like," Zist said soothingly.

"He's a healer, too, so why isn't he down with the other healers?" Cayla retorted. Zist knew she was just showing her nerves.

"He's the best one for the boy," he told her, answering her unvoiced question.

"Because he's half-mad?" Cayla asked, her voice seething with all the protectiveness of an adoptive mother. "And what's he going to find out? Pellar's barely turned three."

"Nothing, if you keep on like that," a voice responded tetchily from the cave. Cayla shut her mouth with a snap, cheeks turning bright red. Zist shot her a not-quite-consoling look. He was too wise to Cayla's ways to give her any look of superiority. Anyway, he knew full well that Cayla understood him well enough to know that *he* wasn't all that sure about consulting with the ex-dragonrider healer.

Cayla glared at Zist and resumed her quiet pacing outside the cave.

"Don't block the light," Mikal called again from the cave, causing Cayla to twitch once and stand still as stone.

Inside the cave, Mikal squatted on the hard floor opposite the child. He held up a piece of glass so that it caught the rays of the morning sun. The glass was three-sided and the light broke into a brilliant rainbow lighting the far side of the cave.

Pellar's eyes gleamed with amazement and his mouth made a big "O" of excitement, but no noise came from his throat.

Nodding to himself, Mikal smiled at Pellar, then drew a number of colored beads from his tunic pocket and spread them out in front of Pellar.

Pellar picked them up and noted their colors: red, orange, blue, green, yellow. He looked up at the rainbow and down at the beads again. In short order he arranged them to match the rainbow in front of him and clapped his hands together excitedly.

"Good," Mikal told him. He held up a finger with one hand and turned so that he could grab some supplies from a low cupboard. Pellar tried to peer around the man's body to see what he was doing.

When Mikal turned back, he noticed the boy's intent look and smiled at him. Mikal placed three small pots of paint down in between himself and Pellar. He raised his still-upright finger somewhat higher, arched his eyebrow, and made his finger dive into one of the open pots as if it were the head and neck of a flying creature. Pellar smiled and his eyes danced at the ex-dragonrider's antics. Mikal's finger zoomed up out of the pot with a small dab of yellow paint. Still holding his finger upright, Mikal nodded encouragingly to Pellar.

Pellar smiled and raised the same finger on his own hand. Mikal nodded again. Gleefully, Pellar thrust his finger into a different pot and zoomed it up again, his fingertip bright with thick red paint.

Silently, Mikal ran his finger over the ground, leaving a yellow snake on the white stone floor of the cave. Pellar imitated him, leaving a red snake on the floor. Mikal held up another finger and daubed up a bit of Pellar's red paint. Pellar gave him a hurt look but Mikal shook his head and held the red-daubed finger up for patience. With a grin, Mikal rubbed his red-tipped finger over part of his yellow snake, creating an orange blob. Pellar saw the color change and, with little encouragement from Mikal, picked up a trace of Mikal's yellow and rubbed it on his red snake to create a duplicate orange spot.

In short order, Mikal introduced blue paint from the third pot and showed the child how to make purple and green by combining blue with red and yellow.

"Can you draw me a picture of yourself?" Mikal asked. "Use any color."

Inspired, Pellar produced a multicolored self-portrait in the way of all those who had only three Turns on Pern, exactly the same way that those who were only three years old back on long-forgotten Earth would have done—complete with arms sticking out of heads. The mouth in the big round head was upturned and smiling.

"Great! Could you draw me, too?" Mikal asked.

Pellar happily complied.

"I see my mouth is pointing down," Mikal remarked of the finished drawing. "Are you saying I'm sad?"

Pellar nodded.

"Why is that?" Mikal asked. In response, Pellar combined all three colors onto one fingertip and drew a

brown shape—a long, sinewy line crossed by another
gull-shaped line.

"Zist, get in here!" Mikal called. Harper Zist raced
inside, looking back and forth from Pellar to Mikal.
"Did you tell him I was a dragonrider?"

"It may have come up," Zist admitted.

"Did you tell him the color of my dragon?" Mikal
pointed to one drawing.

"No, I don't think so," Zist said, examining the
drawing himself. "Come to think of it, I don't think I
ever knew myself."

"Mmm," Mikal grunted. He looked at Pellar and
pointed at the drawing. "Is that my dragon?"

Pellar nodded, eyes sad.

"How did you know what color to paint it?" Mikal
asked.

Pellar raised a paint-covered finger and gently
pointed at Mikal's eyes.

"I want the boy to train with me," Mikal told Zist.
"Healing, painting, tracking, meditation—I'll teach him
everything I know."

Sent from hold, sent from craft,
Whether old, whether daft.
Shunned for good into the wild—
Father, mother, baby child.

Chapter One

"HE'S STILL WAVING, isn't he?" Master Zist called back for the third time. He sat at the front of the wagon as it slowly drew away from the Harper Hall. The last of the winter snow covered the fields on either side of the track. Every now and then the wagon skidded as the workbeast lost his footing on the hard-packed icy snow and struggled to regain it.

"Yes, he is," Cayla agreed, looking back out of the brightly painted wagon at the small figure slowly diminishing in the distance.

"We couldn't bring him," Zist said regretfully. "He'd be too obvious."

At least, Zist thought to himself, the lad was taking it better than he had when they'd first told him their plans.

Pellar had thrown a silent tantrum, had sprawled on the ground in the Harper Hall's courtyard, feet and fists hitting the ground in his outrage. He stopped only when Carissa had started howling in sympathy with him.

"She's crying for me, isn't she?" he scrawled quickly on the slate that was never far from his hands.

"Yes, I suppose she is," Cayla answered.

Pellar swiftly rubbed his slate clean and scrawled a new comment on it, thrusting it under Zist's eyes. "Are you taking her?"

"We have to, she's still nursing."

"We want to know that you're safe, here," Cayla added.

"Aren't I part of your family?" Pellar scrawled in response, tears streaming down his face.

"Of course you are!" Zist declared vociferously. "And we need you, as a member of our family, to stay here out of trouble."

"You are always part of our family, Pellar," Cayla said firmly.

"You've been part of our family since we first found you, ten Turns ago," Zist told him.

"Then why can't I come?" Pellar scrawled on his slate, his mouth working soundlessly in emphasis.

"Because we don't know who abandoned you," Zist told him, catching Pellar's chin in his hand and forcing the youngster to meet his eyes. "It could be some who were Shunned. If you come with us and they see you, they'll know that we're not Shunned."

"You could get in trouble then?" Pellar wrote. Zist nodded. Pellar chewed his lip miserably, shoulders shaking so hard with his unvoiced sobs that he could barely wipe his slate to write a new message. "I'll stay. No trouble for you."

Cayla read the note, thrust baby Carissa into Zist's arms, and grabbed Pellar into a firm and fierce hug.

"That's my boy," she said proudly, kissing the top of his head.

"I'll be here when you get back," Pellar wrote.

"I promise you'll be the first to hear us return," Zist swore, freeing a hand to clap the boy on the back.

"He's stopped waving," Cayla reported. "Oh, dear! His shoulders are all slumped and he looks so sad."

Zist blew out a misty breath and pulled on the reins controlling the workbeast, fighting with himself not to turn the wagon back.

"Murenny promised he'd keep an eye on him," Cayla said, noting how the wagon had slowed. "And this was *your* idea."

"Indeed," Zist agreed, his shoulders slumping in turn. "I think it's absolutely necessary that we learn all we can about the Shunned—"

"I don't disagree with you," Cayla interjected, lifting baby Carissa in her arms and rocking her instinctively.

"Thread will come again soon enough, and what then?" Zist went on, repeating his reasons needlessly. "If there are enough Shunned, what's to stop them from overwhelming a hold or craft hall?"

Cayla didn't have to say a word to make her opinion of *that* clear; she'd said enough before.

"Well, even if they don't, what *will* they do when Thread comes again?" Zist asked reflectively. "It's not right to condemn them all to a death no one on Pern should ever experience."

"I know, love, I know," Cayla said soothingly, recognizing that her mate was working himself into another passionate discourse. She knew from past discussions how vivid the image of Thread, falling mindlessly from the sky, devouring all life, searing all flesh, was engrained in Zist's mind from his reading. "We've discussed this, Murenny's discussed this, and that's *why* we're here in this wagon, dressed like the Shunned—"

"Do you think we should put an 'S' on your head,

too?" Master Zist asked, pointing to the purple-blue mark on his forehead.

"No," Cayla said in a tone that brooked no argument. "And you'd best be right about how to get that mark off."

"It's not proper bluebush ink," Zist reminded her. The sap of the bluebush, used for marking the Shunned, was indelible and permanently stained skin. "Some pinesap, lots of hot water and soap, and it'll come off."

"So you've said," Cayla remarked, sounding no more convinced.

In front, Zist noticed that the workbeast was slowing and flicked the reins to encourage it back to a faster walk.

"Well, I'm glad you're with me," Zist told Cayla, after satisfying himself that they were moving fast enough.

"I'm glad that we left Pellar behind," Cayla said. "Ten Turns is too young to see the sights we expect."

"Indeed," Zist agreed.

"Carissa's so little that she'll remember none of it," Cayla continued, half to answer Zist's unspoken thought, half to answer her own fears.

"There'll be children among the Shunned," Zist remarked. "That's part of what makes it so wrong."

"Yes," Cayla agreed. She flicked a wisp of her honey-blond hair back behind her ear and continued rocking little Carissa. Then she looked back again. "He's gone now."

"We'll be back in less than half a Turn," Zist said after a moment of thoughtful silence. "He'll be all right."

"I hope he'll forgive us," Cayla said.

Zist took the coast road south, toward Hold Gar, Southern Boll Hold, and warmer weather. He and Cayla had guessed that the warmer climes would attract the Shunned, who would find the harsh winters of the north harder to survive.

The road was still snow covered and never more than a pair of ruts running down along the coastline. Even in the protected enclosure of the wagon, Cayla wrapped herself up tightly and nuzzled little Carissa close to her side to keep them both warm. In front, perched on the rattling bench seat, Zist had a thick wherhide blanket spread over his knees and layers of warm thick-knit Tillek sweaters, the same as those used by the Tillek sailors because they kept out the worst of the wet and cold even at sea. Even so, Zist was chilled to the bone every evening when they halted.

They were both relieved when they finally came upon the outskirts of Hold Gar.

Their reception by the holders was sharp and unpleasant.

"Go away!" shrieked the first old woman whose cothold they had stopped at, hoping to barter for food. "Would you have me Shunned, too?"

She hurried them on their way by throwing stones and setting her dogs on them.

"Go back north and freeze! We're hardworking folk down here," she yelled after them. "You won't find any handouts."

Zist shared a shaken look with Cayla who busily tried to comfort a bawling Carissa.

As they neared the next hold, Cayla glanced quickly at the "S" on Zist's forehead. "Maybe I should go by myself," she suggested.

"Bring the baby," Zist agreed. "I'll tend the beast."

Carissa returned later, smiling and carrying a sack full of goods.

"They cost more than they should," she said when she handed the bag to Zist. "The lady fed us, though, and had fresh milk for Carissa."

Two days later they came upon a wagon by the side of the road. It had been burned down to the wheels.

Zist halted. He went to the wreck, crawled around and through it, and came back thirty minutes later, his face grim.

"They were caught while they were sleeping," he told Cayla.

"How do you know it wasn't an accident with a lantern?" Cayla asked. While holders used glows, the Shunned had to make do with what they could scrounge, and that often meant candles or lanterns.

"I'd rather not say," he replied grimly.

"I suppose we should keep a watch at nights," Cayla said.

"Maybe we should turn back," Zist said. "This is beginning to seem more dangerous than I'd feared."

"Perhaps this is what happened to Moran."

"Perhaps," Zist agreed, his face going pale. With a sour look, he gestured to the burned wreck. "There has to be a better way to deal with the Shunned."

"We don't know what happened here. We know that some were Shunned for murder. After being Shunned, what would stop them from murdering again?" Cayla responded. "Perhaps we're only seeing justice done."

"No," Zist said, shaking his head firmly. "That was a wagon much like ours."

Cayla realized from what he'd left unsaid that the occupants of the wagon were much like them, too—a man, woman, and child.

"We should move on before we attract attention," she said firmly.

"I'd like you to keep watch from the back of the wagon," Zist said by way of agreement.

"Of course."

* * *

When they camped that evening, Cayla brought out her pipes and Zist's gitar. They had left their best instruments behind as they had the telltale stamp of the Harper Hall to distinguish them as works of craftsmanship. Instead, they had brought older instruments, as befitted their status of homeless Shunned.

"Let's play a bit," Cayla said as she handed him his gitar. "The baby's asleep and all bundled up for the night."

Zist took the gitar and started tuning it; he recognized her desire to calm them both down from the horrors of the burned wagon.

Cayla adjusted her pipes slightly to match his gitar and then, with a twinkle in her eye, started into a lively reel, daring him to keep up.

Zist smiled back at her, matched her pace, and then exceeded it, nodding a challenge back to her, only to find himself surprised as her fingers seemed to fly over the holes and switched pace and melody at once.

"Very nice," a voice called out from the darkness as they finished the reel in record time. "Have you any other songs?"

Zist stood up quickly, started to grab for the cudgel he'd laid close to hand and stopped, raising his gitar instead. As a weapon it'd do in a pinch and it had the advantage of not being obvious.

A thin, lanky figure stepped out of the shadows toward the fire.

Zist's eyes swept over him, then back to Cayla, who'd turned her back to the fire and was scanning the darkness. She trilled a quick note on her pipes but Zist wasn't fooled—the note was a D sharp, three notes up from C, meaning that Cayla had spotted three others around the fire.

Pretending to check his gitar, Zist glanced behind the stranger and caught sight of the gleam of several pairs of eyes. He strummed his gitar twice, changing chords, as though checking his tuning but really letting Cayla know his tally of two. That made five, total.

"There's a baby in the wagon, she's sleeping," a woman's voice called from the far side of their wagon. Six.

Zist tensed, his jaw clenched angrily.

"Her name's Carissa," Cayla replied in an easy tone to the woman. "Please don't disturb her, she's impossible to get back to sleep."

"What are you doing camped out here on Gar land?" the first man asked.

"We're heading down to Southern Boll," Zist said quickly. "We were hoping to trade tunes and news."

"That's harper's work," the man said.

The man was only visible as a shadow in the night; Zist couldn't see his face. The question was, was the man one of the Shunned or one of Hold Gar? And if he was from Hold Gar, was he the same one who'd burned the other wagon—if that's what had really happened?

Cayla took the decision out of his hands. "We're hoping to sing to those that harpers wouldn't."

"You wouldn't know any healing would you?" the woman at the back of the wagon called out anxiously. "For my Jenni's got a terrible fever."

"I don't know much," Cayla said cautiously.

The woman rushed from the back of the wagon and into the firelight. In her arms she held a tightly wrapped bundle, which she started to thrust into Cayla's hands but stopped, thinking better of it.

"Maybe you ought not," the woman said. "My Jenni's got a terrible fever; I wouldn't want your wee one to get it, too."

"We've probably all got it," the man by the fire grumbled sourly. "Three dead already . . ."

"They weren't the ones in the wagon a ways back?" Zist asked thoughtfully.

"You found them, eh?" the man replied. Zist nodded and the man peered at him thoughtfully. "Thought it was some holder folk who set fire to the wagon, didn't you?"

He saw Zist's reaction and laughed bitterly, shaking his head.

"Other days it would have been," the man said, and spat toward the fire. "Some of them *holders* would do it just for fun."

"You shouldn't say that, Malir," the woman snapped at him. The baby in her arms bawled feebly and she forgot whatever else she was going to say, instead peering down worriedly at the baby and feeling her forehead with her free hand. Horrified, she cried to Cayla, "Oh, she's burning up! Is there anything you can do?"

"When did the fever start and were there other symptoms?" Zist asked, turning to the woman.

"What about those others you mentioned?" Cayla asked, turning to Malir.

Malir gestured to the woman across the fire.

"Yona knows it all, let her tell it," he said, turning abruptly and disappearing into the shadows to confer, Zist guessed, with the others who had kept out of sight.

Zist turned back to the woman, Yona.

"Here, sit down by the fire," Cayla said, gesturing to a comfortable spot.

"Start heating some water," she ordered Zist, "and get the herbals from the wagon." She paused, frowning, frantically reviewing in her head the lore she'd learned from Mikal about fevers. "I think Carissa is safe enough in the wagon for the moment."

"She is, with my man and his crew guarding us," Yona declared.

As Zist set about his errands, Cayla turned to the

other woman, for the first time able to examine her
carefully. Yona's face was lined with dirt, grime, and the
strain of years of rough living. Even so, Cayla noted,
there were laugh lines around her eyes. Life had been
hard on Yona, Cayla surmised, but not unbearable. At
least until now.

"So tell me about the others," Cayla said, making
herself relax in order to encourage Yona to do the same.
"Who got sick first and when was it noticed?"

"Mara was first," Yona said after a moment's reflection. She shook her head, adding, "It's hard to remember, because Kenner got sick just after and then their
baby, little Koria."

She raised her eyes to meet Cayla's and told her, "I'm
the one the others come to for healing in our group.
Not that I know all that much, it's just that they started
asking once and they've never stopped."

Cayla nodded understandingly.

"So it was Mara, Koria's mother, then Mara's mate,
and finally their baby—was that the order?"

Yona nodded.

"And besides the fever, were there any other symptoms?"

"They were always thirsty, and coughing," Yona told
her. "They couldn't drink enough and"—she paused
delicately—"everything they ate came out really quick,
from one end or the other."

Cayla nodded, showing no sign of unease. "What
remedies did you try?"

By the end of the third day there were five sick in the
camp: baby Jenni; an older man named Vero; Nikka, a
young girl; Torellan, Malir's lieutenant; and Yona.
Zist found himself splitting his time between caring
for Carissa and fetching herbs for Cayla, who was com-

pletely immersed in her attempts to find a cure for the fever.

After Zist had finished getting Carissa down for the night, he left the wagon and gathered fuel for the fire. On his return, he noticed that Cayla had fallen asleep, propped up against the wagon wheel nearest the fire's warmth.

He peered down at her fondly for a moment, then shook himself and started to the back of the wagon to get a blanket for her. The sound of footsteps startled him and he turned quickly. It was Malir.

"The baby's dead," he said, his face etched with pain and eyes dull with fatigue. "She died just moments ago."

"I'm sorry."

"Go," Malir ordered. Zist drew a breath to console the distraught man, but Malir silenced him with a shake of his head. "The others think it's your missus's fault; they're talking about burning our wagon—and yours."

"Come with us," Zist suggested.

Malir shook his head. "I'll stay with my kind," he said. He snorted when he saw Zist's expression. "You've had too many meals recently to be one of us," Malir told him. "The others haven't noticed yet but they will, they will."

Malir shook his head, adding, "Anyways, if we went with you, they'd come after us for sure, certain that we were in this together."

Zist cast about for another way to make his argument but Malir forestalled him with an impatient gesture. "Go, now! Before they come after you."

Pellar was the first to hear the returning wagon, just as Master Zist had promised. He ran out under the archway from the Harper Hall. He unshielded the glows in the basket he'd kept ready and recharged for the past six months.

"No, Pellar!" Zist shouted, his voice hoarse and oddly troubled. It took Pellar a moment to realize that the harper's voice was tear-strained. "Get the healer and make everyone stay away." He gestured from his seat to the covered part of the wagon, "They're sick. It might be fever."

It was. Master Zist's wife, Cayla, and their baby daughter, Carissa, were confined to the wagon. Master-healer Kilti tried everything.

Pellar set himself up in a tent nearby, ready to run errands whenever Zist wished. But nothing he nor Masterhealer Kilti could do helped. Even Mikal, who had come at Pellar's first desperate pleading, could find no cure. First little Carissa, then Cayla, succumbed to the fever.

An anguished cry, more felt than heard, startled Pellar out of his sleep and he raced to the wagon to find Master Zist leaning against it, his face buried in his hands. Pellar knew without asking that Cayla had lost her battle with the fever. Tentatively, he reached for the taller harper, awkwardly patting him only to gasp in surprise as Zist grabbed him into a tight embrace. Pellar hugged the older man back tightly until he felt Zist relax.

Then Pellar pulled out his slate and wrote on it, "I should have come with you."

He thrust it under Master Zist's tear-bleared eyes. Zist read it and shook his head. "Then you would have been lost, too."

Pellar shook his head fiercely, gently pulled his slate out of the harper's limp hands, erased its message with a corner of his nightshirt, and wrote once more, "Wouldn't have mattered."

Zist read the new note and shook his head. "You do matter, Pellar. I'm glad you stayed behind, I'm glad you're here." He hugged the youngster once more. "Now, please go tell the healer."

Pellar gave Master Zist a cautionary look, so reminiscent of those Zist had used all too often on his mischievous charge that the harper felt his lips curving upward in spite of his sorrow. Satisfied, Pellar nodded to himself, spun on his heel, and raced off to fetch the Masterhealer.

In the Turn that followed, Pellar was never far from the harper, doing whatever he could to console him in his grief, a grief he himself shared. Pellar helped dig the graves, one so terribly little, with tears streaming down his face as he remembered little Carissa's first and only word: "Pellah!"

He stood up front with Masterharper Murenny and Masterhealer Kilti while Master Zist said his last farewells to his wife and daughter. And he was by Zist's side months later when he planted the first fresh buds of spring on their graves.

And now Pellar stood outside the Masterharper's door, carefully listening to the conversation inside.

"You should have seen them, Murenny," Pellar heard Master Zist saying. "Some of them were no more than skin and bones."

"They were Shunned, they had their chance," Masterharper Murenny reminded him.

"Not the children," Zist responded heatedly. "And some of them were Shunned for no more than not giving *favors* to the Lord Holder or their local Craftmaster. Where's the justice in that?"

Master Murenny sighed in agreement. "But what more can we do?"

"We—" Zist cut himself off. Pellar held his breath so as not to make any sound, but it wasn't enough. With a resigned sigh, Zist rose from his chair, saying, "Hold on."

Before Pellar could scamper out of sight, the door to the Masterharper's quarters sprang open and Zist appeared in the doorway, beckoning to him with a crooked finger. With his head hung low, Pellar slumped into the room, expecting a scolding. Instead, with a glance of confirmation at the Masterharper, Zist said, "You'll hear better on this side of the door."

"Not a harper," Pellar scrawled on his slate in protest. Master Zist read the message and passed it over to the Masterharper with a twinkle in his eye.

Murenny gave a loud guffaw as he read the slate and then said to Pellar, "I wouldn't be so sure about that, youngster. You listen well, as you've just shown."

He gestured for Pellar to take a chair and beckoned inquiringly toward the spare mug beside the pitcher of *klah*. With a wink, he said, "Listening's thirsty work."

Pellar looked inquiringly at Master Zist, who nodded permission. Pellar smiled gratefully and offered the pitcher to the Masterharper and Master Zist, who both declined, before serving himself some of the hot tasty brew.

"I know there's no need to tell you that what we say here is craft secret," Murenny said when Pellar had seated himself and fastened his eyes on the Masterharper. Pellar nodded emphatically.

"Good," the Masterharper said, satisfied. He turned to Master Zist. "Any sign of Moran, then?"

"None at all," Master Zist said, shaking his head. "Of course, we didn't travel very far before we came across those poor sick folk and then—" His voice broke, and it was a moment before he continued, "Cayla insisted we help. When Carissa got a fever, we broke camp as quickly as we could, but . . ."

"I understand," Murenny said softly in the pained silence that fell.

Zist looked up again, his eyes shining. "That's another thing, what about the children? They've done nothing wrong, and yet they're either separated from their Shunned parents or forced to leave with them—mostly on the whim of their Holder—to starve or die without any hope for a future. Is this the justice of Pern?"

Murenny shook his head. "Those who refuse to do their share of work, who steal from others, who commit murder—what else is there to do with them but to Shun them?"

Zist made a face but said nothing, staring at the floor.

"Holders and Crafters can set fines, but if that doesn't bring a person to his senses, what else is there?" Murenny persisted. "Is it any fairer to insist that good, hardworking folk support lazy, shiftless thieves?"

Zist shook his head glumly. He glanced up, saying, "But Thread is coming soon, what then? Shall the Shunned be scoured off Pern by Thread?"

Pellar shuddered. Thread had not fallen on Pern for nearly two hundred Turns. The Red Star, harbinger of Pern's doom, was still only a glowing menace in the night sky. It would be another eighteen Turns before it grew to its ghastly largest size and brought the voracious Thread to threaten all life on Pern for a whole fifty Turns. Pellar would be nearly thirty then, a number unimaginable to him, but he did not doubt the harpers' tales of the First and Second Passes of the Red Star.

To be caught outside of the safe stone of hold or crafthall would mean being exposed to the ravages of Thread, to be burned to a lifeless crisp as the Thread devoured all life. Only Pern's great fire-breathing dragons could save everyone and the planet itself from complete annihilation.

Zist snorted as another thought crossed his mind. "Not that Thread's their biggest threat—there's enough disease and fever to be found, as well."

"Did you get an idea of their numbers, then?" Murenny asked softly.

"No, they were always drifting about, and some of them were mixed in with proper Traders," Zist responded. "The traders don't like them because too many of them steal—what have they got to lose?—and they give the traders a bad name with the Holders.

"And there's another thing," he continued. "They eat so poorly that many of them succumb to the least cold or infection. But they mix enough with crafters and holders that their diseases could be spread to others."

"Have you a suggestion, then?"

"Not any better than my last," Zist replied sourly. "Nor the one before it."

"I thought it was a good idea to get a harper in amongst the Shunned," Murenny said. "It's a shame that we'll never know what happened to Moran."

"It's a great shame," Zist agreed. "I was sure they would have accepted him. Perhaps he could have helped their plight."

"And given us some better thoughts on how to deal with the long-term issues of Thread and the Shunned," Murenny agreed.

Pellar scribbled quickly on his slate, "I'll go."

"No, you won't," Zist said harshly when he read the slate.

"Not a harper?" Pellar scrawled in response.

"That's not it," Murenny said, leaning forward to read Pellar's message upside down. He glanced significantly at Master Zist, and Pellar subsided. The older harper's face was scrunched up in thought.

"I'll make you a harper now," Zist said finally. He

looked up at Murenny. "With Moran gone, I've a right to another apprentice."

"Very well," Murenny agreed, raising his bushy eyebrows to Pellar. "Do you accept?" Before Pellar could write his reply, Murenny held up a hand. "You know how tough he is. Think carefully before you answer."

Pellar's face lit up impishly and he shook with silent laughter.

"I should," he wrote, showing the slate to the other two. He grabbed it back quickly, wiped it clean with his sleeve, and wrote, "But I won't."

He held his answer out until the others nodded that they'd read it, then hastily wiped it clean again to write another note, which he showed to Master Zist. "I'd be honored."

"Well," Master Murenny said in a drawl to Master Zist, "here's a first: a silent harper."

"He might be silent, but he behaves no better than the others," Zist replied. He turned to Pellar. "You should have been my apprentice last Turn." When Pellar made to protest, Zist shook his head firmly, saying, "You can make and play drums, guitar, and pipes already. This Turn you'll be able to pick your wood for a violin."

Pellar's eyes widened in delighted surprise. He was to be a harper!

"So now, Apprentice Pellar, what do you suggest we do?" Murenny asked.

"Go where they steal," Pellar wrote immediately.

"A brilliant suggestion, Pellar," Murenny said, clapping the youngster on the shoulder.

"It is," Zist agreed fervently.

"We don't know where they steal, though," Murenny remarked after a moment of thoughtful silence. Pellar looked crestfallen until the Masterharper added, "But we can find out."

"Pellar, go to the drumheights and ask them to send a message requesting reports of any missing or lost material from all the Holds and Crafts," Zist said.

Pellar smiled shyly, bobbed his head once in acknowledgment, and sped out the door.

"Now that he's out of earshot, why don't you tell me why aren't you thinking of sending him out this time?" Masterharper Murenny asked Zist after the boy had left.

"He's better able to look out for himself than even Moran," Zist said. "Mikal says that he's good in the wild, he survived a full sevenday relying only on his wits. His woodcraft is such that *I* have trouble tracking him." He frowned thoughtfully for a moment, then shook his head. "But no, I think he's better here at the Harper Hall."

"Then who would you send?"

"Me," Zist replied instantly. He spread his hands out, gesturing toward the Harper Hall. "There are too many sad memories here for me now."

Murenny regarded the harper silently for a long while before he sighed and nodded.

"I was afraid you were going to say that," he said. "I can't say that I blame you." In the distance, the Harper Hall's drums rattled "attention." "Just don't forget that you're *my* apprentice."

Zist smiled and shook his head. "As if you'll ever let me forget!"

"Indeed," Murenny agreed, letting his voice go commandingly deep. "And as your Master, it is my pleasant duty to inform you that Lord Egremer has informed me that he is sending two fire-lizard eggs from his latest clutch." He wagged a finger at Zist. "I'd like you to take one."

Zist shook his head adamantly. When the Masterharper drew breath to protest, Zist said, "Give it to the boy instead. He'll need a messenger, and a fire-lizard would be best."

Murenny pursed his lips thoughtfully and then nodded. "Very well."

Pellar had been overjoyed at the prospect of impressing a fire-lizard, then reflective. He stopped in his tracks as they walked back from Fort Hold to the Harper Hall and, with obvious reluctance, put down the pot full of warm sand in which the mottled fire-lizard egg was nestled. Zist looked at him inquiringly but Pellar shook his head and pulled out his slate.

"You should have it," he wrote to Master Zist.

"It was offered to me," Zist told him. "I chose to give it to you—apprentice."

Pellar's face went through a rainbow of expressions, going from stubborn intent through hopeful disbelief to delirious incredulity. He dropped his slate back around his neck and hugged Zist tight. Zist returned the hug with equal intensity, finally pushing the youngster away and pointing down to the egg.

"We'd better get it back to the Hall quickly and near the hearth so that it stays warm."

Pellar picked up the pot gingerly, and in an unusual display of controlled haste, set off again for the Harper Hall.

In the end, Zist was glad of his choice, content to let Pellar spend the next several sevendays hovering around the kitchen hearth in the Harper Hall, happily answering any questions about the egg and anxiously checking it every few minutes.

Pellar was well prepared when the egg finally started shaking and small cracks appeared in the middle of the night. Zist was sure that, had he kept the egg himself, he would have been too tired to notice.

As it was, Zist was rudely jostled awake by Pellar,

who used his foot, his hands being fully occupied with the just-gorged fire-lizard, his face split with a grin and his eyes shining in pure joy. Zist managed to remain awake long enough to ascertain that the fire-lizard was a brown, and to assure Pellar that it was, indeed, the most marvelous creature ever to grace any part of Pern.

Pellar named the fire-lizard Chitter, having first toyed with the name Voice because, as he wrote, Chitter was even better than having a voice—no one complained (much) when the fire-lizard made noise.

Masterharper Murenny had to agree with the youngster's assessment, as the antics of the fire-lizard and his bright-eyed partner were soon the talk of the Harper Hall.

Not everyone appreciated the fire-lizard, however. "Take it away!" Mikal had cried in a hoarse, pained voice when Pellar proudly brought Chitter over to Mikal's cave for inspection. Better was the effect the pair had on Zist, bringing the harper slowly out of the depths of his grief.

They spent more than a Turn gathering information. In that time, Pellar had made his first violin under Master Caldazon's instruction, and had spent as much time as he could working with Mikal, learning about herbal cures and first aid. Summer had come again before Zist made his discovery.

"I think I should go to Crom," he said late one night in a quiet conference with Murenny.

The Masterharper gave him an inquiring look.

"There were those reports last winter of missing coal and there are some more reports just in," Zist said, waving a slate at the Masterharper. "And Masterminer Britell's setting up some new mines far away from Crom Hold."

"Go on."

"Places far up in the mountains that will be isolated during the winter months," Zist continued.

"Good places for things to go missing?" Murenny suggested.

"Along with good places to hide," Zist agreed. "This report from Jofri suggests that there might be some friction between Miner Natalon and his uncle Tarik."

"Wasn't Tarik the one who reported missing a bunch of coal last winter?"

"He was," Zist replied.

"You think perhaps the coal wasn't lost?"

"Cromcoal costs."

"No one would be happy to lose the value of their work," Murenny remarked.

"Jofri's reports lead me to wonder why Tarik didn't complain more," Zist said.

"What are you thinking?"

"Jofri's ready for his Mastery," Zist said. "He should come back here."

Murenny nodded and motioned for the harper to continue.

"So we'll need someone to take his place," Zist said. "And, as I said before, I need some time away from here."

"What about Pellar?"

Pellar had progressed mightily in the past Turn, producing a beautifully toned violin that had practically become his voice. In almost all respects, Zist thought, the boy was ready to walk the tables and become a journeyman.

"Would you leave him behind?" Murenny prompted when Zist made no response.

The other harper shook himself. "Sorry, just thinking."

"I see my lessons have finally paid off," Murenny remarked drolly.

Zist acknowledged the gibe with a roll of his eyes.

"And?" Murenny prompted.

"He should come with me," Zist said. "He can make
his own camp and keep out of sight."

"His woodcraft is excellent," Murenny agreed. "But
why keep him out of sight?"

Zist shook his head. "I don't know," he said. "I just
think it would be better if I appeared the old bitter
harper, unaided."

"Without Pellar," Murenny noted sadly, "you'll have
no trouble filling the role."

Pellar missed his fiddle; it had become the voice he
didn't have and he had rejoiced in it.

"I'll keep it safe for you," Masterharper Murenny
had promised him, reverently placing it in its case and
shaking his head in wonder. "I haven't seen the like,
and that's the truth." He shook a warning finger at
Zist, saying, "You make sure the lad stays in one piece,
Zist. I'll want him back here to pass on his knowledge."
He looked down at the fiddle again and added wistfully,
"If I'd've known, I would have had him building them
Turns back."

"He's a talent with wood, that's for sure," Zist
agreed. He cocked an eyebrow toward Pellar, who had
filled out and shot up in the two Turns since Zist's disastrous trip. "You've the makings of a fine harper."

Murenny nodded in emphatic agreement, and Pellar's
eyes went wide with joy.

"His woodcraft is as good as this?" Murenny asked
Zist, with a hint of a frown as he tore himself away
from the beautiful sheen of the fiddle and turned his attention back to its maker.

"Better," Zist told him.

Pellar looked embarrassed. "I'm naturally quiet," he wrote.

"He crept up on me—caught me completely unawares—even though I'd told him to and was on the lookout," Zist confided. He shook his head ruefully. "He'll not be seen, or heard, unless he wants to."

"Good," Murenny said firmly. "Otherwise I would have to think twice about letting him go." His eyes strayed again to the fiddle and then up to Pellar.

"I've seen you grow from a babe, youngster, and I've watched you more than you might imagine," Murenny told him solemnly. "I need you to understand this: You will *always* have a place in the Harper Hall." He gestured to the fiddle. "*This* just makes us more eager for your return."

Pellar's eyes grew round as he absorbed the Masterharper's emphatic words.

Zist clapped his adopted son on the shoulder. "I told you," he murmured softly in Pellar's ear.

Pellar blushed bright red, but his eyes were shining with happiness.

Flame on high,
Thread will die.
Flame too low,
Burrows woe.

Chapter Two

"COME ON, JAMAL, you'll miss it!" Cristov called as he weaved through the Gather crowd. He looked over his shoulder and frowned as he saw that the distance between him and his friend had widened. Jamal hobbled after him gamely on his crutches. Cristov stopped, then turned back.

"I could carry you, if you want," he offered.

"I weigh as much as you do," Jamal said. "How far do you think we'd get?"

"Far enough," Cristov lied stoutly. "It's only a few dragonlengths to the edge of the crowd."

Jamal shoved Cristov away.

"It'll take forever with these," he cried, waving one of the crutches with his arm. Jamal had broken his leg a sevenday before and would be on crutches for at least two months.

"Then I'll carry you," Cristov persisted, trying again to grab hold of his friend.

"You couldn't do it even if you were the size of your father," Jamal said. Cristov hid a sigh; even if he were the size of Tarik, he'd probably not be big enough to carry Jamal.

"You'll be the proper size for the mines," Tarik had said once when Cristov had complained that all his friends were taller than him.

"I can still try," Cristov persisted. Jamal groaned at him and tried to shake off Cristov's aid.

"There's your father," Jamal said in a low tone. Cristov looked back to the edge of the Gather and saw Tarik. Their eyes locked, and Cristov's heart sank as his father beckoned imperiously to him. "You'd better go. He looks like he's in one of his moods."

"I'll be back," Cristov said as he started away. Not hearing any comment from Jamal, he turned back but Jamal was already hobbling away, nearly lost in the Gather crowd. Cristov wanted to sprint after him, to turn him around, to meet his father with a friend at his side, but—

With a grimace, Cristov turned back to the edge of the Gather crowd and caught the look on his father's face. Tarik repeated his impatient, beckoning gesture and Cristov knew why Jamal had left.

"I just wanted to spend some time with Jamal," Cristov said as he neared speaking distance.

"Never mind him," Tarik growled impatiently. "You'll make new friends up at the Camp, you won't need worry about that cripple."

"He'll be fine when the cast's off," Cristov protested. For all the ten Turns that Cristov had lived, his father had found fault with anyone that Cristov had tried to befriend.

"That's neither here nor there," Tarik grunted. "He's a cripple now and I'm glad you won't be around him." He snaked a hand onto Cristov's shoulder and pulled him tight against him.

"This is Harper Moran," Tarik said, gesturing to the man in blue beside him. Cristov nodded politely to the harper.

"Look! The dragons are starting the games!" Moran exclaimed, pointing up to the sky.

Cristov craned his neck back but found himself bumping into his father's chest. He squirmed forward to give himself enough distance to look straight up into the sky.

"It's a nice day for it," Moran said. "Not a cloud in the sky."

"I hope Telgar wins again," Cristov said. Crom Hold was under Telgar Weyr's protection; it would be the dragons from Telgar who flamed Thread from the sky when it fell. Cristov knew that Thread wasn't due for nearly another sixteen Turns; having only ten Turns of age himself, Cristov could hardly imagine such a distant future.

"Of course they'll win again," Tarik growled. "They won last year, because of their new Weyrleader."

"He came from Igen Weyr, didn't he, Father?" Cristov asked, still amazed that a whole Weyr had been abandoned.

"There wasn't much else for them to do," Harper Moran remarked, "given the drought down that way and that their last queen had died."

"Their loss, our gain," Tarik said. "Telgar Weyr's got nearly twice the dragons the other Weyrs have."

"And twice the duty, too," Moran said.

Cristov lost the sound of their voices, intent only on the dragons flying into view above him.

One group, all golden, burst into view high up above them. The queen dragons.

Moran pointed. "They're going to throw the first Thread."

"Thread?" Cristov gulped. He knew that from the Teaching Ballads that had been drilled into him first by Harper Jofri and then by Harper Zist, just as they were taught to everyone on Pern. He knew that every two hundred Turns the Red Star returned, bringing Thread: a mindless, voracious parasite that ate anything organic— wood, plants, coal, flesh—and grew with such rapidity that a whole valley would be destroyed in mere hours. Water drowned it, steel and stone were impervious to it, and flame, particularly dragon's fire, reduced it to impotent ash.

"Not real Thread," Tarik growled. "Just rope."

"Made to look like Thread," the harper added. "For the games."

"Oh." Cristov turned back around and craned his neck skyward, relieved.

A wing of dragons suddenly appeared in the sky, well below the queens, and moments later the loud *booms* of their arrival shook the air.

"Light travels faster than sound," Harper Moran murmured. Cristov wasn't sure if the harper meant to be heard or was just so used to teaching that he never stopped.

"They look small," Cristov said, surprised.

"They're weyrlings," the harper said. "They're just old enough to fly *between* and carry firestone."

"Firestone?" Cristov repeated, unfamiliar with the word. He made a face and turned to his father. "Is that another name for coal?"

Instantly Cristov knew from his father's angry look that he'd asked the wrong question. Cristov flinched as he saw his father's arm flex, ready to smack him, but he was saved by the harper.

"No, it's not another name for coal, more's the pity," the harper said, not noticing or choosing to ignore Tarik's anger. "You've never seen it, though you might remember it from the Songs."

"I did," Cristov confessed. "But I always thought it had to be coal."

Tarik glared at him.

"You said, Father, that Cromcoal makes the hottest fire there is. I thought for sure that the dragons had to use coal for their flames," he explained, wilting under Tarik's look. Feebly, he finished, "I was sure they'd only use the best."

"Your lad's a fair one for thinking, Tarik," Moran said with an affable laugh. "You can't really fault his logic."

"It's his job to listen to his elders and learn from them," Tarik replied. "He doesn't need to do any thinking."

Moran gave the miner a troubled look. "Thinking comes in handy for harpers."

"He's not going to *be* a harper," Tarik replied. "Cristov's going to be a miner. Like his father and my father before me." He gave Moran a grim smile and held up a hand over Cristov's head. "We're built the right size for the mines."

"I imagine that thinking will be important for miners, Tarik," Moran said, shaking his head in disagreement. "Times are changing. The old mines have played out; the new seams are all deep underground. Mining down there will require news ways of thinking."

"Not for me," Tarik disagreed. "I know all I need to know about mining. I've been a miner for twenty Turns now—learned from my father and he'd been a miner for thirty Turns. It was *his* father that first opened our seam, seventy Turns back."

A ripple of overwhelming sound and a burst of cold air announced the arrival of a huge wing of dragons, flying low over the crowd.

"Telgar!" The crowd shouted as the dragons entered a steep dive, twisted into a sharp rolling climb, and came to a halt, their formation intermeshed with the weyrlings so perfectly that it looked like the two wings of dragons had been flying as one, even though the fighting wing was head to head and a meter underneath the weyrlings.

Cristov gasped as a rain of sacks fell from the weyrlings only to be caught by the riders of the great fighting dragons. Looking at the jacket worn by the bronze rider leading the fighting wing, he saw the stylized field of wheat set in a white diamond—it was the Weyrleader himself!

As one, the fighting wing of dragons turned and dove again, flawlessly returning to hover in the same place where it had come from *between*. As the dragons hovered, their great necks twisted and their heads turned back to face their riders, who opened the sacks they had caught to feed the firestone to their dragons.

"Nasty stuff, firestone," Cristov heard the harper mutter behind him. "Nasty stuff."

The planet Pern was a beautiful world settled hundreds of Turns ago by colonists seeking to forget the horror of interstellar war—indeed, of all war.

But the original survey of Pern failed to notice that one of its sister planets was a wildly erratic rogue. It was not until eight Turns after Landing that the settlers learned of their peril—when the planet they called "The Red Star" came close enough to loose its deadly cargo of Thread across the void of space and onto fertile Pern.

Thread, an alien life-form that streamed into the atmosphere in the form of long silvery strands, devoured any organic material; neither flesh nor vegetation was safe from it. A single Thread burrow could suck the life out of a whole valley in half a day.

The resourceful colonists fought back with the last of their space-going technology while devising a series of long-term, biological defenses, chief among them, fire-breathing dragons that chewed phosphine-bearing rocks—firestone—to create their flames. At birth, in a

ritual called "Impression," the dragons bonded telepathically with human riders who, with their great
mounts, risked their lives fighting Thread. And so Pern
survived.

The Red Star receded and Thread stopped falling. For
two hundred Turns the colonists spread out across the
Northern Continent of Pern. When the Red Star returned, the dragonriders were prepared and flamed the
Thread out of the skies.

Even a pastoral world needed steel for plows, horse-
shoes, and shovels. Pern required more, including steel
buckles and fasteners for the riding harness used by the
great dragons. Making steel required iron ore, coal, and
a host of trace metals. After nearly five hundred Turns,
the original surface seams of coal—easy to find, easy to
mine—had been exhausted.

The Masterminer, Britell, had sent out parties of tal-
ented miners to bore into mountains seeking new seams
of coal deep below ground. Those mining camps that
succeeded in producing coal would be rewarded by ele-
vation to full working mines.

Natalon, who was both Cristov's uncle and Tarik's
nephew, had just opened one such mine. When he'd
heard that Tarik was looking for work, he'd sent word
inviting him to Camp Natalon. Tarik and his family
would leave for the camp the day after the Games.

Tenim stood toward the back of the crowd as the
next wing of dragons started its first run. He let himself
be caught up in the excitement, along with the rest of
the Gather, as they looked up in awe at the sight of
thirty flaming dragons racing across the afternoon sky,
flaming the rope Threads thrown down by the queen
riders high above them, displaying their skill as dragon
and rider worked to reduce the mock menace to dust.

Tenim's eye darted from the spectacle above him back

to his intended victim, a red-faced, corpulent Trader who bellowed loudly as the Fort riders finished their run and the flags on the Lord Holders' stands were changed to Benden.

The crowd roared and Tenim seized the moment. He added his own voice, feigned a slip, and fell roughly against the Trader.

"I'm sorry, so sorry!" Tenim said, helping the Trader to his feet and trying to brush the dirt off the man. He pushed a lock of jet black hair off his face, his bright green eyes tinged with concern.

"Not to worry," the Trader answered genially, backing away. Then he stopped, patting his clothes, and turned back, an angry look on his face.

His purse was in plain sight in Tenim's hands. With a nervous swallow, Tenim held up the purse and put on his most innocent look. "You dropped your purse. Here it is."

"Well, thank you, lad," the Trader said, grabbing the purse.

"You'll not tell my master on me?" Tenim asked, his eyes wide with fear. "He'd beat me if he found out. I'm always clumsy," he added with eyes downcast.

"No," the Trader said kindly. He reached into his purse and pulled out a half-mark. "Not every lad is as honest as you," he said as he pressed it into Tenim's hand.

"Thank you!" Tenim said cheerfully, still in character. "Thank you so much."

He waved at the Trader and started off at a brisk walk, careful not to look back lest the Trader suspect.

Out of sight, Tenim allowed himself one long, explosive curse. His belly rumbled in agreement.

No matter what Moran said, he was too old to beg. It was time to steal.

In the evening there would be gambling; Tenim decided to risk his half-mark on the chance for more.

If he didn't, there were always those too deep in their cups to notice his light fingers late at night.

"So, Harper, what do you reckon?" The question came from a young impetuous man, part of the crowd Moran had cheerfully insinuated himself into earlier.

"It's always difficult to know how these things will turn out, Berrin," Moran replied after a moment's thought.

Someone in the group shouted, "Ah, no, it's easy—Telgar for sure!"

"Telgar for first, I'm certain," Moran said hastily. He couldn't identify the speaker but he knew better than to cast doubt on the local Weyr's chances. "It's which Weyr will come second and third that's hard to know."

"Have you a guess?" Berrin asked. When Moran nodded, the Crom holder fingered the bulge in his tunic and asked, "Care to wager?"

"I don't know if, as a harper, I should bet with you."

"Why not?"

"Well," Moran said thoughtfully, "after all, I've been around, and I wouldn't want you to believe that my superior knowledge bested you."

He caught the holder's greedy look and knew that his deliberate mistakes in their previous conversations had convinced the holder that Moran was a pompous, overconfident fool. The holder glanced at the bulging purse Moran had carefully hung on his belt in plain sight to all. Of course, the holder had convinced himself that Moran's purse was bulging with harper marks, a belief that Moran was careful to cultivate by the overprotective way he clutched at it.

Fools and their money are soon parted, Moran reflected silently, remembering his early years at the Harper Hall.

"Well, now, I'm sure you're a fair man, Harper," Berrin replied in a tone that told Moran that, in fact, Berrin was sure that Moran was a stupid man. "And I'd trust you to be honest with me if you knew something special."

Moran nodded affably.

"So how about a wager for second place?" Berrin asked. Moran raised his hands, feigning nervous indecision. "Nothing much, say a mark or two?"

Moran gave the holder a doubtful look.

"Ah, go on, Harper," one of Berrin's friends called out from the crowd.

"Well," Moran began slowly, clutching at his bag, "perhaps a mark that Benden gets second."

"Benden? I'll take a mark on that," another man called from the crowd. Moran smiled to himself as he recognized the man as another of Berrin's cronies. Privately, the harper was pretty certain that only half of the current crowd was working with Berrin, the rest being innocent but greedy gamblers hoping to exploit Berrin and the harper. Moran was quite certain that in the end he would take money from both groups and come out ahead. He had no qualms with that—there were hungry children at their camp who wouldn't question how their bellies came to be full.

Halla peered worriedly at her big brother as he slid on the slick ground. Jamal winced and bit off a curse after jarring his broken leg.

"Are you okay?" Halla asked him. She helped him get up and made a face. "What's that smell? It's coming from your leg."

"It's nothing," Jamal lied.

"Maybe you should see a healer," Halla said.

"Healers won't see us, you know that," Jamal replied. He waved Halla away. "You go over with the other children, you're supposed to be watching them."

Halla sniffed, but dutifully headed off to a forlorn cluster of youngsters mostly younger than her own eight Turns. She turned to look back as Jamal disappeared once more into the Gather crowd and hoped that he would be okay.

"Of course I'll keep this our secret," Moran promised the disconsolate wagerers as he collected his winnings.

"That's very kind of you, Harper," Berrin told him feelingly, his words echoed by the worried nods of the other losers.

"After all, it was all in good spirits," the harper said, carefully fishing out a few quarter-marks to each of the losing bettors. After the losers thanked him for his graciousness, Moran returned to the miners.

"Didn't I say that Telgar would win?" Tarik declared, soundly slapping the harper on the shoulder. He peered down at him, his eyes shining with an avaricious gleam. "You've some marks for me, I believe?"

"Indeed I do," Moran declared jovially, handing over a two-mark piece that he'd just won as part of his other wagers. He leaned closer to Tarik and said in a softer voice, "And I hope you'll find our other arrangement as advantageous."

Tarik's face hardened for just a moment before he responded, "I'm sure I will. Indeed, I'm certain of it."

Work and living drays do roll,
Taking every long day's toll.
Bearing goods and bringing gifts—
Traders working every shift.

Chapter Three

FOLLOWING MASTER ZIST'S INSTRUCTIONS, Pellar snuck onto one of the trader's drays and hid behind the barrels of goods intended for Camp Natalon. To increase his chances of avoiding detection, Pellar sent Chitter ahead to Zist.

The trip up to the camp took a sevenday. Zist could only manage to sneak him food twice. Fortunately, Pellar had filled his pack wisely and had planned on surviving on his own for at least two sevendays. He left the trader caravan the night before it was due to arrive at the camp and took off into the mountains.

The weather was chillier than at Fort Hold and the Harper Hall. Pellar was dressed well and kept up a hard pace, knowing that his exertions would keep him warm. He pressed on through the night, only looking for a spot to sleep as the sun crested the horizon.

He found the spot in a clearing on an eastern plateau of the mountains that rose up toward Camp Natalon. The plateau was wide, with a thick canopy of trees and lush undergrowth. Grass grew in wide swathes.

Pellar paused before he entered the plateau, scanning it carefully for any signs of life. A tingling feeling, some strange sense of unease, disturbed him and he shrank back tight against a boulder. He waited, taking the time to pull a piece of jerked beef from his tunic, chewing on the tough strip of meat slowly both from necessity and to force himself to maintain his composure as Mikal had trained him.

He peered around the boulder much later and scanned the plateau again. It took him a moment to spot what had first disturbed him—a darker spot of brown underneath one of the trees. He peered at it suspiciously. A breeze blowing up the side of the mountain, fanned by the warming air of the morning sun, caused something bright on the dark mound to flicker. Pellar shrank back against his boulder and waited again.

Finally, he peered back around, examining the whole plateau until he was certain that it was abandoned. He moved around the boulder that had hidden him and walked briskly onto the plateau. He still suspiciously searched the area, stopping to check the ground and scan the areas beyond the plateau that had been out of his sight, resting himself against a tree or crouching down by a boulder. Satisfied, he made a roundabout circle to the brown spot.

The bright something he'd seen earlier resolved itself to a bundle of yellow flowers. Pellar paused, his throat suddenly tight and dry.

The mound was a grave, newly dug—and it was too small for an adult.

He took a deep breath and worked his way closer to the mound, keeping a careful eye out for any signs of footprints. At first he thought he'd found none, then, as he looked near where the flowers had been left, he made out faint signs of disturbed ground. Curious, he got on his hands and knees, and bent close to the ground. The markings didn't look like footprints until he got close enough to see the straight thin lines of bindings and realized that the strange markings around them were those of bark being pressed into the ground. The prints were small, another child.

A child wearing sandals made of bark tied on to the feet with twine.

"You can make shoes out of anything," Mikal had once told him. "Wherhide's the best, of course. But I once made a pair out of bark." He'd shaken his head. "They're brittle, hard to keep on, and don't last long, but they're better than going barefoot, particularly in the cold."

Pellar made a wide circle around the far side of the grave, trying to intersect the bark-sandal tracks as they moved away. He found them. He got down on the ground again, carefully, checking for signs of others. He was about to give up when he noticed some disturbed grass. He smiled to himself.

Someone had very carefully erased his or her tracks. If the small child hadn't felt compelled to put some flowers on the grave site, Pellar doubted if he would have spotted the tracks at all. Now that he knew what to look for, it would be easy to find—the tracks were less than a day old.

A small child had died and been buried here in an unmarked grave without even flowers to mark the passing. Another child—maybe a sister or a brother—had sneaked back to put flowers on the grave before joining the rest of the troop as they headed north toward Camp Natalon.

If he moved quickly, Pellar thought, he could trail the group right to their camp. Pellar was certain that they were Shunned. Tightening his jaw in determination, Pellar hiked his pack farther up his shoulders. But he had not gone forty paces when he spotted the broken stems of flowers snatched along the pathway. They were taken in ones and twos from a clump, so that only someone looking would have seen them. Pellar wondered for a moment if the child who had picked them had done that deliberately or had merely been picking the nicest flowers he or she could find. He looked down at the clump and stopped, his face clouded.

He unshouldered his pack, pulled out a small shovel, and carefully dug up a small outcropping of the flowers.

Carrying them in his hands, he returned to the grave site and firmly planted them on it, going so far as to pour a bit of his precious water over them. Images of Carissa were mingled in his mind with those of another child, older and faceless but another innocent lost because of the Shunned and those who Shunned them.

Nodding to the dead child's ghost, Pellar stood back up from his planting, dusted himself off, and turned back resolutely to his tracking. How long, he wondered, could a child who wore bark shoes survive in the northern cold?

He turned back to face the direction of the tracks and peered into the distance, spotting landmarks and guessing at their general destination. Satisfied that he could pick up the trail again, Pellar turned back the way he came. If he went back to the road, he thought, he could make better time and get in front of the slow-moving band.

Pellar arrived at Camp Natalon in the middle of the night, silently moving through the trees on the plain to the west before breaking out into the camp's clearing and striding boldly, as if he belonged, to the small stone cot that Zist occupied.

The entire camp was sleeping; not even a night shift was working the mine, for that evening there had been a great celebration. Pellar had observed it all from across the lake. When the last of the festivities had died down, he had started his roundabout journey, going west around the far side of the lake, crossing the stream that fed it, and picking his way through the forest.

By the time Pellar reached Master Zist's doorstep, the evening had turned so cold that Pellar could be seen clearly even in the dim light of the lesser of Pern's two moons. As he knocked on the door, his stomach grumbled loudly.

The door opened quickly and Zist stood back, blinking away sleep, to let Pellar in to the warmth.

"Your lips are blue," Zist told him. Pellar could only nod in agreement. Zist grabbed him by the shoulder, turned him, and gave him a gentle shove. "The fire's over there."

Pellar scented succulent smells in the air. "I saved you some food from the feast," Zist said, and Pellar picked up his pace.

He was surprised and grateful when Master Zist thrust a cup of warm *klah* into his frozen hands and pushed him into a chair, making it clear that Pellar was to eat before discussing their business.

As Pellar avidly ate and drank, Zist sat and leaned back in his chair, eyeing the youngster worriedly. Pellar caught the look and interpreted it correctly. He reached under his cloak and pulled out his slate, sliding it over to Master Zist before returning to the excellent food on his plate.

Zist frowned until he saw that the slate was covered with a stiff piece of cloth. He folded the cloth aside and saw that Pellar had written a long missive in carefully precise, tiny letters.

As Zist read, his eyebrows went up.

"You found their camp?" he said in surprise, looking up to Pellar for confirmation. The young harper nodded, grinned, and waved for his Master to continue reading. Zist grunted in assent and bent over the slate once more. He did not read for long before he looked up again. "Mostly children? How are they dressed?"

Pellar pointed to the slate again and once more Zist returned to his reading. The next time he looked up, ready to ask a question, Pellar merely smiled and pointed back down to the slate.

"There's nothing more there!" Zist protested. Pellar nodded in agreement. "So that's all you know?"

Pellar nodded again.

"Winter's coming on," Zist muttered to himself. "Those children will freeze."

Pellar made a grimace in agreement and then emphatically rubbed his belly.

"And starve," Zist agreed. "But I don't understand why they're here. Why weren't they left somewhere else? What use are they up here?"

Pellar stood up, waving his arms to attract the harper's attention and, when he got it, pointed his thumb at himself, put his hand flat over his head, and then lowered it down to his waist while making big and cute eyes.

"They're small and cute."

Pellar nodded and waved a hand, palm up in a general arc, pointed toward the miners' cottages at the edge of the lake, and then gave Zist the same small-child look.

"Well, of course there are children the same age here, but everyone must know all the children in the camp by now."

Pellar gestured for his slate and Zist passed it to him, waiting patiently until the young man passed it back with the new message, "Not at night."

"They're stealing coal at night?" Zist asked, frowning. After a moment's thought he declared, "They couldn't take much, being so small."

Pellar shook his head and dramatically raised a hand

to his forehead, turning back and forth, scanning the room intently.

"They keep watch," Zist surmised. He nodded in agreement. "And, at night, if one of them saw someone he didn't recognize, he could shout a warning or act lost and no one would be the wiser."

Zist leaned back in his chair and gestured for Pellar to sit down. Pellar knew the old harper well: He filled his plate again and nibbled at its contents while occasionally eyeing Master Zist as if hoping to see what the harper was thinking.

"Do you know how much they're taking?" Zist asked after a long, thoughtful silence. Pellar looked up from his plate and shrugged. Zist gave him a small nod of thanks and resumed his musings.

A long while later, Pellar finished his dinner and reached for his slate again.

"Tell me about the feast," he wrote.

Master Zist reached for the slate, read it in a quick glance and grunted in assent. "It was quite interesting," he replied. "Illuminating, really."

Zist proceeded to describe the wedding between Silstra, the daughter of Danil, one of the miners—in fact, the sole remaining wherhandler at Camp Natalon—and a Smithcrafter named Terregar. He went on at length about the singing ability of one of Danil's younger sons and the strains he'd noticed between Natalon, the camp's founder, and Tarik, his uncle.

"And the strangest thing was the watch-wher," Zist added, shaking his head in awe. "It flew over the ceremony, carrying a basket of glows in its claws."

Pellar jerked his head up in surprise. He tucked his thumbs under his shoulders and flapped his arms awkwardly, disbelief clear on his face.

"I know, I know," Zist said, raising a hand to fend off Pellar's skepticism, "it's hard to believe a watch-wher flying and no one's ever reported such a thing before. But then, no one really pays much attention to watch-whers.

"I had a long talk with Danil about it afterward and he claims that he even rode the beast once at night." Zist shook his head at the notion. "Said that the air was thicker at night."

Pellar shrugged, then wrote on his slate, "Not as good as dragons."

"No, certainly not," Zist agreed. "It's one thing for a beast to go where it wants, and quite another to train it to go where *you* want it to go."

Pellar nodded emphatically, recalling his efforts to train Chitter. Zist smiled and shook his head fondly. "There's no love lost between Tarik and Natalon, that much is obvious," he continued. "And I'm afraid in my first few days here I also created some stress between Kindan and Kaylek." He glanced at Pellar, saw his confusion, and explained. "They're two of Danil's boys. The younger one has got the makings of a good singer, while the older—well, he'll do well in the mines.

"Kaylek's got the makings of a bully," Zist added after a moment spent with his lips pursed in thought. "And I'm afraid he may take his anger out on Kindan. I'd hate to have the youngster too scared by his big brother to sing from now on."

Pellar thought, then wrote, "Mentor."

Zist glanced at the word and nodded.

"I suppose that might work," he agreed. It was an old Harper Hall trick to assign some of the more difficult personalities the job of mentoring a younger person. Sometimes the responsibility and the assumption of a mantle of authority succeeded in teaching the "mentor" more than the youngster.

"But who?" Zist asked himself, leaning back once more in his chair.

A yawn escaped from Pellar before he could clamp his jaws shut against it. Master Zist looked up and smiled, shaking his head. "There's no need for you to stay. I can ponder on this by myself." He rose from his chair and gestured to the kitchen. Pellar smiled and charged forward eagerly, opening his carisak as he moved. After twenty minutes of rummaging through Zist's stores, Pellar pulled the strings on the carisak tightly closed and put it on his shoulders. Master Zist smiled, asking, "Did you get your fill of supplies?"

Pellar patted his carisak and nodded. He retrieved his slate, hung it back around his neck, and settled it under his tunic.

"Chitter's guarding your camp?" Zist guessed as they headed for the door, Pellar leading the way. "You can send him here if you need more supplies."

Pellar turned back to the harper, surprised.

"Oh," Zist said with a laugh, "if he's seen I'll just say that he's here on harper business." He winked at Pellar. "And it'll be true, won't it?"

Suddenly, as if on cue, a fire-lizard exploded into the hallway, searching desperately for Pellar and screeching anxiously.

"What is this, is he hungry?" Zist asked. Pellar reached out and coaxed the skittish fire-lizard into his arms, stroking him gently with one hand. Once Chitter had settled, Pellar lifted him away from his body in order to look the fire-lizard in the eye. Zist stood by quietly, still marveling at the way Pellar had learned to commune with the creature.

After a moment, Pellar drew Chitter close to his side again and stroked him softly with a finger. Then he launched the fire-lizard into the air and Chitter went *between* again, leaving only a cold patch of air behind.

Pellar turned to the door with an unmistakable air of urgency.

"Pellar, what is it?"

The youngster turned back, pulling his slate from under his tunic at the same time and quickly writing, "Someone found my camp."

Pellar didn't return to his camp. Instead he spent the night cold and restless crouched nearby, waiting for dawn.

As the sun rose high enough to spread its rays into the deep valley where he'd made his camp, Pellar willed himself to be calm and motionless, doing his best not to give away his position to anyone who might be looking for him.

He had sent Chitter back to Master Zist with a note to say that he was safe and had told the fire-lizard to wait with the harper until he called for him.

Pellar waited an hour before he was satisfied that no one was lurking near his camp, then he slowly made his way toward it. Someone had found his pack, examined it, and carefully rehidden it.

Except—there was a small bouquet of flowers on top of it.

Pellar smiled. It didn't take him long to spot the tracks of bark-soled shoes. He was sure that whoever had found his camp was the same person—a little girl?—who had left the flowers at the grave site.

Quickly he gathered his things, careful to leave his campsite no more disturbed than before. Then he shrugged on his backpack and strode away, determined to find a better campsite, resolved to leave no more clues of his presence.

Pellar found his new hiding place high up in the mountains to the east of Camp Natalon. The site itself was a cave whose narrow entrance looked like it was nothing more than a crevice. Inside, the crevice widened out again. Pellar imagined that part of the mountain had split a long time ago to make the hollow he found. A steady, chilling breeze blew through the crevice and up the natural chimney formed by the mountain's split. Fortunately, part of the hollow was wider and provided a relatively sheltered spot out of the worst of the breeze.

That was just as well, for Pellar was shivering with a bone-deep chill when he finally crawled into the widening part of the crevice and decided to make it his camp. The last rays of the evening sun only partially lit his new hiding place.

He carefully scouted out a collection of small rocks and set them out in a circle, in the center of which he placed the bundle of dead twigs and branches he'd gathered along his way. From one pocket he pulled some dead leaves and from another his precious flint stones.

With the fire going, Pellar rolled out his bedding and pulled off his boots. He made a face when one of the leather laces broke, and made yet another when he reached into his pack for his spare and found only dirtied twine instead. He stared at it dumbly for a moment and then shook his head in chagrin—apparently his flower giver had made him a trade, taking his good leather lace strips for her bark-soled shoes and leaving him her worn-out twine in their place.

With a sigh, Pellar found the least worn, least dirty piece of the twine and cut it off of the rest, carefully knotted it onto his broken lace and laid his boots near the fire to dry. He placed his wet socks on a nearby rock but, mindful of a time early in his training with Master Zist, not so near that they would catch fire.

His feet, socks, and boots were wet not just from the sweat of his exertion in climbing into this new place but also from his trek through a number of streambeds as he worked to hide his trail. Master Zist had told him about the burned-out Shunned wagon that he'd found on his ill-fated sojourn with Cayla and Carissa, and that tale, along with so many others regarding the Shunned, left Pellar certain that at least some of them would think nothing of killing him for his belongings— or even just out of simple spite.

Pellar clenched his jaw as he thought of the little flower girl in the company of such rough men. His thoughts grew darker and he found himself thinking about Moran, Zist's lost apprentice, imagining him tortured and worse after being unmasked by the Shunned. For a moment, Pellar shook in cold fear, but then got control of himself. He had Chitter and he was better, much better, at tracking and fieldcraft than Moran had ever been—Master Zist had said so repeatedly.

Pellar took a deep calming breath and stared at the fire. With a start he realized that some of the cold he felt was from letting the fire burn low. He smiled at his silliness and gently fed some smaller twigs to the fire until it was strong enough to take another branch.

Satisfied, he searched through his pack for some more jerked beef and chewed on it slowly, doing his best not to think of bubbly pies or sliced roast wherry. When his stomach felt fuller, he put the rest of the jerky away.

He stared at the fire, then craned his head around to get a good look at his surroundings.

Chitter, he thought, concentrating on the image of the fire-lizard and sending a mental image of his hiding place.

A rush of cold air burst on him and suddenly the hollow was full of ecstatic fire-lizard, warbling in pride at having found Pellar.

Pellar burst into a wide grin and held out an arm for the small creature to perch on.

You are the best, Pellar thought to him. Chitter preened and stroked his face against Pellar's.

* * *

Pellar soon fell into a routine, meeting every other sevenday with Master Zist while the rest of the time keeping a distant eye on the spot he'd noted at the camp's coal dump where the Shunned were stealing their coal.

Their depradations were small and carefully timed, occurring when fresh coal had been deposited by a night shift but before the coal could be bagged, making it harder for the theft to be noticed.

Pellar was glad of his visits, not only for the warmth and the food, but also for the chance to hear Zist's observations of the miners. He was glad to hear that the harper had taken his suggestion regarding Kaylek and pleasantly surprised to learn that it had worked— Kaylek and Cristov had formed a pleasant attachment, the elder Kaylek learning more restraint and the younger Cristov becoming more outgoing and assured by Kaylek's teachings.

Aside from those visits, Pellar ventured no farther from his cave than he needed, ensuring that he left few tracks. Those tracks he did leave always headed first south before circling back around to the north, and he was careful to break his tracks whenever he could, whether by walking in the middle of a stream or by climbing across several trees.

He never used the same observation point two days in a row, and chose each one so that he could observe his previous observation point from his current one, in case someone had spotted him the day before.

He stayed at his observation point only long enough to see what the Shunned had taken from the coal dump the night before. Because he moved when they were sleeping, Pellar was less worried about being discovered by the Shunned than he was about being discovered by Ima, Camp Natalon's hunter. But his caution worked just as well in keeping him from her sight as it did from the Shunned.

Still, he made it a point to arrive at his day's observation point an hour or two before dawn, and left as quickly as he could.

He had learned in his two months of observations that the night shift, which included the light-sensitive watch-wher, usually finished before the sun crested the horizon, and he kept a careful eye for when they left the mine, not certain how good the watch-wher's sight was and whether it might spot him.

He was surprised one morning when the sky seemed to have gotten lighter than usual and still the night shift hadn't departed the mine shaft. In fact, the sun was now over the horizon and others in the camp were beginning to stir. Pellar smiled as he spotted a distant figure walking sedately from the Harper's cot to Natalon's stone house: Master Zist on his way to teach the children of the camp.

Not long after, his surprise turned to alarm when he noticed a trickle of dark smoke—coal dust—rising out of the mine shaft's mouth. The trickle grew to a torrent and Pellar, with a sinking feeling, realized that something terrible had happened.

He could think of no way to send a warning to Master Zist, nor any of the miners. The torrent of coal was its own alarm, darkening the sky above the camp, marking it in shadow. Miners in the camp noticed the smoke and moved quickly.

Soon the camp was a swarm of activity around the mine entrance. Pellar watched in horror as the tragedy played itself out in the distance. He saw how the women in the camp set up an aid station, saw one boy, about ten or so, rush out of the mine, grab some bandages, and rush back while one of the nurses waved her arms after him scoldingly. Pellar guessed that the boy was one of the victims' sons.

A knot formed in Pellar's throat as he imagined how the youngster must feel and he wished fervently, as if his hopes could change the past, that the boy's father was not too badly injured.

Or perhaps the victim was another boy, Pellar thought as he suddenly remembered that Kaylek was supposed to have been on that shift for the first time. Was Kaylek among the injured?

Feeling an indistinct bond with the lad, who was near his own age, Pellar strained through the distance for any sign of him.

For hours Pellar watched the tragedy, saw the few injured brought up out of the mine, caught sight of a red-haired boy being brought up. Hours later, Pellar gasped in relief as he spotted a youngster emerge from the mine shaft. His relief was short-lived: He saw the figure find the red-haired boy and realized that the other boy was not Kaylek but his little brother.

He kept looking and hoping until he saw one of the women throw a blanket over the two boys and realized that they were the only children in the aid station.

There was no sign of the watch-wher, Dask, of his handler, Danil, or of any of the sons of Danil that had been assigned to that shift. Nor was there any sign of the red-haired boy's father.

Chitter arrived with a cryptic note from Master Zist later the next day: "He can't stay here for a while."

Pellar considered the notion of sending the brown fire-lizard back to the Harper Hall, but he was not at all sure that Chitter would go, nor that he could recall the fire-lizard from such a distance.

Pellar waited several days before making his way cir-

cuitously to the camp. He'd seen the shrouded bodies of
the dead miners brought up—there were nine.

He'd started his journey at the first of the dark, so
there was a chance that the Shunned might also be moving. He sent Chitter ahead to the miners' graveyard to
reconnoiter and followed more slowly, going down the
southern side of his mountain, around west below the
lake, crossing the stream that fed it at the far side before
going east again toward the camp. The night was noisy
with the light winds that carried the cold mountain air
down into the cooling valley.

The graveyard was in a clearing beside a waterfall
that gushed down the cliffside a kilometer west of the
miners' camp.

It was a peaceful place with thankfully few graves—
most of them, sadly, the nine new ones from this latest
accident.

Pellar had picked some yellow flowers on his way and
wasn't surprised to see, among other large floral bou-
quets, small bunches of yellow flowers already at the
graves, each bunch tied together with a blade of grass.
Even though it was possible that the yellow flowers had
been left by one of the miners' children, Pellar was certain that the little girl had left them.

He wondered if the little girl who had left the flowers
did so because she felt somehow responsible. Or was it
just because she was remembering her own dead, and
honoring them by honoring these—as Pellar was honoring Cayla and Carissa.

Pellar's musings were interrupted as Chitter suddenly
ruffled his wings loudly and disappeared *between*. It
was a warning. Pellar pushed himself tight against a
tree, motionless.

A figure appeared near the grave site, not three meters from Pellar. The figure made its way to the graves.
Pellar caught sight of a strand of blond hair around the

person's face. It was a youngster—a girl, Pellar thought—perhaps two years younger than himself. Definitely not the flower girl, who was much smaller and probably younger, too.

Something alarmed her, and she turned toward Pellar's hiding place, reached down, and searched the ground with her hand, coming up with a large rock.

"Who's there?" she called—definitely a girl. "I've got a rock."

Pellar pressed closer against the tree, though he was positive that she couldn't see him in the darkness.

Strangely, the girl sniffed the air. "I can tell you're not from the camp," she called over the breeze. "If you don't identify yourself, I'll—I'll tell Master Zist about you."

Pellar allowed himself a smile; Master Zist would be the least of his worries. But he wondered how the girl could tell he wasn't from the camp, and why she had sniffed the air? The breeze was blowing to her from his direction and he knew that a good bath would not be amiss, but he was certain that no one could smell him at such a distance, particularly in a clearing full of fresh-cut flowers. Perhaps she *could* see him. But if so, why hadn't she thrown her rock?

The girl stayed motionless for a minute more, then dropped her rock and turned back to the camp. She paused once, turned back quickly, perhaps hoping to catch Pellar leaving his hiding place, and called, "Don't say I didn't warn you! Master Zist has quite a temper and won't give up until he finds you."

Pellar stifled a snort of laughter; he was certain that he was more familiar with both Master Zist's temper and tenaciousness than the girl was.

He waited until his feet and fingers were numb before he sent the thought to Chitter to check the way to the camp. Chitter responded instantly, letting him know that the way was clear.

Thirty minutes later, well past midnight, Pellar was ushered into Master Zist's kitchen and handed a mug of warm *klah*. Affectionately, the Master also tossed some small rolls in Chitter's direction; they were caught midair by the hungry fire-lizard.

"Was that you that Nuella ran into at the grave site?" Zist asked as soon as he saw Pellar rest his mug on the kitchen table and pull out his slate.

Pellar didn't pick up his slate but instead drew two curves in the air with his hands and then brought one hand, palm flat, against his chest at the height of the girl he'd encountered.

"Yes," Zist agreed drolly, "that would be Nuella. She thought she'd frightened you away."

Pellar smiled and shook his head.

"I'd prefer it if she didn't find you again."

Pellar nodded emphatically in agreement.

"And I think we should be very careful about your future visits," Zist said. He jerked his head toward the front of the cottage. "I've got a new houseguest."

Pellar raised his eyebrows in surprise.

"Kindan," Zist explained. "One of Danil's sons. He wanted to stay on at the Camp and as none of his kin could take him, I"—the harper waved a hand—"agreed to take him in."

Pellar tried his best to hide his dismay, but Zist knew him too well.

"My predecessor, Harper Jofri, thought highly of him," Zist continued. "His notes show that Kindan has potential as a harper."

Pellar was afraid he knew what was coming next.

"I'm thinking of taking him as my apprentice."

Pellar burst up from his chair, his anger and sense of

betrayal overwhelming him and he pointed emphatically at his chest. "Me! Me!" he wanted to shout.

"Shh!" Zist hissed, waving Pellar back down into his chair. "He's got good ears—he'll hear you and we don't want that."

Pellar's eyes flashed in an obvious response. *Let him!* he thought.

"Jofri has gone back for his Mastery," Zist said, looking sternly at Pellar. "And while it's possible for a Master to have two apprentices—though rare—it's more common to promote one to journeyman."

The color drained as abruptly from Pellar's face as his anger did from his heart and he sat down loudly in his seat.

"Better," Zist said. He cocked his head at Pellar and waggled a finger in his direction. "Although after an outburst like that—" He broke off abruptly and shook his head.

"The truth is that you're still a bit too young to be rated a journeyman," Zist admitted with a sigh. "You need two, maybe even four, more Turns of experience." He caught Pellar's eyes squarely with his own. "But you know everything you need to know—"

Pellar interrupted with a wave of his hands, pointing to his throat.

"Singing, or even speaking, isn't everything," Zist answered waspishly. He glanced back to the rooms at the front of the cottage and added, "In fact, I rather suspect in a short while I'll come to regard your quiet ways with more than a little nostalgia."

Zist frowned in thought for a moment and then nodded. "I'll rate you journeyman, pending more classes back at the Harper Hall. By the time we're done here, I'm sure you'll have earned it.

"Now," he continued, briskly changing the topic, "tell me all your latest news."

It didn't take Pellar long to bring Master Zist up to date with his observations of the past few days. He hesitated before telling Master Zist about the flowers he'd seen at the grave site—he hadn't thought to mention his previous encounter, and he was afraid that Zist would be not angry but perhaps displeased at the omission.

He was right. Zist pressed him for every detail and made him repeat the details about how his leather laces had been exchanged for twine.

"You know you should have told me earlier," Zist told him when Pellar had finished writing out his latest answer. Pellar grimaced and nodded sheepishly. Zist regarded him steadily and then added in a voice tinged with sympathy, "I can see, perhaps, why you kept this to yourself."

"I shouldn't have," Pellar wrote back on his slate.

"I can understand the way you feel," Zist said. "It must have seemed a bit of a betrayal when she took your laces."

Pellar thought for a moment and then rocked one hand in a side-to-side maybe-yes, maybe-no gesture.

"She needed them," he wrote in explanation.

"I'm sure she did," Zist agreed. "But more than you?"

Pellar thought about that for a while before he answered with a shrug.

Zist nodded absently and sat back in his chair, cupping one knee with his hands while engrossed in thought.

"Winter will be coming soon," he murmured after a long silence. He looked up at Pellar and sat forward. "I expect the Shunned will leave the area when the snows come. When that happens, I'll want you to go back to the Harper Hall."

Pellar was disturbed at the notion of leaving Master Zist by himself, and his facial expression made it clear.

"I'll be safe enough," Zist said, waving aside the objection. "Besides, I couldn't live with myself if you froze to death on a fool's errand."

"I could follow them," Pellar suggested on his slate.

"I think you'd be better employed back at the Harper Hall."

Pellar nodded, hiding his own thought that it would be months before winter and things could change.

As the weather grew colder, Pellar grew bolder. He still avoided the area of the Shunned's camp but he spent more of the daylight out of hiding. Partly it was from necessity—he felt a need for more fresh food than he could reasonably ask Chitter to carry from Master Zist's. Partly it was to increase his woodcraft. Partly, also, it was to keep warm by constantly moving in the cold weather. Partly, Pellar admitted when he forced himself to be honest, it was to prove his abilities to himself.

He carefully copied the traps and styles of Camp Natalon's hunter, but avoided setting out any traps where the hunter might operate. If anyone other than Ima, the hunter, came across the traps, they'd attribute them to him rather than someone else.

Pellar chose to seed his traps down the south side of his mountain, toward distant Crom Hold and away from both Camp Natalon and the Shunned.

As the weather grew colder still and the first snows began to fall, Pellar decided that there might be some sense in Master Zist's desire to send him back to the Harper Hall. The snow was not yet sticking but, even so, Pellar had to spend extra care to ensure that he left tracks neither in snow nor in the muddy ground that it produced when it melted.

Pellar's best traps were simple loop snares that, when

sprung, hurled the quarry high up into the trees, out of sight of anyone that might later come along.

Being cautious, Pellar always varied his routes, sometimes starting at one end of his line of traps, sometimes the other, sometimes in the middle—he never took the same route on any given day and he never repeated his pattern.

This day, nearly three months since he'd visited the graveyard, he had decided to work from the highest traps to lowest. The first four traps were all empty. He made a note to consider moving them but decided not to do it just then.

As he approached his fifth trap something disturbed him—something seemed out of place. He stopped, crouching against the ground, listening carefully.

Someone was out there.

He slowly started scanning the ground below him, working his way carefully left to right, bottom to top. He spotted a disturbance of the ground near his trap. He looked up—and suddenly started. Someone was caught in his trap!

It was a little girl, no more than nine Turns old. She was staring back at him, her brown eyes locked intently on him as she hung upside down, one foot caught in the loop of his rope snare. One hand feebly held her tunic up to protect her torso from the cold wind but it flopped down enough on the other side that he could see her bulging belly and bare ribs; her legs were little more than sticks. It was also obvious, from her heaving chest and her bitter look of despair, that she'd exhausted herself in efforts to get free of the trap. On the ground below her, Pellar noted a small knife and guessed that she'd lost it when the trap had sprung. Her clothing—small, patched, and threadbare—merely confirmed his guess that she was one of the Shunned.

Pellar remained motionless for several moments, trying to decide what to do. But when he finally made up his mind to help her and stood up, she waved him down.

No sooner had he crouched back down than he heard the sound of others approaching. They came without talking but not silently, moving in a way that any tracker would be quick to notice. Pellar counted five, including a tall, wiry youth who was probably in his late teens, maybe older.

"Halla!" one of the younger ones called as they caught sight of her. "What are you doing up there?"

"Don't ask silly questions," the little girl snapped back, "just get me down."

"I don't know why," the teenager replied. "You got yourself caught, you should get yourself down."

In that instant, Pellar decided that he hated the young man. It wasn't just his words, or his tone, it was the youth's body language: Pellar *knew* that this teen would have no compunction, nor feel any guilt, about leaving the little girl stuck in the trap to die.

"Tenim, get me down," Halla commanded, her irritation tinged with just the slightest hint of fear.

"I warned you to be careful about where you set your traps. It's a pity you didn't get your neck caught in the thing," Tenim said. "Then you'd be dead by now." He turned back the way he came.

"But Tenim, she's our best tracker," one of the younger children protested. "And Moran—"

"Leave Moran out of this," Tenim snapped to the speaker. "What he doesn't know won't hurt him any.

"Anyway," and here Tenim raised one arm straight out in front of him, "she's not our best tracker."

Pellar was no more than five meters from Tenim and the group. Silently, he felt for the hunting knife he kept sheathed at the top of his boot, still keeping his eyes on the scene in front of him. Would they just leave her to die? Would he?

He heard a strange sound in the sky above him and noticed that Tenim's upraised arm was covered with rough bindings of leather.

Suddenly something swooped down from the sky. For a moment Pellar feared it was Chitter come to protect him, but then he realized that the creature had none of Chitter's sleekness, nor his thin, membranous wings.

This creature was a bird.

"*She* is the best tracker," Tenim said as the bird landed on his arm. His other hand dipped into one of the pouches hung at his side and brought up a thin sliver of meat, which the bird devoured quickly. "Grief, here, is."

"What about the food *I* got you?" Halla called from the tree, her tone growing desperate. "Can Grief feed you all?"

Tenim's features hardened. "At least she doesn't get caught."

"Moran'll know something's wrong when I don't come back," Halla said, trying a different tack.

"So?" Tenim replied, unimpressed. "What makes you think what Moran says matters to me?"

Halla had no answer for that. Her lips quivered and she looked ready to cry.

Tenim glanced from her and back to the bird on his arm, a wicked smile on his face. With a quick command, he flung his arm upward and the bird took flight.

Pellar tensed, ready to spring, as the bird swooped onto the trapped girl, but any noise his movements made was drowned out by Halla's fearful scream. Then, just as Pellar decided to attack Tenim, bird or no bird, Halla's scream turned to one of surprise, followed by a yelp as the bird's beak sliced the rope snare and she fell hard to the ground, curled into a ball and rolling to absorb the worst of the fall.

She was up again in an instant, her arms in a fighting stance.

"Thanks for nothing, Tenim," she snarled, racing up to him. But she recoiled as Grief dropped again from the sky, screeching in her face.

"You owe me, Halla," Tenim told her, a cold smile on his face. The smile changed to a leer as he added, "When the time comes, I'll collect."

The color drained from Halla's face as his words registered. She regained her composure, saying, "If you're still alive."

Tenim smiled but said nothing, instead reaching up once more to retrieve his bird and feed it. He turned away from Halla, muttering soothing sounds to the bird, waved with his other hand for the troop to follow him, and started away up the hill.

Pellar stayed in his hiding place, frozen in thought and anger, with one unanswered question burning in his brain: Why hadn't the girl turned him in?

"You're certain that they said Moran?" Zist asked days later. Pellar had waited until he was certain that his hiding place wasn't in danger and then, taking all his gear with him, had set off carefully, using a route he'd never before used to get to the miners' camp.

Pellar nodded firmly.

"So . . ." Zist's voice drifted off as he frowned, deep in thought.

Pellar knew that Moran had been Zist's apprentice. He dimly remembered a young man full of song and pretensions but Pellar had been still little when Moran had left on his mission to find the Shunned. Turns had passed and no one had heard from him. Zist and Murenny had sadly given him up for dead.

But rumors of a harper named Moran had cropped up in conversations at various Gathers, particularly those of Crom and Telgar Holds. In fact, Zist had chosen Crom Hold partly in the dim hope that he might find Moran, or, at least, find out more about his fate.

Pellar had heard the rumors, too, and had noted that this "harper" seemed surrounded by children, Shunned or orphaned.

When Pellar had brought it up with Master Zist, the harper had waved the issue aside dismissively. "It could be him," he'd said. "Or it could be someone pretending to be him. We'll never know until we find him."

And now Pellar waited patiently, nursing his *klah*, and refilling it in the long silence while Master Zist reviewed his memories. It was a long while before he looked up at Pellar again.

"And only the girl saw you, you're certain?"

Again, Pellar nodded.

"Hmm . . ." Zist's attention drifted away again.

Pellar took the opportunity to refill his bowl with warm stew and had finished it, offering spare tidbits to Chitter, long before Master Zist disturbed him with another question.

"And you're certain that this Tenim thought that the girl was the one who set the traps?"

Pellar nodded fervently.

Zist pursed his lips and stroked his chin, picking up Pellar's stack of slates and reviewing them again.

"There were seven in the troop. Did that include the boy and the girl?"

Pellar nodded.

Zist lapsed into his longest silence. Pellar had two helpings of dessert before the harper looked up at him once more.

"I can't ask you to stay on," Zist began, but Pellar held up a hand, shaking his head. He pointed to Zist,

then to himself, and then grasped both his hands firmly:
We stay together.

"It's too dangerous," Zist protested.

Pellar grabbed for a slate and quickly wrote, "More dangerous alone."

He examined the older man anxiously, saw the look of determination forming in Zist's countenance, and wrote, "Find out about Moran."

Master Zist looked unconvinced, so Pellar swiftly wrote, "Got old sheets?"

Zist read the slate and repeated quizzically, "Old sheets?"

"To hide in the snow," Pellar wrote back. Taking advantage of Zist's surprise, he wrote on another slate, "I could get close to their camp, get a real count, see what they're doing. You know I can, Mikal said I was the best."

"What about the girl?"

Pellar's face took on a bleak look and he gently drew the slate back and wrote slowly, "She's small, not fed well. May not last the winter."

Zist sat long in silence after he read Pellar's reply. Finally he said, "I've two worn sheets you can use."

The Shunned's camp was exactly where Pellar had guessed—a kilometer north and east of the miners' coal dump, and past a line of suspiciously small mounds. The mounds were covered with snow so Pellar had no way of knowing how long they had been there.

Master Zist had insisted that he wait until after the first heavy snowfall and Pellar had decided that journeying as more snow was falling would further hide him and neatly erase his tracks.

He paused for a long moment beside the mounds, trying hard to convince himself that none were long enough for the bright-eyed girl, and in the end grimly continued his trek.

His first signs of the Shunned's camp came in the form of footprints in the snow. He examined them carefully. There were two sets of prints, heading away from him, roughly paralleling his own journey from the coal dump. Both sets of prints were those of adults, both wore shoes, and both were carrying heavy loads.

Coal.

Pellar followed the backtrail far enough to see where the footprints disappeared in the snow and judged that he was half an hour behind.

He took a bearing on the tracks, then he paused for a moment, thinking. From what little he had seen of the youth, Tenim, Pellar guessed that he would be very wary and cautious. That was one reason that Pellar had decided to wait until the second heavy snowfall before he tried to find the Shunned's camp.

The other reason was the bird, Grief. While Chitter was quite willing to pop *between* from a warm hiding place at Master Zist's to a cold snowfall, he doubted that the bird would be up for scouting in the midst of a snowstorm. So, he reasoned, not only would the falling snow make it easier for him to remain hidden but he would have fewer eyes trying to spy him out.

Without the bird to watch out for him, Pellar guessed that Tenim would be extra cautious. Nodding to himself, he decided that Tenim would take a sharp turn to his camp but also double back to it. So first Pellar had to find where the two had turned, then he had to turn back to find their camp. He also had to be very careful—it was just as possible that the two would turn toward him as away from him.

He started forward, cautiously flitting from tree to tree, and then suddenly stopped.

He heard voices.

"I thought I saw someone."

Pellar froze.

"Shards, why don't you shout it," another voice growled in response. It was Tenim.

"Shh," the first speaker hissed urgently.

Pellar held his breath, letting it out again as slowly and quietly as he could. The voices were too near for his comfort.

"There's nothing out there," Tenim pronounced after minutes of silence. "It's just your guilty conscience getting you, Tarik."

"When you said I'd get rich, you never said that I'd have to haul your coal for you," Tarik grumbled in response. "What happened to all those brats of yours?"

"If you're complaining, why don't you bring your own brat along?" Tenim replied. "Not that he'd be able for more than a stone or two."

"You leave Cristov out of it," Tarik warned. "He knows nothing of this."

Tenim laughed cruelly. "He wouldn't think so much of you if he knew what his father was doing."

"It's for him I'm doing this," Tarik replied. "The lad has a right to expect his father to do right by him. The way Natalon's moaning, we'll never earn enough at this mine."

"Not enough for you," Tenim agreed nastily.

"All I want is a place of my own and a chance to rest at the end of my days, not always slaving away for someone," Tarik protested. "I've earned it. I would have had it, too, if it hadn't been for you and the Shunned."

"Well, you don't have to worry about them," Tenim said. "And I said I'd take care of you."

Pellar shuddered, wondering how Tenim planned to take care of Tarik.

"Come on," Tenim said. Pellar heard groaning and

the sound of something heavy being lifted. "Oh, stop groaning, this is the last load. We have to get you back while it's still dark and snowing."

"And you'll want me again the next night it snows," Tarik predicted with a grumble. His voice was farther away than it had been, they were moving.

"Exactly," Tenim agreed viciously. "After all, you want to set something by for the end of your days."

"Why are we hiding the coal way out here? How are you going to get it to market?" Tarik grumbled.

"Don't you worry about that," Tenim said. "When the time comes, this'll fetch a pretty price from the right people."

"How can the Shunned pay for anything?"

The last words Pellar heard was Tenim's response: "Who said anything about the Shunned?"

"I'd thought that they would have to have help from someone at the camp," Zist remarked when Pellar reported back days later. Pellar nodded. "Tarik was my first guess," Zist added, "although I would have preferred being wrong."

"What now?" Pellar wrote on his slate.

Zist didn't look at the note immediately. He acknowledged it with a wave of his hand but sat back, staring off thoughtfully into the distance.

"The boy will have to make his choice," he murmured finally. He glanced at Pellar's note and then at Pellar.

"It would be nice to know what this Tenim plans to do with the coal," Zist observed.

"I could follow him," Pellar offered.

Zist wagged a finger at him. "Only when it's dark and there's snow on the ground. I don't want you caught. In the between times, you'll have to hide here, I'm afraid."

Pellar frowned but Zist didn't notice, once again lost in thought.

"No sign of the younger ones?" the harper asked after a moment. Pellar shook his head.

"A pity," Zist said. "This Crom winter is vicious."

It was awkward, having to hide in the cottage from Kindan, Natalon, Dalor, Nuella, and even Cristov, who was occasionally assigned evening lessons with Master Zist.

When Kindan tripped up Cristov one day, Zist assigned the youngster the job of discovering three of Cristov's virtues. Pellar had found the whole situation amusing, from his position of greater age—two whole Turns—until Master Zist challenged him to do the same when they spoke about it two days later.

"I hardly know him," Pellar wrote in protest.

"You've heard enough about him, haven't you?" Zist asked, arching an eyebrow at him challengingly.

"Words aren't truth," Pellar wrote back.

"Too true!" Zist agreed. "Wiser heads than yours have yet to learn that, you know."

"I listen," Pellar wrote in modest reply.

"Then you should know all about Cristov," Zist replied, returning to his challenge with a twinkle in his eyes.

Pellar was about to write a response when a knock on the side door—the one nearest Natalon's stone house—interrupted him.

"That will be my lesson," Zist said, motioning Pellar into hiding once more.

Swallowing his unhappiness, for he had hoped that Kindan's absence would give him more time to spend with his adoptive father, Pellar retreated to his hiding place in Zist's study. In moments the air was filled with the sound of someone practicing on the pipes. Pellar listened, imagining the fingering and scales while hearing Zist's patient corrections and the young piper's self-deprecating remarks.

Pellar mentally replayed his conversation with Zist and what he'd overheard about Cristov to see if he could rise to his Master's challenge. What did he know about the boy?

He recalled Kindan complaining about how Cristov bragged about sleeping in Kindan's old room and wondered if perhaps Kindan hadn't mistaken Cristov's intent; perhaps Tarik's son was seeking a common ground, some mutual point of interest on which to build a friendship. Pellar knew from what little he'd heard that Cristov had felt very close to Kaylek before his untimely death; perhaps the boy had hoped in a similar way to kindle a friendship with Kaylek's little brother.

It was clear that Cristov respected and honored his father—in fact, most fights Cristov had been involved in had begun over comments about his father. Pellar couldn't blame the lad for being loyal.

Noise of a door opening and voices speaking interrupted Pellar's musings; Zist's lesson had left. Before Pellar came out of hiding, he heard quick steps approaching the front door and the noises of Kindan returning.

He heard Zist quiz Kindan on what he'd learned and was pleased to hear that Kindan listed loyalty as one of Cristov's strengths. Pellar shook his head wryly when Zist demanded that Kindan recount the contents of the cottage—he could have guessed that Master Zist would have had more than one lesson for the lad to learn.

When Zist told Kindan that there'd be a Winter's End celebration the next evening, Pellar fought down a feeling of betrayal, for he hadn't heard of it before and knew that he couldn't possibly attend.

When Kindan had gone to bed, Zist brought Pellar back out of his hiding place, holding a finger to his lips for silence. Pellar gave him a sardonic look and pointed to his lips, shaking his head to remind Zist that there was no fear of *him* talking too loud. Master Zist glared back at him and Pellar's teasing look faded on his face. He knew full well what Zist wanted.

"What did you think?" Zist asked quietly.

"About the house?" Pellar wrote back, referring to Kindan's enumeration of the contents of Tarik's house. Zist nodded. "No surprises, no more than most."

Zist nodded in agreement.

Pellar wiped his slate and quickly added, "A sack full of marks is not hard to hide."

"If he had one," Zist said. Pellar gave him a questioning look, so Zist added, "I don't see why he'd be working here if he already had enough set aside."

"Snow's melting, traders will be here soon," Pellar wrote in response.

"But with the mud and patches of snow on the ground, tracks will be easy to follow," Zist said. "Some traders might wait until later."

"Or Tenim might create a distraction," Pellar suggested.

"*That,*" Zist replied, "is a disturbing notion."

"I could keep watch," Pellar wrote back.

Zist mulled the suggestion over for a long time before he nodded in agreement. "Just don't get caught."

Pellar responded with an indignant look.

"When will you leave?" Zist asked, ignoring the look.

In response, Pellar grabbed his pack.

"It's late enough," Zist said by way of agreement. "Just be careful."

*   *   *

Pellar would have never found Tenim if the other hadn't been with Tarik. It was Tarik's clumsy, irritated motion that had alerted him. Tenim slid through the trees like a wisp of smoke. At the first sign of motion, Pellar froze and slowly pressed himself against the nearest cover.

"Traders will be here soon, and then what?" Tarik muttered angrily as they walked by. "If Natalon finds out that I've been mining the pillars, he'll guess—"

A raised hand from Tenim halted Tarik's tirade.

"What?" Tarik demanded after the barest moment's silence.

Tenim ignored him, turning slowly in a circle where he stood, carefully examining every bit of the terrain.

Pellar desperately wondered if Tenim could sight his trail; he'd been careful to take an oblique approach.

"Nothing," Tenim said after a moment, clearly still nervous. He motioned Tarik onward. "So you're afraid of your nephew, are you?"

"He's too much like his father," Tarik said with a dismissive wave of his hand. "Slow, methodical, never willing to cut corners, but he always gets there in the end."

"What has this got to do with the Traders?"

"He'll figure that someone's been stealing coal, that's what," Tarik growled back.

"Only if he finds out you've been mining the pillars," Tenim observed. "Otherwise he'll think he's only got the coal you and the other shift leaders have reported mining."

"It was easier when it was my own mine I was stealing from," Tarik muttered darkly.

"You still would have had it if it hadn't been for the accident that collapsed the roof," Tenim replied.

"Accidents happen," Tarik said dismissively. "Masterminer Britell's board of inquiry never accused me of anything."

Tenim paused mid-stride and gave Tarik a very piercing look.

"What?" Tarik demanded, sounding just a bit frightened.

"Nothing," Tenim answered with a shrug, gesturing for Tarik to precede him. "Just, as you said, accidents happen."

Tarik looked nervously back over his shoulder. "I've been good for you."

"Indeed you have," Tenim agreed. "In fact, I think we've hauled enough for this evening. Why don't you go back home before your wife and son begin to wonder where you are?"

Tarik glared at the young man. Tenim took the glare with no change of expression, merely leaning down to tie his boots tighter, his hand casually brushing the knife hidden at the boot top. Tarik's anger cooled visibly when he caught sight of the knife hilt and he nodded. "Perhaps I'd better, at that."

"Good," Tenim answered with an unpleasant smile. "You said that there'd be Winter's End festivities tonight? In Natalon's big house?" He didn't wait for Tarik's answer. "I could do with some diversion. Maybe I'll attend—"

"You'd be recognized!"

"—from a safe distance," Tenim finished, his eyes flashing in amusement at the other's blatant terror.

"Don't get caught."

"Have I ever?"

"I found you, didn't I?" Tarik responded.

"Yes, you did," Tenim agreed, lowering his eyes. Considering Tenim's woodcraft, Pellar seriously doubted that Tarik had really found the youth; probably Tenim had *let* himself be found.

"So be careful."

"And you," Tenim replied with a wave as the other turned off toward the camp. Tenim waited several minutes before starting off again—toward the camp.

Pellar followed him cautiously from far behind.

Tenim passed Zist's cottage and then went, more slowly, beyond Natalon's stone "hold." The Shunned youth passed by the camp's cemetery before heading up into the hills and circling back toward the camp.

Pellar waited until he was certain that Tenim was far away before he followed. It took a quarter of an hour of stealthy movement before Pellar reached the top of the cliff and could reinitiate his cautious trailing of the crafty young man.

A sound from the valley below startled Pellar and he froze. The noise sounded like a small rock hitting something more solid. Carefully, Pellar inched to the edge of the cliff, and peered into the valley below.

A glint of white fell—no, was thrown!—from the cliff nearby and landed with a *clack* on the roof of Natalon's stone house.

What was Tenim doing?

Another stone was thrown, landing at the top of the chimney. And another, and another. The stones ricocheted off the roof, landing silently on the soft ground below. A larger stone, big enough to be a rock, was thrown. The impact made a different noise, a sliding noise.

Tenim was trying to block up the chimney! If he succeeded, the fumes from the great hearth fire would quickly overcome anyone inside, including Natalon. And then Tarik would be able to take over the camp, all because of an "accident."

Pellar's response was instant and unthinking. He launched himself from his hiding place and raced along the cliff edge to hurl himself wordlessly upon Tenim.

Even though Tenim was a head taller than him, and twenty kilos heavier, Pellar's mad dive toppled Tenim off balance. They grappled for a moment and then both toppled over the cliff to fall, hard, on the muddy ground behind Natalon's hold.

Tenim recovered first, wrapping his fists around Pellar's throat and squeezing with a manic energy. Pellar, stunned by the fall and the ferocity of Tenim's attack, responded slowly. He strained to pull Tenim's hands off his neck, bucked to try to dislodge the heavier youth, tried vainly to twist to one side or the other—but all to no avail.

Spots appeared before his eyes and his vision turned gray.

Chitter, Pellar thought desperately, wondering what would happen to the fire-lizard without him. Master Zist! And then he remembered no more.

Fire-lizard dance on wing
To the raucous song I sing.
Fire-lizard wheel and turn,
Show me how the dragons learn.

Chapter Four

RED EYES WHIRLING, Chitter scratched awkwardly at the blankets covering the old harper. As gently as he could through his terror, the brown fire-lizard clawed the harper's face. Zist sputtered and twisted, instantly awake.

"What is it?" he demanded, pushing himself up and swiveling his legs over the side of his bed. "Pellar?"

The fire-lizard's whirling red eyes were all that Zist needed to see. He pulled down his nightshirt, slipped a robe around himself, and slid into his slippers.

He hurried into Kindan's room. "Get up," he called, "it's time to change watch."

Certain that it would be a while before the lad would be about and equally certain that Kindan would then rush off in performance of his duty, Zist left the cottage by the back door.

It was still dark outside. Chitter appeared beside him.

"Where is he?" Zist asked, looking up at the gray blur of the fire-lizard. Chitter made an uncertain noise. "Go find him, Chitter! Take me to him."

The fire-lizard chirped an acknowledgment and blinked *between*. Zist cautiously looked around to be certain no one had seen their interaction, and then made his way toward Natalon's hold.

A rustling sound nearby halted him and Zist turned toward it. Someone was moving down by the old watch-wher shed. He peered through the night, straining to see if the figure was Pellar but it disappeared from his view like a mist.

Chitter reappeared, diving to Zist's shoulder and tugging at his robe.

"You've found him?" Zist asked. The fire-lizard chirped and flew off, toward the back of Natalon's house. Zist spared one last glance toward where he had spotted the interloper and then set off after Chitter.

Chitter stopped him before he reached the kitchen door and flew off in a different direction. Zist paused, uncertain, but the fire-lizard returned and tugged at him again.

The reason for Chitter's uncertainty became apparent as soon as Zist rounded the far western corner of Natalon's hold. Right next to the back corner of the house was a crumpled figure.

Pellar. He lay quite still.

Tears misted Zist's vision as he raced to the youngster's body. He paused, swallowing nervously.

If I've killed him, too! Zist thought harshly, remembering his wife and child. Getting a firm grip on his emotions, he knelt down beside Pellar's body, searching his throat for a pulse.

Pellar's neck was red and bruised. It looked like he'd been strangled. Rage thundered through Zist's heart and fury lit his eyes. He swore vengeance on whoever had done this.

He bent down to give Pellar one last fatherly kiss— and felt the faintest of breath.

"You're alive!" Zist cried out, scooping Pellar up and cradling him in his arms.

Pellar came awake surrounded by darkness and fought as best he could, only to discover that he was flailing against Master Zist. He stopped suddenly and looked up. Zist's cheeks were wet with tears.

"Can you walk?" the harper asked. "It's not far to the cottage."

Pellar nodded and regretted it. His throat hurt, his neck ached, and his head throbbed from lack of oxygen. With Zist's help he stumbled up to his feet and back to the cottage.

"In my room," Zist said, guiding the youngster through the front door, guessing that Kindan would be having a cup of *klah* before departing from the kitchen.

After getting Pellar settled into his bed and pulling off his muddy boots, he went to the kitchen to grab cold water and warm *klah*.

"Fire! Help, help! Fire!" Zist heard Kindan's shout from the kitchen and rushed out, fearing that Pellar's attacker had returned and caught the other boy instead.

"Chitter, stay with Pellar," Zist ordered as he left.

Pellar woke to find Chitter resting against his side. The fire-lizard stirred and stared at him warningly. Pellar felt awful and was slow to move. Then he remembered—the chimney! He had to warn the miners. He tried to rise, but Chitter jumped up and sat heavily on his chest. Pellar tried batting the fire-lizard away but he was still too weak and his movements were disjointed and feeble. Chitter nipped at his hand and then grabbed it with his forepaws.

"How'd you find us?" a voice from the kitchen asked. Pellar recognized the voice—it was Dalor, Natalon's son.

"You were late for watch," Kindan replied. Pellar listened intently as Kindan explained how he'd realized the chimney was blocked, had shouted out the alarm, had opened all the doors and windows to the large hold, and had gone in search of Dalor.

Pellar gave a silent sigh of relief and relaxed. Chitter gave him a satisfied look and curled back into his resting spot, clearly convinced that Pellar was going to rest as well. He was right: In moments, Pellar fell into a dreamless sleep.

Pellar woke hungry. The room smelled of cooling soup. He sat up carefully and—as his sore muscles registered—slowly. The room was dark. A small glow was uncovered near the table, its light reflected by the two faceted eyes of Chitter, perched on the back of Zist's chair, keeping vigil.

Pellar's slate was on the table beside the bed. Beside it was a small bowl of soup and a spoon. Written on Pellar's slate in Zist's hand was a note: "Winter's End festivities. Eat slowly."

Winter's End. Pellar's ears picked up the sound of music coming from Natalon's hold. Whoever was playing the pipes was quite good, he decided after listening for a moment. Chitter cocked his head warningly and Pellar ducked his head in wry acknowledgment of the fire-lizard's nursemaiding. Obediently, he picked up the spoon and fed himself.

Swallowing was misery but he was too hungry not to finish the entire bowl. When he had, Chitter flew off his perch and nestled onto the bed in an unmistakable intimation of his expectations for Pellar. Pellar was too tired to argue, and the rich soup was already settling in his stomach. He lay back down and was asleep in minutes.

Pellar woke in the middle of the night to the sound of a commotion.

"Master Zist! Master Zist!" Dalor shouted. Nervously, Pellar wondered if Tenim had returned to finish his job.

Zist snorted and stirred from the chair in which he'd fallen asleep.

"Eh? What is it?" he called out.

"It's my mother," Dalor replied. "The baby's coming early."

Zist wagged a finger at Pellar, ordering him to remain, then shucked on his robe and slippers and left the room.

Pellar heard his muffled order to Kindan: "Go run to Margit's and get her up here." To Dalor he promised, "I'll be along as soon as I get some clothes on. You get on back. Start the cook boiling water, if she hasn't already." He continued in a softer tone. "It'll be all right, lad. Now off with you!"

Pellar looked around the room for Zist's clothes, wondering what the harper would need, and rose from his bed, assembling a kit for him, dimly aware that Zist and Kindan were conferring outside the door.

"Get off, now! We'll cope!" Zist called as he opened the door to his room. His eyes lit as he saw Pellar standing and the clothes laid out, ready for him to put on.

"You'll have to stay here," he told Pellar as he quickly donned his clothes. He gave the boy a warm, worried look. "Lad . . ."

Pellar shook his head and put a hand, palm flat, over his head, then brought it next to Zist's—he was nearly as tall as the harper.

Zist shook his head and grabbed Pellar into a tight hug.

"Man or lad, if I'd lost you . . ." Zist broke off. Pellar patted Zist's back and then broke out of the embrace, firmly steering the harper to the door and gesturing for him to hurry.

"You stay here," Zist called back from the doorway. "Send Chitter if you need."

Pellar nodded firmly and made a brushing motion to

hurry Zist along. But the harper had to have the last word. "Chitter, I'm counting on you to keep him from overtaxing himself."

Pellar was miffed that the harper had let him sleep through until morning, but he couldn't deny that he'd needed it. As it was, he was much relieved to hear that the baby had been born healthy and without undue complications.

"I'll keep watch tonight," Pellar wrote by way of apology.

"You'll do nothing of the sort," Zist told him emphatically. "You'll need at least a sevenday to recover. Anyway, there's a trader caravan due soon and among the apprentices there's supposed to be one with a watch-wher."

Pellar gave him a questioning look.

"With a watch-wher, the miners will be able to start a full night shift again," Zist explained. "With a crew bustling about at night, I suspect it'll be much harder for your friend Tenim to try anything."

"Not my friend," Pellar wrote, pointing to his throat for emphasis.

"And you're to stay away from him."

Pellar gave him a stubborn look.

"You've learned what I wanted to know," Zist responded.

"He might try something else," Pellar wrote.

"He might," Zist agreed. "And we'll have to be careful." He looked sternly at Pellar. "But you would have died if Chitter hadn't alerted me." He took a deep breath and admitted, "And I don't think I could live with that on my conscience."

Pellar looked at the old harper for a long time. Finally, he nodded, realizing that further argument would be pointless; it would only cause the harper further pain and worry.

The traders came that afternoon, only there was no watch-wher with them.

"Apparently someone scared the apprentice off," Zist explained as he prepared for the second celebratory Gather in two days, donning fresh clothes in harper blue and quickly buffing up his boots.

"Tenim," Pellar wrote, cocking an eyebrow at the harper.

"It could be," Zist answered. "But probably not."

Pellar looked surprised.

"The first time anyone noticed that the lad was missing was yesterday, although he might have left sooner; Trader Tarri said he kept to himself."

"Moran?" Pellar wrote.

Zist frowned as he read the slate. "I hope not," Zist said. "It could be, but then why would he not want the watch-wher to come to the mine?"

"Same reason," Pellar wrote.

"I'm not sure that Moran and Tenim have the same reasons," Zist said.

Pellar gave him a questioning look.

"Moran was very worried about the Shunned," Zist explained. "That's why Murenny and I agreed to let him try to make contact." He shook his head. "From what you've described of this Tenim character, I don't think he cares for anyone but himself."

As it was obvious to Pellar that Master Zist didn't want to entertain dark thoughts about his old apprentice, Pellar decided to drop the matter.

"Still need a watch-wher," Pellar wrote, changing the subject.

"Yes, we do," Zist agreed.

"Where do we get one?" Pellar wrote.

"I shall have to think on that," Zist replied, turning to

the door. "If you're still awake when the Gather's through, we can talk some more."

Pellar nodded and Zist gave him a probing look. The harper wagged his finger at the youngster. "Stay here. We'll be all right."

Pellar waited until he was certain that everyone had entered the large hall in Natalon's hold. Then he carefully dressed himself in bright clothes, grabbed a well-used cloak, and went out through the cothold's front door. Regardless of Zist's warnings or even how sore his raw throat still felt, Pellar was going to make sure that there were no more accidents.

Rather than gliding silently past the entrance to Natalon's stone hold, Pellar strode purposely beyond it, looking exactly like someone who was lost but unwilling to ask for directions.

He headed toward the camp's graveyard, planning to find a place beyond it where he could climb to the cliff above and backtrack to a good vantage point near Natalon's hold but away from any possible sighting by the camp's lookouts.

He was just past the graveyard when Chitter appeared from *between*. Pellar gave the brown fire-lizard a fierce admonishing look. He thought he had made it clear that the fire-lizard was to stay in the harper's cothold. Chitter hovered in front of him, wings beating slowly until Pellar understood that, as far as Chitter was concerned, if Pellar felt no compulsion to obey orders, neither would Chitter.

Pellar sighed in reluctant acceptance. Just before Pellar started off again, a noise startled him. Pellar froze. Someone was coming.

He sank to the ground in a crouch, hoping that the cloak would cover him sufficiently.

It did. The person, a small boy, passed him by, moving quickly and purposefully but without taking any particular pains to move quietly.

From the short-cropped blond hair, Pellar reckoned that the boy was either Dalor or Cristov. More likely it was Cristov, he decided, as Dalor would have a difficult time getting away from the evening's festivities.

But what was Cristov doing here?

Pellar followed him quietly from a safe distance. The blond boy made his way to the graveyard, where he stopped in front of one of the graves. Pellar wasn't certain, but he guessed that it was Kaylek's grave.

"Miners look after each other." Cristov's words drifted softly across the night air to Pellar.

Was he making a promise or repeating something he'd been told? Pellar wondered. Or both?

The youngster stood by the grave for a long while in silent communion. Just as Pellar decided that he had no choice but to find an alternate way to the cliff, Cristov stepped back, turned, and moved off quickly—toward the cliff.

Pellar followed him easily, both relieved at not having to lose time sneaking around Cristov and intrigued by the boy's motives. Was it possible that Cristov had been suborned by his father to finish Tenim's task?

Cristov started climbing, following the same route Pellar had taken the other night.

Climbing the cliff was more effort than Pellar remembered. His shoulders and stomach were still sore from his fall, but worse was the torment in his throat as he gulped down the air needed for his exertions. He tried his best to be quiet, but it wasn't good enough.

Suddenly he noticed a pair of eyes staring down at him from the cliff above.

"Who are you?"

For an instant Pellar considered fleeing back down the cliff and eluding Cristov in the forest—he knew he had more woodcraft than the boy—but before he could put his plan into action, Chitter appeared and started scolding Pellar and Cristov with equal intensity.

"Is he yours?" Cristov asked, his voice full of amazement and yearning.

Pellar nodded. Chitter caught his eye and looked back and forth rapidly between him and Cristov. Pellar knew that the fire-lizard was trying to tell him something, but he couldn't decide what.

"Did you block the hold chimney?" Cristov asked, his voice cold with outrage.

Pellar shook his head firmly. Cristov peered at him and reached forward to touch his neck.

"Someone tried to choke you," the blond boy declared, his fingers brushing Pellar's throat gently. He gave Pellar another intense look. "Did you try to stop someone from blocking the chimney?"

Pellar nodded.

"And they tried to choke you?" Cristov asked rhetorically. "And now you can't talk?"

Pellar nodded and then shook his head to answer both questions. Cristov looked confused.

Pellar reached to his side, then paused, looking questioningly at Cristov who, in his turn, looked confused. Pellar held up both his hands to show that he had nothing in them and then flattened one hand and poised the other over it in an imitation of writing.

"You want to write something?" Cristov asked. "I've got nothing to write with—oh! You do."

Pellar nodded, smiling, and reached for his slate. He was bigger than the boy and older by at least two Turns, but if Cristov grew afraid or alarmed, his shouts could easily bring the entire mining camp out, and Pellar didn't even want to think about what might happen then.

"It's dark, I don't know if I'll be able to read," Cristov began, only to stop when he saw that Pellar had a slate and stick of white chalk. "Maybe if you write big, then."

Pellar wrote carefully, "Name Pellar."

"I'm Cristov," the other replied, holding out his hand. Pellar pocketed his chalk and let go of his slate which dropped around his neck, held in place by the ever-present string, and solemnly shook Cristov's hand. Cristov pursed his lips for a moment, then asked, "You aren't Shunned, are you?"

Pellar shook his head emphatically, reached again for his slate and chalk, and wrote, "Shunned blocked chimney."

"And you stopped them?" Cristov asked, his eyes brilliant with awe.

Pellar shook his head and held up a finger.

"There was only one of them?"

Pellar nodded.

"What about your voice? Will it come back?" Cristov blurted, obviously overwhelmed with curiosity.

Pellar shook his head.

"Oh," Cristov said, crestfallen. "Does it bother you that you can't talk?"

Pellar shrugged, then waggled a hand in a so-so gesture. Then he smiled at Cristov and tapped his ear meaningfully.

"You listen more?" Cristov guessed. Pellar nodded. "I'll bet you do. And so that's why you were here? To listen?" Pellar nodded, surprised at how quickly Cristov had guessed. "For the Shunned, right?"

Pellar's nod merely confirmed Cristov's suspicions.

"So you're listening for the Shunned," Cristov murmured to himself thoughtfully. "Do you work for Master Zist?"

Pellar's startled look was answer enough for Cristov. Pellar grabbed his slate and hastily wrote, "Secret!"

"From whom?"

"Everyone," Pellar wrote back.

"Why?"

"Shunned," Pellar wrote back. He pointed to his throat, rubbed his slate clear, and wrote, "Hurt people."

"If they found out, they might hurt more people?" Cristov asked, trying to guess at Pellar's meaning. Just as Pellar started to shake his head, Cristov shook his own head, dismissing the thought. "No, that doesn't make sense."

Pellar waved a hand to get the boy's attention and wrote, "Watch now. Think later."

Cristov gave him a sheepish grin. "You're right," he said, extending a hand to Pellar to help him up the cliff.

Shortly they were in the same position Pellar had seen Tenim occupy the previous night. Pellar leaned forward and painfully craned his still-sore neck over to peer down into the valley below.

Light from the great room of the stone hold outlined the far corner at the east and dimly lit the western corner, but the nearest corner was barely distinguishable. After a while, Cristov said, "I think I can see the chimney."

Pellar followed the boy's outstretched arm and peered carefully into the night. It took him a moment to make out the shape of the chimney.

Cristov looked around where they were sitting and picked up a fist-sized rock. Pellar turned at his motion and grabbed Cristov's hand, shaking his head.

"He threw rocks, right?" Cristov asked, dropping the rock from his hand. Pellar nodded. "They pulled one of the chimney bricks out of the chimney. If Kindan hadn't come by—" Cristov's voice broke. "—they'd all be dead."

Pellar grimaced in agreement.

"And the baby wouldn't have been born," Cristov added quietly. He was silent for a longer moment. When he spoke again, it was in a slow, uncertain tone. "If they had died, my father would have been the head miner."

For the barest instant, Pellar froze. Then he felt Cristov's eyes on him and he shrugged carelessly, gesturing for the boy to sit down and doing the same himself, sitting on his butt, his knees raised and legs splayed to provide extra stability. Cristov's gaze intensified, so Pellar wiped his slate clean and wrote a response. To read the slate, Cristov sat down beside him.

"I watch," he wrote.

"So we're safe?" Cristov guessed, then added, "As long as no one attacks you."

Pellar gave him a pained look as he nodded in agreement.

"What would the Shunned want here?"

"Coal," Pellar wrote.

"But we'd notice, we'd know it when someone stole coal from the dump," Cristov protested. "And they wouldn't try to sneak into the mine."

Pellar nodded in agreement. Chitter, who had flown out over the cliff for his own inspection, flew back and perched on one of Pellar's knees.

"Could I touch him?" Cristov asked shyly. Pellar glanced at Chitter. The fire-lizard inclined his head toward Cristov and then stretched out his neck in invitation. Pellar indicated his agreement with a beckoning wave of his hand.

Slowly Cristov brought up his hand and gently touched the side of Chitter's head. The fire-lizard rubbed his head against Cristov's outstretched fingers enthusiastically.

"He's beautiful," Cristov said. "A regular dragon in miniature, not at all like a watch-wher." He glanced up at Pellar. "My father had a fire-lizard egg once, but the fire-lizard went *between* when it hatched. My father says that Danil's watch-wher, Dask, frightened it."

Pellar gave Cristov a dubious look and the boy shrugged.

"My father says that fire-lizards would be far more useful in the mines than watch-whers," Cristov said. "He says that he's going to get another egg soon and he'll let me keep it." His voice fell uneasily. "But he says that I'll have to keep it a secret."

He looked down at Chitter, stroking his head firmly. "I don't think I'd like that."

They sat in silence for a while, and then Cristov stood up.

"I think I'd better get back," he said. "Will you keep watch?"

Pellar nodded.

"I'll keep your secret," Cristov promised as he strode off.

Master Zist was extremely annoyed with Pellar's disobedience, even after he read Pellar's painstakingly detailed account of his meeting with Cristov.

"You can't imagine how I felt," Zist scolded him fiercely when Pellar returned the next morning, well after dawn. "I didn't know where you'd got to, or whether you'd gone of your own free will, and even Chitter wasn't here to send after you."

"Had to keep watch," Pellar wrote in his defense. It was a feeble defense and he knew it.

So did Zist, who snorted angrily. "What sort of

watch did you keep? You were caught and then, later, you fell asleep."

Pellar nodded miserably.

"If you can't do as you're told, and you won't rest when you need it, then I shall have to send you back to the Harper Hall," Zist said.

"Can't make me," Pellar wrote defiantly, his eyes flashing angrily as he shoved his slate under Zist's nose.

Zist bit back an angry response and let out his breath in a long, steadying sigh.

"Well, at least we now know what the Shunned are trading for coal," he said, forcing himself to change the topic.

Pellar gave him a quizzical look.

"Fire-lizard eggs," Zist told him. He looked fondly at Chitter. "I should have thought of it myself. Any holder or crafter would exchange top marks for a chance at a fire-lizard."

Pellar nodded in agreement, one hand idly stroking Chitter's cheek. The fire-lizard luxuriated in the attention, preening his head against Pellar's fingers.

"I wonder if that's how they got to Moran," Zist said to himself thoughtfully.

Pellar shook his head and wrote, "Tenim has bird."

Zist looked at him thoughtfully. "You think that Tenim wouldn't have a bird if Moran had a fire-lizard?"

Pellar nodded.

"And a hunting bird at that," Zist said. "I suppose— they wouldn't need a bird if they had a fire-lizard. So Moran wasn't offered a fire-lizard. Although perhaps he was, and Tenim couldn't Impress a fire-lizard. From your description, the bird seems a better match for his personality."

Pellar nodded, his expression bitter.

"And now we know at least one reason Tarik has to

hate watch-whers," Zist said. Pellar gave him an inquiring look, so Zist explained, "He blames the watch-whers for the loss of the fire-lizard."

Pellar frowned and held up two fingers. He wrote, "Watch-whers awake at night."

Zist grunted in agreement to Pellar's correction, then his expression changed. "Maybe we should find a watch-wher."

"Where?" Pellar wrote, his eyebrows raised questioningly.

Zist pursed his lips thoughtfully for several moments and then he looked Pellar square in the eyes.

"I think it's time for you to disappear," Zist replied, his eyes twinkling with mischief. It took Pellar only a moment to guess his master's thinking. Pellar grinned.

Pellar returned to Crom Hold with the trader caravan, his passage arranged by Master Zist and secured by his agreement to use Chitter as a messenger in case of emergency—and his willingness to help spread gravel to shore up the roadway.

Trader Tarri ordered the caravan to set out slowly, with the domicile caravans in the rear, which not only made good sense but made it easier for Pellar to creep on board the last one, which happened to be Trader Tarri's.

"Put these on," she said as soon as she saw him scramble aboard. "And join in the work the next time we stop."

Pellar nodded mutely and waited until the trader had left before donning the loose-fitting tunic and trousers she'd tossed him.

He found his brawn called upon almost immediately, when the caravan stopped at the next bend.

Tarri had arranged that the foremost dray be filled with gravel and discarded rock from the miners' diggings. She ordered the larger stones to be laid down first and packed with the backs of the shovels, then covered by a thinner layer of the light gravel.

After half an hour, Tarri was satisfied and sent the first dray carefully over the repaired road.

From that point on, Pellar found himself at the forefront of the workcrews, patching and filling the road as the caravan made its slow, cautious way back downhill to Crom Hold.

When they stopped for the night it was all he could do to find the rearmost wagon and crawl in.

"No, you don't!" Tarri barked at him when she saw his muddy boots. "There's food to eat first."

She led him back to the communal fire and made sure that he, and everyone else, ate before she did. None of the traders spared a glance in his direction, acting as though he didn't exist.

The next morning, with the sky still gray, Pellar woke to the sound of someone moving beside him and the smell of fresh hot *klah*.

"Brought you something to break your fast with," Tarri said, pushing a roll and a mug of *klah* into his hands. "I'll be up front as soon as it's light. You can stay here but listen for my call, or come if the caravan stops."

Pellar nodded.

Tarri gave him a thoughtful look, then patted his arm. "You did good work yesterday."

Pellar nodded in acknowledgment of the compliment, for he knew that was the best he could hope for from the gruff trader.

"With luck, we'll see Crom Hold before this evening," Tarri added. Pellar looked surprised and the trader laughed. "The journey's faster going downhill than up."

She turned to leave, then turned back again. "What are you going for, anyway?"

Pellar searched for a place to put his mug. Noticing, Tarri took it from him. He nodded gratefully, stuffed his roll in his mouth, and pulled out his slate. He wrote, "Secret."

Tarri laughed. "And don't you think I can keep secrets? Nor Master Zist? If so, why'd he ask me to take you?"

Pellar reddened and shrugged apologetically. Tarri laughed again and waved off his embarrassment. "We traders know a fair bit about trading. It seems like Zist has sent you to find something," she said. She wagged a finger at him. "Finding things is also something we traders are good at."

Pellar pursed his lips in thought for a long time before he wrote, "Watch-wher egg."

"Oh!" Tarri nodded. "That makes sense, given the way the last apprentice with a watch-wher scarpered when he heard he was coming to Camp Natalon." She gave Pellar a shrewd look. "But a watch-wher egg would be no good unless there was someone there to Impress it."

Pellar nodded but wrote nothing in reply. Tarri gave him another appraising look and laughed. "If you won't talk, you won't talk."

Pellar started to write a protest, but she laughingly waved him back to stillness.

"You know what I mean," she said. "But I'll do you a favor, little though it is. The only one who could get you a watch-wher egg is Aleesa, the Whermaster. She's got a gold watch-wher she sometimes breeds."

"Where?" Pellar wrote.

Tarri shrugged. "I don't know." She tapped her temple. "There's not much call to trade for watch-wher eggs, so it's not something I keep in here. Maybe you can find out more at Crom Hold."

The Whermaster, Aleesa, was so hard to locate that for the first month Pellar doubted her existence. It took him another two months to track her down.

His journeying had hardened him in ways he would not have imagined beforehand; when he boldly made his way into the small camp that was reputed to be Aleesa's demesne, he was rake thin but whip tough.

He had traveled with the traders when he could, and the Shunned when he had no other choice. His fire-lizard made him a welcome guest among traders and Shunned alike, who considered the fire-lizard's Impression a character reference. The small groups of traders or Shunned were particularly grateful, seeing the fire-lizard as a source of communications in an emergency.

Over time, his nervousness with the Shunned had faded. He discovered that they were very much like the traders, with one vital difference: The traders were aloof of Hold and Crafthall from choice, the Shunned by decree.

Still, with the Shunned Pellar found himself called upon more often to prove himself, either by providing for the communal pot, prescribing for the sick, or, more often than he liked, proving his strength.

His fights were always with those near his own age who looked upon him as an easy challenge and a good way to improve their standing in the community. After painfully losing his first several encounters, Pellar got quite adept at seeking quick solutions and less concerned about any bruises he gave his assailants.

Even though food was not plentiful and he was expected to share, Pellar thrived, filling out and growing tall. So tall, in fact, that as time progressed he found himself challenged by older, taller lads, many Turns older than his own thirteen.

Upon taking his leave of Trader Tarri at Crom Hold, Pellar found passage on one of the barges heading downstream from Crom Hold, continuing his search for Master Aleesa. He worked the passage, helping pole the barge when necessary and tying it up at night. The family who owned the boat didn't trust him and made him sleep on deck, although by the end of the sevenday journey, they had grown so fond of him and his fire-lizard that they pressed a well-worn half-mark on him.

A bad piece of advice sent Pellar eastward, to Greenfields, and then on to Campbell's Field, a journey that took over a month.

It was only at the small hold in Campbell's Field that Pellar heard that Aleesa had set up a hold of sorts somewhere around Nabol Hold. That was all the way back west of where he was. He sent word to Master Zist, returned to Crom Hold, and took passage once more on a barge downriver. This time he left at Keogh, a minor hold at the bend of the Crom River.

At Nabol Hold he learned that Aleesa's hold was north in the mountains, but no one quite knew where.

The mountains north of Nabol were mostly forested and uninhabited. Pellar found himself slowed by the necessity of having to forage for food. After three sevendays of searching without success, his strength ebbing, and the last days of summer fast approaching, Pellar was just about ready to give in when he remembered that watch-whers flew at night.

So he ate early, put out his fire, found a clearing at the top of a nearby hill, and waited, eyes eagerly scanning the horizon.

It wasn't until the middle of the night, when Pellar's body was so bone cold that he could no longer shiver, that he caught the merest glimpse of something darting in the sky high above him.

He quickly woke Chitter, pointed to the watch-wher, and launched the fire-lizard into the sky.

As soon as Chitter and the watch-wher were out of sight, Pellar crouched down to the stack of wood he'd piled up before him and carefully sparked a small—and oh, so joyously warm—fire.

Chitter returned, quite pleased with himself, late that morning. Shortly thereafter, with a stomach freshly full of jerked beef, Chitter led Pellar to the Whermaster's hold.

Pellar hadn't known what sort of reception to expect, but he didn't count on having an arrow whiz toward him to strike the ground just in front of his foot.

"That's far enough!" a voice in the distance shouted in warning. "State your business."

Pellar looked crestfallen, not at a loss for words but at a loss for a way to convey them. He held his hands up, palms out, to show that he was unarmed and waited.

Another arrow answered him. "I said, state your business!"

Pellar pointed to his throat and shook his head, making a face.

"You won't talk?" another voice suggested. This voice belonged to an old woman, while the other had clearly been a man's.

Pellar shook his head and pointed to his throat again.

"You can't talk?" the woman asked, this time sounding intrigued.

Pellar nodded vigorously and smiled as broadly and kindly as he could.

"Do you trust him?" the man called to the woman.

"I don't know," the woman shouted back.

"Maybe we shouldn't take any chances," the man replied. "If he's one of the Shunned and he reports back—"

Pellar's eyes widened. They were talking about killing him.

Pellar stood stock-still for a moment, concentrating on Chitter. The fire-lizard chirped nervously in response but finally, if reluctantly, went *between*.

"Where'd he go?" the man called angrily.

"He could have gone anywhere," the old woman responded. When she spoke again, her tone held a grudging respect. "That's what you intended, isn't it?"

Pellar nodded firmly.

"If he's trained his fire-lizard well, the little one could lead others back here," the old woman continued. There was a silence, then she spoke again. "You can come here, to me. Just remember that Jaythen has a bow trained on you."

Pellar took a deep steadying breath, hitched up his pack, and carefully walked toward the sound of the woman's voice.

He had been walking for several moments before the woman's voice, near but now to his right, called out, "Stop."

Pellar, still very aware of a bowman somewhere out there, obeyed, standing motionless. For several moments, nothing happened. Then he heard a movement behind him and rough hands grabbed him, pulling him backward off his feet.

He fell back, mouth open in an O of silent surprise. When he landed on his pack, his look was both angry and confused—hadn't he done everything they'd asked?

Instinctively, he grabbed for his slate. Someone stooped over him from behind, pressing a knife against his chest.

"Don't," the man, Jaythen, said.

Pellar let his hands go limp.

"Let him up, Jaythen," the old woman said. Another shadow fell over Pellar; he looked up and saw a thin old woman with white hair woven into a braid that hung down her back. "He told the truth; he can't talk. If he could, he would have made some noise when you pulled him over like that."

His pack weighing him down, Pellar rolled onto his side before shakily standing up. The woman was taller than him. Jaythen stood behind him, doubtless with his knife ready.

Gingerly, Pellar reached for the strap around his neck and was first surprised and then horrified at how easily it moved. Forgetting everything, he felt in his clothes for his slate and was devastated when he found that it had cracked in half from his fall.

"Is that what you write on?" the old woman asked, her voice sounding more kindly than before. "And it's broken?"

Pellar nodded miserably to both questions.

"Well, we'll replace it, then," the woman declared. She held out her hand. "I'm Aleesa."

Pellar shook it and then pointed to himself and regretfully to his broken slate. He fished out his chalk and wrote his name on one of the pieces.

"Pellar, eh?" Aleesa repeated when she read it. She nodded to herself. "I've heard about you."

"So have I," Jaythen growled menacingly from behind. "The Silent Harper, everyone calls you." Jaythen spat in disgust, then added, "But the traders said you were a good tracker."

Aleesa's eyes flicked beyond Pellar to the man standing behind him and she said, "He walked in here, there's no other way out."

"Unless his fire-lizard went to fetch a dragonrider," Jaythen growled.

Aleesa frowned and then shrugged. "We'll be moving again soon enough," she declared. "If the dragonriders come, they'll find another empty camp."

She gestured for Pellar to follow him. "Come along, youngster, there's *klah* and something warm at the fire."

Pellar was still somewhat dazed by the turn of events, but he remembered his manners and bowed politely to the old woman, then crooked his elbow toward her in an invitation to hold on to his arm.

Aleesa laughed, a deep hearty laugh that brought out the crow's-feet around her eyes. She latched onto Pellar's arm and called over her shoulder, "See, Jaythen? This one has *manners*!"

Behind them, Jaythen grumbled.

Aleesa's camp was hidden behind a hillock and nestled against the rising Nabol Mountains. Pellar suppressed a shiver as they went into shadow deeper than the early morning. Beside him, Aleesa shook herself and shivered.

"My bones don't like this cold," she admitted to him. "I'm too old."

At the foot of the mountain there was a small opening, and Aleesa led him inside. To the right side there was a small crevice; on the left, a larger opening with the smell of *klah* and stew. Aleesa led him to the left.

The opening widened to a natural cave that reminded Pellar of the cave he'd found up by Camp Natalon, except that this cave was far more spacious and had several alcoves. Young children played noisily in the center of the cave, while around them a couple of women bustled, washing, cooking, or keeping the children out of the worst of the mischief.

"Those that aren't resting are on watch," Aleesa said.

She gestured to the women. "These are just the child minders."

One of the women looked up at the oblique introduction, smiled at Pellar, but was instantly distracted by the movements of a baby crawling toward the open fire.

Pellar nodded at Aleesa's explanation, keeping his expression neutral. He got the impression that Aleesa wanted him to believe that the camp had many inhabitants, but a quick glance at the food stored in the pantry and the size of the pots told him that there could be no more than two or three others in the whole place—and that with them all on short rations.

Aleesa herself served him up a cup of *klah*. Pellar nodded and smiled in thanks, cupping his hands gratefully around the warmth. The *klah* was thin and watered down.

Aleesa gestured toward a pile of furs placed to one side of the cave and took a seat on the largest pile. Pellar found another fur nearby and sat.

"I'd heard that you've been looking for us for several months now," Aleesa said.

Pellar nodded.

"You found our old camp over by Campbell's Field?"

Pellar shook his head, his surprise obvious.

"I told Jaythen no one would find it," she said with a bitter laugh. Her look turned sour. "Except maybe the dragonriders."

Pellar carefully schooled his expression to be neutral but he didn't fool the old woman.

"They don't like us," Aleesa continued bitterly. "They say that watch-whers steal food meant for their dragons." She snorted in disgust. "That D'gan! Him with his high airs. He's got it in his mind that the watch-whers ate him out of Igen Weyr."

Pellar looked surprised. He knew that D'gan was the Weyrleader of Telgar Weyr, and that Igen Weyr had been combined with Telgar a number of Turns back, but he hadn't heard anything about watch-whers being involved.

"He says that they are abominations and shouldn't exist," Aleesa said with a sniff. She looked up at Pellar. "I know they're no beauties on the outside, but they've hearts of gold when you get to know them, hearts of gold." Her eyes turned involuntarily toward the entrance to the cave and the crevice beyond.

"And there are so few left," she added softly.

"So few," she repeated, nodding to herself, her gaze turned inward. After a moment, she glanced back up at Pellar and told him conspiratorially, "I think *she's* the last one, you know."

Then her tone changed abruptly and she demanded, "So what do you want and why should I let you live?"

It was then that Pellar realized that the Whermaster was quite insane.

In the course of the next few days, Pellar discovered that Aleesa's camp was a desperate place full of desperate people. It took of all Pellar's tact, winsome ways, and hard work to earn their grudging acceptance—and his continued existence. For, unlike the Shunned, these people were not only desperate, they were fanatics dedicated to the continued existence of the watch-whers.

Realizing how desperate the camp was for game, Pellar offered to set and tend traps, which he was allowed to do, though he was often shadowed by Jaythen or one of the other men of the camp. He gladly accepted even the worst jobs and did his best at them all, to the point where even Aleesa commented on how brightly he'd shined the pots assigned him.

Good as her word, Aleesa had one of the men find suitable pieces of slate to replace Pellar's broken one and help with the difficult task of boring holes on

which to string it. Pellar took advantage of the supply
to lay aside other pieces for the future.

Because he was not trusted, Pellar often found himself stuck entertaining the camp's three young children,
none of them more than toddlers. It was difficult, particularly as he couldn't *tell* them what to do, but he
quickly found that they were entranced by his expres-
sive ways, charming games, and magical pipes.

As soon as he could, he gathered enough reeds to
fashion three more pipes, each a different note, and
taught the children how to play one of the more popu-
lar Teaching Songs. The mothers were pleased and vo-
cal in their pride of their children; Aleesa was not.

"Teaching Songs!" she snorted when she heard it.
"What do we need of those? 'Honor those the dragons
heed!' " She shook her head disgustedly.

Pellar gave her a quizzical look, surprised by her ve-
hemence.

"Dragonriders care nothing for us," Aleesa continued
in a bitter voice. "It was D'gan himself, *Weyrleader* of
Telgar, who sent us packing from our last camp."

" 'Your beasts will eat all the herdbeasts and leave
nothing for the fighting dragons,' " she quoted. She
shook her head, her eyes bright with unshed tears.

"Fighting dragons!" she snorted. "No Thread has
fallen any time in over a hundred Turns! What do they
fight?" She shook her head dolefully.

"And he turfed us out, just like that, like we were
Shunned." She sniffed. "One of the babies died on the
way here, for want of food." She shook her head again.
"Anything the watch-whers ate, they earned. They kept
watch at night for nightbeasts eager to devour the
herds, they caught and killed tunnel snakes, frightened
away wherries—even the herders were glad to have
us—but he sent us packing.

"No," she said, looking at Pellar, "I'll hear nothing of

dragonriders in my camp. They sent us out to die, and the last queen watch-wher with us."

The look of shock on Pellar's face was so obvious that Aleesa, when she saw it, gave him a sour laugh. "You think all dragonriders are perfect and can do no harm?" She shook her head derisively. "You have a lot to learn, little one, a lot to learn."

She turned away from him, toward her sleeping alcove. Her gaze rested briefly on the youngsters all snuggled together, surrounded by their parents.

"This place is too cold," she declared, shivering. She nodded to the children. "Come winter, there'll be less of them."

She looked at Pellar.

"You've the watch," she told him. From a corner, Jaythen looked up sharply at her declaration. "You wake Jaythen next."

Pellar nodded.

"Don't bother the watch-wher," Aleesa warned him. "If you hear any noise, send your fire-lizard to tell her." She rolled her eyes in disbelief. "For some reason, she *likes* him. She'll check anything out; she's got the best night eyes on Pern."

Pellar waved in acknowledgment, strode to the entrance of the cave, and settled down cross-legged, with his back to the distant fire.

Chitter made a quick tour of the surroundings and returned to curl up near Pellar, resting his head on the youngster's leg. Pellar smiled and idly stroked his fire-lizard, his mind turning over his conversation with Aleesa.

He had heard enough rumors about D'gan, the Weyrleader of Telgar, on his journeying. His trip from Crom Hold to Keogh had been through lands looking to Telgar Weyr for protection when Thread came again. Also, Campbell's Field. He remembered that the holders, particularly the herdsmen he met at Campbell's Field, had been very wary of talking about Aleesa and her watch-whers. When he'd convinced them that he wasn't working for D'gan and they found themselves comfortable talking to him—usually after a few glasses of wine—they told Pellar exactly what Aleesa had said, though in different words.

"Best thing against a nightbeast I'd ever seen," one herder said of the watch-whers, shaking his head sadly. "We lost more herdbeasts the first sevenday after they left than we gave for the protection of the watch-whers in the last half Turn." Hastily, he added, "Not that I mean any disrespect to our Weyrleader."

Pellar's opinion of D'gan had been formed earlier, when he'd heard how Telgar Weyr had repeatedly won the Weyr Games. The gossip around the Harper Hall had not been very flattering.

"He's such a bad winner, I hope he never loses," was the one comment Pellar had heard most often from the older journeymen.

A noise from behind, followed immediately by something butting against his back, caused Pellar to startle and jump. When he turned back, he saw the large glowing eyes of a watch-wher staring back at him. It butted him again, politely. Beside him, Chitter leaped up and hovered near the watch-wher.

Pellar looked curiously at the watch-wher, and realized that it was the gold. He wondered what the watch-wher wanted and was at a loss for some way to communicate when Chitter landed on his shoulder and started tugging at him.

Oh, you want to go out, Pellar thought to himself. He stood aside, and the watch-wher lumbered out of the crevice into the dale. You're welcome, Pellar thought, just as he did with Chitter.

The gold turned back for a moment and nodded her

head toward Pellar before turning back, taking one giant stride, and jumping into the air.

Well, they're related to dragons, Pellar mused, so why wouldn't they move well in midair?

He was still trying to absorb this new thought when a voice behind him cried out and he felt a rush of air. Suddenly there was a second watch-wher in the air, climbing frantically after the queen.

A rush of feet behind him alerted him in time to turn and see Aleesa come pelting toward him.

"You! Send your fire-lizard away!" she ordered. As Pellar's brows furrowed questioningly, she added, "It's a mating flight! You'll not want him around."

A mating flight? Like dragons? Pellar grabbed for Chitter and locked eyes with his brown. Chitter protested twice but finally agreed and, just after Pellar released him, vanished *between.*

"Have you ever seen a mating flight?" Aleesa asked, her voice filled with a reverence that made Pellar uneasy.

Pellar shook his head.

"Have you ever *felt* a mating flight?" Aleesa asked with a hint of a leer in her voice.

Reluctantly Pellar nodded. Others were awake now and rushed out of the cave. Jaythen approached Aleesa with a wild light in his eyes and Pellar realized that the bronze watch-wher was bonded to him.

"Do you want to do this, Aleesa?" Jaythen asked, his voice rasping with barely controlled emotions. "She's old."

"She'll outfly your bronze if you keep jabbering," Aleesa replied, turning toward the younger man. She spared one last glance at Pellar. "Have Polla get the children and the others prepared and stay with them."

Pellar nodded and ran back to the cave. He found Polla, one of the older women, already organizing the children into groups. He was surprised to see some of the younger women eyeing him consideringly.

"It'd only be for the flight," the woman said when she caught his gaze. "Nothing more than that."

Pellar nodded, not sure of his own feelings, and wondered how many of the children were the results of previous mating flights—he'd heard enough about them during his time at the Harper Hall.

"They'll be needing food and warmth after the flight," Polla warned, brusquely setting the children to play near the fire.

Who, Pellar wondered, the watch-whers, Aleesa, or the children?

"How many Turns have you, anyway?" Polla asked, regarding Pellar carefully.

Pellar hastily pulled out his slate and wrote 13.

Polla read it and laughed, nodding toward the younger woman. "Arella's nearer your age, she's only three Turns older."

Pellar found it hard to believe that the other woman had only sixteen Turns; he would have guessed her nearer to thirty. Life with the watch-whers was clearly very demanding.

"Come sit by me, then," Arella called, patting a spot near her.

Pellar crossed around the fire and had just sat, nervously, when the watch-whers mated.

Much later, Arella whispered in his ear, "Now you are one of us."

"He is *not* one of us," Jaythen declared loudly the next day, staring angrily at Pellar and Arella but directing his speech to Aleesa.

The old woman looked very tired. She shook her head slowly. "Perhaps," she said, "perhaps not." She cast a secretive glance toward Arella. "Time will tell."

"Mother," Arella said, "it was a *mating* flight. He knows."

Knows what? Pellar wondered. That watch-whers mated? That they were enough like dragons that people felt the intensity of their emotions?

"It might be her last mating flight," Aleesa said, her voice betraying her own fatigue and sorrow. "If there's no queen egg . . ."

Pellar looked up at the mention of eggs. Jaythen and Aleesa both noted it.

"You're here for an egg?" Jaythen demanded, towering menacingly over Pellar.

Pellar nodded.

"You would steal an egg, why?" Aleesa asked.

Pellar shook his head. He slowly drew out his slate, very aware of Jaythen's menacing presence, and wrote, "Not steal. Trade."

"Trade what?" Jaythen growled derisively. He turned to Aleesa. "We've been through his pack; he's got nothing of value."

Pellar kept a neutral look on his face; he'd known that they had searched his pack the first night he arrived. He had guessed that they would.

"He'd've hidden anything of value, Jaythen," Arella said to the older wherhandler, not attempting to keep her sense of derision from her voice.

"What's valuable enough for a watch-wher's egg?" Jaythen demanded.

Pellar felt all eyes on him. Hastily he wrote, "Warmth. Fire. Fuel."

He passed his slate to Aleesa, who looked at it and frowned, passing it on to Polla.

"Warmth, fire, fuel," Polla reported.

It was then that Pellar realized that Aleesa couldn't read. All the other times, he hadn't realized that she'd let someone else read his slate because she couldn't; he'd thought she'd done it to prove her authority.

Pellar gestured urgently for the slate. Polla passed it back to him, her brow creased in concern. Pellar made sure that no one else saw what he wrote before he passed it to Aleesa.

Aleesa frowned at it, then passed it to Polla. Polla read it, gasped, and gave Pellar a hard look. Pellar gestured for her to read it. Polla glared at him, then glanced nervously at Aleesa.

"Well?" Aleesa demanded.

"It says, 'lessons,' " Polla reported.

Aleesa snorted. "In return for which, I'm supposed to teach you how to talk, I presume?"

Pellar stood up, backing away from Jaythen, whose attitude, if anything, had grown more frosty during the exchange. He bowed low to Aleesa, stood up again, and gestured to the children. From inside his tunic, he pulled out his pipes, mimed putting them to his lips, put them back in his tunic, and then made like he was holding a guitar.

"You claim you're harper-trained just because you can make pipes?" Jaythen asked incredulously. He laughed derisively. "A pretty poor excuse you are for a harper if you can't speak!"

Pellar nodded and then shook his head, cupping his ear and frowning intently.

"He hears better than those who talk," Aleesa guessed. She laughed, and not bitterly.

"And he's got a fire-lizard, Mother," Arella pointed out. "If he can keep one of those, he'll be able to bond with a watch-wher."

Pellar shook his head emphatically and made a waving-off gesture with one hand. He retrieved his slate from Polla and wrote, "Not me."

"Who, then?" Aleesa asked. "Would you bring a horde upon us?"

Pellar gave Aleesa a long, thoughtful look. "Good idea," he wrote finally.

"Good idea?" Jaythen snorted when he read the slate. "What makes that a good idea?"

"Sell the eggs," Pellar wrote. "Herdsmen, miners."

Polla's eyes widened when she read his response, and her tone was very thoughtful when she told Aleesa, "He's thinking you could sell the eggs to herdsmen and miners."

"Sell them?" Aleesa repeated. She looked at Pellar and frowned. "And what would we sell them for?"

"A year's coal," Arella answered immediately. She looked defiantly at her mother and then at Pellar. "The chance of an egg for a year's supply of coal."

"Chance?" Jaythen repeated.

"They'd have to get by Aleesk," Arella pointed out.

Aleesa barked a laugh. "I like it!"

"The herdsmen could offer a year's supply of food," Polla added, looking at the youngsters huddled together by the fire.

"Or gold," Jaythen said, his eyes glowing thoughtfully. "Better than marks: You can buy anything with gold."

Aleesa raised a hand, silencing the group. She gave Pellar a long, appraising look.

"It's a deal," she said finally. Pellar's eyes brightened until she raised her hand. "If you stay here, make the arrangements, *and* provide for your replacement as harper when the time comes."

She held out her hand to him. "Will you do it?"

Pellar thought for a moment and then, slowly, took her hand and shook it firmly.

"Heard and witnessed!" Arella declared. From the watch-whers' cave came a chorus of acknowledgment.

* * *

Pellar's new duties, it seemed, didn't absolve him of his old duties; he found himself working twice as hard. Arella's behavior toward him was much warmer and full of playful banter, which was good, as Jaythen seemed to grow more distrustful with every new day.

So it was more than a month before Pellar found the time and the timber with which to fashion the frame of a decent drum. He started with a well-formed section of tree trunk, carefully carved out the center, and slowly expanded the hollow until the frame was only a few centimeters thick. With all the other work he had, the process took him two sevendays.

"What are you doing?" Arella asked him late one night as she watched him carefully rub a rough stone against the outside of the frame. She peered curiously around the fire in the middle of the largest cavern.

Pellar paused, carefully placing his stone tool and work to the side before dragging out his slate, on which he wrote, "Sanding."

Arella made a face. "I see that, but why?"

Pellar looked at her, picked up the frame, and mimed pounding on the hole where a skin should be. Arella looked at him with a creased brow before she relaxed in comprehension. "You're making a drum?"

Pellar nodded. Arella crossed around the fire in quick strides and sat down close by him. She leaned in to peer at the drum in his hands and begged, "Teach me how."

Pellar thought for a moment, nodded, and handed her the frame and rough stone.

Arella looked down at both in awe and then looked up at Pellar. "What do I do?"

"Sand," Pellar wrote in reply.

The next morning, Pellar set out in search of a good hide for the drum. As he trotted from one trap to the next, he suppressed his irritation at Jaythen trailing him. Grinning, he glanced back over his shoulder to where Jaythen was hiding. Rather, where Jaythen was *trying* to hide, for Jaythen's skills were only slightly better than none at all.

Pellar had taken pains to remain easily tracked in the past several sevendays—although he occasionally applied more of his craft just to learn the limits of Jaythen's skill. He was always careful never to lose Jaythen for too long, lest the older man guess Pellar's true abilities.

So far, after three traps, Pellar had nothing to show for his efforts. What he really wanted was a wherry foolish enough to fly into one of his large aerial traps—wherhide would make an excellent drumhead—but he'd settle for one of the larger furbeasts. What he didn't expect was half a furbeast and a busted trap. He had barely time to recognize what he was looking at before an arrow flew by his shoulder and landed near the broken trap. Pellar whirled around to see Jaythen waving at him frantically and gesturing for him to run. Pellar had only taken his first confused step when Jaythen stiffened, notched another arrow to his bow, and let it fly—straight at Pellar.

Pellar dived to the right out of the arrow's path, landing hard on his shoulder, curling up as soon as he hit the ground, and turning around to face the sounds coming from behind him. He pulled his knife from the top of his left boot and cradled it in both hands close to his chest while coming up to a crouch, for the volume of the sound told him he was facing something big and fast. And the grunting noise told him it was a wildboar—one of the most dangerous creatures on Pern.

Pellar only had an instant to spot Jaythen's arrow sticking out of the wildboar's left eye before he dove to the side and flung himself atop the wildboar. It lurched under his weight and squirmed to dislodge him. Pellar wrapped his numb right arm around the beast's haunches and dug deeply into the wildboar's neck with his knife. The boar squealed and bucked, throwing Pellar off.

Pellar fell hard, banging his head on a rock and rolling over another with his sore shoulder. He would have screamed out loud if he could. His face pinched in pain, he grabbed the rock his head had hit on the way down and threw it at the wildboar.

"Are you mad?" Jaythen yelled in the distance. "Run!"

But Pellar shook his head, knowing that even as injured as the wildboar was, he was too slow to outrun it.

The wildboar charged toward him, its good eye blazing balefully.

Pellar dodged to the left just in time, grabbing at his knife as he did. The knife wouldn't dislodge, but that was fine with him: He was hoping to drive it deeper. With a sudden squeal, the wildboar's legs splayed out from under it and it fell to the ground.

Jaythen rushed up. "Did you kill it?"

Pellar shook his head. Jaythen threw him a puzzled look, which cleared up as he saw that the beast was still breathing.

"You cut its spine," Jaythen surmised, drawing his own blade and deftly delivering the mercy blow. The wildboar gave one last surprised sigh and collapsed.

Pellar exhaled heavily, carefully wiped his blade, returned it to his boot, pulled out his slate, and wrote, "Hide mine."

Jaythen snorted when he read the note. "It's yours," he declared. He gestured at their kill and said with a broad grin, "There's a sevenday's eating here."

Pellar nodded, smiling in return. Wildboar made great eating.

With a laugh, Jaythen patted him on the shoulder and declared, "*Now* you're one of us."

Arella took charge of the carcass as soon as Pellar and Jaythen brought it in. Pellar was surprised to see how deft she was with a knife, even more so when she presented him with a perfectly cut hide. She also took great pains to get as much blood on Pellar as herself, dragging him off to the nearby bathing pool as soon as she'd set the meat to smoking.

Pellar played and cavorted with her but refused to be drawn into anything more serious, pointing to his various injuries. Arella's angry frown was immediately replaced by a tender look and she insisted on bandaging him when they were done with their ablutions and had returned to the main cave of what Pellar had started to think of as the wherhold.

"So when are you going to arrange these trades?" Aleesa demanded at dinner that evening. Her abrupt manner was as close to praise as he'd ever heard from her.

Pellar held up a hand politely, finished chewing his food, fished out his slate, and wrote, "Eggs."

"You know I can't read," Aleesa told him curtly, sliding the slate toward Arella. Pellar grabbed her hand, caught her eyes, and shook his head slightly. Gently he pulled the slate back and carefully drew three small ovals piled on top of each other. He slid the slate back to Aleesa and gave her a challenging look.

"Eggs?" Aleesa said, glancing at the drawing. Then she glanced up at the letters above. "That says eggs?"

Pellar nodded. Aleesa glanced down at the writing once more, her gaze intent on absorbing and remembering every aspect of the letters before her.

After a moment, Pellar touched her hand and gestured to get the slate back. He carefully rubbed out the letter "s" and two of the three ovals and slid the slate back to Aleesa.

"Egg?" Aleesa guessed. When Pellar nodded, she squinted at the slate, examining it carefully. "That little squiggle at the end, that makes the 'sss' sound?"

Pellar nodded, smiling encouragingly.

"That's the letter 's,' Mother," Arella told her.

Pellar nodded and gestured for the slate again. Aleesa released it with just a hint of reluctance. Pellar acknowledged her expression and carefully erased the letters and drawing. He wrote the letter "s" and handed the slate back to her, this time handing her the chalk as well.

"You want me to write the letter?" Aleesa asked. Pellar nodded. Aleesa frowned, then bent over the slate, carefully sliding the chalk on the slate. She muttered to herself as she drew and finally looked up, holding the slate toward Pellar with a sour look.

"Mine doesn't look as good as yours," Aleesa said.

Pellar held up one finger.

"You're saying that it's my first?"

Pellar nodded.

Aleesa pursed her lips, but Pellar's face burst into a smile as he danced his finger up and down in front of her and cocked his head invitingly. He held up two fingers, then three, four, and finally five.

"You want me to try five more times?"

Pellar nodded.

Aleesa's lips thinned rebelliously, and Arella smiled at her and mimicked, " 'Five times to learn, Arella.' "

Aleesa frowned and stuck her tongue out at her daughter playfully. She turned back to Pellar, bit back some comment, and carefully drew four more copies of the letter.

When she was finished, Pellar examined her handiwork carefully and then nodded emphatically, not failing to note the slight sigh of relief that Aleesa tried to keep hidden from him.

And so began Aleesa's education.

In the days that followed, though both she and Pellar found themselves exasperated by their mutual difficulty in communicating—his in speaking and hers in reading—neither one would permit it to sour or break their bargain.

" 'I go soon,' " Aleesa repeated nearly ten sevendays later. She shook her head at Pellar. "Shouldn't it be: I'll be going soon?"

Pellar nodded in agreement but pointed at the slate.

"Oh, I see," Aleesa said. "The slate's too small."

"Be sure not to use that drum of yours until you're far away," Jaythen warned.

"And be prepared to run—you're likely to draw every one of the Shunned upon you," Aleesa added.

Pellar nodded understandingly. They had discussed his plans in detail over the past several sevendays. Jaythen had been the first to point out that if in the watch-wher eggs they had something to trade, they also had something for the Shunned to steal.

"I'm convinced they get a lot of their money from trading in fire-lizards' eggs," he had said.

"Hunting birds," Pellar had written in response, opening himself to a long line of questioning from Aleesa, Jaythen, and Arella in which he explained his encounter with Halla, Tenim, and Tenim's hawk. Arella had drawn him out, and Pellar had found himself explaining about the flowers and the tragedy at Camp Natalon. Tears welled in his eyes as he recounted how he'd found the small snow-covered mounds.

"Working underground!" Jaythen exclaimed when Pellar explained the expected watch-wher's role.

Aleesa took on the abstracted look that Pellar had

come to recognize meant she was communicating with her watch-wher. "Aleesk says that watch-whers like the dark and would enjoy it," she reported a moment later.

"Dask did," Pellar wrote in response.

"Very well," Aleesa said. "You may tell this Zist of yours that we'll trade. A winter's worth of coal for a chance at an egg."

"Chance?" Pellar wrote back.

"Whoever wants it has to get it from Aleesk," Aleesa replied with an evil grin. "I'll let her have the final say."

"Fair enough," Pellar had written in reply.

"When will you go?"

"Tomorrow," Pellar wrote back.

"Tomorrow it is, then," Aleesa agreed. Beside her, Arella gave a sob and raced out of the main cavern. Aleesa followed her daughter's anguished departure with her eyes and looked back to Pellar. "She is hoping that when you come back, you'll stay."

Pellar nodded.

"And?"

Pellar shook his head sadly.

"It's a hard life with the watch-whers," Aleesa said with a sigh. Her eyes twinkled as she added, "It has its compensations, like mating flights, but I won't deny it's hard."

She caught his gaze and held it with her own.

"You could make it better, though," she told him.

Pellar's mouth quivered, but finally, he shook his head, wiped his slate clean, and wrote on it, "Shunned."

Aleesa read it and nodded slowly. "You don't like putting flowers on graves."

Pellar nodded.

"You're a good lad, Harper Pellar," Aleesa said. "I'll not force you, but remember this—you've a home here if you want."

Pellar grabbed her hand and squeezed it in thanks, rose, and bowed slightly, then sprinted off after Arella.

He found her outside of the main compound, up near a stand of trees.

"I'm not staying," Arella told him as he approached. He arched an eyebrow at her. Whether she saw it in the dark or guessed at it didn't matter. She was crouched on the ground, cradling her knees with her arms, her chin rested on one knee. "I'll be here when you get back, but I'm not staying."

Pellar sat down beside her. She sidled up next to him and laid her head on his shoulder.

"One of those coming for an egg will want help, I'm sure," she said. "I'll go with him. There's more than watch-whers, worry, and empty bellies in this world, and I *want* it."

Arella pulled away from him and stood up. Pellar stood up beside her. She looked at him half-defiant, half-hopeful. He shook his head slowly—no, he did not love her.

"I knew that," Arella said. But Pellar could hear the lie in her voice.

He tugged at her, gesturing toward the cave. Arella followed reluctantly. Her resistance grew when he turned toward their sleeping quarters, but he waved aside her objections with a hand and begged her with his eyes to wait. Suspiciously, Arella followed him.

From under his sleeping furs, he pulled out a small, perfect drum and presented it to her solemnly.

"For me?" Arella asked, carefully turning the drum over in her hands.

Pellar nodded and wrote quickly. " 'Arella. Emergency.' I come."

He had taught her how to drum her name and the emergency signal several sevendays before.

"If I need you, I can call for you?" Arella asked, her eyes gleaming again.

Pellar nodded firmly.

Arella smiled and drew him toward her for a kiss. Not the kiss of lovers, but the kiss of friends who once had been.

Pellar took the most difficult route out of Aleesa's wherhold: He went straight over the mountains. It took him a full day to get to the far side. He pressed on at first light the next morning and was glad to find himself within sight of Keogh, a minor hold of Crom, before the sun set that evening. He found a good camp but did not wait to set up before unlimbering his drum, checking the bindings of the wildboar hide, and rolling out the quick beat of "Attention."

A huge grin split his face as he heard no less than three drums return the "Ready" signal.

His grin slipped a little as he sought to compose his message. He finally settled on: "For Zist. Aleesa will trade."

He would send Chitter on with a longer explanation.

As the drums pounded back their acknowledgment, Pellar spread out his sleeping roll and gestured for Chitter. His note to Master Zist was terse but explained most of the details.

Chitter waited patiently for Pellar to roll the small piece of paper and tie it onto his harness, but Pellar could tell that the fire-lizard was increasingly eager at the thought of the tidbits he'd find at Master Zist's table—just as Pellar had hoped.

With a final chirp, the fire-lizard bade Pellar farewell, leaped into the air, and blinked *between* before he was more than head high above Pellar.

Greedy guts, Pellar thought with a grin as he pulled

off his boots and socks and settled in for a well-earned rest.

Chitter was back the next morning with a small breadroll, a note from Zist, and a belly that had clearly been stuffed to the gills.

Pellar merely smiled and shook his head; he intended to keep Chitter working for his food. The fire-lizard caught his mood and did a quick twirl in the air, standing almost on his tail, before returning to Pellar's shoulder with a satisfied chirp.

At Keogh, Pellar earned his meal and a place to sleep with his pipes and his slowly told tales of watch-whers and watch-wher eggs. He left before first light, certain that on his return he would not only get another night's food and board, but also at least two holders committed to trade for the privilege of a watch-wher egg.

But Keogh wasn't his primary goal. He had in mind, instead, the herders he'd met near Campbell's Field, and some of the wiser traders he'd met along the way.

The herders' need for watch-whers was obvious, and Pellar felt a small twinge of satisfaction at the notion of arranging things so that D'gan would have no choice but to accept the creatures—he couldn't argue that they were useless if they were set to protect the very herd-beasts his dragons dined on.

He traveled fast, prepared to get rides where he could and ready to steal them where he couldn't. Aleesa had told him that Aleesk had already clutched and that it would be only four sevendays before the watch-wher eggs hatched. He planned to be back at least a sevenday beforehand, ready to acknowledge those with whom he'd set up trades and fight off those with whom he hadn't.

What he hadn't counted on was the dragonrider. He was three days out of Keogh and worried that he was falling behind on his schedule when he noticed a strange shadow on the ground before him. Chitter squawked and flew up out of sight. As Pellar craned his neck up to follow the fire-lizard, he found his eye distracted by the sight of a large bronze dragon, wheeling downward on its wingtip, circling right above him.

Pellar froze, unable to react. The dragon was huge. Its eyes whirled the blue of contentment. Did that mean that the dragon was happy to find him, or glad to have caught an intruder?

Pellar was not at all sure how a dragonrider of Telgar Weyr would react if they knew his mission.

He forced himself to relax—the dragonriders wouldn't know his mission unless someone had told them. And the only people who knew were Aleesa's people and Master Zist.

Pellar waved. The dragon was low enough now that Pellar could make out the dragon's rider and he waved back.

Shortly the dragon landed and Pellar realized once again how *huge* bronze dragons could be. The dragon's head was nearly twice as tall as Pellar and its body could easily have circled three, maybe four, of the traders' large workdrays.

Pellar bowed low, first to the dragon, and then to the rider who quickly dismounted and pulled off his headgear.

"Are you Pellar?" the rider called out, striding quickly toward him.

Pellar nodded.

"Master Zist sent me for you," the rider said. "I'm D'vin of High Reaches." He gestured back to his dragon. "This is Hurth."

He saw Chitter hovering near the dragon's left eye and added with a laugh, "I see that your fire-lizard has introduced himself already."

D'vin eyed Pellar carefully. "Master Zist asked me to bring you back."

Pellar gave him a questioning look.

"Isn't it true that the watch-whers are living on land that looks to High Reaches?" D'vin asked.

Could High Reaches want the watch-whers to leave? Pellar wondered in horror.

D'vin must have guessed his thoughts. "Master Zist asked Weyrleader B'ralar to extend the protection of the Weyr to Master Aleesa and the watch-whers.

"He said that you'd told him about Master Aleesa being driven out of Telgar lands by D'gan," the bronze rider added, in an odd tone, one that strived not to be disapproving.

Pellar nodded.

"Let me bring you to Zist," D'vin said. Pellar looked startled—what about his mission?

"Afterward, I'll help you on your way."

Pellar bowed in thanks and then looked back at the dragon, trying to keep his eyes from going wide. He had never ridden a dragon before.

The dragon, Hurth, swiveled his long sinewy neck so that both eyes peered down at Pellar. For a moment, Pellar was lost in those huge, whirling eyes that were nearly as large as he was tall. He felt the same keenness of attention that he got from Chitter, only more so. He had a sense that something about him amused and intrigued the dragon.

Hurth inclined his head slightly and Pellar heard a voice in his head tell him with a laughing lilt, *You think that you can't talk to people. You do it all the time.*

Could the dragon hear his thoughts? Pellar wondered, eyes wide in amazement.

Yes, came the reply. Pellar noticed the crispness of the voice, strangely devoid of tone yet still full of inflection and meaning. *So can your little one.*

Chitter chirped and flew a quick circuit between Pellar and the huge dragon.

He can? Pellar asked, both awed and thrilled. He had always thought that he had a special relationship with the fire-lizard; he'd felt and hoped that Chitter understood him but—to have a dragon confirm it! Pellar looked at his small friend and thought hard. Chitter flipped in the air and flew straight into Pellar's arms, made a satisfied noise, and stroked Pellar's chin with his face.

He is very lucky, your little one, Hurth said. Pellar felt that he both knew and didn't know what the dragon meant by the remark, but before he could reply, he got the distinct impression that the dragon was occupied elsewhere, listening to a voice Pellar could not hear.

D'vin—the name was spoken with a warmth that awed Pellar—*says that we should go. He is glad you can hear me. He asks if you can give me the image for Master Zist and Camp Natalon.*

Image? Pellar asked himself, bewildered. Then he remembered that dragons were like fire-lizards, and that they needed to visualize their destination first. Pellar had never ridden a-dragonback. Image, he thought. He scanned the sky for the sun and then visualized as clearly as he could the fork of the road leading into Camp Natalon, Zist's stone cothold, the larger stone hold of Natalon, the shed where Danil's watch-wher had lived, the other road curving right and uphill toward the coal dump.

You give good coordinates, Hurth complimented. *Very clear, very clean.*

"You'll want to put these on," D'vin said, pulling a pack off his back and removing something blue. He shook it out and handed it across to Pellar.

Pellar shook his head and waved the offer aside, appalled that the dragonrider would offer him the clothes of a full apprentice harper.

"They'll fit," D'vin said, extending his hand again. "Master Murenny swore on it."

Pellar gave the dragonrider a questioning look.

"He said that they're yours," D'vin told him in reply. For a moment the confident rider looked uncomfortable as he asked, "You're not upset that there's no proper ceremony, are you? Master Murenny seemed assured that you'd take these from a dragonrider."

Harper clothes? Apprentice? A full apprentice? Proper? Pellar dodged past the clothes and grabbed the rider in a fierce hug, clapping him firmly on the back.

Even though Master Murenny and Zist had said he could be an apprentice, he had always been half-afraid that they didn't mean it, that maybe they were just humoring him—until now. Proper clothes! He really *was* a harper!

I have told D'vin that you are honored, Hurth said, adding a low rumble to Chitter's high, happy warbling.

Pellar stepped back and bowed apologetically to D'vin.

The bronze rider smiled, drew himself up to his full height, steadied his expression, held out the blue garments in both hands to Pellar and said formally, "Pellar, I have been requested by Murenny, Masterharper of Pern, to present you the formal garb of a harper apprentice. Do you accept?"

With equal formality, Pellar nodded and gave the dragonrider the same half-bow he'd seen other apprentices give on their induction into the Harper Hall. Then he took formal delivery of the precious blue garments.

D'vin excused himself to inspect Hurth's riding harness while Pellar changed into his harper blue. He was sorry that he couldn't clean himself up better; it had been days since his last bath. Inside the new blue-stained wherhide boots Pellar was quite pleased to find clean socks.

He was surprised to notice that his trousers and tunic both contained several large pockets—not standard.

D'vin, alerted by Hurth, turned and told him, "Master Murenny told me that you'd wonder about the pockets. He said to tell you that he expects you to carry more burdens than most."

Pellar looked surprised.

"He also said that he was sure you'd be up to them," the dragonrider added. "From the little I've seen of you, I'd say he underestimates you."

D'vin gestured to Hurth's shoulders. "This time, however, Hurth stands ready to carry *you*."

The bronze dragon snorted and nodded in agreement.

A dragon. Pellar looked again at the huge beast. He felt uneasy.

You're not afraid of me, are you? Hurth asked, sounding slightly hurt.

No, Pellar responded immediately. *But you are rather big.*

I am as big as I need to be, Hurth replied. *If I were smaller, how would I be able to carry you and D'vin?*

Pellar smiled at Hurth's logic. His smile was echoed by D'vin's laugh.

"Come, Harper," D'vin declared, holding out his hand. "Let me get you up on the big one before he decides he really *is* too small for both of us!"

D'vin sat in front. When he was settled, he turned back to Pellar, both hands in fists with the thumbs up. Pellar returned the thumbs-up gesture with a nervous grin. He was actually on a dragon! He was actually going to fly! No, he *was* flying! He looked down for a moment as the ground shrank slowly away from him. A moment's dizzying sense of perspective sent a thrill of fear through him and then Pellar realized that this was the most amazing moment of his life.

Thank you, Pellar thought to Hurth.

My pleasure, Hurth responded. There was that pause again as the dragon spoke with his rider and then Hurth continued, *Remember,* between *only takes as long as it takes to cough three times.*

Only? Pellar thought to himself. And then he was engulfed in blackness. He couldn't feel the dragon beneath, D'vin in front of him, or anything around him. His heart beat loudly in his body, he felt his blood coursing through his veins—nothing else. He realized that he was holding his breath and never remembered doing so. He wondered how long he could hold it. He felt cold, a bone-numbing cold, so cold, so very cold, worse than the coldest night in winter. Would his skin freeze?

And then they were in the sunlight again, Pellar's breath came in a rush, and the cold became a swiftly fading memory.

Pellar looked around. They were at Camp Natalon.

You give good coordinates, Hurth said again. *Very clean. D'vin wonders why you were never Searched.*

Searched? Pellar mused. *Him?* For Impression? To be a dragonrider? But dragonriders have to talk, to be heard.

I hear you quite well, Hurth told him.

Me, a dragonrider? Pellar thought. Chitter burst out in the sky beside them, gave a satisfied warble, and banked tightly to close in to Pellar's side.

Good for you, Chitter, Pellar thought fondly. *You followed us just fine.*

Chitter chirped smugly.

Zist does not want me seen, Hurth said. *Is there a place I can drop you?*

Pellar thought that a bronze dragon was pretty hard

to disguise, but then he realized that Hurth had come in close to the east mountain and flown back behind it almost instantly.

There's a plateau, he responded, remembering the small grave site. He had a sudden wish to see how it had survived through the spring thaw—and an echoing curiosity about the other mounds he'd seen when tracking Tenim and Tarik.

I see it, Hurth replied, veering toward it. *I can land there.* The dragon started a precipitous descent. *What makes you so concerned about little mounds?*

Pellar found himself overwhelmed by the question and its answer, his mind awash with many different memories—of Cayla and Carissa, of little Halla hanging upside down, of the yellow flowers.

Dragons go between *to die,* Hurth responded. He sounded sad and somewhat confused. *I suppose earth is like going* between *for people.*

Pellar was startled by the comparison and stunned by Hurth's astute observation. He didn't have much time to consider it, as D'vin was already helping him down onto Hurth's huge leg.

Once Pellar had scrambled to the ground, D'vin told him, "Let Hurth know when you want to be picked up."

Pellar nodded, and waved in acknowledgment.

Step away, Hurth cautioned. Pellar moved a dragonlength away. With a great bound of his hind legs, Hurth leapt in the air, his huge wings beating mightily to gain altitude, and then dragon and rider winked out of sight, *between.*

Pellar was surprised to see only a faint bubble of mist where the dragon and rider had been a moment before. He stared for a moment longer, then shook himself from his musings and started off over the hill and down to Camp Natalon.

He was surprised to find Master Zist waiting for him at the bottom of the hill.

"We haven't much time," Zist said brusquely. "I've already heard that the Shunned know about the sale of the watch-wher eggs."

Pellar nodded grimly. He had guessed that something as rare and valuable as watch-wher eggs would attract the attention of anyone desperate enough to become Shunned.

"Murenny has asked B'ralar, the High Reaches Weyrleader, to provide protection for Aleesa and her watch-whers," Zist continued. He put a hand on Pellar's shoulder and shook him gently. "I need you to convince Aleesa to accept the protection and arrange some signal that either you or the watch-whers can send to the dragons if the need arises."

Pellar shook his head, drew out his slate, and hastily wrote, "When."

"*When* the need arises," Zist agreed solemnly. Pellar raised a hand palm up to stop Zist from saying anything more, cleaned off his slate, and wrote, "Must move."

Zist read the note and nodded. "You're saying that they'll have to move after the eggs are distributed?"

Pellar nodded, wiped his slate clean, and wrote, "Want harper."

"They want a harper?" Zist guessed. Pellar nodded. Zist stroked his chin thoughtfully for a moment, then looked back up speculatively at Pellar.

Pellar shook his head, pointed to himself, and followed that gesture immediately by waving both hands in front of himself—his way of saying "no" since he was a baby.

"Not you," Zist gathered. He cocked an eyebrow at his adopted son. "Is that your choice or theirs?"

Pellar raised both hands, one with a single finger raised and the other with all fingers outstretched.

"All of you, then," Zist guessed. He shrugged. "Well, I won't say I'm not relieved, but I can't say when we'll have a replacement."

"I stay until," Pellar wrote.

"That's probably for the best," Zist agreed. "Your Chitter can tell us when they move and where." He waved aside Pellar's rising reaction. "The dragonriders will need to know so that they can provide protection."

Pellar mulled on Zist's words for a moment and then nodded.

"Good lad," Zist said, slapping him once more on the shoulder. This time he released his grip on Pellar and pushed him lightly away. "Now, go to Master Aleesa and get her to agree to the protection. Tell her that Natalon will provide the coal."

Pellar turned to leave, but then turned back and wrote, "D'vin bring you?"

"When it's time for the hatching?" Zist asked. Pellar nodded. Zist shook his head. "No, we'll have to get a rider from a different Weyr, so that we don't give away Aleesa's location."

Pellar frowned for a moment before nodding slowly in agreement—the lands protected by a Weyr were vast, but not so large that a determined group couldn't locate Aleesa and her watch-whers if they knew which Weyr protected them.

"Telgar," Pellar wrote as a suggestion, knowing that D'gan would never let the watch-whers back under his protection.

Zist caught on to the implications immediately and snorted in laughter. "Great idea!"

Pellar bowed slightly, waved, and turned back the way he'd come.

He was so immersed in his thoughts that it seemed

only moments before he was back on the plateau. He paused instinctively and scanned for any sign of others. When he was certain that he was alone, he thought of signaling Hurth but stopped, deciding first to visit the little grave.

It was right where he remembered. The mound had shrunk a little as the snow had thawed into mud and the mud had settled, but it was still unmistakably a grave.

They were no flowers. It looked forlorn and sad. Barren.

Pellar decided that it would have been more pleasant with a blanket of snow. He closed his eyes for a moment and imagined a small bundle of yellow flowers, the image being the only gift he could leave. He turned north and west and imagined the other mounds he'd seen in the snow following Tarik and Tenim; he closed his eyes again, imagining flowers on each of them and wondering once more which one was occupied by Halla, the girl with the flashing eyes and bark shoes.

He felt a spasm of anger run through him as he remembered Tenim and their fight. Unconsciously his hand went up to his throat and massaged it.

With a deep sigh, Pellar opened his eyes again. One day, he swore to himself. He knew he would meet Tenim again one day.

He scanned the plateau once more and then walked carefully to where he'd last seen the great bronze dragon.

Hurth, I'm ready.

What's that large and ugly thing?
A watch-wher, who shuns daylight's sting.
Night's its friend, its dark ally
Only in the cold to fly.

Chapter Five

PELLAR WAS CAREFUL to send Chitter on ahead to the camp before he approached. The fire-lizard returned immediately, eyes whirling with fear, and wrapped himself around Pellar's neck, clutching tightly and painfully.

I'm going in, Pellar thought to his frightened friend. Chitter gave a plaintive but resigned mewl in response.

It was still daylight and so not at all hard for Pellar to spot Jaythen's hiding place before Jaythen spotted him. He was sure that if he hadn't he would never have avoided the arrow Jaythen sent whizzing his way. The arrow buried itself up to the shaft in the hard-packed dirt where Pellar had been walking.

It will be hard to hide in blue, Pellar decided, abandoning any notion of using his woodcraft to elude Jaythen.

Pellar broke into a run, zigzagging and moving in a wide arc to the far side of Jaythen. He dodged another arrow, and another. He was running blindly, without any plan, his only thought to get to Jaythen, to convince him *somehow* that he meant no harm.

"Did you sell us out for finery?" Jaythen yelled as the fourth arrow missed. He threw his bow aside and pulled a long dirk from his belt. "How good do you think it'll look when your blood's on it?"

Pellar dodged again, only to find himself gape-mouthed in unvoiced pain. He looked to his left and noticed an arrow sticking out of his left forearm. Someone else had shot him. He caught the sight of Arella rising up from her hiding place, eyes streaming with tears as she notched another arrow and aimed for his heart.

"I trusted you," she yelled at him as she shot at him.

Aleesk! Pellar cried in his head as the arrow flew at him. Chitter launched himself—too late—toward the stone-tipped missile.

Time slowed for Pellar and suddenly the arrow was stuck in the air, crawling toward him. Chitter was hovering in place, getting nearer to the arrow as slowly as the arrow was approaching Pellar, and Pellar could see that the arrow would hit him before his fire-lizard could intervene.

But none of that mattered. What mattered was Aleesk, the gold watch-wher. For in that instant, Pellar felt himself a part of another in a way that he'd never felt before. He found himself in touch with Aleesk in a way he'd only imagined, even more than he'd felt with Hurth.

And he only *felt*. He was feeling: pain in his arm, pain in his laboring lungs, fear in his heart, sadness, grief, anger, loss, defeat, and above all that a burning shame and anger that this *need not be,* that if only Pellar had done something different, if only, if only—

Time moved again and the arrow whizzed toward him. Chitter's cry of anguish filled the air and Pellar looked at his own death, a mere instant away.

Then suddenly the air was full of gold, of noise, of movement, and of anger, of understanding, of contrition.

Aleesk shielded Pellar with her body. The arrow

struck her in the side, penetrated, and bounced out again. Aleesk bellowed, more in defiance than in pain, her head and eyes turning to Pellar, her mouth open, fangs bared.

She cried out to Pellar, then closed her mouth and nuzzled him, crying again in supplication, sorrow, concern.

I'm all right, Pellar told her. He found power he'd never known he'd had and stumbled over to her, grabbed her around the neck, and hugged her tightly. *I'm all right.*

The air was rent by a loud, outraged bellow, and suddenly the sky above was dark as a fully grown bronze dragon burst into existence above them.

I'm all right, Hurth, Pellar called to the dragon, fearing the wrath implied in the bronze's huge red whirling eyes.

Jaythen lurched for his bow and notched it, aiming at the dragon.

No! Pellar cried in his head. Aleesk shrieked, and the sky darkened again as a bronze watch-wher emerged above them, its cries directed at Jaythen, its body shielding the dragon.

"Jaythen, stop!" Aleesa's shouted.

Jaythen dropped his bow, his eyes wide in shock and horror.

"We do not attack dragons," Aleesa declared, moving forward stiffly toward Aleesk. "Aleesk has said so."

Jaythen looked at her in astonishment.

"She spoke?"

"She made me *feel,*" Aleesa said, holding her side at the same place as Arella's arrow had hit the gold watch-wher.

Aleesa looked over to Pellar, her eyes hard as flint.

"You played your game well, little one," she told him, her voice broken. She glanced up at the dragon hovering above her. "Now they will kill my Aleesk and there will be no more watch-whers, just as they wanted." She shook her head, tears rolling unchecked down her cheek. "I trusted you, I truly trusted you."

A sound from behind caused them all to turn sharply. D'vin had jumped off his dragon. He landed in a ball and rolled, jumping up quickly, his hands outstretched.

"You were right to trust him," the dragonrider declared.

Jaythen snorted derisively. "He's even ensnared the watch-whers."

"Has he?" D'vin asked, turning to Aleesa. "What does your watch-wher tell you?"

"Watch-whers don't talk, dragonman," Aleesa responded, raising her head and glaring at him. "They feel, and act."

"What did her actions tell you, then? What do her feelings tell you?"

Aleesa frowned thoughtfully. She looked at the gold watch-wher in an abstracted way, communing with her.

"Watch-whers are simple, uncomplicated beings," she said after a moment. "She trusts him." She glared at Pellar, hatred in every fiber of her being and then said to D'vin, "And he's sold her to you."

"I trust you, Pellar," a voice called from the distance. Arella trotted in from her hiding place. She patted Aleesk apologetically, then threw her bow down to the ground and looked at her mother. "I felt you, I felt you and—"

"We are not your enemies," D'vin declared, glancing from Arella to Aleesa and back. "Your watch-whers know this." He glanced at Jaythen. "They know not to harm dragons."

"And how do dragons think of them?" Jaythen demanded angrily.

They are our cousins, Hurth declared. Pellar looked

up at the dragon and then noticed that Jaythen, Aleesa, and Arella were also staring up at the dragon, mouths open wide in surprise. *They are our kin, as are the fire-lizards.*

"Cousins?" D'vin echoed. He looked over at Pellar. "Do the harpers know this?"

Pellar shrugged.

"Cousins?" Aleesa repeated, turning her gaze from the bronze watch-wher to the bronze dragon.

And they do not like the light, Hurth added. *You are to believe them. They are leaving now.*

Suddenly the watch-whers were gone.

They are very nimble, Hurth remarked in a surprised tone. *They are in their weyr; they like the dark.*

Into the silence that followed this last draconic announcement, D'vin spoke. "I am D'vin, rider of bronze Hurth, wingleader at High Reaches. I have been sent by Weyrleader B'ralar to offer the protection and aid of High Reaches Weyr."

"Dragonrider," Arella said, bowing low, "on behalf of our watch-whers and the last of the golds on Pern, I accept your offer."

"I am sorry for our behavior," Aleesa said, shaking herself out of her shock.

"She's the last gold?" D'vin asked, turning to the watch-wher with a horrified look on his face. He turned back to Arella. "And you shot at her?"

Arella flushed and gestured angrily at Pellar. "I shot at him," she declared, "to protect her."

Pellar strode over to the two, waved his hands for attention, grabbed their hands and pulled them together, forcing them to shake.

Hurth, Pellar thought to the dragon hovering still above them, *tell them to stop bickering, and that I'm about to faint.*

Pellar says that you are to stop bickering and that he

is going faint, Hurth dutifully reported just as Pellar crumpled to the ground.

"So, when will you be ready to continue?" Arella asked Pellar as his eyes fluttered open.

Pellar gave her a look of outrage and Arella laughed. "I thought that's what you'd do."

Pellar closed his eyes again and felt for Chitter.

He is sleeping here with me, Hurth reported. Pellar got the impression of a small brown fire-lizard curled on the forearm of a large bronze dragon. *I am glad you are well. He was quite upset. D'vin says that we can go whenever you wish. Aleesa says that the hatching will come any day now.*

"Are you able to stand?" Arella asked. It was then that Pellar realized that she was lying next to him, her body's heat warming him. Arella guessed his thoughts from his expression and smiled wryly at him. "Don't go getting any ideas, Harper Pellar. There's no mating flight for months yet. I am here because it was my arrow in your arm, and I owe you."

Arella's eyes were bright as they looked deep into his. He reached over and stroked her cheek. She leaned into it and then drew back again, all business. "Are you ready to earn your keep?"

Pellar nodded and rolled over, trying to rise and finding himself terribly weak. His left arm was sore and stiff, and his mouth opened vainly to cry in pain.

Arella's strong arms grabbed at him, steadied him, and lifted him up.

"You're as weak as a hatchling," she told him, helping him up to a stool.

Pellar looked around for his slate. When he didn't find it, he spread out his hands imploringly to Arella, then brought them together frantically, one flat like a slate, the other fisted like someone holding chalk.

"Your slate's broken. You'll have to talk through the dragon," Arella informed him.

Hurth? Pellar thought to the dragon.

Tell me what you want and I will tell her, the dragon responded. *D'vin is ready to help if you need.*

Pellar glanced quickly down at his naked body, blushed, and decided that he would wait before taking the dragonrider up on his offer.

Arella bustled about him efficiently, throwing undergarments at him and helping him with them only when his attempts failed piteously. Trousers and his blood-stained tunic went on next, then Arella pushed him back onto the stool and gently slid socks onto his feet. She tugged his boots on carefully, keeping her eyes on his face for any signs of pain, but Pellar only winced twice as her movements jostled his arm.

"I would have killed you for betraying the watch-whers to their deaths," Arella told him softly. "You understand? Wouldn't you do the same if someone tried to kill Chitter?" She turned her head toward the watch-whers' quarters. "And she's the last of her kind."

Pellar stared at her for a long while before nodding slowly. Tears rolled down Arella's cheeks and she grabbed his right hand tightly. Pellar clenched back, and pulled her toward him. Surprised, Arella looked up from her kneeling position and crawled forward until her torso was cradled between his legs. Pellar pulled her hand back more, drawing her head toward him, and kissed her lightly on the forehead. Arella let out a sob and dropped her head against his shoulder.

"Besides," she sobbed against his chest, "you left me. I loved you and you left me."

Pellar let go of her hand and wrapped his free hand around her back, hugging her tight against him. He patted her soothingly. He knew he loved her, too, and he tightened his arm, but even as he did so he closed his eyes and saw a small mound with a thin bundle of yellow flowers.

Tears rolled down his face, dropped onto Arella's cheeks, mingled with her tears, and rolled with them onto his stained blue tunic.

With Hurth's wings, D'vin's assistance, and Arella's support, Pellar managed to find candidates for all the twelve other eggs that Aleesa said Aleesk had clutched.

"She'll outlive me," Aleesa had confessed to Arella when they were ready to leave. "And then what happens? Will you bond with the last watch-wher on Pern or let her go *between*, the last of her kind with no queen to follow?"

Arella pursed her lips tightly and shook her head indecisively.

Aleesa decided not to press the issue and turned her attention to Pellar. She gave him a piercing look, like the first look she'd ever given him but weaker, a pale imitation of the one mere months before. For the first time Pellar realized how frail the thin Whermaster was and how tired she was of her old body, how worn out and sore she felt.

"Make sure you get some joint-ail medicine, Harper," she told him firmly, as though guessing his thoughts. "I don't move like I used to."

Pellar nodded and then surprised himself, leaning forward and hugging her with his good arm. Awkwardly Aleesa patted him back and then pushed him away, spreading her gaze between him and Arella.

"Go now, or it'll be too late."

They returned three days later. Hurth bellowed a warning that Chitter repeated in quieter counterpoint. From within the watch-whers' cavern came an echoing response.

"You've reason to be proud, you know," Arella murmured in Pellar's ear as they spiraled down toward the ground. She was perched behind him, while D'vin was in front. She reached forward and squeezed his thigh for emphasis. Pellar nodded and covered her hand with his.

"Some of them are already here," D'vin noted as they circled down for their landing. Above him, a dragon bugled; he peered back over his shoulder. "Those are *Benden* colors. The Weyrleader!"

Hurth suddenly lurched sideways, clearing a path for the great bronze dragon bearing Benden's Weyrleader. As the bronze descended, Pellar caught a glimpse of three passengers: Natalon with his eyes scrunched firmly tight, Zist, and Kindan. The youngest son of Camp Natalon's last watch-wher handler looked a little green with fear, but his eyes were wide with excitement.

"I need to get down," Arella muttered from behind. "I need to help Mother."

As if in response, Hurth tucked into a steep dive, backwinging only a dagger's length above the ground and landing firmly. Arella was in motion immediately, nimbly scrambling down the dragon's front leg. She patted him absently before darting into the crowd gathered in the hollow.

D'vin turned in his seat and said, "Pellar, I think it might be a good idea to keep you out of sight. As long as those down there don't know that you're here, they won't know if you know the location of the watch-wher's lair."

Pellar nodded. He and Arella had bargained well for the watch-wher's eggs, and the Whermaster and the rest of the camp would find their lives easier for Turns to come, but news of their riches would certainly spread to the Shunned, who would have the double incentive of those goods and the watch-wher eggs that could be traded for more.

"I, on the other hand," D'vin continued, "have to mingle amongst our guests. They don't know where this camp is, all having come a-dragonback, but Zist is hoping they'll draw the obvious conclusion."

Pellar quirked an eyebrow at the bronze rider. D'vin smiled and waved a finger at him. "You're a harper—surely you've noticed the only Weyr not represented here?"

Pellar looked around at the other dragons, some aloft on watch, some perched on top the hill below. He found the riders and their markings—Fort, Ista, Benden, and High Reaches. Suddenly he found himself holding his sides in silent laughter. Only Telgar was not present. Any devious mind would quickly conclude that Master Aleesa's camp was still on Telgar lands!

"So where *are* they?" Tenim shouted, angrily pounding his fist on the table. A sudden hush filled the tavern. Hold Balan had grown up as natural stopping point for barges and drays on their journey between Miner's Hold and Campbell's Field. The holders earned much of their trade providing the bargemen and draymen with lodgings and meals, so they were used to a raucous, constantly changing crowd. Even so, patrons turned nervously toward him. Some tossed back the last of their drinks and made their exit with indecorous haste.

Moran made calming gestures with his hands. "They're checking."

"Checking? *Checking?*" Tenim roared, the veins in his neck standing out like ropes. He pounded the table again, ignoring the worried expressions of the few remaining patrons and the cowed look of the owner with whom he'd already shared harsh words and short jabs, concentrating instead on Moran's worried face. Oh, he thinks he hides it, Tenim thought, but I know. I know who's in charge here, and it's not this fat old fool.

"Checking," Moran repeated firmly. "Halla's report is from Crom; we've still Telgar to hear from, and Miner's Hold to the east—who knows?"

"*We* don't," Tenim growled. "There's a fortune changing hands and we don't even know where." He gave the harper a cunning look. "Think of the children you could help with *that* sort of money."

Tenim smiled to himself as he saw his remark hit home. Oh yes, I know your loyalties, he thought, wondering how he could have ever thought of the older man as anything but a weakling.

Sure, it was true that Moran had found him, fed him, nursed him back to health when no others would so much as raise a hand for the son of a Shunned father and no one had the time for his spineless mother. He never wondered anymore what had happened to her; the last he'd seen of her was the night she'd turned on his father and he'd struck her down. Tenim had learned not to argue with his father at an early age; in fact, at the same time Tenim had learned that even if she'd had a will, his mother would have never used it in his defense.

"If you hadn't sold all the coal we'd stolen for your brats, we'd have enough now to pay for decent information," Tenim added. "I told you to hold on to it."

"Who would we sell the egg to?" Moran asked. He wondered again how he had come to this pass, how the boy he'd succored so long ago had turned into this sour young man, and again he remembered the many petty compromises, lies, wheedles, and thefts that the harper had made to provide the next day's food, to feed just one more helpless mouth, make one more small difference, only to find himself repeating the effort the next day, this time to feed even more mouths with even more theft and lies.

"Anybody," Tenim replied sourly. "Think of what we could get. They say that Tarik's camp promised a whole winter's supply of coal for their *chance* at an egg. What would they pay for the real thing in their hands, no questions asked?"

"Somebody would ask questions," Moran protested. "There aren't that many watch-whers—"

Tenim cut him off. "What makes you so certain? Why would they care where it came from?"

"I suppose they might not," Moran said, unwilling to press the point. "Not that it matters—we don't know where they are. The eggs might have been distributed already."

Tenim snorted. "If they had, then Tarik would have told us." He took a sip of his ale. "You didn't hear how much he complained about the waste." He frowned thoughtfully and took another long pull on his drink, then threw it back altogether, draining the mug and slamming it on the table. He rose and headed for the door.

"Where are you going?" Moran asked. "We have to wait for the rest of the children."

Tenim snorted. "You wait if you want. I know where one egg will be, and I know what'll be paid for it. I'll get that for certain."

"There's an egg left," Aleesa announced as the last of the party left.

"Is there anyone else who wanted to trade?" D'vin asked Pellar. Pellar thought for a long moment before shaking his head. He stifled a yawn, gave everyone a sheepish look—which grew deeper as others yawned in succession—and then shook his head again firmly to be certain he was understood.

"Aleesk won't move until the last egg's gone," Aleesa told the others.

"If she doesn't move, there's a good chance you may be found out by some of the Shunned," D'vin replied.

"So now we'll see the worth of a dragonrider's word," Jaythen responded, eyeing the bronze rider challengingly.

For a moment it looked as though the young dragonrider would respond to Jaythen's barb, then D'vin relaxed and smiled. "Yes, you will."

Aleesa slapped Jaythen on the arm. "You apologize, Jaythen. They've kept their word and more."

Jaythen's jaw clenched as he locked eyes with the dragonrider. Then he drew himself up to his full height and gave D'vin a low bow. "Aleesa's right, dragonrider. You've done everything you've said you would; I had no call to doubt you."

D'vin waved the apology away. "We've all been working hard, we're tired."

"It's not just that," Jaythen replied as he stood up. "We—" He waved a hand to include Aleesa, Arella, and the rest of the wherholders. "—have had to be wary for so long that it's hard to trust anyone."

"No problem, I understand," D'vin told the man, his eyes full of warmth at Jaythen's candor and integrity.

"I think it *is* a problem, bronze rider," Jaythen disagreed mildly. "We have fewer friends when we treat them like enemies."

"Hmm, I imagine that's so," D'vin replied. He held out his hand to Jaythen. "Will you be friends with a rider from High Reaches?"

Jaythen nodded and took the hand, shaking it firmly.

"There's still an egg left," Arella reminded them. "If we're to trade, we'll need to act fast."

Aleesa shook her head. She looked over to Pellar. "That boy, Kindan, he was a worthy lad," she said. "If his egg doesn't hatch, we'll give him this one."

"And what if his egg hatches, Mother?" Arella demanded.

Aleesa sighed. "Then the hatchling will decide what's necessary."

Arella and Jaythen both paled, and Pellar looked inquiringly at them.

"It'll go *between*," Arella explained.

"Forever?" D'vin asked, aghast.

Arella nodded.

Aleesa looked Pellar straight in the eyes and said, "You go, be sure that egg hatches, and come back to help us move and keep your part of the bargain."

Pellar nodded. D'vin gestured for the harper to follow him. In moments Pellar was airborne, and an instant later, *between*.

They arrived in daylight, hovering over the grave plateau, hidden from the miners by the mountain peak to the east.

After Pellar dismounted, D'vin looked down at him and said, "You know that if this lad's egg hatches, Aleesa will be expecting *you* to bond with the other hatchling."

Pellar nodded, grimacing.

D'vin pursed his lips thoughtfully before continuing, "Don't forget that your future is your own to choose, not hers."

Pellar shook his head, pulled out his slate, and wrote, "Oath."

D'vin craned down to read the slate. "Your oath was to teach her and be harper, not to become a wherhandler."

Pellar felt that D'vin wasn't saying all he thought. With a sudden insight he pointed his finger at D'vin and at Hurth and then back at himself and shook his head firmly—there was no way that *he* could become a dragonrider.

D'vin says that you should know that dragons choose

whom they will, Hurth informed him. *You are the right age,* the bronze added on his own.

Pellar threw up his hands. *Thank you, thank D'vin. Please, I must go now.*

Call when you have need, Hurth said. *I like the sound of your voice.*

Pellar waved and turned to the path around and down the hill. He had been marching a long time before he realized that Hurth had referred to his "voice." He stopped, momentarily stunned that anyone had ever heard his voice. Hurth could hear him. Really hear him. Pellar's face split into a huge grin. The rest of his journey to the miners' camp disappeared behind that amazing thought.

Perhaps he *could* be a dragonrider. Chitter burst forth from *between* a short distance above him and made it clear that he was *sure* that Pellar could be a dragonrider. After all, Pellar was his mate, so why not something bigger?

Pellar gave Chitter a shushing gesture—they were too near the camp and he didn't want to attract attention. In fact, he thought with a sudden chill, he wasn't sure how Master Zist would feel about his sudden arrival.

Reflecting on that, Pellar decided to wait until dusk before approaching the camp. Chitter wasn't happy with the decision, projecting more and more pointed images of mouthwatering food and warm fires as the bitter evening chill drew down upon them.

All the same, Pellar held out until dark. If his approach to the camp afterward was perhaps more influenced by his grumbling stomach than his caution, he felt Chitter was to blame.

Whatever the reason, Pellar was surprised when he stumbled across someone crouched in a bush outside of the shed that had housed the late watch-wher.

Believing the worst, Pellar grabbed his victim around

the throat, determined to repay his attacker for every bruise and indignity.

"It's me," a young voice gasped out hoarsely. Pellar let go instantly and sprang back, dropping into a defensive crouch as he revised his estimate of the situation. The other person was smaller than him and younger—neither Tenim nor Tarik. But the voice sounded vaguely like Tarik's.

Cristov.

What was he doing here? Pellar wondered. It didn't matter. He moved close and carefully massaged the boy's throat the same way he'd done his own after Tenim's assault.

"Sorry," Pellar wrote after Cristov recovered.

"You—" Cristov stopped, swallowed, and massaged his throat before continuing. "You thought I was Tenim."

Pellar nodded.

"Are you afraid he might steal the egg?"

Pellar's eyes widened at the thought. It was a good idea that neither he nor Aleesa had had. Certainly Tenim knew where Camp Natalon was and would have no trouble finding the watch-wher egg. It would be easy for him to steal it before it hatched. In all the efforts of his dealings to find homes for the eggs, Pellar hadn't considered the possibility that, once placed, the egg might still be in danger from the Shunned.

"Father says it's a waste of a winter's coal," Cristov said. He looked Pellar straight in the eyes. "Even if it is, it'd be worse if the egg was stolen, wouldn't it?"

Pellar nodded in agreement with the boy's logic.

"I decided I could help and keep an eye on it," Cristov explained. Pellar got the distinct impression that Cristov was not telling him all of his reasons; in that moment he got the distinct impression that Cristov was a rather lonely youngster, someone looking for an older friend.

Pellar knew the feeling well, and recalled how well his suggestion that Zist get Kaylek to mentor the youngster had worked. Could it be that Cristov was hoping to see Pellar again? The thought made the young harper feel confused—both flattered and embarrassed.

Chitter appeared at that moment, hovering nearby. Pellar got the impression that the fire-lizard had seen everything but had been confused by both Pellar's actions and Cristov's reactions.

"He's beautiful," Cristov exclaimed, tentatively holding his hand up to Chitter. Pellar gestured to Chitter and sent the fire-lizard a thought; Chitter chirped an assent and dropped down to hover just in front of Cristov's outstretched hand.

"Can I touch him?" the boy asked Pellar, eyes wide with awe. In answer, Chitter snaked his head forward, jaw canted so that Cristov's fingers were touching his favorite scratching spot. Cristov needed little prodding and was soon happily scratching Chitter's jaw and rubbing over his eye sockets, totally absorbed with the fire-lizard's enthusiastic responses.

"Will the watch-wher be the same?" Cristov asked, taking his eyes off the fire-lizard just long enough to look at Pellar.

For a moment Pellar wondered whether Cristov was asking about the watch-wher's appearance or its behavior. Guessing that he meant the behavior, he nodded in agreement, remembering Aleesk's staunch defense.

"It won't be as pretty as you, though," Cristov told Chitter, fearing that he might offend his newfound friend. Chitter agreed with everything Cristov said, especially when the miner boy brought up his other hand and scratched both sides of Chitter's face.

After a long time, Cristov looked back to Pellar. "Are you here to guard the egg, too?"

Pellar thought quickly, and made his decision. He shook his head and wrote, "No. Ask you."

Cristov's eyes got very big. "Me? You want to ask me to guard the egg?"

Pellar nodded.

The younger boy swallowed hard. "I'm not very big," he admitted.

Pellar grinned and wrote, "Big enough."

Cristov still looked dubious, so Pellar cleaned his slate and wrote, "Trust you."

As the young miner absorbed this, a woman's voice called out, "Cristov!"

Cristov shook himself out of his reverie and his eyes lost their shine. "I can't stay up late," he confessed sadly. "My mother would find out."

"Only day," Pellar wrote hastily.

"And you'll watch at night?" Cristov said. "You and your fire-lizard?"

Pellar nodded.

Cristov mulled this over, the shine returning to his eyes.

"Cristov!" his mother called again.

"Deal," Cristov said, holding out his hand to Pellar. Pellar took it and shook it firmly, convinced that Cristov was nothing like his father.

"Gotta go," Cristov explained, then turned quickly and shouted, "Coming!"

Pellar waved at the retreating form and then wiggled into the bush Cristov had been using.

Pellar's improvised guard schedule worked perfectly over the next three days. Cristov's "guard" was unnoticed by the rest of the camp as he lived right next to the shed where the watch-wher egg had been placed, and his presence made it easy for Pellar to sneak into place for his night watch and sneak away in the morning.

When Pellar arrived for his watch on the fourth

evening, Cristov was there to greet him, his face clouded.

"It hatched," he said in a dull voice. "I haven't seen it yet."

Pellar gestured for Cristov to say more.

"You're going to leave now, aren't you?" Cristov asked with a deep sigh. Pellar nodded. Cristov screwed up his courage to ask, "Will I ever see you again?"

It was obvious to Pellar that Cristov was looking for a friend, a surrogate older brother, someone to train him in what was right and how to live in the world. Pellar was amazed that the boy had already decided that Tarik was no such guide, had decided to abandon the teaching of his father and look instead for some other mentor. He understood Cristov; a wave of sympathy and regret swept over him. He'd promised Aleesa. He was needed back with the Whermaster.

"Not soon. Turns," Pellar promised on his slate, not wanting to set the boy hoping for his early return even though he wasn't sure how long it would be before Masterharper Murenny or Master Zist arranged for his replacement at the wherhold.

"Turns?"

"Promise," Pellar wrote in response.

"Turns," Cristov repeated, eyes downcast. He looked up at Pellar. "How will you recognize me? How will I recognize you?"

Pellar smiled and pointed to Cristov's heart and then his own.

Cristov nodded slowly in response, but Pellar felt that the boy was still disheartened. He held up a hand for a moment, then shrugged off his backpack and rummaged through it.

Cristov watched wide-eyed as Pellar searched his pack. His eyes got even bigger when Pellar pulled out a lovely pipe and ceremoniously handed it to him. No one had ever given him something before.

"Is this for me?" Cristov asked in disbelief.

Pellar nodded. He wiped his slate clean and wrote on it, "Zist teach."

"You want me to ask Master Zist for lessons?" Cristov squeaked in surprise. When Pellar nodded, Cristov confessed, "I don't know if I'd be any good."

"Try," Pellar wrote in response.

"Okay," Cristov promised. Pellar sealed up his pack and shouldered it once more. As he turned to go, Cristov said, "I'll try real hard."

Pellar turned back and grabbed the youngster in a big hug. Then as quick as he could, Pellar vanished into the darkness.

Two hours later, Pellar stood again in the plateau clearing.

Hurth, I'm ready, he thought.

We come, the dragon responded immediately. *You sound sad.*

I am, Pellar responded. How many children on Pern, he wondered, were like Cristov—trying to do their best without example?

Pipes for playing, pipes for song,
Pipes to help the day along.
Pipes for laughter, pipes for joy,
Pipes for sorrow, pipes for boys.

Chapter Six

MASTER ZIST WAS SURPRISED when Cristov stayed behind after the end of the morning class. He was even more surprised by the boy's request to be taught the pipes.

"I don't know if I have any spare pipes," Zist said, not sure why he'd want to do Tarik's son any favors.

"Someone gave me one," Cristov replied, his face a mix of sorrow and surprise.

"May I see it?" Zist asked, holding out a hand. The pipe that Cristov reluctantly gave him was immediately familiar to the Master. He had made it himself not too many Turns before. In fact, Pellar had been just about Cristov's age when Zist had presented him with this very pipe.

"Did Pellar give this to you?"

Cristov looked surprised but nodded. "He said he'd see me again but it would probably be Turns," he explained.

"Well," Zist replied, "if he said it, then it will be so."

Zist twirled the pipe in his hand. The Ancients would have called it a recorder. The mouthpiece was at the top of the pipe, not at the side as with the more common flute. A recorder was much easier to learn than a flute, but at the expense of the dynamic range it could produce.

Zist nodded to himself in sudden decision. He looked at Cristov. "I'll teach you."

"Thank you," Cristov said, smiling. Then his smile faded as another thought crossed his mind. "Can we not tell my parents?"

Zist considered the question carefully. "I see no reason why we can't wait until the appropriate time to surprise them," he allowed, his eyes twinkling with a sense of mischief that Cristov had never seen before.

"Thank you," Cristov said.

"Let's see if you thank me after your first lesson," Zist replied. He handed the pipe back to Cristov. "And your first lesson will be on breathing."

Breathing? Cristov thought to himself in dismay. He'd heard how Kindan and Zenor had both been as limp as rags after an hour of Zist's "breathing" lessons! Well, he *had* asked.

"Egg?" Tarik repeated to Tenim in disbelief. "What would you want with an egg?"

"Not me," Tenim said. "Others. They'd pay full marks, too."

"The egg hatched two days ago," Tarik replied. "It's bonded with the brat now."

"Bonded?"

"Yes, the thing bit the boy and now it follows him everywhere."

Tenim's features soured as he scowled. They were in the kitchen of Tarik's new cothold and it was dark. Tenim's journey had taken two more days than he had planned: profitable days, to be sure, considering the increased bulk of his well-hidden purse, but perhaps not profitable enough to make up for missing a chance at the egg.

"Hmmph," Tenim snorted in disgust. "It's no good to me now."

"It's a green," Tarik said thoughtfully. "That means it'll mate someday." He smirked at the thought of how young Kindan would deal with *that*.

"Greens aren't as good as golds," Tenim snapped, having absorbed that much lore from Moran's teachings. "Not green fire-lizards, nor green dragons. I'm sure it's the same for those uglies, too."

"Then the best price would be paid for a gold egg, wouldn't it?" Tarik suggested, carefully keeping his tone neutral. Tarik would breathe easier if Tenim took up the wild watch-wher chase.

Tenim cocked his head quizzically at the suggestion. It was a good idea, so good it surprised him. He pursed his lips and furrowed his brow while he examined Tarik, wondering what thoughts were going on in the older man's head. Still . . . it was a good idea.

"No one knows where the queen watch-wher is," Tenim said.

"No one?" Tarik asked. "From what I've heard, there were several buyers vying for watch-wher eggs."

"No one's told me anything," Tenim said, gazing intently at the miner.

Tarik returned Tenim's intent look with a bland one of his own, waiting with growing anxiety that he worked desperately to hide. As the silence grew uncomfortable, he suggested, "Perhaps your harper friend might learn more?"

"Him!" Tenim snorted at the suggestion.

"What's he doing now, I wonder," Tarik said, sounding as though he were talking to himself.

Tenim nodded thoughtfully and rose from his seat, heading for the door.

At the door, he stopped and said, "I'll find out." He

waved a finger at Tarik. "When I come back, I'll expect you to have more coal set aside."

Tarik nodded, knowing that there was nothing else he could do—except hope that perhaps Tenim wouldn't come back.

Halla said nothing as she watched Moran scan the landscape in front of them, just as she'd said nothing when Moran announced their sudden departure from the environs of Hold Balan, even though some of the older boys had grumbled about missing Tenim.

"He'll find us, no worries," Moran had replied lightly. Halla had been the only one close enough to see his face in the dark night, and she'd seen the deep lines and worry written on it. To her it had looked like Moran was more worried about Tenim finding them than not, but perhaps she was just assigning her own feelings to the harper.

Little Tucker bumped into her. He did that often to get attention. Halla ignored him this time, knowing that the child was still half-asleep.

"We'll need food soon," she said to Moran. Moran gave her a surprised look; usually children told him that they were hungry. It was a sign of Halla's forced maturity that she thought the way she did.

"It looks pretty barren," he replied, but he eyed the girl hopefully. After Tenim, Halla was the best hunter. Astride his shoulders, little Nalli stirred.

"I'll take her for a while," Halla said, holding up her arms to grab the toddler.

Although he still wore a backpack, Moran's step grew more energetic after Halla had taken Nalli from him. After a few more steps carrying Nalli, Halla could see why—there was so little in their packs that the weight of an undernourished toddler more than doubled the load. Little Nalli, who had roused slightly during the transfer, soon fell back to sleep, resting her small head on Halla's and providing warmth for the back of her neck and shoulders.

At a sound from behind them, Moran stopped and turned.

"Perri," Moran said in a tone that was equal parts exhaustion and worry.

Halla half turned and warned, "There's no more feverroot."

Moran rushed back to the fallen youngster. Perri had been bitten by a tunnel snake when he was playing at the outskirts of Hold Balan—or that's what Halla guessed, for the toddler had never been much of a talker and refused to say anything about his injury. The wound had festered in the past several days, and he'd walked through the night in a half-fever.

Some noise or sigh caused Halla to stop and turn all the way back to the others. Instead of trudging after her, they were grouped in a semicircle. Moran was kneeling in the center.

As soon as Moran lifted his head up and looked at Halla, she knew. She sighed, too tired for anything else, wordlessly passed Nalli back to Moran, and grabbed at the handle of the shovel that hung down from her backpack. She was getting too good at digging graves.

A half hour later they trudged on, Halla more grimy than she liked, and only a few withered yellow flowers for the mound she left behind. She'd liked Perri, he'd just started to smile.

They look to you, Moran thought to himself as he led the group of children away from yet another grave, and you let them down.

How many graves did that make? He wondered idly and realized with dull relief that he couldn't remember. This isn't how things were supposed to be, Moran told himself. I was to find the Shunned, to set up meetings, to help them, Moran recalled. He had always wanted to make a difference, have ballads composed about him, make up for his unknown origins. Instead, somehow, he'd found himself only surviving one crisis to fall into another, never seeming to find the right place, the right answers, and always coming up with more complications. Every time he'd sworn that he'd locate the next harper, report in to the Harper Hall, something had happened to change his mind. He wanted to report his success; he could not bring himself to report failure. And so the Turns had passed. Turns, and Moran's dreams had gone from saving the Shunned to simply finding food enough for those waifs he'd found along the way. Worse still, at times he'd squandered their spare marks for drink, or an evening's comfort. Always, at the time, Moran had told himself that he deserved it—the drink or the warm company—and after, seeing the mute looks of the hungry children, had sworn never again. But again and again, he would give in to his base desires. With such dismal failures, how could he face Murenny or Zist?

He shifted Nalli on his back, looking hopefully back at Halla in hope of a trade. Her face was streaked with tears.

Moran swore at himself for his selfishness and trudged on.

"Egg hatched—green," were the words written on Pellar's slate as he met with Aleesa and the rest of the wherhandlers when he arrived at the wherhold that evening.

"So did ours," Arella replied. "She was a green, too."

A small form butted its head up from under her skirt. Chitter flittered down to the young watch-wher and gave it a polite chirp. The watch-wher sniffed back at the fire-lizard, then ducked behind Arella's skirt once more.

"You'll be first watch come morning," Jaythen told him. "There's a bit left in the pot, so get some food and get some rest. Aleesk will wake you."

Pellar nodded once more, stifled a yawn, and wandered over to the cooking fire. Polla smiled at him as he found a clean dish and served himself.

"I'll bet you're glad to be home, aren't you?" she asked, her grin more gap than teeth.

Again Pellar nodded but his heart wasn't in it, any more than his stomach was enticed by the smell of his dinner. He ate quickly, spread out his bedroll in his old place, and quickly fell asleep. Tomorrow he would see about looking for reeds or wood for a new pipe.

When Arella came to bed later, she set her roll apart from his.

The next day was no different; neither the next sevenday, nor the next month. Pellar found himself overcoming the difficulty of teaching others to read when he could not speak, Aleesa grew proudly proficient in her abilities and took to writing a journal, the watch-whers grew older, and the camp slowly found its supplies dwindling once again to their old meager levels.

Pellar grew and thickened up. The last of his childish looks sloughed away; his chest grew wiry from his work with trap, drum, and knife. He improved his tracking, always remembering his encounter with Tenim, now several months past.

Polla had flirted with him, but he'd ignored the older woman, just as he and Arella found themselves ignoring each other—although with increasing difficulty. Some of the older girls Pellar had been teaching had started flirting with him, too. Pellar politely redirected their attention, while he worried about what might occur the next time Aleesk rose to mate. His best hope was to be far away before then.

Halla didn't like Conni or her daughter, Milera, but Moran had decided to accept them into their band when they passed through the meeting of the three rivers between Telgar and Crom Holds.

Halla didn't need for Conni to part her hair to guess at the big blue "S" that had been painted there with bluebush ink. Young as she was, Halla had a good idea of what had caused Conni to be Shunned by her Lord Holder, and she liked neither the way that Conni looked at Moran—like a tunnel snake ready to pounce on its prey—nor, worse, the way Milera slavishly emulated her mother. And while Conni might be a few Turns past her prime, Milera had just gone from child to woman.

Halla had been around Moran too long not to guess that there was more to the harper's acceptance of the two than just the kindness of his heart. Even with the death of Perri behind them by a sevenday there were still too many mouths to fill and nothing with which to feed them, despite Halla's best efforts with her traps.

And Conni's offer to share her food did not warm Halla to the pinch-faced, sharp-eyed woman with her long straggly hair, nor to her simpering doe-eyed daughter.

Conni's food lasted no more than a meal. A meal, Halla had noted, which fed Conni and Milera more than the rest of the troop put together. That meal had been three days since, and still Conni and Milera always seemed to get the best or the most of what meager pickings Moran's band acquired.

Conni, Halla decided, would be better matched with Tenim than with Moran. Although, Halla conceded, perhaps Conni would find herself losing out to the younger Milera in winning Tenim's affections.

Whichever way it was to be, Halla was certain that neither Conni nor Milera would have tolerated Halla or anyone of the littler ones were it not for their ability to gather food, either by trapping it or stealing it from local cotholders.

Although she preferred hunting and trapping, it never bothered Halla much to steal from a wealthy holder or crafter, but none of the holdings they'd seen in the last sevenday were wealthy; Halla was certain that their thefts had meant empty bellies for the rightful owners. It bothered her to steal from those who worked as hard for their food as she did.

Her line twitched and she tugged at it. Another bite. She gently played the line with her free hand, gauging the size of the fish by its heft on her line.

It had been Conni or Milera who had secured their passage on the small riverboat. Halla was not sure which and didn't want to think long on it—both because she hated being beholden to either in any fashion, and because of the satisfied smirk both had displayed the morning after they'd spent the night in the little cabin below deck with Moran and Geffer, the grizzled old man who owned the boat.

Halla finished her battle with the hapless fish at about the same time as she finished her thoughts about the night before. She deposited the fish in the bucket where two more vainly circled. There, that was enough for a good meal. She looked forward to gutting the fish, a smellier task than dressing land animals, but all the better to wash the stench that the presence of Conni and Milera lent their party.

"That one's too thin," Milera's whiny voice piped up just behind Halla. "You ought to throw it back—it's as skinny as you are."

Halla did not betray her surprise that she had been so lost in her thoughts that she hadn't heard Milera's approach. She merely threw her line back over the side of the boat and trawled it out carefully.

"The sun's just barely past nooning; I didn't think you'd be up," she said carelessly, keeping her attention on the line.

"I get up when I'm hungry or bored," Milera answered. "I'm both now. Moran says that you're to feed me."

"I'll share my catch," Halla replied, "when the time comes."

"The time's for Moran to say," Milera snapped.

"Yes," Halla agreed, with a slight incline of her head. "Until he does, I'll go on fishing."

"And I told you that Moran said to feed me," Milera returned venomously. "The two big ones ought to do. You can fish for more when you've finished cooking mine."

Halla's eyes flashed and she set her jaw, prepared to give Milera a piece of her mind when she heard footsteps climbing up from the cabin.

"Are you getting fed, Milera?" Geffer called as he approached. He cackled. "Wouldn't want you to lose your strength, would we?"

Halla felt her whole face turn red with anger, embarrassment, betrayal, and a sense of shame.

"Halla's just about to gut the fish," Milera purred back. "She's only caught three, but I suppose that's as good as she can, being still a child."

Halla turned back to her fishing to hide her anger.

"She's a good fisher to get three in such a short time," Geffer allowed.

"It's good that she's got so many talents," Milera agreed. "A plain girl's got to have some craft to trade on."

Geffer laughed agreeably. "Will you come back down when you're finished eating?"

"Whatever you want," Milera replied.

Geffer laughed again and Halla heard him pat the girl, mutter something that caused Milera to giggle, and then turn back to go below.

Milera was silent only until Geffer was out of earshot, when, in icy tones, she declared, "I'll take my fish now."

Halla bit her tongue and nodded sullenly. Times had changed; they would change again.

It took another fortnight for Halla's predictions to come true, though not in the way she'd imagined. When the boatman, Geffer, pulled in to the wharf at the highest part of the River Crom, Milera remained behind, much to Conni's evident disgust. "You can do better than that."

At least that's how it seemed—until Milera met up with them on the far outskirts of the small river hold, her cheeks red with exertion and face bright with mischief.

"I got his money," she crowed to her mother when she found the group. "Just waited until he fell asleep, is all."

"That's my girl," Conni said, patting Milera on the back and holding out her hand. "How much did you get?"

"All of it, of course," Milera said, pulling out her purse and gleefully emptying it into Conni's hands. "You know I can't count."

"Thief!" a voice—Geffer's—shouted.

Other voices took up the cry. "Thief!" "Thief!"

Milera's gloating look dissolved into one of worry, then outright fear as Conni clenched her hands and scarpered off, calling over her shoulder, "Fool! He wasn't supposed to wake up!"

"Scatter!" Halla told the other youngsters. She took her own advice, dissolving into the crowd and then circling far around to come up behind their pursuers.

But someone grabbed Halla before she could slip away, a tall man with bad breath and a strong grasp. "There's one!"

"She was with them," Geffer said, as the crowd gathered around. "She didn't steal nothing—'twas the prettier one."

Halla flushed.

"Put an 'S' on her just so others know, then," someone in the crowd shouted.

"Yes, Shun her!"

"Shun the thief!"

Halla struggled against her captor, kicking and squirming futilely until she collapsed into a pathetic heap, sobbing silently with uncontrollable terror and despair.

"She didn't steal nothin'," Geffer shouted over the crowd. "It was the other one, the tart, that did it."

"Let her go, then," a deep voice chimed in.

"Should mark her just to know," someone muttered in the crowd.

"I see them!" the deep voice called. "They're over there!"

The crowd surged forward, around Halla, and charged off.

"Here, let me take her," the deep voice spoke to Halla's captor. "She's scared and needs a rest."

"Needs a good thrashing," Halla's captor objected and then looked carefully at the owner of the deep voice. "Oh, Harper, I didn't know."

Halla's arm was thrust into the harper's grasp.

"That's all right," the harper replied. "I'll take her now."

"I'll leave her to you, then."

Halla waited until the stranger disappeared and then looked up into Tenim's eyes. She didn't even wonder where he'd found harper garb.

Tenim stayed silent, looking around the clearing until he was certain that they wouldn't be overheard. When he spoke again, it wasn't in the deep voice he'd used before but in his natural baritone. His tone was deadly. "Where's Moran?"

At the far east edge of the river hold, Moran gathered the remains of his band and set off hastily across the path that led east toward Keogh. He could only find six of his original dozen orphans, but he dared not wait longer because Conni had never left his side. Her resemblance to Milera was too close, and only Moran's quick thinking in throwing a spare cloak over her had kept them both from being caught.

Moran might have been able to talk his way out of the ensuing unpleasantness, but he was certain that Conni, with the blue "S" of the Shunned so prominent on her forehead, would find herself in mortal peril. Judging by her biting grip on his forearm, Conni felt the same.

She had played him for a fool, Moran realized. A sideways glance at her features, haggard, hawklike, bitter, confirmed to Moran that it was full proper that Conni had been Shunned—she was a voracious taker, stalker, and menace to all. Worse, she had raised her daughter to copy her ways. Whether Milera would escape the holders today was of no importance; one day she wouldn't, and then she, too, would wear the blue "S" of the Shunned until her nature finally betrayed her to her death. Just as it would be for Conni.

"If I'm caught, I'll see that you get yours, too," Conni hissed beside him, her hard features showing that she'd guessed at Moran's thoughts. "I'll let them know that you're no harper."

Moran nodded and gave her a worried look. Her not knowing that he truly *was* a harper might be his salvation; he didn't want to lose that advantage just yet.

"Whatever you say," he told her.

"I say we lose these brats," Conni replied, scowling at the small children following them.

Moran's heart sank as he realized his mistake. Quickly he temporized, "Not here. They won't survive, and then we'd be wanted for murder, as well."

"It wouldn't be the first time," Conni replied with a bitter laugh.

"Not children," Moran said. "Shunned or not, they'll hunt you to your death if you abandon children."

"You're a fool," Conni said, lips pursed remorselessly.

"The next cothold we find," Moran said. "We can leave them there."

"What about the others?" Conni asked. "My daughter?"

"She's smart, she'll survive," Moran said with a shrug. "The others will manage, too."

Conni gave him a sour look and said nothing. Moran accepted his small victory without any outward sign. It was, after all, only a small victory.

He had to find a way to lose this woman before she got them all Shunned.

"I've found them," Halla announced proudly to Tenim when they met in the river hold's main concourse late the next evening. The five missing youngsters crowded close by her, eyes shining with the light of the night's moons.

"And I've found *her*," Tenim said, flicking his head toward the shadow at his side.

Halla nodded, keeping her expression neutral. It was obvious that Tenim valued the pretty girl more highly than he did the missing youngsters—or herself.

During the day's searching, Halla had found herself several times looking in a still pool of water or a shiny pot. Her reflection did not displease her.

She was still young and the features of her face were still not fully formed, but they were serviceable. Probing brown eyes looked out from behind dark brown hair that could do with a wash. Her nose was straight and thin, her teeth were mostly white and strong, her lips were thin—perhaps they were too thin and that was the trouble, but she liked her smile. She had to admit that her eyes danced mischievously when she smiled, but she didn't think that was such a horrible thing.

No, Halla decided, where she was most lacking was in the curves that Milera and, more so, Conni so proudly displayed. Halla couldn't quite remember if she had ten or eleven Turns—Moran had insisted on teaching her to read and count, while Tenim had insisted on teaching her to hunt and track—but she was certain that she would have to be older and better fed before she'd develop any curves of her own. Anyway, she wasn't even sure that she wanted such curves; it seemed to her that they would make running more awkward.

"Did you find Moran?" Tenim asked.

"I want my marks," Milera added darkly from beside him. Halla gave the older girl a careful look; it was obvious that she'd grown more like her mother through the terror of the day's events.

"We'll find them," Tenim said reassuringly. Halla had never heard Tenim use that tone of voice before—the same soothing tone Moran had used with Conni.

"Just the marks'll do," Milera said.

*   *   *

For nearly a month, at least three sevendays and more, they trudged along the track that skirted the Crom hills until they finally came to the edge of the Crom River, which flowed westward toward Keogh and then southward past Nabol Hold and into the Bay of Nabol.

They were lucky to get a ride with some traders. No, Halla admitted, it had not been "luck"—for once again Milera's simpering looks earned approving glances and sparked a hurried conversation amongst the unattached traders. Halla could not understand why any trader would believe Tenim's story that he was Milera's half brother, given the way he hovered near her.

The traders were a cautious lot; they insisted on checking every one of the children to ensure that none bore the mark of the Shunned. Halla suppressed a shudder at the memory of the holder's arm-wrenching grasp of her and the crowd's fierce desire to mark her with the blue "S." She'd no doubt that if Tenim hadn't intervened she'd be wearing that mark now; nor did she doubt that if she'd been marked, Tenim would have cast her aside rather than lose his ride with the traders.

If the traders were disappointed with Milera and her hovering "brother," they were more than pleased to take advantage of Halla's good eyes, strong legs, and productive traps.

The best part of meeting up with the traders was Tarri. Tarri was much older than Halla, outspoken, sharp-eyed, with a ready laugh and smile. What was more, Tarri shared Halla's opinion of Milera.

"Looks don't last," Tarri told Halla one night as the male traders vied for Milera's attention. Halla gave her a bland look and Tarri laughed. "You don't have to worry, you know."

"I've been told," Halla replied glumly. Her response

set Tarri off into more laughter, but the trader was all the while shaking her head.

"I've seen many people grow up in my time," Tarri told her. Halla had her doubts and her expression showed it. Tarri nudged Halla playfully, saying, "I'm a trader, I travel; so I see more."

She gave Halla a considering look before continuing, "You might even have trader blood. I've seen your features before. Or Boll blood—they get swarthy down there."

Swarthy? Halla thought to herself. She'd never heard the word before.

"Your skin tans faster than others," Tarri continued. "Some find your dark hair and eyes very attractive. When you get older, your features will sharpen and you'll be glad you've got strong legs to run from all the men chasing you."

Halla snorted.

Tarri shook her head and patted Halla consolingly. "And when you're old, really old, you'll still have that great skin, lithe figure, and flashing eyes, while Milera will be a sagging, toothless, lardy mess."

Halla could never imagine herself as old, but she could easily imagine Milera as toothless and lardy.

Tarri took in Halla's expression and smiled, then rose from the fire.

"We'd best turn in," she said. "We'll be moving early, and they'll want you to check your traps for breakfast."

Halla nodded and stood, too.

"You can sleep in my wagon, tonight," Tarri offered. "I've got spare sheets and a blanket."

"But I'm dirty!" Halla protested, shocked that anyone would consider letting her near *sheets*.

"No more than I am," Tarri said, grabbing Halla's hand and dragging her along. "But we'll solve that.

"Come on—up," Tarri said, pointing to the stairs

leading up into one of the nicer wagons. "Through the curtains."

Halla obeyed and gave a startled gasp as she parted the curtains and entered the wagon proper. It was beautiful.

Tarri stepped up beside her and started rummaging. She carefully folded back the plush carpet that lined the floor and pulled down a large pan and a smaller bucket.

"There's towels and clothes down there," Tarri said, pointing to one of the many doors that lined the lower half of the wagon. "Pull out two, no, four of each while I see about this."

Halla turned in time to see Tarri disappear back under the curtain with the bucket dangling from one hand. Mystified, Halla opened the indicated door and found herself staring at large fluffy towels. She hadn't thought that anyone except maybe a Lord Holder knew such luxury!

She had just pulled out the towels and smaller clothes—shirts and pants—and was wondering what to do with them when Tarri returned, carefully moving the heavy bucket so as not to jostle it.

She eyed Halla appraisingly and said, "There should just about be enough."

Enough for what? Halla thought.

"That is, if you're willing to let me show you," Tarri said, dimples appearing on her cheeks. Her voice sounded odd, shy. "Then we could sleep in the good sheets."

"Show me what?" Halla asked.

"It's not a proper bath," Tarri continued quickly, "but it gets the job done all the same."

"Bath?" Halla repeated blankly. The big pan was way too small for a bath, even for Halla, but the thought of a bath, of getting properly *clean*, was appealing beyond all reason. "Can we start now?"

"Certainly!" Tarri replied, grinning at Halla's fervor. "You first," she said, pulling a curtain from one side to give Halla some privacy.

Halla splashed happily for several minutes and then stopped, pushing the bucket back out with a foot and poking her head out from around the curtain.

"I could do your hair, too, if you'd like," Tarri offered, quickly dampening a washcloth in the bucket. Halla accepted the offer with a huge grin.

While Tarri worked the soapy water into Halla's hair, Halla closed her eyes and reveled in the feeling of Tarri's fingers running through her hair and across her scalp. A pleasured sigh escaped her lips and Tarri's fingers stopped moving.

"When's the last time someone did this for you?" Tarri asked her.

"Never."

Tarri smiled and gently tweaked Halla's nose. "Then I'll be sure to do an extra special job."

Halla smiled back, thrilled that the trader liked her so much. As she drifted off in the sensual luxury of having her hair washed, Halla's last thought was of hanging upside down from a trap with a pair of bright blue eyes peering back up at her. Whatever had happened to that trapper? she wondered.

"If you decide to sleep in," Tarri said, "I might be able to give your tunic a wash and have it dry by the time you wake up."

"Sleep in?" Halla repeated. She was always up with the first light or sooner, either to deal with traps or a cratchety youngster.

"Yes, sleep in," Tarri replied. She gave Halla an appraising look, adding, "I thought the concept was only foreign to traders."

"But the traps—"

"—can wait until the sun's properly up, I'm sure," Tarri cut her protest short.

Before Halla could reply, Tarri pulled out a large multicolored blanket and some soft sheets, and produced a bed that was nearly the width and length of the wagon. She flicked back one corner, and with a flourish and smile, gestured for Halla to precede her. "Ladies first."

Halla smiled back and crawled into the bed. Tarri crawled in next to her and Halla moved over to give her room, amazed to find herself with a whole *half* of a bed. She was asleep in an instant.

When she awoke, the wagon was moving. It took a few moments before Halla's sense of time informed her that it was past noon. She'd never slept that late before.

She heard voices coming from the front of the wagon. One was Tarri's, the other was a deeper voice—a man's. Halla couldn't make out the words they were saying because of the noise the wheels of the wagon and the rest of the caravan were making, but she could tell from the tone that the man was angry and Tarri was trying to soothe him.

The man's voice reminded Halla of the holder who had wanted her Shunned. She got up as quietly as she could and searched in the dim light for her tunic. She found it and was surprised at how clean it smelled. She forced herself not to dwell on that for long; the man's voice made her nervous.

When she tried the wagon's back door she found it was locked. Were they keeping her prisoner? Was there no escape? Halla looked at the small windows gaily clad with curtains still closed to keep the light out—the windows were clearly too small.

There was no way out but through the curtains leading to the front of the wagon and the angry man.

Halla overcame her fearful shuddering with a deep, slow breath. If she came out on the far side of Tarri, she might be able to avoid the man and run away before anyone knew what had happened. None of the traders had any fleet-footed animals, and she was as good at hiding as she was at tracking. She stood a better chance at running than she did trying to deal with such anger.

She strained to distinguish the conversation over the noise of the wagon.

"For the last time, Veran, she didn't have anything to do with it," Halla heard Tarri say. "She was asleep here with me."

"If you say so," Veran replied. "But what's to say that she wasn't hoping to steal from you, too?"

"She wasn't."

"And what makes you so sure?"

"Because I asked if she'd like bangs," Tarri replied.

"Bangs?"

"You know, hair cut across her forehead," Tarri said with a hint of exacerbation.

"But she didn't have the mark of the Shunned," Veran replied. "Why would it worry her?"

"That's not the point," Tarri said. "If she were living with people who were Shunned she would have known immediately what I meant and would have reacted differently."

"So you've reached your judgment on a hunch," Veran declared.

"As have you," Tarri responded, her tone gently chiding.

"Hmmph," Veran muttered thoughtfully. There was a moment's silence while the trader reflected on Tarri's point. "So why do you want to let her go?"

"She could lead us to the others," Tarri said.

Halla pushed her head through the gap in the thick curtains and said, "I can track them if they've stolen from you."

Tarri glanced back at her and smiled. Before Tarri

could utter a greeting, Halla's face clouded and she asked anxiously, "My traps?"

"Checked, cleared, removed, or recovered before we set out," Tarri told her, adding with a grin, "We've got breakfast *and* lunch thanks to you."

Halla sighed deeply, and said with relief, "I'd hate the thought of leaving trapped animals to die."

Veran, who was a good ten Turns older than Tarri, gave her a startled look, which settled into one of keen appraisal.

"Why would you track the others?" he asked in a deep rumble.

"Because I don't like walking, I like running even less, and I hate the thought of spending all my time worrying that someone might brand me Shunned," Halla told him honestly.

"How did you come to be with the others?"

"I don't know who my parents were," Halla said. In fact, she had only dim memories of a sad-faced but smiling mother, and none of her father. "Moran says he found my brother and me wandering around a Gather Turns ago—"

"Where's your brother?" Tarri asked, her forehead creased in a frown.

"Dead," Halla said. "He broke his leg and the wound festered." She was surprised that she hadn't thought of Jamal in so long, and ashamed that his memory had faded so much from her thoughts.

"But—" Veran started to protest and then cut himself off. "Was he Shunned, then, that he couldn't get to a healer?"

"No," Halla said. "But to see a healer you've got to be known to the holders or the crafters.

"If they don't know you," she continued, shrugging, "they don't even ask if you're Shunned."

"A trader, then—"

"Traders want marks," Halla said. "Or trade." Her tone when she said "trade" made Tarri blush.

Veran blustered at her words. "We traders—"

"—were happy enough to see that girl yesterday," Tarri interjected. "At least the men."

Veran weighed her words; from his expression it was obvious that he couldn't argue with them but he didn't like the way they set on his mind either. He peered critically at Halla and demanded, "So tell me that you've never stolen, then."

"I won't lie," Halla replied, torn between shame, anger, and a strong desire to tell the truth.

"I trap when I can, earn my food and keep like everyone else—" She met his eyes squarely. "—but when I'm starving or the little ones have gone without food so long they can't even cry anymore, then I'm not above taking from those who've more and won't share even with a starving baby."

"I'd do the same," Tarri admitted.

Veran frowned thoughtfully for a moment, glanced away from Halla's intense eyes, and finally nodded in reluctant agreement.

"If there was another way, I'd do it," Halla declared, her brown eyes flashing fiercely. "Whenever there *is* another way, I do it."

Veran could only glance in her direction for a moment before the intensity of her gaze proved too much for him again.

"The little ones," Halla asked after a moment, "where are they?"

"We've got them," Veran said.

"So who left?"

"The girl and the lad," Tarri said.

"What'd they take?"

"You don't sound surprised," Veran growled.

"She learned from her mother," Halla said. "Her mother had bangs."

Tarri gave Veran a meaningful look.

"I see you don't name her," Veran said pointedly.

"Her name's Milera," Halla replied. "Her mother's name is Conni. We were looking for her and Moran—"

"Moran?" Veran interrupted. "That's the second time you've said that name. That wouldn't be Harper Moran, would it?"

"You mean he's really a harper?" Halla asked in surprise. When Veran nodded, she explained, "He taught me to read but I was never sure."

"Master Zist's had the word out about him for Turns now," Veran said. Tarri looked at him quizzically—obviously this was news to her, as well. Veran shrugged and sighed before continuing, "What I heard was that Zist had sent Moran to work with the Shunned—"

Halla snorted derisively and Veran nodded in agreement.

"They say," he continued, "that the Harper Hall is worried about what will happen to the Shunned when Thread comes again."

"Thread?" Halla peered up to the skies, wondering if the dreaded menace would fall at any moment.

"We've Turns before then," Tarri reassured her. She looked to Veran. "Why would the harpers worry about the Shunned?"

"They didn't say," Veran replied. "But we've talked about it among ourselves, and it's thought that perhaps the Shunned might cause problems when Thread falls."

"They'll all die," Halla declared in a dead voice. "They've nowhere to go; the Thread will devour them in one Fall." She looked up imploringly at Veran. "Would you take the little ones? They didn't do anything wrong, you know."

"Of course we would," Veran declared stoutly. "We

traders know what's right and we do it, even if the holders and crafters don't.

"Besides," he added quietly, "there's been dealings between traders and Shunned before."

Halla nodded. She'd heard as much and expected as much. The Shunned were rootless and desperate, the traders were rootless by choice; it was obvious that the two groups would be in contact, sometimes to mutual advantage.

"We don't like to admit it," Tarri confessed. "If the holders or crafters found out we were helping . . ."

"Besides, some of the Shunned were traders who went bad," Veran said. He raised his eyes to Halla's and nodded emphatically. "Most of the Shunned were sent out for good cause."

"I don't know what my parents did," Halla told him. "But my brother didn't do anything more than he needed to survive, nor do I."

"Then you'd make a good trader," Veran declared.

"I'd like to settle someplace, I think."

"That's harder," Veran replied, shaking his head. "Holders don't like giving up their lands."

"I thought Pern belonged to everyone," Tarri said.

"That's what the traders say," Veran replied with a smile.

"The little ones, would you take them *now*?"

"We'd have to talk it over," Veran said. "But there are some who've lost children recently and—"

"Of course we'll do it," Tarri said, overriding Veran's caution. "You can stay, too."

Halla shook her head. "I've got to find Moran."

"What about the others?" Veran asked.

"I'd prefer to avoid them," Halla confessed.

Veran nodded understandingly. He pursed his lips thoughtfully and then declared, "Tell us about Moran and the others, and you can go with a pack full of food."

"The truth?" Halla asked.

"Traders don't trade in lies," Tarri warned her. Halla looked at her quizzically while she absorbed her words then nodded in assent.

She spoke for a good twenty minutes, surprised by what she said and how well Tarri and Veran drew her out. She was relieved to unburden herself and glad not to have to worry about shading the truth or having to decide what to leave out of her tale.

"I've heard of Conni," Veran said when she'd finished. "I hadn't heard about her daughter."

"She's a woman now," Tarri said. Veran gave her a funny look and it took Halla a moment before she realized that Tarri was several Turns older than Milera and so a woman herself.

"They say some men died near the mother," Veran said, his voice cold. "Enough was proved that she was Shunned."

"Where was the father?" Tarri asked.

"The father was the first to die," Veran told her. Tarri and Halla shuddered. Veran gave Halla an admonishing look. "You stay clear of both of them."

Halla nodded in agreement.

"You could stay with us," Tarri offered once more.

Halla shook her head again, sadly.

"You can come back if you want," Veran told her.

"Thank you," Halla said, smiling. "I'd like to visit again, at the least."

"I'll spread the word," Tarri told her. "You'll be welcome at any trader fire across Pern by the end of the next sevenday."

Veran disappeared behind the curtains into the back of the wagon and reappeared some time later with a pack, full, as promised, with provisions.

"Fair trade," he said, offering the pack to her.

"Thanks."

" 'Fair trade' is what you say," Tarri corrected her.

Halla smiled. "Fair trade."

"Fair trade," Tenim said as he left the body lying in the gully. Milera had been a pleasant diversion, but she'd been a fool to think she could stab him while he was sleeping. She'd gotten closer than he'd liked; his shoulder was sore and hot where the dagger had scored.

She'd forfeited her purse and her life when she'd tried to take his. Now Tenim traveled by himself with a pack provisioned for two.

He turned his attention to the trail ahead. Not only had his purse profited—twice—from his stay with the traders, but he'd gained considerably on Moran and Conni. Soon his purse would be even fuller. Tenim liked the idea. A full purse could buy a full belly, a good night's rest, even a willing partner.

Conni's purse had bought them a good berth on the barge that sailed down from Crom to Keogh. Her mouth had bought them an abrupt dislodgement on their arrival.

"He was rude," Conni muttered again, her face buried in a mug full of cheap wine. She was drunk and getting nastier with every sip.

Moran eyed her distastefully. He had allowed his passion to cloud his thinking—again—and, again, he was paying far too much for his error. At least, he consoled himself, the bargeman's wife had looked upon his charges kindly, so he had reason to hope that they'd be adopted, clearly a better fate for them than remaining close to Conni. Now all he had to do was achieve a similar distance and perhaps he could return, prodigally, to the Harper Hall.

For a moment Moran imagined the look on the faces of the harpers as he returned from his impossible mission. Why, he might even gain his Mastery straight out. He was old enough, nearing his thirtieth Turn even if he looked older.

His pleasant rumination was rudely interrupted by a clatter as Conni's fingers let slip her mug, and her head fell to the table, insensate. Moran looked at her critically for a long while, reached carefully to remove her hidden purse—at least that's what she believed it to be—and rose in one fluid motion to head for the door.

"What about her?" a voice growled.

Moran turned and a mark flew out of his hand directly into the innkeeper's. "She'll need a place for the night."

The innkeeper nodded and smiled, the gaps in his teeth showing only slightly darker than the rest of his teeth. "She'll have one."

As he left, Moran found himself wondering less where Conni would be sleeping than how far he would be from wherever that was when she woke.

As he made his way out of Keogh, following the river southward, he made a decision and turned sharply right, to the west hills.

Three days later he began to regret his decision. The weather was cold in the foothills, and he could see only mountains ahead of him. His food ran out that night.

The next morning, Moran wished he hadn't always left the chores of hunting and trapping to Tenim and Halla. He wasn't a bad trapper—he had taught Tenim when he was little, and Tenim had passed his knowledge on to Halla—but his skills were long-unused.

He caught nothing in a nearby stream, and although he'd been smart enough to remove his pack and boots and roll up his trousers, a misjudged step had sent him into the cold, snow-fed stream so now he had warm feet and a cold backside. He pressed on, knowing that his exertions would soon warm him back up and his body heat would dry his clothes.

Snow started falling before nightfall. Moran found a sheltered cave with difficulty and huddled into it.

Moran woke, shivering. It was still dark. He thrust his head out of the cave opening and looked up into the night sky. It was clear of clouds. The stars shown brightly above him. It was late; both of Pern's moons had set. Moran paused, listening intently for whatever it was that had disturbed him.

There! Something moved overhead in the night. He cocked his head sideways, trying to track it. A meteor? A pair of meteors? The lights almost looked like dragon eyes, but Moran had never heard of dragons flying at this hour. A fire-lizard? No, they were even less willing to fly at night. The brilliant lights grew larger, were coming toward him, and then, just as suddenly, were gone, whizzing over the mountain.

Moran skidded back into the cave and hastily folded his sleep roll and donned his gear. As soon as he could, he set off after the creature, hopeful of finding food or game.

The air was freezing and his breath came in wisps, but he ignored it as he scampered up the hillside. He quickly lost sight of the flying eyes, but he continued climbing, his breath coming in increasingly faster gasps, his lungs protesting the effort, his tired legs threatening to cramp with each upward step.

Finally, just as he felt he could breathe no more or take another step, Moran reached the summit of the hill. He paused, his breath coming in white clouds and searing his lungs, his legs trembling with exertion.

He scanned the new vistas before him. His breath returned to normal and his legs stopped trembling before he finally spotted it: some imperfection in the distance, something that didn't look natural.

It was a camp, he was sure of it. Perhaps a camp for traders or some Shunned. He doubted that it was a regular hold or temporary quarters—it was too high in the cold mountain air for that. No, whoever was there hoped not to be found. But the wisp of smoke, just barely visible in the dark of night, gave the camp away. For better or worse Moran started toward the camp; he knew he did not have enough supplies to return to Keogh.

He stepped out briskly, eager for his journey's end and a warm fire, too briskly, his eyes on his goal and not on his footing. Whether it was the snow or the rocks underneath didn't matter; the slip caused his left calf to spasm into a tight, painful knot, and then he was sliding down the hillside on his right side. His painful slide was finally halted when his head struck a large rock and he remembered nothing more.

Pellar was out inspecting his traps when he spotted the tracks. He checked the back trail—the tracks were headed nearly on a straight line for the wherhandlers' camp. Pellar quickly removed his traps and started obliterating the trail, replacing it with one that led northward, away from the camp.

Pellar paused, sent a thought to Chitter and smiled when the little fire-lizard appeared directly above him from *between*. The fire-lizard had brought a pocket of warm, campfire air with him, and that air mixed with the cold air to produce a fine mist that dissipated almost before Pellar noticed it.

Pellar wrote a quick note, tied it to Chitter's harness, and carefully constructed a mental image of Aleesa for the fire-lizard. Chitter chirped once—happy at the thought of returning to the warm fire—and disappeared *between*.

Pellar was about to start once more on his work when a nearby noise startled him. He looked around quickly and saw the trail of a rock rolling not far from him. Another rock landed nearby. It came from behind him. Pellar twirled around—and spied a small figure in the distance behind him. The figure was vaguely familiar. It raised a hand to its mouth in a shushing gesture, then held up both hands in a gesture of peace and started walking toward Pellar.

The figure stopped when it was close enough for Pellar to recognize it as a girl.

"I've seen you before, haven't I?" the girl asked, still keeping her hands out. Pellar recognized her. She was Halla, the trapper who had been caught in one of his traps. The girl who had kept his existence a secret.

Pellar nodded in answer to her question.

She looked around and gestured to his handiwork, saying, "That's good work you've done, disguising the trail.

"That's Moran's trail," she continued. She looked at Pellar. "Have you seen him?"

Pellar shook his head.

Halla's eyes narrowed as she considered his answer. Finally, she declared, "You're changing his trail because of the direction he's taking."

Pellar gave the girl a long, frank look before, with a sigh, he nodded. She was too smart to fool, and he decided that trying to would only raise her suspicions further.

"That's a good idea," Halla said, moving cautiously closer. "I think Tenim's after him. Moran's got a purse full of marks, and Tenim wants it.

"What's your name?" she asked as she drew closer.

Pellar shook his head and waved in front of his mouth

to show that he couldn't talk. Cautiously he pulled out his slate and wrote on it.

Halla noted his caution and cocked her head at him quizzically. "Do you trust me?"

Pellar gave her an appraising look. She was small, taller than when he'd met her last, but still not much more than skin and bones. He couldn't imagine that she'd be all that tough if she chose to fight him. And she hadn't betrayed him back at the camp. He nodded, yes, he trusted her.

He beckoned for her to come closer, lifting the strap of the slate over his head and placing it on the boulder, then moving warily away from her.

Halla raised an eyebrow in surprise. After a moment she shrugged, approached the boulder, and lifted the slate.

"Pellar," she read aloud. She looked up from the slate to meet his eyes. "Is that your name?"

Pellar nodded.

Suddenly Chitter burst into the air. Halla ducked and stepped back, her eyes wide with fear until she identified the fire-lizard, then she cautiously stood back up, her eyes shining with excitement.

Chitter chirped when he found Pellar and quickly flew to him. The fire-lizard had a message. With one eye on Halla, Pellar carefully removed the message and read it: Come quick, need healer.

"I thought it was Grief," Halla admitted as she stood up straight once more. Pellar looked questioningly at her. "Tenim has a falcon that spies for him."

Pellar pursed his lips tight. If Tenim could use his bird to track, then perhaps the camp was already in danger.

"If there's anything at your camp of value, Tenim will want that, too," Halla told him.

Pellar nodded in agreement; he remembered too well his fight with the larger lad. He gave Halla one more frank appraisal and then passed the message over for her to read.

Halla read it quickly and glanced back up at him. "Do you want me to follow you and hide our tracks?"

Pellar nodded and grinned, glad that this little girl was so quick in her thinking.

Halla frowned. "If Tenim follows the false trail, it'll end here and he'll backtrack. He'll probably find our trail no matter what we do."

Pellar wiped his slate and quickly wrote, "Hurry, hope for snow."

"That might work," Halla agreed. While Pellar wrote a note and sent Chitter back, Halla worked on extending their false trail to a realistic dead end, a nearby stream that was not completely frozen over. She ended the trail opposite some wind-exposed rocks in the hope that Tenim might decide that Moran had climbed out the other side of the stream by the rocks.

When she turned back she was surprised to see Pellar watching her with great interest. He smiled oddly at her and waved a beckoning hand: "Let's go."

Watch-wher, watch-wher in the night,
Keep us safe from fear or fright.
Watch-wher, watch-wher guard our Hold,
Keep us from those cruel or bold.

Chapter Seven

MORAN WOKE UP warm and disoriented. He was wrapped in blankets and he could smell a coal fire burning nearby. He could also smell the cold winter air billowing in from some distant entrance.

"He's awake," a young girl's voice declared. Halla.

"Wh-where's Tenim?" Moran asked, surprised at the weakness of his voice.

"Not far," a deeper voice replied. A face came into Moran's view. The face was hard-edged and looked bitterly upon him. "You've done us no favors, Harper."

Oddly, the last words weren't directed at Moran but at someone else. Moran swiveled his head around and regretted it as pain lanced through his joints. He guessed that he must have fallen hard. His head throbbed.

An amazingly painful sound clawed at his ears, the sound of chalk on slate. Moran winced more as he found the origin of the sound—was that Pellar?

"Your leg is broken and you have a nasty knock on your head," an old woman told him. "Pellar here set your leg and nursed you."

A face swam into view. The woman was old, much older than Moran.

"Why'd you come here?" she asked, eyeing him without favor.

Moran shook his head and again regretted the motion. "I was cold and saw the fire."

"Put out the fire, Jaythen," the woman ordered. The hard-faced man moved to obey. The woman turned to Pellar. "What are we going to do now?"

Pellar scrawled an answer on his slate. The woman read it and frowned thoughtfully. She looked back down at Moran.

"Do you know who I am?"

"No," Moran replied feebly, having learned not to shake his head.

"I'm Aleesa and you've stumbled on our hold."

Aleesa. The one who was selling watch-wher eggs. Moran tried to sit up. He could only imagine what Tenim would do if he found them.

A hand forced him back down.

"Pellar says to lie still," Halla told him. Another scraping noise and Halla turned to peer at Pellar's slate. "He says he's got a plan, but you'll have to agree to it."

"A plan?" Moran repeated. He licked his lips and continued, "Tenim wants a watch-wher egg—"

"They're all gone!" Aleesa declared with a derisive snort.

"But he doesn't know that," Halla said, rereading Pellar's plan. She looked up at the older boy and warned him, "If he catches you—"

Moran realized he was too sick to move. If Tenim arrived, he'd want his marks, if not more. He decided it was a good idea that Pellar not be dissuaded from his plan, so he cleared his throat and asked, "What do you want me to do?"

It all depended upon Chitter. Chitter and the falcon, Grief. Tenim's falcon had to spot Chitter, and Chitter had to lead Tenim to Pellar's trail. But not too soon, not until Halla had managed to disguise Pellar's original track and blend his trail in with Moran's.

Pellar set out as soon as he could finish constructing his bait. The pack was heavy and its straps tore into his shoulders as he trudged along in the cold winter countryside, heading north and west in a large loop around Keogh.

If Tenim found him anytime in the next three days, it was likely that the older lad would corner him before he could complete his plan. At least, Pellar thought ruefully, Tenim couldn't make him talk.

Pellar looked down at Moran's huge shoes as he trudged along in them and regretted that part of the plan, too. His feet were already raw and chafed and he'd only traveled for a day. But it was vital that Tenim think he was following Moran.

Pellar hoped that Halla would be all right. In some ways she reminded him of Cristov, both needing a better example in their lives.

Pellar allowed himself a fond smile as he thought of the little girl waving after him as they parted. She had insisted on leading the youngest of the wherhold's children back to the safety of Keogh despite both Moran's and Pellar's protests.

"I'll be fine," she assured them. "And with the fires out, they'll perish here."

She'd been right about that, Pellar realized, thinking of the small cold children all bundled up in the freezing caves of the wherhold. Moran had admitted reluctantly that Halla had a way with children, even those slightly older than herself, and that it would be best to get them out of the way of the harsh winter or any trouble that might come.

That part of Pellar's plan—leaving Moran behind as harper—had worked out better than he'd imagined.

While neither Aleesa nor Jaythen were likely to ever look upon the older harper without distrust, it was obvious that they were willing to take advantage of his presence. After all, there were some things that were best explained without chalk and slate.

Pellar stumbled on an icy patch and caught himself, berating himself for his inattention. The snowy night wind howled around him and he started forward again, hoping to spot the lights of Keogh in the distance but not really expecting to see anything until late the next day at the earliest. He paused for a moment to glance at the mountains around him before setting on again, making a slight correction in his direction. He didn't need to get turned around in the middle of the night.

The next evening, just after he spotted Keogh to the south and west of him, Pellar allowed himself a broad grin.

It was time to start the next phase of his plan. Gratefully he built a small fire and laid some stones around it for heat. Satisfied that the fire was going well, Pellar unlimbered his pack; he rooted around in the special pocket he'd had added, pulled out his bait, and made sure that a little of the protecting sand scattered on to the ground around him before he placed the bait to warm by the stones.

Tenim swore long and slow to himself as he lost Moran's tracks for the third time in the past several days. It was obvious to him that the harper knew he was on his trail. Tenim's pack had grown lighter faster than he'd expected and his stomach was now emptier than his purse. He snorted to himself as he imagined Moran getting gaunter from all the exercise—the harper rarely put on such a hefty pace.

But if Moran was carrying so many marks, why didn't he simply buy his passage? The answer came to

Tenim as quickly as the question—because neither he nor Moran were willing to risk that there wasn't someone else eager to take their hard-won marks. Just as Moran had decided he'd no further need of that useless Conni. Tenim snorted as he remembered her ranting and raving when he caught up with her at the tavern.

When he picked up the harper's trail again, he found signs that Moran had stopped at last. A fire—a day old. Some rocks gathered around. Something placed near the fire. What? Tenim wondered and peered closer. He sifted among the ashes. Sand? Why would the harper be carrying sand? And keeping it warm?

With a curse, Tenim sprang up and broke into a steady trot. Moran had found a fire-lizard egg or, better, a watch-wher egg.

One day. If he could catch up with Moran before Crom Hold, he'd have more than a fortune. He'd have a winter's worth of coal, or the same amount of marks.

Pellar was glad to see the great walls of Crom Hold rising up in the morning sun as he approached. So far his plan had worked—Chitter had spotted Tenim a full day behind. Now all he had to do was get to Camp Natalon and Master Zist. Faced with a camp full of miners and a harper with a complete set of drums at his command, Tenim would have to give up the chase.

He paid for some provisions and sped through the far side of Crom Hold, catching up with a trader caravan that was heading near Camp Natalon. He was surprised that the traders would risk the snowy passes in the dead of winter.

"It's good to see you again," Tarri said cheerfully.

"And you," Pellar wrote. "Although, I'm surprised you're venturing up to the camp at this time of year."

"Cromcoal's worth a lot," said Tarri, the young trader who'd agreed to his passage. "Master Zist worked out a good deal and we've got a well-paved road—unless some of it's washed out."

She eyed his pack warily but said nothing as Pellar climbed aboard.

"You ride up front," she said, crawling through the curtains to the back of her wagon. She threw him a thick blanket. "Use this against the cold."

Pellar nodded in thanks. Tarri kept an eye on him until she was certain that he had the workbeasts well in hand and then she went back through the curtains. A while later she emerged.

"It's only warm," she said, handing him a mug of *klah*. "We keep heated rocks in a pail so's we don't freeze entirely."

Pellar took the mug gratefully and drained it quickly. The residual warmth of the mug itself he used to heat his cold fingers before regretfully passing it back to Tarri.

The trader kept her eyes on him as they drove. To Pellar's relief, she took the reins in some of the more difficult passes.

When not driving the wagon, Pellar dozed off, glad enough of the thick blanket Tarri had loaned him.

Shortly after dusk the snow picked up and was soon falling so thickly that they couldn't see the road.

"We'll stop," Tarri told him, pointing to the large drays behind. "You and I are first watch."

Pellar nodded and got down from the wagon, walking back to the end of the short column of workdrays. Tarri's was the only sleeping wagon—everyone slept in shifts, and there were only three work drays in the caravan.

"Less to lose, better prices," Tarri had explained when Pellar had first joined up.

In two hours Pellar was relieved and trudged back to

his place at the front of Tarri's wagon. He was freezing cold.

Tarri's head poked out from the curtains.

"Come on inside—it's too cold and we've another watch before we move out," she told him.

Gratefully, Pellar crawled inside. He was immediately warmer. With a few gestures he asked permission to spread his sleeping roll; at Tarri's nod, he removed his boots and socks and crawled in.

Tarri gave him an amazed look and snorted, "You'll freeze if you try to sleep like that. You need to get out of those clothes."

Pellar nodded and smiled back, carefully removing his clothes while modestly hidden in his sleeping roll. He pulled them out and laid them beside him.

Tarri laughed. "I'm not as deft as you, so I'd appreciate it if you looked the other way."

Pellar nodded and rolled over.

Moments later, Tarri crawled under her pile of blankets and called out, "You can turn over now."

She was answered by Pellar's soft snores.

Tenim spread his marks liberally to get information. Yes, there had been a suspicious lad with a large pack. No, no signs of a harper. The lad couldn't talk, that was odd, managed to get a ride with the traders heading up to Camp Natalon. Daft to head up the mountains in midwinter, no matter what the price of coal, even with the improvements that had been put in. Tenim had bought another round or two of drinks before disappearing into the night.

Egg or no, purse or no, this "lad" owed him. He'd taken Tenim in, convinced him for three days that he'd been following Moran and a sack of marks or, better, a watch-wher's egg. Now Tenim was sure that he wasn't following Moran, and he had his doubts about the egg, too.

So this "lad" had decided to play Tenim for a fool. Moran would have to know, would have been in on it, Tenim was certain. What was the harper to the lad that he'd go out of his way to protect him? Why would the lad risk his life for a broken-down man who claimed he was a harper but spent most of his time stealing?

Or was the lad protecting something else? Had Moran stumbled on something the lad felt he had to protect? Something to do with watch-whers?

Tenim had smiled coldly to himself as he strode out of Crom and up the mountain path to Camp Natalon.

He'd find out soon enough; he'd been close behind the traders all day and he knew they'd stopped for the night. The lad might not talk, but when Tenim was done with him, he'd wish he could—and he'd still tell Tenim all he wanted to know. And, after that, well, no one who made a fool of Tenim lived to tell it.

Dawn was coming. He stopped and removed his pack. It was heavy and cumbersome, but the extra weight was worth it. His sources had said the lad had a fire-lizard.

Tenim unlaced the special compartment, reached in with a well-gloved hand, and restrained the falcon resting inside. With the other hand he finished opening the compartment, exposing it to the cold morning air.

"Come on, my pet, I've got a job for you," he crooned as he settled Grief onto his hand.

Pellar woke the instant the hand touched his shoulder. He twisted his head quickly and looked up to see Tarri above him.

"Our watch," she said. "You get dressed and search for kindling. I'll keep watch here and ready some *klah*."

Pellar nodded and Tarri left the wagon. He dressed

quickly, rolled up his bedroll and left the wagon, waving to Tarri.

The caravan had stopped at a bend in the road, crouching close to the mountainside. On the other side of the road the mountain fell away in a cliff. Pellar looked over and saw a stand of trees and a stream in the distance below. He shrugged to himself and started carefully down the cliffside to the only source of kindling.

Chitter joined him as he reached the plateau, chiding Pellar against the cold morning air. Pellar nodded and waved in companionable agreement—yes, it was cold and only fools would climb down cliffsides in search of kindling. He unshouldered his pack and put it down by a tree, looking around the clearing. Why, he wondered to himself, would Chitter have stirred from his warm spot in the wagon?

The thought made him go suddenly cold and still, his eyes moving over the terrain in front of him. Had something disturbed the fire-lizard?

There! Pellar spotted a movement in the trees high above him, moving very fast. It was a bird, diving. He formed a warning in his mind for Chitter and was just about to send it when the fire-lizard dove in front of him, screeching a warning of his own.

Chitter was too late. A hard fist landed behind Pellar's ear and he stumbled in pain. His last sight was of Chitter and claws and a beak—and then the air was filled with shrieking and green ichor. And then he was falling into the stream, cold water engulfing him.

Wail at night, cry by day,
Never right, always fey.
Make the cairns with rocks piled high,
To mark the spot where loved ones lie.

Chapter Eight

"WHEN HE DIDN'T show up, we sent out a search party, and we found this," Tarri said, holding up the mangled body of a fire-lizard for Master Zist's inspection.

"And this." A pack, torn and shredded. There was some sand and shards still inside it.

"I need you to take me there," Zist said.

"It's half a day away on foot," Tarri protested.

"Please," Zist begged, "I've got to see."

"We can take my wagon," Tarri said. "That will save us some time."

The day was cold and clear—the clouds that had brought snow the night before had dissipated. Tarri easily followed the trail the drays had left on their way up to Camp Natalon. When she reached the bend, she pulled the wagon to a halt.

"Right over there," she said, pointing across Zist to the cliff on their right. "Down the ravine."

Tarri showed Zist the way down. The site where they'd found the fire-lizard and Pellar's pack had been trampled down by the trader's boots as they searched.

"We think he fell in the water here," Tarri said, pointing to a depression on the bank of the fast-moving stream. "There's a fall just down there," she added sadly.

Zist grunted his acknowledgment, shading his eyes against the sun to peer farther into the distance. He sighed and turned back to the trampled site, particularly examining the ground where the snow was stained green by Chitter's ichor.

Zist remembered the brown fire-lizard's battered body. Some sharp object had cut through Chitter's neck just where it joined the shoulders. There were claw marks on his sides—some large bird, or a very small wherry. Zist guessed it was a bird, probably a falcon, because he'd never heard of a fire-lizard being so surprised by a wherry that it couldn't get *between* to safety.

There was a large patch of sand not far away and some shards. What had Pellar been carrying in his pack? And why had someone murdered him for it? Had the attack by the bird been an unhappy accident or part of a plan? Why had Pellar been on his way to Camp Natalon?

"We may never know," the harper said softly to himself.

"Pardon?"

Zist shook himself and rose from beside the ichor-stained snow, saying, "I'm sorry, I was talking to myself." He pointed up to the wagon. "I'm ready to go now."

But it seemed to Tarri as she watched the harper climb feebly up the ravine he had so vigorously descended only moments before that Master Zist was not at all ready to go—that, in fact, he left a large part of himself behind in that ravine.

They rode back toward Camp Natalon in silence and the setting of the sun.

*   *   *

After tens of Turns in his cave near the Harper Hall, Mikal had learned to cipher the drum codes. He always perked up when a message came in from Zist, wondering about Pellar and his fire-lizard.

But the message wasn't good. "Chitter dead?" Mikal whispered to himself as he deciphered the message. He closed his eyes from the pain of the ancient loss of his own dragon, now relived in the loss of the fire-lizard he had been afraid to meet.

The message continued and Mikal's face drained of all color. "Pellar?"

Wordlessly, sightlessly, he reached around for a flask of wine and remorselessly, hopelessly tried once again to blot his pain by getting drunk.

Tenim was in a foul mood as he entered the kitchen of Tarik's cothold. He had gone up to the mine, taking the long route around to the coal dump and then out of sight beyond the crest of the hill to come back around to the mine, only to discover from the miners' chatter that Tarik's shift had been relieved by Natalon. If he hadn't been on his guard he might have been caught.

The thrill of Grief's deadly strike on the fire-lizard—Tenim had never dreamed the attack would be so successful—had completely drained from him in the ensuing events: first, the boy's unexpected fall into the river and, second, the infuriating discovery that the boy's pack held only a fake egg made of clay. Tenim had been led on a wild wherry chase for no profit.

"What are you doing here?" Tarik asked as Tenim let himself in. The miner was sprawled in a chair, a bottle of wine on the table in front of him and a mug in his hand.

"I might ask you the same," Tenim said. "Let's just say that I'm here to see how we are doing on our investments.

"Only," he went on, gesturing toward the mine, "I discover that you've been relieved." He gave Tarik a sour look. "Something about skimping on the wood joists, I hear."

Tarik flushed angrily. "Natalon's a fool. He'd have us use three times as much wood as we need."

"So you decided to profit on your own initiative?" Tenim asked, glowering down at the miner. "And, instead, we stand to lose everything."

Tarik took an angry breath, caught the murderous look in Tenim's eyes, and let it out with a deep sigh.

"I thought you weren't going to be back until spring," Tarik said.

"My plans changed," Tenim replied, dragging up a chair opposite Tarik. The miner gestured to the bottle on the table, but Tenim shook his head irritably. "One of us needs to keep his head clear enough to think."

"Why bother?" Tarik said. "Natalon's as good as sacked me. I'll never find work after this." He shook his head dejectedly. "His own uncle, and he'd throw me out."

"You're no use to me if you're thrown out," Tenim said, eyeing Tarik thoughtfully. The older man was too much in his cups to recognize his peril.

"I should be the master here," Tarik grumbled, "not him. I've Turns more experience in the mine, helped train him, too."

Tenim's murderous look altered subtly as he listened to Tarik.

"Where's Natalon now?"

Tarik quirked an eyebrow at him, saying querulously, "In the mine, my shaft, shoring up the joists, of course."

Tenim rose from his seat in one fluid motion, like a bird rising to swoop on its prey.

"Stay here," he ordered Tarik. "Don't let anyone in the mine."

Tarik looked up at him in confusion. "I'm not in charge."

"Yet," Tenim replied curtly.

"Master Zist? Master Zist?" Cristov called at the door to the harper's cothold.

The mine had collapsed and Tarik had forbidden anyone to enter it, declaring it too dangerous. He'd even hit Kindan when the lad had insisted on going in with his watch-wher.

"That dumb animal's no use now," Tarik had sworn angrily.

Someone had to take charge, someone had to do something. Cristov had run down to Zist's, hoping the harper could restore order.

"Master Zist?" he called again, inching inside the door. His resolve grew and he walked all through the cottage, calling Zist's name.

In the kitchen, on the table, he spied the grisly remains of a brown fire-lizard. The memory of stroking that fire-lizard's cheek woke an anger in Cristov that he had never before felt. He turned on his heel and strode out of the cottage.

He was going to get his axe.

BOOK TWO

Dragon's Fire

Miners, dig in streets so black,
Find the coal, bring it back.
When cold winter comes to stay,
Your warm coal keeps chills away.

Chapter One

TOLDUR GENTLY LAID the most injured of the rescued miners down on the floor of the lift. "Let's go up, Cristov."

Cristov grabbed one of the lift's ropes while Toldur grabbed the other, and together they winched themselves and the lift up from the bottom of the mine.

At the top, helping hands reached out to grab the injured miner from them and haul him out of the mine. Toldur stepped out behind him only to pause as he noticed Cristov holding back.

"Are you all right?" Toldur asked, peering intently at the young miner.

"Yes."

"You should be proud of yourself," Toldur said, clapping one of his huge hands on Cristov's back. "Though you've just turned twelve, today you did a man's job—and made a man's decision."

They reached the mine entrance and found themselves lost in a throng of torches and milling voices. In the distance, Cristov could make out a number of shining eyes peering down from the hillside—dragons.

Alarmed, he picked out several dragonriders in the

crowds, wondering if he'd have to defend his actions tonight.

"Is that the last of them, Toldur?" asked Margit, the camp's healer. She squinted when she noticed Cristov. "I didn't think *he'd* be here."

"He helped," Toldur explained, patting Cristov on the back once more. "Without him we wouldn't have been in time."

Margit started to say something but thought better of it, shaking her head and turning away.

Around him, the noises and the cheering of the rescued and rescuers faded in Cristov's ears as he imagined what Margit wanted to say. He felt numb, lost.

And then, across the crowd, his gaze locked with his father's.

Instead of smiling at him or giving him any sign of recognition, Tarik turned his head sharply away from his son, as though disowning him.

Cristov felt his face burn in shame, even though he knew it wasn't right, that *he* was the one who should be ashamed of his father.

As he watched, Masterminer Britell and two miners he didn't recognize approached his father.

"Tarik, I think you should come with us," Britell said. "There will be an investigation."

"I didn't do anything," Tarik growled angrily.

"Precisely."

Cristov was wondering if he should follow when a hand on his shoulder stopped him.

"You need to drink some of this," Toldur said, pressing a warm mug into his hands. "And then you'll need to get some rest."

"But my father—"

"He'll have to accept the consequences of his actions," Toldur said, his voice flat.

* * *

Three days later, after Masterminer Britell, his assistant, Master Jannik, and Harper Zist had conducted an extensive investigation, the whole camp was summoned to the great room in Natalon's house.

Cristov was familiar with the room; he had taken classes from Harper Zist there. The room was arranged as it usually was when Harper Zist was teaching, with one small table placed at one end and the remaining tables arranged in two long rows perpendicular to it. Cristov and his mother, Dara, sat near the end of their table, closest to the small table where Zist, Britell, and Jannik sat.

When everyone was seated, Masterminer Britell rose. "We have completed our investigation," he told the room. "And I have communicated my findings to Lord Holder Fenner."

A ripple of surprise spread through the room as people wondered why the Masterminer had needed to communicate with Crom's Lord Holder.

Britell gestured to a group of men standing in the doorway and silence fell as Tarik marched into the room, flanked by two guards.

"Miner Tarik," Britell said to him. "I have heard evidence that you did purposely steal the wood intended to shore up your mineshaft and that you did purposely mine the pillars of your shaft. Will you explain what you did with the wood and the coal?"

"Who said I did any such thing?" Tarik demanded, seeking out Natalon among the crowd and glaring at him. "It's all lies—"

"Among others, miners Panit and Kerdal?" Master Zist's voice cut across Tarik's outburst.

A vein bulged in Tarik's forehead as he tried to jump out of the grasp of his guards, lunging toward Panit and Kerdal.

"You're dead!" he shouted to them, struggling against his guards. "Dead!"

"Silence," Zist said, his voice not loud but command-ing.

Tarik fell silent, still glowering at Panit and Kerdal.

"Would you answer our question?" Britell said.

Tarik looked nervously around the room. He opened his mouth to speak but decided against it, shaking his head.

"Very well," Britell said. "Miner Tarik, it is our con-clusion that your actions did severely endanger the safety of the mine and directly caused the death of two miners. Further, it is our conclusion that you took your actions repeatedly, in full knowledge of the dangers you were creating and against the directions of Camp Nat-alon's leader. Your actions were taken, we believe, for your own gain."

Beside him, Cristov could see his mother shaking as silent tears wracked her body.

"Beyond that, when the mine did collapse as a result of your negligence, you purposely refused to allow any rescue attempts to the extent that you struck a child un-conscious to prevent him from attempting a rescue," Britell continued, his voice harsh with repressed rage. "There is also some question as to whether your orders to pump air into the mine after the shaft's collapse were not an attempt on your part to ensure that there would be no survivors."

"That's not so," Tarik protested feebly. He raised his head to look Masterminer Britell in the eyes. "I didn't know, I swear!"

Britell glanced down to Masters Zist and Jannik. Master Zist made a dismissive gesture with his hand. Britell shrugged in response and nodded to Zist. With a slight sigh, Master Zist rose and faced Tarik.

"Are you prepared to hear our judgment?" Master Zist asked him.

"What about the Lord Holder?" Tarik protested. "Doesn't he get a say?"

"He does," Master Zist agreed. "And he has." He lifted a small roll of parchment from the table. "I ask again, are you prepared for our judgment?"

Tarik shuffled on his feet as he nodded.

"Your actions indicate a disregard for the lives of others," Zist said. "As such, it is our opinion that you should be released from the company of men."

"Shunned?" Tarik cried in disbelief.

Cristov's eyes went wide. Beside him, Dara let out a moan.

"Shunned and Nameless," Masterminer Britell said.

Nameless? Cristov thought in despair. His father's name would be taken away from him, never to be spoken again. Beside him, Dara collapsed.

"Further, for the rest of your days you will work at the pleasure of Lord Holder Fenner," Britell continued.

As Cristov tried desperately to rouse his mother, a voice spoke softly in his ear, "Let's get her out of here."

It was Toldur. Dalor and Zenor stood beside him, faces grave and concerned.

"It's all right," Cristov protested as Toldur lifted Dara's limp body over his shoulder.

"We miners take care of our own," Dalor asserted, patting Cristov on the shoulder.

But as they left the crowded room with all eyes upon them, Cristov wondered how true that would hold for him and his mother in the Turns to come.

Gather, gather, gather!
Frolic, play, and laughter!
Juicy bubbly pies to eat —
Gather day's the best all week.

Chapter Two

CRISTOV FELT AWKWARD wending his way through the Gather crowd at Crom Hold. There were more people at the Gather than in all of Camp Natalon. It was overwhelming. He was sure that they were all looking at him.

"They're not looking at you," Toldur said from behind him, guessing Cristov's thoughts from the lad's hunched shoulders, the way he kept his elbows close to his sides, and his bowed head. "At least, they're looking at you no more than they're looking at everyone else."

Cristov paused long enough to give Toldur a sour look and then turned his attention back to the crowd.

"There's a good crowd this time," Toldur judged. "I'm surprised."

"Why?"

"Because Telgar Weyr's won the Games for the past four Turns."

"And they'll win again," Cristov replied loyally.

"Over there," Toldur said, pointing over Cristov's shoulder toward a raised platform. "The Masterminer will be over there, with Lord Holder Fenner."

Cristov changed his course. Again he wondered why

the Masterminer had sent for him. Surely if he'd done something wrong, Toldur—or even his Uncle Natalon— would have told him.

He looks a lot like his father, Moran thought to himself as he watched the gangling youth heading through the crowd toward the Lord Holder's stand. Same bowed head, same surly look. Yes, he might do, Moran decided. He might do indeed, if it worked out that way.

Imperiously, Moran raised his arm and beckoned. "There's your target."

"He was Jamal's friend," Halla objected when she caught sight of her prey. "I remember him. About three Turns back, just when Jamal broke his leg."

"He was, and his father helped us, too," Moran agreed. "So there's no reason he shouldn't be your friend, too."

"But—"

Moran silenced her with a finger to his lips. "Go, if you want to eat tonight," he told her. When she still looked rebellious, Moran added, "If you want the young ones to eat tonight."

Halla glared at him, her jaw set, weighing the alternatives. There were none, and Moran knew it. Moran controlled the food, the wealth, and all the secrets. She had even been relieved when he'd arrived at Keogh to bring the wherhold children back to Aleesa—she'd found it harder than she would have believed to beg enough food to keep them fed. It was natural, afterward, that Halla and Moran continued on to Crom Hold, just as it was natural that Moran had collected a new group of children, orphaned or Shunned.

Halla could do what he said or suffer the consequences. When Jamal had been alive, Halla had held hopes that they might escape from Moran somehow.

But the fever that had seeped in through his broken leg had sapped him first of strength and then of life.

She'd been all of eight when he'd died. With Jamal dead, there'd been no one but Moran—she doubted he was a real harper—to look after her. And now, when she was nearing twelve Turns, there were other young ones to look after—and perhaps save.

Halla knew that Moran had followed the same reasoning, had tied her to him out of her pity for the young ones just as he had tied her brother Jamal to him out of Jamal's worry for her. And, even so, Halla couldn't imagine leaving the young ones to deal with Moran alone. She, more than any, knew what that was like—she'd experienced it after Jamal's death; the harper off at all hours of the evening, her never knowing if the harper would return, and, if he did, whether he would come with enough food for them or none at all and him drunk instead on the marks that he'd begged for their food.

"Just follow him," Moran told her. "Listen to what's said and report back to me."

Halla nodded and headed off after her quarry. When she looked back, Moran had disappeared into the crowd. Probably looking for some wine, Halla thought, wondering if she'd have to deal once again with the harper's drunkenness later that night. She felt herself chill at the thought.

Cristov found it easier to look at the youngsters scampering about the Gather than the older folk. He stopped and twirled around to follow the antics of a small pair of boys as they raced through the crowd, chattering incessantly. His eye fell on one girl, maybe one or two Turns younger than himself. She looked forlorn and hungry.

"Toldur, can I borrow a half-mark?"

"I'm sure we'll be asked to eat with the Masterminer," Toldur began, then paused as he followed the lad's look. "Oh, certainly. You've more than that coming to you."

The tall miner fished in his pocket and handed the token, branded with the Minercraft mark, over to Cristov.

"Thanks!" Cristov called back as he walked over to the girl.

"You look like you could use some bubbly pies," he said to her. The girl froze for a moment, giving him a frightened look.

"I'm going to be with the Lord Holder," Cristov continued, "and I'm not sure if they'll serve bubbly pies." He had the girl's attention now, he could tell. "You remind me of a friend I knew here many Turns back; his name was Jamal. Would you do me a big favor?"

The girl's eyes widened.

"Please?"

The girl nodded. Cristov smiled and pressed the half-mark into her palm. "Would you go and see if the bubbly pies are still good? Get as many as this will buy and eat them all for me? Can you do that?"

"Yes," the girl said woodenly.

"Thank you," Cristov said. "That way at least I'll know that one of us will get bubbly pies." He smiled at her. "I'm Cristov, of Camp Natalon."

"Halla," the girl said and then, as if she'd reached the limit of her words, she darted off into the crowd. Cristov tried to follow her progress, but she was soon lost from sight. He turned back to Toldur.

"Sorry," he told the older miner, for it was Toldur's mark he'd given away.

Toldur clapped him on the back. "There is nothing to

be sorry about," he exclaimed. "You did a good thing there."

"Masterminer, how are you?" Toldur called out as he and Cristov climbed up the stands, all eyes upon them. Cristov cringed, wishing he could stay behind. Everyone was looking at him.

"Toldur!" Masterminer Britell exclaimed as he caught sight of the miner. He gave a cry of surprise when he spotted Cristov. "Is that Cristov?"

"It is indeed," Toldur agreed, gesturing for Cristov to stand in front of him.

"When did you get so tall?" the Masterminer asked in astonishment. "And where did you get all those bulging muscles?"

"Where else but the mines?" Toldur answered for him. Cristov failed to keep the flush off his face. He didn't think he was all that tall, and he still felt that he was as "scrawny" as when his father last griped about it.

"Lord Fenner, this is the one I was telling you about," the Masterminer said, grabbing Cristov by the arm and turning him to Crom's Lord Holder.

Cristov didn't know if he was more shocked by his introduction to the Lord Holder, or at the way the Masterminer grabbed him—it was just like his father!

Lord Holder Fenner, Cristov was surprised to note, was not all that much taller than himself and did not look very imposing. In fact, Crom's Lord Holder looked less imposing than the Masterminer, with a friendly face and kind eyes.

"A pleasure to meet you, Cristov," the Lord Holder said, holding out his hand. Cristov shook it awkwardly, feeling like a little boy. His unease increased with the Lord Holder's next words: "You've the look of your sire."

An awkward silence fell upon them until Toldur coughed and said, "I think he takes more from his mother's side of the family, myself."

"Do you?" Fenner asked, peering at Cristov. "Hm, I suppose you're right at that." To Cristov he said, "And how is your mother, boy?"

Cristov gave Toldur a bleak look, but the Masterminer answered for him. "I'm afraid Dara had an accident. She'd not been well since . . ."

The Lord Holder looked nearly as embarrassed as Cristov felt. "I'm very sorry to hear that," he said after a moment. "She was always such a kind, vivacious lady. She will be sorely missed."

"Indeed," Britell agreed.

"She died of shame," Cristov said, startling the older men around him. He remembered his mother's eyes that day, when Tarik was Shunned. He had seen the life go out of them slowly in the days before the trial, as her hopes dwindled.

When the sentence was read, she had been the first to turn away from Tarik, even before Cristov had turned his back on his father. He had seen her eyes and the tears spilling from them, and he had seen her heart harden and wither, and he knew, even before Tarik was sentenced to the firestone mines, that if the sentence had Shunned Tarik, it had killed Dara.

"I wish she hadn't," Britell replied gravely.

"Why don't you stay up here and watch the Games with us?" Lord Holder Fenner offered awkwardly.

"That's a marvelous idea," Britell agreed.

"Thank you, we'll be delighted," Toldur said for both of them. "It's not every day one is invited to sit in the Lord Holder's stands, is it, Cristov?"

"Thank you, my lord," Cristov said with a slight bow to the Lord Holder, remembering his manners.

"If you look over there, the queens should be appearing," Lord Fenner said, pointing to the ridgeline to the east of the Gather field.

As if on cue, a group of gold dragons burst into view.

"Look carefully, lad, you won't see all the queen dragons of Pern together every day," Britell said to Cristov.

"Isn't that dangerous?" Toldur asked. "Won't the queens start fighting?"

"Only if one of them is ready to mate," Lord Fenner replied. "You're thinking of the Queen's Battle, aren't you?"

"Yes, my lord."

Fenner laughed and waved away Toldur's worry. "That was back in the First Pass, nearly five hundred Turns ago," he said. "All the dragons were crowded into Fort Hold back then."

"In the Hold? I thought they were always in the Weyrs," Cristov exclaimed, adding guiltily, "my lord."

"No, after the colonists crossed north, everyone lived in Fort Hold for a while," Lord Fenner said. He gave Masterminer Britell a teasing look and said, "I thought you miners were all taught the Teaching Ballads before you went underground."

Cristov's face drained of all color in embarrassment; he was startled when the Lord Holder of Crom Hold clapped him on the shoulder and said, "Oh, give over, lad! I was teasing. I know that you've been taught by Master Zist, so I've no worries about your knowledge."

"I'm afraid the lad isn't used to your ways, Fenner," Britell said, giving Cristov a reassuring nod.

Cristov, relieved, looked around and noticed that, beside the plush chairs and lush appointments and the Crom Hold pennant, the flags of the five Weyrs were displayed prominently in front of the stand. Near them were three empty flag holders, set at different heights.

"That's where we indicate who is to fly," Masterminer Britell said, noting Cristov's glance. "And the other two are added when the judging is complete—for first, second, and third places."

"These Games are to keep the dragonriders ready and trained," Lord Fenner explained. He turned to the Masterminer. "Provided they've enough firestone to train with."

Masterminer Britell grimaced. "We've got one mine working, now," he told the Lord. "It's enough."

"For the moment," Fenner allowed.

One mine? Cristov wondered. He knew of at least six coal mines and had heard of four mines for iron ore. One mine seemed insufficient to produce firestone for all the dragons of Pern. Was that why he had been sent to Crom Hold? To set up a new mine?

A wing of dragons suddenly appeared in the sky well below the queens. Moments later the loud *booms* of their arrival shook the air.

"They look small," Cristov marveled.

"They're weyrlings," Britell replied. "They're just old enough to fly *between* and carry firestone."

A ripple of overwhelming sound and a burst of cold air announced the arrival of a huge wing of dragons, flying low over the crowd.

"Telgar!" The crowd shouted as the dragons entered a steep dive, twisted into a sharp rolling climb, and came to a halt, their formation now aligned just below the weyrlings so perfectly that it looked like the two wings of dragons had been flying as twins, even though the fighting wing was head to head and a meter underneath the weyrlings.

A rain of sacks fell from the weyrlings and were caught by the riders of the great fighting dragons. Cristov looked at the jacket worn by the bronze rider leading the fighting wing and gasped when he saw the stylized field of wheat set in a white diamond: It was the Weyrleader himself!

As one, the fighting wing of dragons turned and dove again, flawlessly returning to hover in the same place where it had come from *between*. The great necks of the flying beasts turned back and the riders opened the sacks they had caught from the weyrlings to feed the firestone to their dragons.

"That's the same entrance as last Turn," Britell said, shaking his head.

"Don't they always come the same way?" Cristov asked.

Britell snorted. "Indeed they do, more's the pity. A bit of change would do them some good." He sighed. "Still, I suppose D'gan's worried about the firestone."

"Nasty stuff, firestone," Cristov heard the Lord Holder mutter behind him. "Nasty stuff."

"Indeed," Masterminer Britell agreed. "It's the hardest of all to mine."

"No mine lasts too long, either," Toldur added.

"Why?" Cristov asked.

"They blow up," Lord Fenner answered with a shrug.

"If the gases don't suffocate the men first," Masterminer Britell added mournfully.

"But we must have it," Lord Fenner said. "Without firestone, the dragons could not protect Pern."

Cristov knew that. Harper Zist had taught him long ago that the dragons needed to chew firestone in order to breathe flames. Without the dragons' flames, there was no way to destroy Thread in midair, before it reached the soil of Pern and sucked it of all life, turning lush valleys into lifeless dust bowls.

"Look, here comes Benden!" Lord Fenner called out, pointing to the sky.

Cristov followed the Lord Holder's finger and spotted a single bronze dragon in the sky. He squinted as he noticed that something was flapping down from the dragon's neck.

"What's that?" Toldur asked.

Two more bronze dragons appeared below the first one and, in a move so quick Cristov couldn't comprehend it, grabbed at the flapping object with their front claws. Cristov cheered as the flapping object was pulled taut and revealed itself to be a huge flag, in the diamond shape of the Weyrs, colored in the deep red of Benden Weyr and marked with the large "II" symbol of Pern's second Weyr.

Below him, Cristov saw the crowd of Crom Hold echo his astonishment, pointing up into the sky and exclaiming to each other.

"Benden!" "Benden!" voices cried in the crowd, impressed despite their loyalty to Telgar Weyr, the Weyr sworn to protect their Hold.

"Very nice," Lord Fenner remarked. "But Telgar will still win the Games, you'll see."

"No doubt, my lord," Toldur agreed, his eyes still glued to the amazing aerial display.

"They must have spent ages practicing," Britell murmured.

"Let's see what the others do," Lord Fenner said, scanning the skies for signs of the other three Weyrs.

As soon as Moran saw Nikal he knew he was in trouble. He altered his course, but the holder was too nimble and quickly caught up with him.

"Moran, a word with you!"

"Oh, it's you, Nikal! I was just looking for you," Moran said in mock surprise.

"You were, were you?" Nikal asked suspiciously. "Does that mean you've got my coal? You said months back you'd have it delivered."

Moran took a step back from the angry holder. Nikal took a quick step forward and grabbed the harper.

"If you haven't got it, I'll have my money back," the holder growled.

"I've had to make alternate arrangements," Moran said, calling upon all his training to sound believable. Desperately he pointed to the Lord Holder's stand. "See there? See those two with the Lord Holder?"

"They work for you?" Nikal asked dubiously.

"In a manner of speaking."

"I don't care how it's said," Nikal replied, "as long as my allotment of coal's in my lockers in the next seven-day."

"You may rely on it," Moran said, stepping back out of Nikal's grasp and drawing himself up to his full height. "My word as a harper."

"That was the same word you gave that I'd have my coal by now," Nikal noted sourly.

"There was a problem with my supplier," Moran said. "It was totally beyond my control."

"It's already getting cold at nights," Nikal complained. "I can't afford the prices charged for Cromcoal—the harvest hasn't been that good. I won't have my family and kin freezing because of you."

Moran sensed the hidden desperation in Nikal's words. "I'm sure," he said unctuously, "that your Holder will provide for you, just as you tithe to him."

"You know full well that I tithe to no Lord," Nikal growled. He grabbed at Moran again. "You don't have to be marked to be Shunned." Angrily, he pushed the harper away. "My father was Shunned and my mother went with him. I grew up without a Lord, moving from place to place, eating only when we were lucky. And now I've got a family of my own and a chance to start fresh, to make my own holding."

He gave the harper a deadly look.

"I'll not have you taking that away from me," he swore. He turned away, and then back again to say, "You've the sevenday, and then I spread the word on you, Harper."

"How much do you think your word would count against a harper?" Moran snapped angrily.

"With some folk," Nikal said, "more than you'd like."

Fort Weyr's arrival was not as dramatic as Benden's, but it was still awesome. In one instant three full wings of dragons burst into the skies over Crom Hold, with a long streaming banner in the earth brown and black of Fort Weyr carried by each rider. The Gather crowd clapped and cheered politely, but Cristov felt the lack of enthusiasm.

"Old G'lir was hardly trying," Fenner muttered, referring to the Fort Weyrleader. "There'll be a new Weyrleader there, soon, mark my words."

Britell nodded in agreement.

Ista Weyr's arrival was heralded by a steadily growing pyramid of dragons, each rider dropping an orange-and-black flag. The crowds below first looked on the display with puzzlement and then with hoarse cheering as the flags together formed a giant image of Ista Weyr's famous volcano.

"That was the best yet," Toldur shouted to Cristov above the crowd.

"Ah, but they're no good in the Games," Lord Fenner said.

"They weren't last Turn," Britell agreed. "But who knows what they've planned?"

"A point," Fenner replied thoughtfully. He scanned the skies expectantly. "Only High Reaches Weyr to come, and then we'll begin the Games."

"I wouldn't expect much from B'ralar," Masterminer Britell said.

"I don't know," Fenner replied, "B'ralar's more open to change than G'lir."

"I can't see much inspiring about jagged spires on a field of blue," Britell remarked, referring to the emblem of High Reaches Weyr, reflecting the Weyr's lofty mountain home and the deep blue skies which surrounded it.

"Indeed," Fenner agreed. "They are a dour lot up high in those northern mountains." He gestured to the nearby mountains of Crom Hold. "They say the cold in the High Reaches gets into your bones and stays there."

"And they don't have Cromcoal to cut the chill," Masterminer Britell agreed with a laugh.

A change in the sky attracted Fenner's attention. "Here they come," he said, pointing.

Above them several bubbles of fog appeared, out of which burst blue dragons. A second group of dragonriders—all on bronze dragons—appeared from *between,* creating another set of bubbles, outlining the first with a bronze border.

"Look at that!" Britell cried. "Did you know they could do that?"

"They brought the cold moist air of High Reaches with them," Fenner guessed. "That air would turn to fog in our heat."

The blue riders released black streamers. The lower blue dragons caught the streamers and held them. In a moment, the blue of the dragons and the black of the streamers resolved itself into a huge re-creation of the High Reaches Weyr symbol, black mountain crags on a blue background.

"Well, that's *much* better than last Turn," said Lord Fenner.

"I wonder if they'll fly any better," Britell muttered.

"Not enough so that it matters," Fenner said. He turned to Toldur. "Care to place a little wager?"

"No, my lord," Toldur said, "unless you want to bet against Telgar."

Fenner snorted. "Not likely." He looked at Cristov. "How about you, lad?"

Cristov shook his head. "No, my lord," he said, "I stand loyal to Telgar."

"Wise choice!" Britell declared. "Besides, it's not as though there's likely to be competition."

"Certainly not the way the other Weyrs have been grumbling," Fenner agreed. "I'm not sure I am entirely opposed to their views."

"In what way, my lord?" Toldur asked, curious.

Fenner gestured to the Masterminer to answer.

Britell frowned. "It seems that more firestone is going to D'gan and his Weyr than to all the other Weyrs combined."

"That doesn't seem right," Toldur said. "How did this happen?"

Britell gave the Lord Holder a sheepish look before he answered. "It appears that both Lord Holder Fenner and I were giving Telgar preferential treatment."

"That would be enough for Telgar to get four times what the others receive," Fenner said, "but we've also discovered that Weyrleader D'gan was appropriating firestone for his Weyr directly from the mine itself."

"He was stealing?" Cristov asked in amazement.

"Not so much stealing as, perhaps, taking more than his fair due," Lord Fenner said judiciously. "But we'll sort that out now that we've discovered our error."

"Perhaps Telgar will get a *little* more firestone than the other Weyrs," Britell suggested.

"No," Fenner said with a shake of his head. "I think that D'gan's got enough firestone stockpiled now to last him until the Pass. Perhaps it's time to be concerned with the other Weyrs, too."

"High Reaches Weyr flies Thread over upper Crom," Britell noted.

Lord Fenner smiled at the Masterminer. "Indeed they do," he agreed. "But I think we've got to look to all Pern's needs. Without enough training, any Weyr might fail to stop Thread."

A young harper, an apprentice by his shoulder knots, came running up to the stand.

"Kindan?" Toldur shouted in surprise. "Is that you?"

Kindan nodded and gasped in a deep breath. "It is," he said with a grin. "I've just arrived from the Harper Hall," he explained. He nodded respectfully to Lord Fenner.

"My lord, my greetings," he said, adding, "I have been asked to tell you that Weyrleader D'gan says that all the Weyrs are now present and could you have the drums sounded to start the Games?"

"Of course," Fenner agreed. He turned to Cristov. "Seeing as this young harper's all winded, Cristov, would you be so kind as to wave the Hold flag and start the Games?"

At the mention of Cristov's name, Kindan gave Cristov a nod of recognition and a grin, waving while still panting for breath.

Cristov grabbed the staff from which the Hold flag was flying and waved it from side to side. As he did so, he saw that all eyes were on him. Lord Fenner had given him a signal honor. Perhaps he hadn't been ordered here to be punished after all.

"Let the Games begin," Lord Fenner shouted as Cristov waved the flag.

From the far hill, drums beat out a rapid tattoo. High above, dragons' flames answered.

*Dragonmen, your beasts must learn
When to flame and swiftly turn.
Keep the burning Thread away,
Live to fight another day.*

Chapter Three

THE EARLY MORNING air was colder in the center of
the Weyr Bowl than it had been in the Living Cavern,
which was warmed by the hearth fires that had been
stoked high to cook the breakfast that the dragonriders
had eaten early in anticipation of the day's events.

D'vin could see the gleaming eyes of dragons arrayed
all around him. Behind him, Hurth craned his neck
around to watch the proceedings.

"You're as ready as we can make you," B'ralar told
him quietly. With a smile, D'vin acknowledged his
Weyrleader's hidden taunt. B'ralar was in the middle of
his sixth decade, forty Turns of which he'd been a dragonrider. Of those forty Turns, he'd been Weyrleader for
more than twenty, whereas D'vin had only been a wingleader for two Turns and had Impressed Hurth only five
Turns ago.

"I wish we'd had more firestone to practice with,"
the Weyrleader continued, "but with the wet weather,
it's been hard to keep hold of our stocks." Dampness
was a danger with firestone, which would explode on
contact with water.

D'vin nodded but said nothing; he had already aired
his concerns about their allocation of firestone in the
Council Room with the other wingleaders. Here, in

front of his riders and the rest of the Weyr, he would not.

"We'll do our best," D'vin said.

"I know you will," B'ralar said, clapping him on the shoulder. "You and your Wing have earned the right."

"Thank you."

B'ralar shook his head. "I only set the standards; *you* exceeded them." He mounted his dragon. "The queens have gathered. Now it's time for the opening ceremonies," he said. "I'll have Kalanth tell Hurth when we're ready for you."

Kalanth kicked off from the Weyr Bowl and beat his wings strongly to climb out of the Bowl before going *between.*

"You heard the Weyrleader," D'vin called to his wing. "Mount up. We'll gather by the Star Stones. The exercise will warm us up for the Games."

D'linner and P'lel, the wing's two youngest riders, cheered exuberantly, while the others looked on with the amusement of veterans.

The wing did not have long to wait at the Star Stones before the signal from the Weyrleader came.

Let's go to Crom Hold, D'vin told his dragon, barely able to control his excitement.

As one, thirty dragons and their riders winked out of existence over High Reaches Weyr and reappeared over Crom Hold.

"The first event is a single rider competition," Lord Fenner explained to Cristov. "Each Weyr picks two riders to represent them. The queens throw the rope Thread down, simulating a normal fall, and the riders flame it."

Cristov listened attentively. He knew that the rules for the Games were changed each Turn, and this event was new to him.

"How do they determine the winner?" Toldur asked.

"Each rider has one pass at the Threadfall, and the one who chars the most Thread without letting any Thread get past wins," Fenner replied.

Fenner turned to Kindan. "Harper, can you wave the Fort Weyr flag?"

Kindan nodded and took the Fort Weyr flag, waved it high, and placed it in the center stand to indicate that Fort Weyr was to fly Thread.

"Look up, lad," Masterminer Britell told Cristov in a kindly tone. "You'll never see the like of this again, I'll wager."

Cristov needed no urging; he looked up first to the queens hovering high above and then toward the cluster of Fort Weyr riders.

Presently, one dragon—a blue—separated from the formation and flew low over the Lord Holder's stand, waggling its wings in acknowledgment before pulling up higher to take station at the starting point. The blue breathed a burst of flame to signal its readiness.

A hush came over the field as all those at the Gather looked up in anticipation of the forthcoming "Threadfall." Cristov, along with the entire crowd, gasped as the air beneath the high flying queens suddenly turned silver with squiggling rope Threads.

"Can they really get all that?" Toldur asked in astonishment.

"The queens are throwing more Thread than one dragon would fly in a real Threadfall," Kindan informed them all. "My understanding is that the Weyrs always try for harder Falls than they expect."

"A good precaution," Britell said approvingly.

All the same, Cristov was awed at the speed at which the blue flew through the wide swath of falling Thread, flaming continuously and seemingly everywhere as it battled the Fall.

It seemed mere moments before all the Thread was gone. It took the crowd some time to register this fact, and then the air was filled with a great roar of cheering.

"That was magnificent," Lord Fenner murmured.

"Fancy a wager?" Masterminer Britell asked, with a gleam in his eyes.

"I'd wager that D'gan is furious," Fenner said drolly. "But, as a bounden Holder, I'd not bet against my Weyr."

"It's not your Weyr, just the best rider," Masterminer Britell responded in cajoling tones.

Lord Fenner waved the correction aside. "I'll bet that Telgar wins the Games."

Britell grimaced. "I'd not bet against *that*."

Kindan, meanwhile, had removed the Fort Weyr pennant and, with a look to the Lord Holder, had placed the Benden Weyr pennant in the starting position.

A large brown dragon descended over the stand, waggled his wings, and took station. Again, a blizzard of Thread was unleashed by the queens high above, and again Cristov and the crowd were amazed at the speed with which the brown dragon turned all of it into harmless ash.

"What if one of the ropes is still burning when it hits the ground?" Toldur asked.

"I've ground crews standing by to put it out," Lord Fenner told him. "The same ground crews that would fight Thread burrows in a real Fall."

"Burrows?" Cristov repeated, wondering how they'd be dealt with in the Games.

"Oh, we're not testing the dragonriders on burrows," Lord Fenner said with a chuckle.

"That'd be for the ground crews," Britell agreed. "Is there a separate event?"

"No," said Fenner. "But I might suggest it to the Conclave of Holders. Usually, though, each Lord

Holder is responsible for the effectiveness of his ground crews." He told Kindan, "We're ready for High Reaches, now, lad."

A blue dragon represented the northern high mountain Weyr first. It flew through the Threads faster than the other two dragons and drew a great cheer, which changed into a puzzled noise as more and more people noticed one uncharred Thread slithering to the ground.

"Oh, missed one!" Fenner exclaimed. "Well, there's still the second candidate."

"He's disqualified?" Cristov asked, thinking that it was a shame, since the dragon had been fastest of the three.

"Indeed he is," Fenner agreed.

"Speed's not the point when it comes to Thread, lad," the Lord Holder expounded. "Except, perhaps, for the speed with which the ground crews dispatch such a burrow." He peered over to where the Thread had fallen and grunted when he saw a black flag being waved.

"Harper, put a black flag over High Reaches's pennant," Fenner said to Kindan. To the rest of the group, he explained, "The black flag shows that the rider was disqualified."

Tell D'linner he did his best, D'vin thought to Hurth.

He and Delth are both very disappointed, Hurth responded after relaying D'vin's message.

Well, there's still P'lel and Telenth, D'vin said. Beneath him, Hurth rumbled in agreement. Together the two watched Telgar's first entrant, a green, dive through the next Threadfall. The green's speed was greater than Delth's but her accuracy was even worse. *Pity.*

In the distance D'vin could see Telgar's Weyrleader screaming at the hapless dragon and rider. D'vin schooled his expression, aware that several of his riders were gauging his reaction. He didn't want to give either them or the Telgar Weyrleader a chance to disparage his behavior.

The next dragon, an Istan green, was ridden by one of the older riders, but neither rider nor dragon could be faulted for speed or accuracy.

And then it was time for Fort's second entrant, a brown. D'vin was surprised at the choice of a brown— the larger dragons were usually better at endurance than speed—but the brown proved itself up to the Fall thrown down by the queen riders and advanced to the next round. Benden's second entrant was a more conventional blue who performed quite creditably.

D'vin mused to himself that while the purpose of the All-Weyr Games was mostly to assure the Holders of the abilities of the Weyrs to fight the Threadfall that would come with the next Pass of the Red Star, it also allowed the five Weyrs to become comfortable with each other's abilities.

Tell P'lel good flying, D'vin said to Hurth as it came turn for High Reaches's second entrant. D'vin saw P'lel wave at him before he and Telenth dove over the Lord Holder's stand and rose up again to take their position.

D'vin could feel the tension in his wing as they waited for the queen's wing to drop the Thread. In a moment he spotted it. The pattern, whether by design or the churning of the air from all the flaming before, was oddly clumped. It would be a hard fall for a bronze to fly, let alone a small green. Still, D'vin grinned as P'lel and Telenth dived toward the first clump and flamed it easily into blackened char. The pair continued their run, but it was becoming obvious to D'vin that they were both getting tired as they neared the end, with three clumps still to char. Suddenly Telenth disappeared, only to reappear, wheeling on a wingtip, just below the center of all three clumps. It was a wild tactic and one D'vin wasn't sure he'd approve for a real Threadfall, but the green's agility on wing and length of flame just managed to char all three clumps at once. Far below, D'vin could hear the crowd cheering more loudly than they'd ever cheered before.

Overcome with joy, P'lel and Telenth rolled quickly upside down and right side up again, to the renewed cheers of the crowd.

Tell Telenth well done, D'vin said. *And tell P'lel, no more fool stunts!*

The chagrined green rider rejoined his wing, but his discomfort quickly evaporated in the congratulations shouted by the rest of the wing.

Telgar's second entrant performed adequately, if a trifle slowly, as if reluctant to repeat his weyrmate's mistake.

Ista's rider, a grizzled veteran on a blue, seared the Threads out of the sky so quickly that it took a moment before the crowd reacted.

That's how it's done, D'vin told his dragon. Hurth rumbled in agreement while D'vin tried to fix in his mind what it was about the blue dragon that had made it so effective. It almost seemed as if dragon and rider had anticipated the fall of the Thread and arrived *before* the Thread itself. Years of training, D'vin thought to himself in awe.

And then they were into the second round. The queens spread out somewhat and prepared to drop even more rope Threads for the next Pass. The first Fort and the first Istan entrants were disqualified in this round. In the third round, the queens practically doubled their original distance and the Fall was something truly frightening to behold.

In the third round, Benden's first entrant was disqualified, then Fort's second entrant, and finally, with a gasp from the crowd, Telgar's last blue was disqualified.

But that still left three dragons, from Benden, Ista, and his own High Reaches, for the fourth round. As the queens spread out yet more and prepared to drop a veritable rain of Thread down, D'vin was convinced that the victory would go to High Reaches's larger green Telenth. He could not imagine either of the two blues even completing the course, much less without error.

But they did, with Ista's blue clearly putting in the most amazing performance. D'vin could find no fault with P'lel's flying or with Telenth's work, but it was obvious to him that the Istan blue dragon was simply the master of the situation.

From above he heard the queens' bugle, announcing a tie. He looked down to the Lord Holder's stand, wondering how Crom's Lord Holder would decide.

"Ah," Lord Fenner said as the sound of the queens far above floated down to them, "I was afraid of that."

Cristov and the others looked at him expectantly.

"In the event of a tie, the Lord Holder must judge," Fenner explained to them. He smiled deviously. "And, as Lord Holder, I have decided to enlist you all in my decision making."

"My lord?" Toldur said.

"Indeed," Fenner replied. "I think a show of hands amongst all of us, for first, second, and third place should do it."

Toldur caught Cristov's look of surprise and whispered down to him, "I'll bet you didn't expect to be judging dragonriders today, did you?"

Cristov gulped.

"Just do your best," Kindan told him. "It's not as though they'll find out."

"And be grateful that our own Weyr dropped out of the running, or our decision would be more difficult," Masterminer Britell added.

Cristov sidled over to Kindan and asked softly, "Have you ever done this before?"

Kindan shook his head, a nervous smile plastered on his face.

"For first place, all those for Ista?" Lord Fenner asked. He counted easily, as all hands were up. "As I expected, then," he said contentedly. "And all those for High Reaches for second place?" Again, all hands went up. "That would leave Benden in third place," he said. "Harper, if you would so arrange it. Be sure to wave each flag high over the stand before you put it in its placeholder."

Kindan nodded and removed the Ista Weyr pennant from its stand and waved it high from side to side.

As the crowd roared its approval, Lord Fenner said, "See, we've chosen wisely." He waved back at the crowd before turning once more to Kindan. "And now, Harper, if you'd be so kind to wave the Crom Hold pennant, that will let the dragonriders know to come down."

Kindan gave the Lord Holder a surprised look, and Fenner laughed. "I've not lost my senses! They're only coming down for a break, young harper. The Games will start up again in a half hour. That'll give the riders a chance to slake their thirst and fill their stomachs before the next event."

D'vin waited until the Fort and Benden Weyr riders dismounted in front of the Lord Holder's stand before ordering his riders down. After he dismounted, he bowed to the Lord Holder.

"Greetings from High Reaches Weyr," D'vin called.

"Greetings to you, bronze rider," the Lord Holder called back with a jaunty wave. "There are refreshments in the stalls. Please invite your riders to take what they need for their comfort."

"I will, thank you," D'vin replied. As he turned, he caught sight of two youngsters in the stands and turned back again, surprised. "Are these your heirs, my lord?"

Lord Fenner laughed. "No, indeed! These two scally-wags hail from Camp Natalon. Kindan's the harper, and Cristov is the miner."

"Do you mine firestone?" D'vin asked. He had hoped to strike up an acquaintance with one of the firestone miners.

"No, my lord," Cristov said, blushing in embarrassment. "We mine coal at Camp Natalon."

"He's being modest, my lord," Fenner said, clapping Cristov on the back. "Camp Natalon has the best coal in all Crom."

"Well, I'm glad to hear that," D'vin said. He nodded to Cristov. "Good to meet you, miner." He turned away and then back once more. "My Lord Holder, could you point me to a vendor of bubbly pies?"

Lord Fenner looked surprised by the question, so D'vin explained sheepishly, "I've not had one in a long time and just caught a whiff as I landed."

Lord Fenner shook his head and was about to reply when Cristov's hand shot up, pointing. "My lord," he said, "I think if you ask that girl there, she'll lead you right." He waved and shouted to the girl, the one upon whom he'd bestowed his half-mark earlier. "Could you lead my Lord D'vin to the bubbly pies, Halla?"

Halla's stomach had rumbled in anticipation as she followed her nose to the bubbly pies. A miner half-mark entitled her to four, so she paid for two and got a quarter-mark back. She ate one pie immediately despite its burning warmth, and then turned to scan the crowd for her benefactor and quarry.

She was surprised to see him on the Lord Holder's stand. What did Moran want with this one? she wondered. Still, orders were orders, especially from Moran, so she worked her way close to the stand, careful not to be obvious and also not to jostle her second pie.

The Lord Holder's stand was constructed on a high knoll, giving it not only a great view of the Games but also of the whole Gather spread below. Halla had to work carefully to keep herself close enough to the stands to hear what they were saying but far enough in the crowd to avoid being spotted.

So she jumped when Cristov called her name. She couldn't help shivering in fear. Had she been discovered? Had Moran been apprehended? Had he turned her in to save his own skin?

She was ready to run, almost ready to drop her precious bubbly pie, when the full extent of his words registered with her.

"Bubbly pies?" she repeated blankly, drawing closer to Cristov and the stand, like a moth to a flame.

"Yes, Lord D'vin would like some. Could you lead him to the baker?" Cristov repeated, frowning at the young girl. She was terrified. To assuage her fear, he offered, "Would you like me to come with you?"

Dumbstruck, Halla nodded. Cristov muttered excuses to the others and climbed down the stands. He gestured for the dragonrider to precede him, but D'vin politely demurred.

The crowd parted for them and they approached Halla. "My lord, this is Halla," Cristov said.

"Halla," D'vin said, with a nod. Halla could only nod in reply. "Can you show us the way?"

Halla nodded again, and turned. She strode off, glancing over her shoulder to see if they were still following her.

How could this happen? she asked herself. Now I've got a *dragonrider* following me!

In fact, she realized as she glanced around again, the dragonrider had caught up with her and was walking at her side.

"Do you come from Crom Hold, Halla?" D'vin inquired.

"No, nearby," she said.

"Are you excited about the Games?"

Halla nodded. D'vin, sensing her reticence, let the conversation drop and trudged along beside her companionably, waving politely to anyone who called out or acknowledged him.

D'vin paused and sniffed the air. "Bubbly pies! I can smell them."

"We're close," Halla agreed, feeling some relief at the prospect.

"We'll need you to lead us back," D'vin warned her. "I got quite lost in all that crowd."

Halla's eyes grew round in alarm.

Meanwhile, Cristov had been watching her closely. Suddenly, he asked, "Did we ever meet before, Halla?"

Should I tell him? Halla wondered. Or, she thought fearfully, did he see me up at the mine?

"Once, three Turns ago," Halla said.

"Is Jamal your brother?" Cristov asked, his face brightening. When Halla nodded, Cristov continued excitedly, "No wonder I recognized you! You look just like him! It's been ages since I've seen him!" He looked around wildly. "Where is he?"

Halla's face fell and Cristov's expression changed. "He's all right, isn't he?" he asked. "He had the cast on his leg when we met, but he's all right?"

"The break got infected," Halla murmured.

Cristov stopped dead, grabbing Halla's arm in alarm. "Where is he?"

Halla pointed to the cemetery. "He died not long after he met you," she told him. "He'd hoped to see you again."

"I'm sorry," Cristov told her miserably. "I never knew."

"How are you getting along, then?" D'vin asked. His gaze took in the state of her clothing, and the gauntness of her frame.

"I'm making do, my lord," Halla said, dipping her head in an apparent gesture of respect but really trying to hide her eyes from the dragonrider's probing glance. To change the subject, she looked up again and pointed. "There's the baker, my lord."

"Thank you," D'vin replied, picking up his pace. Sonia's words from months back echoed in his head: *I swear, D'vin, you'd take in every stray that crossed your path!*

The baker was so pleased at D'vin's patronage that she sent to the tent next door for fresh berry juice and set a special table out in front of her stall just for them.

Neither Halla nor Cristov were used to such deferential service, but D'vin did everything he could to make them feel at ease, while praising the baker's and juice-maker's efforts loudly to the bustling crowd.

Halla watched the dragonrider surreptitiously, surprised at his easy ways and the manner with which he dealt with the merchants. It was clear to her that he knew his praise would help their sales, and that he didn't overdo it—he said just enough to ensure that both vendors would have plenty of custom for the rest of the Gather.

Cristov watched neither of them. Instead, he explored his last memories of Jamal. Memories of a Gather three Turns past.

"Cristov?" D'vin's voice startled him.

"My lord?"

"Was he a good friend?" the dragonrider asked softly.

Cristov shook his head. "He might have been," he said, "but we never got the chance to find out." He looked up. "My father didn't approve of him."

Cristov didn't notice the startled look Halla gave him but D'vin did.

With a sigh, D'vin got to his feet. "We'd better get back—the next event will start soon."

Shunned from hold, Shunned from craft,
Steal the grain, steal the haft.
Take without returning too
And it will be Shunned for you.

Chapter Four

"GET UP, you lazy oaf!" Gerendel, the foreman, roared in his ear.

Tarik struck out feebly from his cot with one hand, trying to fend the foreman off.

A cold splash of water inundated him and he came up suddenly, arms swinging but meeting only air.

"I was on watch!" Tarik complained, sitting back on his cot.

"You were asleep on watch last night, so you'll pull a full shift," the foreman growled. He nudged Tarik with the empty bucket. "Get up now, or we'll put you back in the stocks."

With a bitter look, Tarik grudgingly stood up. He lunged suddenly toward the foreman, but Gerendel was too quick for him and jumped back out of his grasp while at the same time smashing him on the head with the bucket. Tarik crashed to the ground and lay there, clutching his head and groaning.

"Get up now, you useless Shunned no-named oaf," Gerendel growled.

Wearily, Tarik pulled himself to his feet, his hands clenched firmly to his side, not daring a repeat of Gerendel's beating. He found his boots at the end of his cot and dragged them on.

"My name's Tarik," he growled to the foreman as he trudged out of the room.

"No, it isn't," Gerendel spat. "You were Shunned, and lost your name along with everything else." He laughed as Tarik turned back to glare at him. "You might win back your name one day, but with you—I doubt it."

The building they came out of was rough-hewn, built out of wood. Tarik remembered the others laughing at him when he'd complained of not sleeping in a proper hold. But for more than a Turn since he'd been Shunned, he'd done just that—working as a drudge in minor holds around Crom.

"If you were so bothered about that, you'd not be Shunned," Maril, one of the Shunned, guffawed. He spat. "If you want to live like a Lord, you've got to please 'em!"

"No spitting," Gerendel roared at him. The other miners scowled at Maril, not the foreman. Gerendel wagged a finger at Maril. "You'll find yourself in the stocks if you do that again, Maril!"

"But we're not in the mine," Maril protested.

"If we were, you'd likely be dead," Gerendel said. "I don't want you thinking you can spit anywhere lest you forget when you're in the mine." He turned to Tarik. "You remember that, firestone's fickle with water. If it doesn't explode, the fumes'll kill a man."

Tarik had remembered so well that he'd spent the first night in the stocks, after being caught trying to escape.

"Think you're the first one who thought of escaping?" Maril had asked him as Tarik sat, his feet, neck, and arms locked into the wooden stockade. Maril kicked a loose pile of dirt up from the ground and rubbed it in Tarik's face. "The rest of us'll have to work extra while you laze about here," the scrawny miner snarled. "You think about that the next time you try something. Think hard."

In the two months since then, Tarik had been in the stocks twice more, and beaten, once, in the middle of the night. He was certain that Maril had been one of his assailants.

But neither Maril nor Gerendel frightened Tarik as much as the mine.

"This is the last working firestone mine on Pern," Gerendel had told him when he arrived. He gave Tarik an evil grin as he added, "Mine number eight blew up a Turn back and set the whole valley around it in flames.

"It's only a matter of time before this one blows," Gerendel continued malevolently. "But there are always those who think themselves above all others, those who don't care about other people, and they'll get Shunned. And the Shunned work the firestone mines." He nodded to Tarik. "You're the first miner that's been Shunned here."

Tarik was shocked. How could they mine if they weren't trained?

Gerendel laughed. "Oh, you're thinking that mining requires special skills? It's naught but hard work with a pick and a shovel, shift after shift."

"What about shoring up the shaft?" Tarik asked in spite of his resolution against helping in any way.

"That'd be *your* specialty, wouldn't it?" Gerendel said, leering. "Skimping on the shoring?" He noticed Tarik's look. "Oh, we heard all about you, miner. Where'd you sell all that extra lumber, that's what the lads wondered." Gerendel shook his head and pointed at Tarik's threadbare clothing. "It's not done you much good, has it?"

Tarik glowered but said nothing.

Now he was going into the mine again, forced on a shift after a night's watch duty because someone had caught him sleeping. Tarik grimaced at the indignity of it all. It wasn't as though anyone would want to steal anything from the camp!

Tarik had thought once of trying to convince the others to murder Gerendel in his sleep and escape as a group. But there were too many dragonriders arriving at all hours, looking for firestone or dropping in supplies—there was no proper road up to the mine, so everyone was brought in a-dragonback.

Besides, with a big blue "S" on their foreheads, where would they go? They'd be fugitives searching for their next meal, animals on the run with only another mine to work, or worse, if they were caught. Gerendel had warned him on his first day that the nearest dwelling was over three days' march away over the mountains, adding, with a smirk, "At least, that's what they tell me. But no one's ever come here except on a dragon."

At least no one that was *seen,* Tarik thought. He wondered how long it would be before Moran appeared; the harper was always going on about the Shunned and their needs. Tarik wondered if, now that *he* was Shunned, Moran would still deal with him—it would only seem logical, given how much coal he'd handed over for Moran's brats. Privately, he hoped not. Especially if Tenim was still around.

"Come on, grab a pick," Gerendel said as they left the crude shack that served as their only dwelling.

The others were already milling about the shaft entrance. Sourly Tarik noted that Maril had managed to get the cart, the softest job of the lot. Tarik hefted his pick, eyeing the back of Gerendel's head thoughtfully.

Maril shouted, pointing at Tarik, and Gerendel wheeled around.

"Right!" Gerendel shouted, snatching the pick out of Tarik's hands. "It's the stocks for you!"

"I did nothing!" Tarik protested as Gerendel gestured toward the stocks.

"Only 'cause Maril warned me," Gerendel replied. He gestured to the others, shouting, "Well, lads, this one's decided he needs another day in the stocks. Why don't you let him know how you feel about that?"

The other Shunned miners roared with wrath and bounded up to grab Tarik. Roughly, they dragged him to the stocks, and shoved his feet, neck, and hands into the position, locking him in. His back immediately began to ache from the awkward half-sitting, half-standing posture the stocks forced him into. He knew that by the end of the day he would be in agony.

"I did nothing wrong!" he shouted again. "I was just testing the heft!"

The others ignored his protests.

"You'll get half rations for the rest of the sevenday," Gerendel said as he gave the lock on the stocks a final test.

"He shouldn't get any," Maril growled. "The drag-onriders only provide food for the firestone mined." He turned to the others. "He'll be eating our share of the food—what do you think about that?"

"If he doesn't eat, he'll just die," Renlin objected. "And we'll still have to do his work and more." The small, rat-faced miner shook his head. "Let him serve his time and learn his lesson."

"You're too soft," Maril growled. "Next you'll be wanting to leave him a drink and a snack."

"No food," Renlin disagreed. "But some water. He's no use dead, and we'd have the trouble of burying the body."

"See to it, Maril," Gerendel ordered, gesturing to the others. "Come on, we've wasted enough daylight."

Grudgingly the other fourteen Shunned miners trudged to the entrance of the firestone mine.

Maril lounged by the stocks until the others had disappeared inside the mine and then, with a rude gesture, turned to follow them.

"What about my water?" Tarik shouted after him.

Maril waved dismissively over his shoulder, grabbed the rope on the cart, and tugged it into the mine after him.

If there was a center to camp at firestone mine #9, it was the stocks. Beside them was a large fire pit, carefully shielded by rocks and a large cleared area, where the miners cooked fresh meat on the rare occasions they got some.

The stocks faced the mine entrance. They were set just off the path from the miners' shack to the mine entrance. The wooden rails that led from the mine entrance to the only stone building in the camp curved in front of the stocks before curving farther to the stone-walled firestone storage building on the far side of the hill.

Every hour or so, Maril would come trudging out of the mine, muscles straining as he hauled the full cart up the hill and down to the firestone building. About fifteen minutes later, he would reappear, riding the empty cart on the down slope back into the mine.

Every time, Tarik shouted to him, asking for water. And every time, Maril smiled evilly and waved as he reentered the mine.

By noon, Tarik was too parched to call out. His legs, back, shoulders, arms, and neck all burned with the searing pain of his enforced stance.

A burst of laughter from the mine entrance startled him, and he lifted his aching head enough to see that the miners were breaking for lunch.

They grumbled and cursed at him on their way past him to the shack. Tarik's stomach lurched with hunger as they returned with plates full of fresh tubers and jerked beef.

Renlin carried a large cook pot. In a short time there was a roaring fire in the fire pit, and the cook pot was bubbling with the most amazing smells as tubers, beef, and herbs simmered into stew. Perhaps it was the work, or the setting, but Tarik had never disagreed with the miners' assertion that Renlin was the best cook they'd ever met.

As the others emptied the last of the stew onto their plates, Renlin came over to Tarik.

Gerendel scowled. "You can't feed him, Renlin."

"Yes, how will he learn?" one of the others grumbled.

"He looks parched," Renlin said, peering closely at Tarik.

"Did you give him water, Maril?" Gerendel asked.

"Oh, I must have forgot!" Maril exclaimed in tones that fooled no one.

"If he dies, you'll do his work as well as your own," Gerendel replied.

"I'll get you some water, Tarik," Renlin promised. The miner passed his plate off and returned with a bucket of water. He ladled some out and poured it into Tarik's mouth.

Tarik coughed on the first mouthful. Renlin tried again. Tarik's parched throat absorbed the liquid eagerly.

"Don't give him too much, Renlin, or he'll get sick," Gerendel warned.

"Thanks," Tarik said to Renlin, his voice thick and husky.

"I'll leave the bucket here," Renlin said. He turned to Maril, saying, "Then it'll not be too much trouble for you to check on him."

Maril glowered but said nothing.

Shortly afterward, Gerendel chivvied the crew back

to work. On his first trip out of the mine with a cart-load of firestone, Maril paused on his return trip long enough to fling some water at Tarik. "There!"

Tarik was still thirsty enough to lick the drops off his face; Maril laughed.

Maril ignored him on the next trip, and again on the next. On the third time, Maril paused beside Tarik.

"Thirsty?" he asked, scooping up a ladleful of water from the bucket.

"Yes," Tarik admitted.

"Pity," Maril said, pouring the water from the ladle back into the bucket.

"Please . . ." Tarik began, begging. He cut himself short. He had lost everything else when he was Shunned; he refused to lose his pride.

"Beg for it, miner," Maril said, bending down to peer into Tarik's face. "Beg for it, and maybe I'll give you some."

Tarik stared back stonily. He knew that he'd be free of the stocks soon enough, and then Maril would pay for his insolence.

"You won't beg?" Maril asked. He stood up and grabbed the bucket. "Then you'll have to get it your-self." Laughing, he carefully placed the bucket just to the left of Tarik's booted foot, then, with a derisive snort, returned to the mine.

The air was dry; the mountain morning's chill had worn off, replaced by an afternoon heat that bore down on Tarik. Thirst consumed him. At first he ignored the bucket by his foot, determined to last until either Maril relented or the shift ended.

Maril passed by him again with another cartload of firestone. On the way back, he rode the cart down into the mine, waving tauntingly at Tarik as he passed.

Tarik looked at the bucket. Maybe, he thought, he could hook the handle with his boot and drag it close enough to grab with his hand. He'd have to be quick; he didn't know how long it would take before Maril appeared with another cartload of firestone. He was certain that Maril would take the bucket away if he thought Tarik could get it.

Tarik eyed the bucket, eyed the mine entrance, and paused. If he didn't get the bucket, if it tipped over, what then? He was close enough to the mine shaft that the water from the bucket might flow to the entrance. Of course, he reminded himself, there was a deep gutter dug in front of the mine to carry any water away—water in a firestone mine would be disastrous.

Tarik's thirst won out over his caution. He strained his toe forward and flicked it up. The first time, the end of his foot slid off the handle, flicking it up and back down again before he could get his foot under it. He paused and tried again. This time the handle flew up and he quickly kicked with his foot, hoping to get it under the handle before it fell back to the bucket's side.

He kicked too hard. The bucket shuddered and fell over away from him. With a hoarse cry, Tarik watched as the precious fluid flowed away from him, downhill, toward the mine.

Everything would have been all right, if Maril hadn't emerged from the mine at that moment. The water had lapped over the wooden rails the cart ran on; Maril, pushing from behind, didn't see the stain of liquid and was taken off guard by the sudden change in resistance of his load. His pushing jarred the cartload, and a few pieces of firestone fell off the cart.

Tarik's voice was too dry for more than the hoarsest of shouts, "Run!"

Maril didn't hear him. He leaned over instinctively to retrieve the errant stone just as it fell into the water and burst into flame.

In an instant, the disaster was complete. The fire startled Maril, who leaped backward, tripped, and, struggling to stay upright, tugged the cartload of firestone back toward the mine. The cart of firestone caught flame even as it rolled back over Maril's leg and into the mine, gaining speed on the slope.

A huge ball of flame, taller than a man, burst out of the side of the mountain where the firestone mine had been. The blast caught Tarik and threw him, still in the stocks, backward like a straw doll.

The flames licked the nearby trees, withering their limbs. And then the fires subsided, leaving the mine shaft a huge, black, smoking hole in the side of the mountain.

A silver swath falls from the sky,
Dragon and rider rise on high.
Practice fighting Thread with flames,
'Tis the purpose of the Games.

Chapter Five

D'VIN LEFT THEM at the stands. Cristov climbed back up and, when he turned back, found that Halla had disappeared. He regretted that; he wanted to talk with her more about Jamal.

"They're off again," Fenner said as wings of dragons reassembled above the crowd. He turned to Cristov. "The next competition is for whole wings fighting Thread."

"How is that judged, my lord?" Toldur asked politely.

"It's about the same, I believe," Lord Fenner said. "The queens throw Thread and the wings fight it. If any gets through, the wing is disqualified. If all wings succeed in fighting the Thread, the queens spread out and throw more."

"Will we have to judge a tie again?" Britell asked, a hint of worry in his voice.

Fenner laughed. "No, this continues until there's a clear winner."

"That's a relief," the Masterminer said with a sigh. In response to Lord Fenner's questioning look, he explained, "I'm afraid we'd hardly be considered impartial if every event was a tie and we had to judge."

Lord Fenner snorted in agreement. "I daresay you're right."

At Lord Fenner's nod, Kindan waved the hold's flag high over his head, signaling that the games were to recommence. Again, the drummers on the far hill drummed their tattoo, and again dragons up high flamed their readiness.

Cristov craned his neck back to spot the queen dragons. He was amazed at how far up they were.

"How high can dragons fly?" Cristov asked Kindan in a low voice.

"It depends on the dragon and the rider," Kindan replied. "The queens can fly higher than most, but the air gets too thin eventually."

"What happens if a dragon flies too high?" Cristov wondered.

"I've been told that as the air gets thin, the riders start to feel as if they're drunk," Kindan said.

Cristov raised his eyebrows in surprise, wondering if Kindan was teasing him. Kindan caught his look and said, "No, seriously, I've heard that from many dragonriders. One even said that the color went out of his eyes and he only saw shades of gray until he got back down on the ground."

"That can happen in the mines, too, if there's not enough air, as you two know," added Toldur, who had been listening in. Cristov and Kindan shuddered in memory.

The cave-in at Camp Natalon had been Tarik's fault. He had skimped on the planking for the tunnel his shift was digging. Natalon had discovered this and, in the process of trying to repair the faulty tunnel, had been caught with most of his shift in the cave-in. Kindan, Toldur, and Nuella, Natalon's blind daughter, had defied Tarik's order that no one go into the mine.

Cristov remembered the shocked look on Kindan's face when he'd arrived with his axe to offer help.

Even with his help and the use of a secret passageway Natalon had dug when the mine was first surveyed, the rescue party was nearly overcome by the coal dust that had filled the mine after the cave-in. In the end, they discovered that the trapped miners were too far away to dig out, but Kindan somehow managed to convince Nuella that she could ride his watch-wher, Kisk, like a dragon *between* to rescue the trapped miners.

And somehow, the strange journey Nuella and the watch-wher made had bound the girl and the watch-wher together, allowing Kindan to pursue his desire to become a harper.

Cristov envied Kindan his freedom to follow his dreams. Wistfully he recalled one of his conversations with Jamal when they had stared up skyward at the last Games. Jamal had pointed up to one of the dragons and exclaimed, "I'd like one like that!"

"A bronze?" Cristov said, peering upward.

"Sure," Jamal replied. "And then I'd become Weyr-leader." He blew out a sigh and asked wistfully, "Do you think the dragonriders will Search when the Games are over?"

Cristov shrugged. "I dunno."

"Wouldn't you like it, Cristov? Wouldn't you love to Impress a dragon?"

Cristov looked over at Jamal, then back up to the brilliant formation of dragons—bronze, brown, blue, and green. For a moment he imagined himself on the Hatching Grounds, the excitement as the dragon eggs burst open and the dragonets scrambled awkwardly out of their shells, multifaceted eyes whirling anxiously, searching for their life mates. Cristov imagined how he'd feel, his face splitting wide in surprise and joy as a dragon—*his* dragon—spoke telepathically to him and told him that he would forever have a friend, a champion. He tried to imagine how his father would react—and could only see him frowning.

"It'll never happen," he had said firmly, turning away from Jamal. "Father says I'm only fit to be a miner."

And now Tarik was Shunned, and Cristov stood here next to the Masterminer and Crom's Lord Holder not knowing what was in store for him, and Jamal was nearly three Turns dead.

Cristov locked his eyes on one of the high-flying bronze dragons and tried not to be envious of his rider.

The pace picked up immensely as Fort began its second run. The sky that seemed practically black with the Thread that the queen riders had thrown down was suddenly bursting into flame. And then the sky was clear—except for one strand that sailed harmlessly to the ground.

A groan of sympathy rose up from the Gather crowd as they realized what had happened. Kindan waved a black flag to show that they'd been disqualified.

The rest of the Weyrs completed the second round. The wing from High Reaches was disqualified in the third round. For a moment it even looked like Telgar had let some Thread through but, as the crowd watched anxiously, it broke up into harmless char just before hitting the ground.

"Now they'll have to fly three times as far," Lord Fenner muttered as the queens spread for the fourth round.

Benden flew flawlessly but just a little too slow to get to the last of the Thread before it hit the ground, so they were disqualified.

Kindan, who was friendly with Benden's Weyrleader, M'tal, groaned sympathetically.

"Third place isn't bad," Toldur assured him.

It was down to Telgar and Ista. The Telgar wing flew the extended, thickened Fall flawlessly with a speed that seemed to Cristov like lightning. The Istan wing got off to an even faster start, and it looked certain that there would be a sixth round.

"Look!" Fenner shouted, pointing skyward. "They missed some!"

Sure enough, a clump of rope fell to the ground uncharred.

Britell raised an eyebrow at Crom's Lord Holder. "Didn't you say that Telgar would win?"

"I did," Fenner agreed, "but this—!" He gestured to the sky and shook his head. "Ista flew well and deserved to win."

"Ista placed second, so they're ahead on points," Britell noted.

"There's still the final competition," Lord Fenner reminded him. He cocked an eye speculatively at the Masterminer. "Are you willing to wager, then?"

Britell snorted. "Telgar will win the final event, I'm sure."

"What if they don't?" Toldur asked.

"D'gan will be impossible," Lord Fenner replied with a shudder.

"They have to win the next event or they'll only be able to tie with Ista," Britell noted.

"At best," Lord Fenner agreed with a grimace.

Cristov looked puzzled. Toldur noticed.

"The overall placing is based on points," Toldur explained. "First place is worth five points, second place is worth two points, and third place is worth one point. The Weyr with the most points at the end of the Games is the winner."

"There's a lot of gambling on the outcome," Kindan added.

"But Telgar always wins," Cristov declared loyally.

"Which is why most people bet on which Weyr will place second and third," Lord Fenner told him with a twinkle in his eyes.

"If Telgar wins the last event, they'll have ten points, and the best Ista could get then would be second place in the event for a total of nine points," Kindan continued.

"And if either High Reaches or Benden wins the next event, they'll tie with Ista," Masterminer Britell noted.

"That won't happen," Lord Fenner declared stoutly.

"One thing's certain," Britell said, "the betting's going to be fierce."

Cristov, casting an eye over the crowd below and seeing how excitedly people were talking amongst themselves, silently agreed.

D'vin looked at the movement of the crowds far below him. He could see enough to spot bettors exchanging marks and wished he had a few to wager himself. Certainly things were interesting, and he was glad they were. Of all the events, the relay was his favorite—the one event he felt most tested a Weyr's true ability to fight Thread.

The first round of the relay would be nothing special: Three wings from each Weyr would fly against the rope Thread in rapid succession. It was the next round, when the queens spread out more and thickened the fall of Thread that things would start to get interesting.

Far below him, someone on the Lord Holder's stand waved Fort's flag. Nearby, a Fort dragon belched flame. The relay began.

Fort did well, as did all the other Weyrs, just as D'vin had expected. He turned back from his run on Hurth with all three wings of High Reaches dragons warbling in elation at their run. They'd done well.

The queens spread out more. And then Fort's flag was waved again for the next run.

Soon it would be High Reaches's turn.

Make sure everyone has enough firestone, D'vin reminded his dragon.

Telenth needs more, Hurth responded. D'vin craned around to spot the small blue and saw P'lel wave as a weyrling appeared from *between.*

Just as suddenly as the weyrling had appeared, there was a brilliant explosion by its side. The deafening sound shook the afternoon sky.

As D'vin's eyes recovered from the flash of the explosion, he saw that the weyrling had disappeared.

Where are they? D'vin asked Hurth.

They are gone.

"By the egg of Faranth!" Lord Fenner declared, staring in horror at the brilliant fireball above them.

"What happened?" Toldur asked.

"The firestone must have come in contact with some water," Britell said, shaking his head sorrowfully.

"It exploded?" Cristov asked. Britell could only nod, eyes wide with shock.

"And the dragon? The rider?" Cristov looked from the Masterminer to the Lord Holder, but the expressions of both were identical.

"At least it was quick," Fenner said somberly.

"They're dead?"

"Nasty stuff, firestone," Britell murmured, still shaking his head in disbelief. "The slightest bit of water and . . ."

All around him, dragons keened for the lost weyrling. D'vin shook his head angrily. *That* shouldn't have happened!

His thoughts returned to the instant, still seared in

his eyes, when the weyrling emerged from *between*, trying to see what had caused the explosion, but he couldn't. Firestone was too difficult, too impossible to handle. He could remember at least three times when the storage cavern at High Reaches had exploded.

It burns, Hurth agreed. D'vin nodded absently. The large bronze must have felt the movement of his rider's body on his neck, for he dropped his neck suddenly in an expression of irritation. *It burns* wrong.

D'vin cocked an eye down at the huge neck of his friend. Firestone had always been dangerous. He couldn't imagine how the dragons survived it and was appalled at the risks he'd taken as a weyrling when it had been his task to haul it to the older riders.

D'gan asks if you'll withdraw, Hurth reported.

Withdraw? D'vin shook his head angrily. What tribute would that be to the lost rider and dragon?

We will continue, D'vin replied. *Tell the rest of the flight.*

D'gan says good luck, Hurth told him.

D'vin looked over to where the Telgar flights were arrayed and gave them an exaggerated wave. Good luck, indeed!

Let's show them what High Reaches can do, D'vin told his dragon.

The crowd cheered encouragement as High Reaches began their next run. As the queens threw down a new hail of ropes, D'vin's wing raced forward, flaming it all to char, backed by High Reaches's other two wings.

They almost made it. Just at the end, two riders headed for the same cluster, missing a single clump that fell behind them. At D'vin's urging, Hurth dove toward the clump, but Hurth was out of flame and the clump fell, unburned, to the ground. Below him, the crowd groaned sympathetically.

Sorry, D'vin said to his dragon. *We tried.*

"That's a pity," Britell remarked, "but it's not unexpected."

Lord Fenner looked less sanguine, and the Masterminer gave him an inquiring look.

"I don't deny their prowess, nor that they've suffered a tragedy," the Lord Holder explained, "but I hope that the Weyrs can recover more quickly from their losses when Thread really *does* start to fall."

"I think they will, my lord," Kindan said from his place by the flags. "That's part of the purpose of these games, to train for the worst."

Fenner and Britell both nodded.

Cristov wasn't listening. He was too busy wondering why the dragons depended upon such a dangerous rock as firestone for their flame. Coal was bad enough, but something that exploded on contact with water was just incredible. How could anyone work with such a difficult mineral?

The explosion above the crowd was all Tenim needed to make his greatest theft of the day. He'd been by the Smithcrafthall tent early on and had spotted the lovely dirk set proudly on display—well guarded by no less than three apprentices.

"That?" A journeyman had said in response to his questioning. "That dirk's been made special for Lord D'gan, the Weyrleader himself."

It was a beauty, Tenim decided. Its hilt was decorated with several rare jewels and embossed with gold. The blade itself was sharp enough to cut wherhide, as was demonstrated by the proud Smiths. It was a valuable piece.

And Tenim wanted it. He had had too few pretty

things in the past several Turns. It was time his luck changed. And the explosion in the sky was all the change he needed.

In one swift moment he jostled against the apprentices, pocketed the dirk, and took off before anyone could react.

Far enough to be lost in the crowd, he flipped over his tunic and ruffled it up, while at the same time removing his cap and patting down his hair. He switched his belt around and changed the buckle for a Smithcraft piece. No one would recognize him now.

Yes, his luck had changed.

It was then that he spotted Cristov up in the Lord Holder's stand. Tenim's lips tightened and he frowned. He knew that Moran was hoping to use the lad the same way they'd used Tarik.

Tarik had cost him dear. Except for a quiet visit in the dark of the night, Tenim was certain that Tarik would have talked and cost Tenim even more dearly. Tenim was still not ready to have an "S" brushed on his head.

But the price had been the coal they'd stashed. It had taken little work on Tenim's part to expose it and break a trail that led to it, a trail marked only with Tarik's boot prints.

All the wood that Tarik had stashed had been found, too.

In the end all Tenim got for all his efforts was a small sack of coal, the only one he dared keep from the hoard that he and Tarik had laid down. The sack of coal hadn't been worth more than three marks.

Tenim had learned quickly enough that his final plan had been ruined by Cristov, when the boy had helped save Natalon. Tenim felt that he owed little Cristov—though he was no longer quite so little—the same treatment that his father had been given. Wouldn't it be fitting for Cristov to get the same blue "S" his father wore?

Yes, Tenim decided, nodding to himself, it would. He felt the dirk hidden under his tunic and smiled. He knew just how to do it. The dirk would be a small price for such a sweet revenge.

The horror of the weyrling's loss was soon overcome by the excitement of the last event of the Games. Ista had been eliminated in the first round, and High Reaches had fallen out at the second round. Fort, Benden, and Telgar competed with astonishing passes in the third round. It seemed as though the sky was alive with the rope Threads. The crowd gasped in regret when Fort was disqualified by a single Thread in the third round. The fourth round was only between Benden and Telgar.

"Telgar, without a doubt," Fenner declared loyally. Masterminer Britell nodded in agreement.

"It'd better be," Kindan quipped to Cristov with a grin. "I've heard that D'gan's commissioned a fancy dirk for himself as a reward."

"It's never a wise course to bet on your success," Toldur opined.

Kindan nodded, but added, "It'll be his solace if he loses."

"Oh, so he plans on the dirk either way?" Toldur asked. When Kindan nodded again, the older miner continued, "Then why does he wait for the outcome?"

"If he wins, he'll have Lord Fenner present it to him ceremoniously," Kindan said.

"And savor the reward all the more," Britell remarked.

"Look! Benden missed some!" Lord Fenner shouted, drawing them back to the event overhead.

"So Telgar's the winner," Cristov said.

"Only if they complete this round without letting Thread through," Kindan corrected, shaking his head. "Otherwise it's a tie."

"If they tie, they'll split the points and Telgar will win anyway," Britell noted.

Cristov frowned at that, while trying to do the math in his head. First place was worth five points and second place worth two, so Telgar would earn only three and a half points if they tied with Benden. Add that to the five points that Telgar already had for winning the wing event and Telgar would have eight and one half points. Ista had seven points and Benden would add three and a half to its two points, so neither would beat Telgar. Satisfied, he nodded in agreement.

"Did that without moving your lips," Britell said to Cristov with a smile. "I'm impressed."

Cristov turned red with embarrassment.

A cheer erupted around them and Cristov looked up. The skies were clear of the rope Thread. Telgar Weyr had won.

"Raise the Telgar flag," Fenner instructed, but Kindan was way ahead of him, raising and waving the Telgar flag to indicate the winner of the Games.

"D'gan will be well pleased," Britell said.

"And he'll get his dirk," Kindan said to Cristov with a smile and a broad wink.

Cristov smiled back, wondering what sort of dirk a Weyrleader would covet.

A crowd rushed toward the stand.

"Here comes D'gan!"

Some enthusiastic revelers rushed up onto the stand itself, pushed by the cheering crowd. Cristov was bowled over and had a hard time getting up, buried under the crush of several holders.

When Cristov stood up again, his clothes felt different, heavier. He started searching his clothing for what had changed.

"Cristov, stand up, D'gan's coming," Toldur hissed in warning.

Hastily Cristov straightened up and sidled over to Toldur, peering out over the stand to where the crowd had parted wide to let one group pass through.

The dragonriders all bore the strange, hot, burning smell of firestone and the lean look of those who'd mastered their craft. They looked haughty, proud, determined— and they had earned the right.

As D'gan stepped upon the platform, the holders and crafters in the Gather burst into cheers.

"Telgar! Telgar! Telgar!" they shouted.

D'gan nodded and waved at them, his face beaming with pride.

"Lord Fenner," D'gan called out, extending his hand imperiously. "Do you have something special to mark this occasion?"

Fenner turned to the group of smiths who were approaching and told D'gan, "I believe that the Smithcrafters of Telgar have created something special for you, Weyrleader."

"My lord," the eldest of the smiths called out, in despair, "it's been stolen!"

"Stolen?" D'gan cried in amazement.

Cristov suddenly identified the strange weight in his clothes. With a metallic clatter it fell to the ground.

"There it is!" one of the smith apprentices exclaimed, pointing to Cristov's feet.

Before Cristov could react, he found himself grabbed roughly from all sides.

D'gan strode over to him and bent to retrieve the dirk. He eyed it carefully for damage, then held it up, point first, under Cristov's chin.

"You dare steal from a dragonman?"

"No," Cristov said, shaking his head fiercely. "No, my lord. I never saw it before!"

"A likely tale!" someone from the crowd shouted. "Shun him!"

Halla heard Tenim shouting, "His father was Shunned, Shun him, too!" She followed his voice to spot him standing right before Lord Fenner's stand, urging the crowd on, and Halla knew that Tenim had planted the dirk on Cristov. Tenim glanced her way, smiled, and nodded evilly.

"Speak up if you want to join him," Tenim told her.

"He's innocent!" Halla shouted, but her small voice was lost in the crowd. Desperately, she strode forward to the steps and shouted once more, "He didn't do it!"

Tenim's gleeful look vanished from his face and he slipped back into the crowd. Even if she couldn't convince others, he didn't need Halla pointing her finger at him.

"Shun him!" the crowd shouted.

Up on the platform D'gan waved for silence. The crowd slowly subsided, pressing forward eagerly, sensing that the Weyrleader was ready to make a proclamation.

"He's innocent!" Halla shouted once more.

"Indeed, he is," a loud voice shouted from the back of the crowd. The crowd parted as another group of dragonriders strode through. Halla recognized D'vin.

"This is a Telgar matter," D'gan declared, turning away from D'vin.

"With all due respect, Weyrleader," D'vin replied, "it seems to me that this is a matter best left to the Lord Holder of Crom."

D'vin strode past Halla and up the steps to the platform. He turned to Fenner and pointed at Cristov. "My lord, I happen to know that this lad was here on the platform for the entire Gather, except when he accompanied me on your request. Is that not so?"

"Well, yes," Fenner replied, glancing uncomfortably at D'gan, "yes, he was." To D'gan, he explained, "Cristov and Toldur were invited to attend by Masterminer Britell."

"And why was that, miner?" D'gan demanded.

"I asked that they be here because they are being promoted in rank," Britell replied. "Toldur to Master and Cristov to journeyman."

"Is it your habit then, miner, to promote thieves?" D'gan ask in a vicious tone.

"No, it is not."

"Yet am I not correct in remembering that this lad's father was just recently Shunned?" D'gan continued. "And now we find him with this dirk, a dirk commissioned especially for me."

"There was a rush to the stands a while back," Toldur interjected. "Perhaps someone dropped the dirk then."

D'gan laughed. "That seems hard to believe!"

A throbbing sound overwhelmed Cristov. He was going to be Shunned. Shunned on the day he was to be made journeyman.

The throbbing grew. He looked around, aware that others had stopped speaking and were also looking around. A dragon bugled imperiously and the silence grew.

The throbbing remained. In the silence, Cristov recognized the sound as distant drumming. A nearer drum picked up the message and amplified it. And then another.

"Firestone mine number nine has exploded," Kindan reported.

"Number nine?" D'vin echoed, turning in alarm to D'gan. "Is that the last mine?"

D'gan sheathed the dirk in his hands and spun on one heel, shouting to his men, "To your dragons! To the mine!"

"I'll come!" D'vin shouted after him, jumping off the platform.

D'gan twirled back to glare at the younger dragonrider. "Stay where you are, High Reaches. This is a Telgar matter!"

And with that, he was gone.

D'vin turned to Masterminer Britell with a questioning look. "Shouldn't some of the miners go, too?"

Britell shook his head. "There were no miners at the firestone mine."

"Cristov," Kindan said softly, stepping close to him, "wasn't your father at that mine?"

Slowly, Cristov nodded.

Dragon fly, dragon flame,
Dragon char, dragon tame.
Rider watch, rider fight,
Rider aim, rider right.

Chapter Six

D'GAN SWORE as he circled down over the wreck of firestone mine #9. He swore at the miners, he swore at the Shunned, he swore at his luck. Hadn't everything been going too well? And now this!

The camp was a smoking ruin, all the firestone consumed in the explosion of the mine. A gaping hole in the side of the mountain was all that remained.

Firestone mine #8 had gone much the same way, although it had operated for nearly thirty Turns before disaster struck. Prior to that, well before D'gan's time, the records showed that the last mine, #7, had been completely mined of ore without incident for over a hundred Turns. Privately, D'gan wondered if the old Telgar records hadn't been altered to disguise some earlier mismanagement. He knew that such things happened. He certainly saw no reason to leave records over which his eventual successor might one day gloat.

Firestone mine #9 had lasted only two Turns. It had been hard enough to locate a new vein of firestone. Many Shunned had been killed in the search.

Well, D'gan thought to himself, there're plenty more scum to hand. His thoughts turned back to Tarik's son.

A movement caught Kaloth's eye, and the great dragon banked tighter, circling back. *There.*

I see it, D'gan answered. Covered in bits of wood and debris was the body of a man. It had moved. *Tell the others that we're landing.*

Kaloth obeyed, then circled in for a neat landing not far from the body.

"Over here," came a voice.

Great, D'gan thought, there's a survivor. His worries about finding someone with enough lore to locate firestone abated. His elation lasted only until he got a good look at the survivor.

"I know you," D'gan swore, pulling his dirk from belt and waving it threateningly, "You're Tarik. Your son tried to steal my dirk!"

Still in shock from the explosion, Tarik flinched and tried to scramble away from D'gan, but he was still pinned by wreckage.

"Over here!" D'gan shouted to his wingriders. Six of them ran over immediately. D'gan issued a crisp set of orders, and Tarik was freed from the rubble only to find himself restrained on either side by two burly dragonriders. D'gan strode up to him, toying thoughtfully with the dirk in his hand and eyeing Tarik with evident distaste.

"What happened here?" he asked, gesturing behind him at the ruin of the firestone mine.

"There was an explosion," Tarik replied. D'gan's eyes narrowed in a frown and he tightened his grip on the dirk. Hastily, Tarik added, "Someone kicked over a bucket of water. I tried to warn them, but it was too late. The mine exploded and blew me over here."

"What were you doing in the stocks?" D'gan asked, nodding toward the pile of rubble in which Tarik had been found. He watched Tarik's reaction shrewdly and noticed how the ex-miner's eyes widened in alarm, only to narrow again in calculation.

"I'm a miner; they wouldn't listen to me," Tarik said. "The foreman was afraid of me."

"If he was afraid of you, why didn't he kill you?" D'gan asked, advancing toward Tarik, dirk held tightly in his hand.

"He needed me," Tarik replied with an edge of desperation in his voice. "I know too much about mining."

At Tarik's words, D'gan paused. The miner had a point.

"Toss him that shovel," D'gan said to a wingman, gesturing for the ones holding the miner to release him.

As Tarik caught the shovel, D'gan sheathed his dirk and told the Shunned miner, "I'll be back in the morning for a hundredweight of firestone."

"A hundredweight?" Tarik protested. "But the mine's been destroyed!"

"Build another," D'gan commanded and turned away to his dragon.

"What about food?"

"Tomorrow," D'gan called over his shoulder. "You don't want to be wasting time on something that trivial today."

"But if I don't eat, I'll die," Tarik cried.

D'gan climbed up Kaloth's leg and vaulted into his position astride the bronze dragon's neck before responding. "If you don't have my firestone in the morning, I'll kill you, and then neither you nor I will have to worry about your belly."

"But—but who will mine for you then?" Tarik shouted back in terrified amazement.

"The Shunned," D'gan replied. "There's plenty of them, as you well know."

Before Tarik could muster another protest, D'gan and his wing of dragons leapt into the air and disappeared *between*.

The wing reappeared over Crom Hold an instant

later. The moment Kaloth touched ground, D'gan leaped off, ordering his dragon back into the air so that the rest of his wingriders could assemble behind him. With gratifying speed and precision, his wingriders formed silently behind him and D'gan strode off briskly, heading back to Lord Holder Fenner and the others who were still on the platform. Waiting respectfully, as they should, D'gan noted to himself.

His face tightened when he caught sight of Tarik's brat. The brat had blond hair and blue eyes, while Tarik had both brown hair and eyes, but the shape of the face was the same.

Same vapid look, D'gan thought to himself. Same whining ways.

With a nod to himself, D'gan decided that the boy was as guilty as the father. Justice would be served.

"There were no survivors," D'gan said. "The mine was totally destroyed." He let that sink in for a moment before adding, "It looks like the miner caused the explosion. Sheer carelessness, overturned a water bucket. We won't be getting any more firestone."

This last he said with a sly look at D'vin and a sharp cut of his eyes to Tarik's brat.

Only the Shunned worked the firestone mines. Why not arrange to have two miners and two mines? The idea appealed to D'gan not just for its redundancy but also for its efficiency—if both son and father died in the mines, then D'gan was doing all Pern a favor, weeding out a bad bloodline. And if they survived, Pern would benefit from the protection their labors helped provide. Yes, he told himself, a good solution.

He turned his attention to Fenner. "We'll need new miners."

Lord Fenner and Masterminer Britell exchanged a quick, worried look.

"My Lord D'gan—" Britell began, only to be cut off by D'gan's upraised hand.

"You can start with him," D'gan said, pointing at Cristov, setting off a cacophony of protests.

"It's not clear . . ." Britell protested.

"I'm sure he didn't do it," D'vin declared.

"The matter shall have to be decided," Fenner said.

"I'll do it," Cristov said. The others looked at him in shock. He waved aside Toldur's unvoiced objections and the worried look of the Masterminer. "I'll go in my father's place. He destroyed the mine. Pern needs the firestone."

D'vin had been watching D'gan carefully and now spoke up. "The mine was destroyed?"

D'gan nodded absently, savoring the look of misery on the brat's face. He *should* be ashamed, he thought, with a father Shunned.

He is not bad, Kaloth remarked from up on the fire-heights, punctuating his thought with a low rumble.

It's for the good of Pern, D'gan responded, wondering what in the name of the Shell of Faranth had prompted his dragon to make such an observation.

D'vin glanced up at rumbling from D'gan's bronze and made a snap judgment. "Cristov can mine at High Reaches."

"High Reaches?" D'gan snorted in disgust. "No one's ever mined firestone there."

"There is firestone at High Reaches," Kindan piped up suddenly. Britell and D'vin turned to him questioningly. "I remember from a map at the Harper Hall."

In response to their surprised looks, Kindan added, "I recall large areas in the mountains, mostly to the north by the sea."

D'vin extended a hand to Cristov with a firm nod. "So, Journeyman Cristov, will you mine for High Reaches?"

"Yes, my lord," Cristov said in a daze.

"No!" D'gan exclaimed angrily. "He should stay here!"

Lord Fenner looked at the Weyrleader consideringly. "Granted that you have a grievance with the lad, wouldn't it be better all around to give him a chance to prove himself outside the lands that look to you?"

D'gan gave Crom's Lord Holder a sour look followed by a curt nod, which he repeated to Masterminer Britell. He snorted at D'vin and turned to leave, only to turn back to Toldur, who had been watching the events intently. "What about you? Would you mine firestone?"

Toldur lined up beside Cristov with a firm nod, saying, "I will, my lord."

D'gan was elated with his response. He held out a hand invitingly.

Toldur shook his head regretfully.

"I will stay with Cristov, my lord." He nodded at the startled youngster and gave him a reassuring smile. He glanced at D'vin then turned to D'gan. "We miners take care of our own. Journeyman Cristov will need a Master's instruction."

"Well said, well said!" Britell exclaimed, nodding fiercely.

"What about Alarra?" Cristov asked, referring to Toldur's mate.

"I would like to have her join us," Toldur said, looking inquiringly toward D'vin, and then back to Cristov, as he added, "But not until we've got a proper house for her."

"I can arrange a dispatch to Camp Natalon," Britell offered.

D'gan's eyes flicked angrily from Toldur to the other men before settling on Fenner.

"I'll need more men to start a mine," D'gan told him.

"Wouldn't it make more sense to get men for Cristov, my lord?" Fenner said.

"High Reaches can fill his needs," D'gan snapped. He pointed to the hills in the distance, saying, "*I* want men for a mine there."

He turned to the others. "I think it's a good idea to start two mines, so that we don't find ourselves without firestone when Pern most needs it."

"There is that," Fenner said, glancing to Britell and the others. Then he shook himself and said regretfully, "But I've no Shunned at the moment. Perhaps you might find some at Telgar Hold, my lord."

D'gan scowled.

"I should get going," D'vin said. He glanced back at Toldur and Cristov. "Would you care to come with me now or later?"

"I think now would be best," Masterminer Britell said, nodding firmly. He looked at Toldur, adding, "There's an extra hour of sun at High Reaches—it would give you a better chance to get settled today."

D'gan hissed but said nothing, stomping off toward his wing, circling his arm over his head in an ancient gesture. Over his shoulder, he shouted to Fenner, "Start the victory ceremonies."

"As you wish, my lord," Fenner said with a bow. Turning to Kindan, he said, "Kindan, place the banners in their order."

Kindan first picked Fort Weyr's banner, raised it high, waved it from side to side, and then placed it in the fifth-rank stand. The Gather crowd clapped politely. Kindan next picked High Reaches Weyr's banner and, after the flourish, placed it in the fourth-rank stand. The crowd again applauded politely.

As Kindan reached Benden Weyr's banner, Fenner raised a hand and told him, "Wait a moment, lad. Some of the bettors are a bit drink-fuddled."

A momentary look of puzzlement crossed Kindan's face to be replaced by a smile of understanding—not everyone of the Gather crowd would have figured out the final rankings, so Lord Fenner was giving the gamblers a bit of suspense.

After a long moment during which the noise from the crowd changed from one of excitement to one of confusion, Fenner waved a hand at Kindan, saying, "I think now will be good enough."

With a nod, Kindan picked up Benden's banner, to the murmured approval of the crowd, waved it overhead, and placed it in the third-place stand. The crowd clapped approvingly. Their applause grew when Kindan repeated the performance with Ista's banner.

"Now watch them go *really* wild," Fenner said as he nodded to Kindan to proclaim the winning Weyr.

As Kindan raised the Telgar Weyr banner, the crowd erupted in a huge roar of approval that seemed to go on forever. Only when it finally died down could the sound of the crowd's clapping hands be heard. Slowly the applause died away, only to rise again to a new crescendo as all the dragons of Telgar Weyr, in fighting formation, flew a low circuit of honor over the Gather grounds, while the dragons of the four other Weyrs kept station far above them. When they completed their circuit, the dragons from fifth-placed Fort Weyr vanished *between*.

The dragons of Telgar Weyr continued their circuit three more times; at the end of the second circuit, fourth-placed High Reaches vanished *between*, at the end of the third circuit, third-placed Benden Weyr went *between*, and, finally, at the end of the fourth circuit, second-placed Ista Weyr departed.

The dragons of Telgar Weyr performed one final lap and then, they, too, went *between* with a huge, resounding explosion of sound.

As the last echo died away, Cristov felt as though he'd woken from a dream.

"Well, that's that," Lord Fenner said, "at least until the next Turn."

As dawn broke over the surrounding hills, the unmistakable sound of dragons coming from *between* erupted over the remains of firestone mine #9.

Tarik looked up at the sound and was not surprised to see a full wing of thirty dragons descending toward him. He identified D'gan in the forefront. Wearily he raised an arm and waved at the dragonriders as they landed. He swallowed nervously when their dragons took station on the hilltops and valley exits, but then schooled his expression to project a calm he didn't feel.

As D'gan strode directly toward him, his wingriders arrayed themselves in a circle, cutting off any chance for Tarik to escape. D'gan's hand hovered over his dirk.

"Your son knows that you're dead now, Shunned one," D'gan said, his eyes looking hard for Tarik's reaction.

Tarik merely grunted, in a response that grated on D'gan's nerves.

"Where's the firestone?"

Tarik bowed low, gesturing behind him with one arm. "Over there, Weyrleader."

D'gan nodded to one of his men, who strode off and quickly located a mound of filled sacks.

"Two hundredweight of firestone," Tarik added, rising slightly from his bow, his eyes just avoiding D'gan's.

"Two hundredweight?" D'gan exclaimed derisively. "No man can mine two hundredweight in a single day." He drew his dirk and advanced on Tarik. "You're a liar just like your son."

"Weyrleader!" the detailed dragonrider shouted.

"There's over two hundredweight of high quality fire-stone here!"

D'gan halted, his menacing look replaced by one of surprise. With a curt nod to Tarik, he said, "Explain."

Tarik straightened some more, still careful to keep himself slightly hunched in obeisance. With a wave of his hand around the ruins, he explained, "My lord, I could not find a suitable site for a new mine. However, I was able to recover some firestone from the ruin of the mine and the storage shed."

D'gan pursed his lips, his brows furrowed in angry contemplation of the useless man standing in front of him. With a lunge, he swung, hitting the Shunned miner with an open backhand. Tarik recoiled, his eyes wide with a mix of fear and anger.

With a wave to his riders, D'gan ordered, "Take the firestone."

"My lord?" Tarik inquired obsequiously. D'gan favored him with a glare. Tarik licked his cut lip before continuing. "I know where you can get more firestone."

D'gan gave the Shunned miner a considering look and frowned. "Where?"

"Near Keogh," Tarik said quickly. "Still in Crom lands, but high up in the north hills."

"And how do you know this?"

Tarik looked to the ground, acting subservient while hiding the triumphant gleam in his eyes. "I came across it when I was looking for more coal mine sites," he muttered.

"Coal and firestone are never found together."

"As I discovered, my lord," Tarik quickly replied. "At the time I hadn't seen firestone, but I learned that any prospect that included it was not a good prospect for a seam of coal."

He risked an upward glance to gauge D'gan's response and continued, "I know exactly where it was. And it was a large site, a full valley."

"Hmm," D'gan murmured. "In Keogh, you say?"

"Near it," Tarik said. "It was difficult to locate— barely accessible—but I'm sure I could find it again."

"And you'd have to be on foot to find it, wouldn't you?" D'gan asked suspiciously. "And the ranges over there are so steep that anyone could get lost without much trouble. Is that what you were hoping?"

"No, my lord," Tarik protested quickly, waving his hands in supplication. "Nothing of the sort. I couldn't find the site on dragonback, but once found, you'd have no problems flying in."

D'gan snorted. Cocking an eyebrow at Tarik, he said, "So you're asking us to trust you."

"If you please," Tarik said, lowering his head once again.

"And what is your price, nameless one?" D'gan demanded, knowing very well what the miner would ask.

Tarik straightened and looked D'gan square in the eyes. "My name and life."

D'gan shook his head. "Your life you left when you were Shunned and marked with the blue 'S.'"

"My name, then," Tarik responded, slumping once again, his voice barely more than a whisper. "And to be foreman."

"Ah!" D'gan exclaimed, tossing his head. "Now we see your true price. You would want to be master to others."

"I was a miner, my lord," Tarik said. "If I could mine your stone, I'd be a miner again."

D'gan gave Tarik a long searching look. The miner was hiding something, he was certain. Still . . . the notion had possibilities.

"If you desert us, the dragons will be able to hunt you down," he warned.

"I had guessed, Weyrleader," Tarik replied.

D'gan nodded slowly, his lips still pursed thought-fully. "And how many men would you need?"

"It would depend upon the richness of the vein, and of your needs," Tarik told him, knowing that D'gan already knew that. Seeing D'gan's eyes narrow angrily, he added hastily, "With eight men, I could have a mine producing a hundredweight of firestone every day within two sevendays."

D'gan snorted. "I'll give you four men, and a sevenday."

Tarik bit off an angry protest, let out his hastily drawn breath in a slow sigh, and nodded. "As you wish, Weyrleader."

"Yes," D'gan said, steel in his voice. "As I say." He wagged a finger at Tarik. "And remember, nameless one, that if I wish, I can leave you to the wild, or take you to the sea and let you swim for your life. For you're Shunned and no man will lift a hand to help you."

Tarik swallowed angrily, his eyes lowered, and nodded in resignation.

"I'm glad that we understand each other," D'gan responded with the cold of *between* in his voice.

Tarik kept his head lowered until he was ordered onto the back of a green dragon. He looked up only once the dragons rose into the air, and his eyes were gleaming in triumph.

Even though he had two purses filled to near bursting, Tenim's earnings weren't enough. Especially if he was to share them with Moran and the harper's starving brats. Sure, Moran had fed him and reared him ever since he'd found him, but the price had been paid; he was ready to move on. Large numbers attracted attention, and too many might remember him with Milera.

No, it was best, Tenim decided, to finally part ways. He glanced around to be certain that none of Moran's brats were in sight, particularly the nosy Halla, and started to fade into the deepening night.

He had no idea where he would go next, not that—with both purses so full—he would have to worry about food or lodging.

He was about to set his course when he noticed a disturbance over the hills in the distance. North of Keogh were the unmistakable signs left by dragons' coming from the cold of *between* into the warmer moist evening air.

Why would dragons head there? Tenim wondered. They would have to be Telgar dragons; D'gan would permit no interlopers. Tenim frowned, wondering what could be keeping the Telgar riders from their victory celebrations.

What, Tenim decided with narrowing eyes, but finding firestone?

Word of the disaster had fanned throughout the Gather and the drums had spread the word throughout Pern. Tenim guessed that the dragonriders, particularly D'gan, would be desperate to found a new mine immediately. From all he'd heard after the disaster with the firestone and the weyrling, Tenim knew that the Weyrs stored only the barest minimum of firestone—no more than that needed for a sevendays' worth of training.

If the Weyrs were without firestone, what would they pay to get it? His musing look grew more contemplative. D'gan had been stingy with the rations. What would the other Weyrs pay for extra?

Certainly far more than for coal at the start of a cold winter. With a calculating frown, Tenim set off in the direction of the dragon sign.

*   *   *

"He's gone," Halla told Moran as the last of the small ones reported in to her. "We should be going soon."

Moran turned slowly around the churned field that had earlier that day been thronged full of spectators recovering from their revelries of the night before. Gone? Moran had never considered that Tenim would leave. What would the lad do without him?

"Moran," Halla said urgently, "we have to find a place for the small ones to sleep soon." She waved at hand toward two of the toddlers. "They'll fall over soon enough, and the ground's too cold and moist."

Where had the lad gone? Moran wondered again, ignoring Halla's pleading tone. He made another long, slow, scan of the grounds. In the far distance, he spotted a pinprick of light—a wood fire in the distance, toward Keogh.

Tenim had been evasive when asked about Milera, and violently abrupt when questioned about his whereabouts. Moran had known that the lad had spent the time since then attempting to locate Aleesa's wherhold. As long as Moran controlled the purse strings, Tenim stayed close by. And that was as Moran preferred it. He needed the lad's greater speed and strength to protect the small ones, just as he needed Tenim's quick fingers to provide the marks needed to feed these small outcasts of Pern. If Tenim were gone, Moran worried, how would the children be fed?

What if—and Moran's stomach shrank in fear—Tenim had decided to find the wherhold, and had left him with the children in order to slow him down? Would Moran find the wherhold a ruin littered with shattered remains? He shuddered. Aleesk was the last gold on Pern. If anything happened to her, there would be no more watch-whers.

He turned to Halla. "I have to go."

"Go?" Halla repeated, alarmed at the harper's tone. "Go where? What about the children?"

Halla was still a child, Moran told himself, glancing down to meet the challenge in her upturned eyes. Her brown eyes blazed at him, full of determination.

A child, yes, Moran thought to himself, but she's been mother to so many that she's a child only if measured by Turns.

A part of Moran shrank at that assessment. Well, no matter. He would not let Tenim's greed destroy the dragons' cousins.

"You can take care of them, I'm sure," he told her. "You've always done so."

"And where will you be?" Halla demanded.

"I'll be back in a sevenday, not much more," Moran responded evasively. He unhitched his purse and tossed the sack to her. Halla caught it easily. "That should be enough until I'm back."

Halla weighed the purse in her hand. "There's more than a sevenday's worth here."

"Extra, just to be sure," Moran replied lightly, hoisting his sack to his shoulders. As he strode away, he called back over his shoulder, "Anyway, it's safer with you."

Halla glared at the harper's back, her mind full of guesses at the reason for his sudden desertion. Then one of the smaller children started whining, and Halla found herself engulfed in the issues of dealing with eight small ones all by herself. She hefted the purse once more and scanned the now empty field. The lights of Crom Hold burned bright in the cliffs above her. Decisively, Halla started chivvying the children toward the Hold's walls.

"What are you doing out this late?" a voice called from in front of her an hour later. Halla's feet were sore from stomping on the hard-packed road that led up from the foothills into Crom Hold proper. She had one of the smallest perched on her shoulders, another held to her side, and a third dangling off her free hand.

"We're looking for lodging for the night," she said, working to deepen her voice. The effect was not quite what she'd hoped.

"Where are your parents, lad?" the guard asked, angling a glowlight down to shed its eerie glowing green light on them. He peered closely at Halla. "Why, you're just a girl!"

Just a girl! Halla bristled and bit back a quick retort.

"Where are your parents?" the guard asked suspiciously, glancing at the small children draped around her. "What are these young ones doing out so late?" he added with a shake of his finger, "You're sure to get a tanning, missy."

"If you please, we've lost our parents," Halla said, picking up on the guard's guess.

"You have, have you?" The guard bent over to peer more critically at Halla. With one hand he reached down and swept her hair off her forehead, looking for the telltale blue "S" of the Shunned. Halla suppressed a shriek, the image of the outraged holders from two Turns back suddenly in her mind.

"Maybe you have at that," the guard allowed. He stood upright, drew his dirk, and beat a quick tattoo with it on his shield.

"We'll let the guard captain deal with you," he told Halla, sheathing his dirk once more. "If you're lucky, he'll let you go with no more than a scolding."

"I hope so," Halla said fervently.

"You'd better," the guard agreed. "Elsewise you're likely to be seeing Lord Holder Fenner himself. He'll not appreciate being disturbed this late at night."

Halla was not lucky. An hour later she found herself wrapped in a blanket with a mug of warm milk, perched on the far end of one of the great tables in Lord Holder Fenner's Great Hall, small children nestled all around her.

When Lord Fenner entered the room, dressed in his nightrobe, Halla's heart skipped at the sight of his angry, stiff expression.

"Out at night!" he bellowed, waking the smaller children who started whimpering fearfully. He stormed up to Halla and wagged a finger down imperiously over her.

"Your parents must be frantic. My captain has told me that you've refused to name them. That's all the worse for you, for now you have not only them to deal with but me as well." He paused to see how his words registered with Halla, and then his expression changed to one of confusion. "I've seen you before," he declared. "Where was it?"

"I was at the Gather, my lord," Halla mumbled, her insides shivering as the Lord Holder's angry intensity overwhelmed her.

"I *know* you were at the Gather," Fenner barked, waking up the rest of the children. Startled, and sensing Halla's fear, they began to cry quietly.

Tears started in Halla's eyes. Tears of fear, tears of sorrow, tears of rage.

"Wait a minute," Fenner said, kneeling beside her and peering close at her dirt-stained face. "You're that girl Cristov pointed out. The one that found the bubbly pies."

He looked past her to the sobbing youngsters. He raised a hand and told his guards, "Get someone to settle them in a guest room."

The children's wails rose as the guards tried to remove them from Halla, and Halla grabbed at them impulsively.

"No, no, no," Fenner told her irritably. "No one's going to hurt them."

"Where are they going?" Halla demanded, rising to her feet, her eyes flashing a challenge at the towering guards and darting around the Great Hall searching for avenues of escape. But it was futile. The guards were too many, too big, and Lord Fenner stood directly in her way.

"Halla!" Fenner declared, his face brightening in memory. "That's your name. I remember now." He noticed that Halla was still resisting the guards' attempts to pick up the other children.

"No, no, leave off that!" he scolded her. "They're only taking them to bed. You'd think they were going to be Shunned the way you're—" Fenner abruptly stopped speaking, his gaze intent on Halla's forehead. Slowly, almost apologetically, he reached out his hand and parted her hair. He grunted to himself when he saw that she was unmarked. Halla's relief was short-lived, however, for Fenner's eyes narrowed again critically.

"A number of Turns ago," Fenner began slowly, "there was a theft and attempted murder at Three Rivers." He watched Halla carefully. "And a girl matching your description was caught. The crowd was ready to mark her Shunned, but she escaped."

Halla swallowed hard and lowered her head. She *knew* that she would never escape the mark, the sign of those to whom no aid would ever again be given. Her parents had been Shunned; Halla had expected no other fate. Turned from hold, turned from craft, how long could she survive in the wild by herself?

"Please," Halla said in a whisper, tears streaming down her face. "The little ones. They did nothing."

Halla started as Fenner's strong hands grabbed her. Would the Lord Holder strangle her here and now? she wondered frantically, clawing at him with all her might.

Maybe if she broke free she could rescue the others, too.

"*Stop* struggling!" Fenner's voice boomed over her. Halla went limp, sobs wracking her small body, eyes scrunched tightly closed. She felt herself being lifted. Huge arms wrapped around her and hugged her tight. Was he going to crush her in his arms? Halla wondered anxiously. She squirmed once more.

"I said, stop," Fenner growled. "By the First Egg," he continued almost to himself, "it's as though you expected me to Shun you on sight."

The impact of his words registered in his ears and he peered down at the figure shaking in his arms.

"It's all right," he told her soothingly. "It's all right, little one."

Some inner flame, some core of her being flared to life inside Halla once more and she looked up, eyes glaring, and declared, "I'm not little."

"Yes, yes, of course," Fenner agreed hastily. "Why, you must be all of—nine Turns."

"I've twelve Turns," Halla growled back defiantly.

"No!" Fenner responded, his heart sinking. The child in his arms was light for nine, skeletal for twelve. He looked down at her and wrapped a large hand against the back of her neck, pulling her head gently toward his chest. "Why, my youngest is the same age as you."

Lord Fenner had children? Halla found herself wondering, her neck still resisting his insistent hand.

Fenner let go of her head and looked down at her, telling her frankly, "I haven't hugged anyone your size in Turns. Would you humor me?"

He smiled down ingratiatingly at her, making his eyes go wide and waggling his eyebrows. He kept his bright blue eyes focused on her warm brown ones until he felt her relax, and then he gently pulled her head against his chest. With a contented sigh, he started rocking from side to side.

"We can talk in the morning," he said softly, still rocking. "After you've eaten."

Her fragile reserves of energy all consumed by her previous struggles and desperate panic, Halla felt a warm lassitude spread over her. She nodded muzzily in agreement. Yes, morning would be good.

Slowly Lord Fenner carried Halla to the sleeping chambers where the other youngsters had been sent. As he walked, he hummed contentedly to himself. By the time he got to the bedroom, Halla was fast asleep, lips curved in a soft smile.

Lord Holder, your role is assured.
Lead the hold, help all endure.
Set the pace and show no slacking;
Let the lazy ones go packing.

Chapter Seven

WHEN HALLA WOKE the next morning, she gasped in surprise. She was in a bed with fresh sheets. She shouldn't be in a bed, she was too dirty!

Memories rushed back, and Halla struggled to get out from under the sheets only to discover that she was surrounded by the warm bodies of the children Moran had placed in her care. It took several moments of careful maneuvering before she could extricate herself, leaving the sleeping children behind. She spared only a moment for her embarrassment when she discovered that she had on only her undergarments—blushing red at the thought of Lord Fenner skinning her out of her dirt-encrusted tunic—before locating a huge plush towel and wrapping it around her.

She listened at the door for a moment before opening it swiftly, hoping to catch anyone outside off guard.

"Daddy said you'd be up by now," a girl down the corridor called out to her. The girl looked like a thinner, smaller version of Lord Fenner, only with blond hair instead of brown and eyes, that if anything, sparkled more than those of Crom's Lord Holder.

The girl bore down on Halla and held out her hand. "I'm Nerra."

Awkwardly Halla took the proffered hand.

"Are you hungry?" Nerra asked and Halla saw that she carried a basket in her other hand. "I've got some rolls, but not much fruit and all of it dried."

"Dried fruit would be nice, my lady," Halla said, trying her best to imitate the curtsies she'd seen Hold ladies use.

Nerra smiled so widely that her face dimpled. "Oh, but the rolls are fresh and I've got butter."

"Fresh?" Halla repeated blankly.

"Cook told me to bring them specially," Nerra said. She gestured back to some distant spot in the large Hold. "She said I was to feed you before your bath and to watch the children if they woke." Her face fell as she confided, "I don't know how I'll manage eight."

"I can have a bath?" Halla repeated, her skin crawling with excitement at the very notion. She turned her head to peer around the hallway. "Where is the bucket?"

"Bucket!" Nerra snorted. "We don't have a bucket, we have a bath room."

"A whole room?" Halla exclaimed, eyes wide.

"Certainly," Nerra replied in a surprised tone. She gestured back to the room. "But first we should eat."

And so, twenty minutes later, Halla found herself lowering her small, lean frame into a whole tub of warm water. She came out again only when she heard Nerra's frantic knocking, and the other girl's frantic cry, "Help, they're all over the place!"

Halla found herself issuing orders to the Lord Holder's daughter and the Hold guards while clad only in a pair of thick, plush towels. Soon, to Nerra's obvious amazement, she had restored order and got the two younger ones into a bath where, after several moments of panic, they were now happily splashing, cavorting, and thoroughly drenching the guard captain.

Much later the guard captain, properly dried off, escorted Halla once more into the Great Hall, with Nerra chatting away happily at her side.

Halla felt nervous in the rich surroundings and the old clothes Nerra had loaned her.

"Don't worry, he's not the growler he pretends," Nerra whispered to Halla, stopping, and—suddenly all formal—curtsying to her father.

"Greetings, my lord," she said, doing nothing to ease Halla's fears. "I bring the prisoner for your judgment."

Prisoner? Halla's eyes widened and she found herself once again searching for the best exit from the Great Hall.

"What are her crimes?" Fenner called out from his seat at the end of the hall.

"Complicity in theft, flight from a crime," Nerra replied formally. Quietly, in a totally different tone, she confided to Halla, "But I told him you didn't do it."

"Lady Nerra, please stick to the forms," Fenner growled in exasperation.

Nerra gave her father a grumpy look but nodded. "What is your pleasure, my lord?"

"The rule of Crom lands rests with the Lord of Crom," Fenner intoned severely. He crooked a finger at Halla, beckoning her forward. With a slight push from Nerra, Halla found herself walking down the long way to the Lord Holder's chair.

When she was directly in front of him, Fenner held up a hand for her to stop.

"What is your hold?" he asked her, his tone still formal.

Halla shook her head in silence.

"What is your craft?"

Again Halla shook her head.

"So you claim no hold or craft?" Fenner asked, his tone full of solemn disapproval.

"None, my lord," Halla said honestly, her arms hanging limply at her side. He had seemed so nice, too.

"And did you steal as accused?"

"No," Halla answered honestly.

"Were you not identified as a thief and nearly Shunned?" Fenner asked, leaning forward to gaze directly into her eyes.

"Yes."

"How plead you?" Fenner asked solemnly.

Plead? Halla looked at him questioningly. She shifted on her foot nervously. Was she supposed to beg for her life? Or did he expect her to tell him that Milera was the thief? If Milera ever found out—and Halla wondered where she'd been so long—she'd choke her for sure.

"Not guilty," Nerra whispered stridently to her. Halla turned to face her with a questioning look. "Say 'not guilty,' " Nerra whispered again.

"Not guilty," Halla said. Hastily she added, "My lord."

"Good," Nerra murmured approvingly. "Now demand justice."

Halla nodded and swallowed. "My lord, I demand justice."

"In what name?"

"My name. Halla."

"Very well," Fenner replied. "Justice is asked and will be given."

He closed his eyes for a moment in thought. When he opened them again he looked straight at Halla.

"The issues against Halla of no hold are dropped," he declared. "The judgment is that the children traveling with you will become fosterlings of Crom Hold, under my protection until they come of age."

Halla opened her mouth to form a protest, but Nerra

nudged her foot so sharply that Halla was afraid for her balance.

After a moment of silence, Lord Fenner looked up at Halla again and smiled. "Well, now that that's done, I think it's time for some lunch, don't you?"

Halla could only nod in shock.

Moments later she found herself seated at the great table in the kitchen while Nerra bustled about, arranging for the feeding of the eight new fosterlings.

"I swear that I'll treat them as my own," Fenner said when he caught Halla glancing nervously at the children. Once he was certain that she had heard him, he allowed himself to cast a glance at the eight youngsters, the newest additions to Crom Hold. They were all very thin and haggard. Fenner hoped that they would fill out with enough food. "I'm surprised they survived."

"Not all did," Halla admitted in a dull voice, her thoughts full of shallow graves and yellow flowers.

"Why did you not ask for the mercy of the Lord Holder?" Fenner asked, his face full of honest curiosity.

Halla flushed and shook her head. "I didn't know."

"Who was with you before?" Nerra asked. Halla gave her a startled look which Nerra waved aside. "You were little once; someone had to look out for you."

Hastily, Halla sought a safe answer. "My brother, Jamal."

"What happened to him?"

"He broke his leg and it got infected."

"So where is he?" Nerra asked, glancing around as if expecting to see him any moment.

"He died three Turns ago," Halla replied.

"Then he wasn't the last one to help you," Fenner declared. "Who was?"

Halla pursed her lips tightly. Fenner reached over and lifted her chin lightly with his forefinger until her eyes met his. "I have a reason for asking," he told her. "I am trying to contact the Shunned, you see."

Halla gave him a startled look. Why would a Lord Holder want to contact the very people he'd Shunned?

"Thread will be coming soon," Lord Fenner said in answer to her unspoken question. "I think now is the right time to set aside lands for the Shunned and give them the right to hold what they can."

Halla blinked in surprise, crying, "But they're Shunned!"

"Some I've Shunned myself," Fenner confessed. "When I can see a way, I let holders and crafters be. For murder, repeated manslaughter, repeated theft, even sheer laziness, I have to consider the good of all."

He pointed to the ceiling. "Thread is coming back. We need to start storing the food we can now in case we aren't so prosperous in future Turns. That way we'll have sufficient in reserve for any disaster Thread might inflict on us."

He sighed and spread his hands, indicating his entire hold. "I can't ask one man to toil in the hot sun when another does nothing."

"What if one man has no tools?" Halla asked. "Or his fields are full of rocks?"

"We give him tools, and we all work to clear the rocks from fields," Fenner said. "When Thread comes, we will all need everything we can get—shorting one man makes no sense."

Halla nodded, wondering why Moran hadn't told her this. Of course, she thought sourly, he was a fat man.

"But if you give them tools, wouldn't that make you Shunned also?" Halla asked after a thoughtful silence.

"Before that, we have to contact them," Fenner said, "which is where you come in."

Halla was surprised and it showed.

"I'd like you to contact those of the Shunned who are

willing to settle," Fenner told her. Halla looked questioningly at him. He nodded. "You are young enough to present no threat and bright enough to know when to speak.

"And the Traders speak highly of you," he added, smiling at Halla's look of surprise. "As Lord Holder, I am supposed to know what goes on in my Hold."

"He does, believe me," Nerra added fervently.

Fenner waved at his daughter for silence; to Halla's eyes, the gesture spoke of an affection greater than she'd ever seen.

"But I'm only a little girl," Halla protested feebly.

"Yes," Fenner agreed, eyeing her carefully. "I suppose you are."

Halla caught the challenge in his tone and her face flashed with anger.

"I'll do it," she told him defiantly.

"But you're right, you are young," Fenner responded.

"Don't push it, Father," Nerra said acerbically. "She's agreed to go."

Fenner smiled at Halla. "I'd hoped you would."

"We'll have to go higher, my lord," Toldur called to D'vin from behind the dragonrider as they flew over the precipitous mountains north of the High Reaches. "I can still smell the sea."

In front of him, D'vin nodded, and Hurth suddenly banked and veered inland.

Cristov was wedged in between the bronze rider and Toldur, still somewhat in shock at the speed with which events had moved. It had taken less than a day to gather tools, maps, and equipment, and it had taken only three short seconds to move halfway across the continent from Crom Hold to High Reaches Weyr.

There, Toldur and Cristov met with B'ralar, the Weyrleader, to discuss their plans. Cristov took the time to stroll around the Weyr, examining dragons and quarters with nearly equal interest, marveling at how the ancient builders had managed to produce such straight, smooth corridors, at the size of the individual weyrs, and at the sheer bustle and energy of everyone in the Weyr.

He was even more impressed and somewhat daunted by the tour of the firestone caves, especially when he was told that the replacement cave had taken the weyrfolk three Turns to construct. Another cave was a mere open sore at the base of the Weyr—testament to the power of firestone and its combustibility.

It took another hour for Toldur and Cristov, referring to the wind-rattled map, to find a suitable place for mining. Once they'd settled on a location, it took mere seconds for Hurth to land them and their supplies.

"I'll be up to check on you every day," D'vin promised. "Let me know if you need help."

"Certainly," Toldur said, waving a thanks to the dragonrider. "We'll have our first site by noon tomorrow."

After D'vin departed, Cristov and Toldur selected a suitably flat site and set up a hasty camp under a rock outcropping. The two collected kindling and larger branches and quickly built a roaring fire. As the night wore on, Cristov grew increasingly grateful for the fire's warmth and light.

"It's colder up here than at Crom," Toldur observed as he slipped into his sleeproll. "We'll need to be careful if snow comes."

Cristov grunted in agreement, too tired and wound up to talk. He was soon asleep.

"This is a bad time to mine," Toldur remarked the next morning as they chipped cautiously away at the grass and soil covering a nearly sheer cliff. Toldur frowned as a drizzle of dirt rained down on him from above.

"At least the ground's soaked enough to keep the dirt from sliding too much," Cristov said as the slide tapered off.

Toldur frowned, shaking his head. "I'm not sure I like the idea of wet soil meeting firestone."

They peered at the bare rock their labors had exposed and smiled.

"There's a clay layer here," he said happily. "It would protect any firestone beneath it."

Cristov nodded, looking at the exposed rock for the telltale dark gray and dark yellow crystals. When he found a candidate, he would silently point it out to Toldur. Four times he pointed, and four times Toldur shook his head. When he pointed for the fifth time, Toldur nodded, saying, "It looks like it to me, too."

Toldur gingerly tapped a small section out of the hillside. Cristov caught the shards as they fell, grateful that he and Toldur had found a creosote bush nearby in the valley. They'd rubbed their hands on it to stop their palms from sweating, a precaution they'd learned from the Weyrlingmaster at High Reaches.

They took their samples over to a nearby stream.

"Ready," Toldur said, eyeing the stream carefully and nodding to Cristov. Cristov tossed the contents of the bucket into the stream. Toldur peered intently for telltale signs of gas, then shook his head.

D'vin had explained that firestone gas only exploded in large quantities. In smaller quantities, the gas was deadly if inhaled.

Cristov and Toldur had agreed that tossing the suspect rocks into a running stream was a safe way to detect firestone—if the rocks were firestone, they'd emit the characteristic gases that immediately exploded on contact with air.

"I don't know," Toldur said as Cristov gave him a questioning look. "Perhaps we'll have to use the bucket instead."

Neither of them liked the idea of filling a bucket with water and dropping suspect rocks into it; the dangers of inhaling fatal gases or of ruinous explosion were too high.

Cristov pursed his lips in thought. "Perhaps we could use one of the cooking pans."

"Get the big one," Toldur suggested. Cristov nodded and raced back to their campsite. When he returned, he was moving more slowly, as the big pot was not only heavy but bulky, restricting movement in the undergrowth.

They selected a wide clearing near the river, placed the pot close to the river's edge, and used the bucket to fill it with water.

"Now all we need are more samples," Toldur said.

Cristov shook his head. "We need a dry bucket, too."

Toldur grunted in agreement. With a shrug, Cristov turned back to the campsite.

"I'll head back to the rock site," Toldur called as Cristov moved away. Cristov raised an arm in acknowledgment, still moving briskly toward their camp.

Ten minutes later they were back beside the pot, close together. Cristov tossed the contents of the dry bucket into the water in the pot, while Toldur watched carefully. The water bubbled, and the bubbles burst into flame on contact with air.

"Firestone," Cristov whispered in awe. Toldur's amazed and wary look was all the agreement he needed.

"We've got to work quickly," Toldur said, his voice full of urgency. His legs gave meaning to his words and he outpaced the shorter Cristov. When Cristov caught up again, Toldur said, "We've got to build a full entrance before nightfall; we don't want a late night snow or downpour to destroy our site."

They worked quickly. Cristov's hands blistered as he hauled away load after load of clay while Toldur bared the entrance fully and dug into the face of their firestone vein, squaring it up.

Cristov would dump a load of clay and return with planed wooden beams for shoring.

Working carefully, he and Toldur constructed a proper shaft entrance. They glanced at the entrance for a moment before Toldur groaned, "The first drop of water will set off the mine."

They went back for some clay, which they placed on top of the mine entrance to keep any melting water from entering the mine.

It was a tough race, but by night, bone weary, Toldur and Cristov stood in front of a proper mine entrance, the roof and sides protected by layers of protective clay.

Early the next morning, when D'vin arrived, Toldur surprised him with a sack full of rock.

"No more than an eighth hundredweight," the miner said diffidently. "But we wanted to give you some ore to test."

"Well, then," D'vin said, "let's see if you've found some firestone."

Ready? he asked his dragon, patting Hurth's neck affectionately.

It's not a lot, Hurth responded, warily eyeing the sack D'vin held. However, he opened his great maw and let D'vin throw him the largest of the chunks to chew and swallow.

It seems about the same, Hurth said after a moment. Hurth raised his head and emitted a bellow of fire.

Cristov jumped in surprise.

"That's definitely firestone," D'vin said. "The quality's good, too."

"Is he okay?" Cristov asked, looking up at Hurth worriedly.

"Have you ever heard of the hot peppers from Southern Boll?" D'vin asked. Cristov nodded. "Imagine that you'd eaten a whole mouthful of the ripest, hottest of those peppers."

"That bad?" Toldur asked, shaking his head in awe at Hurth's constitution.

"If our ancestors created the dragons, why didn't they create them so that eating firestone wasn't so painful?" Cristov asked.

"A good question," D'vin said. "And one that's talked about often in the Weyrs." He shook his head resignedly. "Our best guess is that our ancestors didn't have the time to make things perfect."

"But doesn't the pain of chewing firestone distract the dragons from fighting Thread?" Cristov asked.

"No," D'vin said, "they are willing to endure it for Pern's sake." And so am I, he added to himself, casting an apologetic look toward his dragon.

It is the only way, Hurth agreed, his second stomach feeling bloated and his throat sore.

D'vin nodded in agreement and turned to the miners. "This is high-quality firestone," he said again. "How soon can you get the mine into operation? What do you need from us?"

Cristov and Toldur were prepared for those questions, having thought about both for a long while.

"We don't ask for dragonriders to help in the mining," Toldur began, "but any help would speed things up, particularly among those miner-trained."

D'vin sighed and shook his head. "I'm afraid we can't help you there. None of our weyrfolk have mining experience."

"We'd thought as much," Toldur said. "But if your weyrfolk could help in making the wooden shorings and beams, then we'd have more time to put them in place and flesh out the mine head."

"That we can do," D'vin replied, nodding vigorously. "Anything else?"

"Do you suppose you have someone who could rig up some pumps?" Cristov asked. He pointed to a waterfall in the distance. "I was thinking if they could use the power of the waterfall to run the pumps, then we could pull any gases out of the mine."

"If we don't have an automatic way to clear out gas buildups, we'll have to run the pumps by hand," Toldur explained. "That would mean only one of us in the mines and . . . well, I'm afraid that the mine and the miner would be short-lived."

"Very well, I'll get with the headwoman and see if we can't solve that problem," D'vin said. "If we can't, I'm sure the Mastersmith can."

Cristov turned to Toldur, eyes shining with amazement as he mouthed the word, "Mastersmith."

Toldur laughed and clapped him on the back. "You think too little of yourself, journeyman! All Pern relies on our efforts now, so why wouldn't all Pern pitch in and help?"

"Indeed," D'vin agreed. Why wouldn't all Pern help? Toldur's question echoed in his mind. Was there a way to get more help—help D'vin hadn't ever previously considered? Weren't the Shunned also part of all Pern? What would B'ralar say to his radical thought? What of the Lord Holders and Craftmasters?

"But with two of us, even if the pumps are automatic, we can hardly mine enough for all the Weyrs," Cristov said.

Toldur gave him a thoughtful look, then turned to the dragonrider. "How much firestone do the Weyrs need?"

"As much as we can get," D'vin said promptly. Seeing Toldur's surprised look, he expounded. "We like to keep only a little on hand because it's so dangerous. Typically a dragon needs at least a hundredweight of firestone for a full Fall, sometimes two or three. With three hundred fighting dragons in a Wcyr, that works out to a minimum of fifteen tonnes per Fall." He paused, stroking his chin, debating whether to say more and finally added, "My search of the Records indicates that in a typical Fall, a Weyr needs closer to forty tonnes."

"Forty tonnes?" Cristov murmured, glancing to Toldur and then on to the mine, unable to imagine how they could mine such a huge number every sevenday.

"For one Weyr," Toldur noted. "We'd need five times that number for all the Weyrs."

"Probably more," D'vin corrected. "Telgar flies with the strength of nearly two Weyrs."

"Two hundred and forty tonnes every sevenday," Cristov said, awed.

"I think we're going to need some help," Toldur said.

D'vin waved a hand, dismissing the issue. "Not for some time, however. The first thing is to get you up and running. Aside from pumps, what other needs have you?"

Toldur took on a distant, thoughtful look. "We'll need a good storage site; plenty of firestone sacks; maybe some hands to help load the firestone; a good set of rails and carts to haul firestone to and from the mine—I think that's it."

D'vin laughed, shaking his head. The two miners looked at him in surprise. "Weren't you ever planning on sleeping?"

"Well, yes," Toldur said, wondering why the drag-onrider had brought up the issue.

"Or eating?"

The two miners nodded.

"Then I suppose you'd like a place to live and perhaps a cook to take that burden off of you," D'vin said.

"We can sleep in our camp," Toldur said, surprised at D'vin's generous offer. "And we cook well enough."

D'vin shook his head, holding up a hand to forestall further comments from the miners. "The least the Weyr can do is to provide you with a warm place to sleep, hot meals, and hot water with which to bathe."

A look of joy and amazement flashed across Cristov's face only to be replaced by bemusement as he wondered why the Weyr would consider treating two mere miners so well.

"It's the least we can do," D'vin said in answer to his unasked question. "And, if you think about it, it's for the most selfish of reasons—every waking moment you're not mining firestone means less practice time for us."

" 'Dragonmen must fly when Threads are in the sky,' " Cristov quoted, realizing that dragons without firestone were helpless against Thread.

In the days that followed, Cristov and Toldur found themselves pampered by weyrfolk morning and night, with hot food pressed upon them and a sturdy shelter quickly built. Beyond that, the weyrfolk quickly erected a waterwheel and a crafty set of pumps to continuously suck the air out of the mine, built tracks, and assembled ore carts to haul out the ore.

The actual mining, however, fell to just Toldur and Cristov. And while they managed to produce a steady amount of firestone, both were depressingly aware that it was much less than the High Reaches, let alone the other five Weyrs, needed just for practice.

Tarik yelped and twisted over in his bed the second time a foot kicked him, not too gently, in the shoulder. The light of a low glow dimly lit the tent.

"You!" Tarik growled as he made out the figure towering over him. "What are you doing here?"

"I've come to renew our contract," Tenim answered, his eyes glinting green in the glow's light.

"I've lost *everything* and you want—" Tarik's protests were cut off in a gasp as Tenim dropped his hands around Tarik's throat and squeezed tightly.

He lifted the miner's head by the neck, his face nearly touching Tarik's. Tenim watched emotionlessly as Tarik's frantic efforts to free himself and gain breath grew feebler and feebler. Finally, as Tarik's fight for his life was reduced to no more than a frantic look in his eyes, Tenim let go and threw Tarik back onto his cot.

As the miner lay gasping in rasping breaths, Tenim whispered to him calmly, "Everything? Think again."

He glanced around, found a folding chair, pulled it up, and sat down close to Tarik's head.

"I hear that the dragonriders are desperate for this firestone," Tenim said. "I'm sure that they'd pay more for it than Cromcoal."

"D'gan pays nothing," Tarik said, his voice still hoarse from Tenim's crushing grip.

"So? Aren't there other Weyrs?"

"He knows how much we're mining," Tarik replied warily. "There's only so much a person can do in a day."

"In a day," Tenim agreed. "What about a night?"

Tarik considered the notion. "The workers would tire out too quickly. He'd notice."

"Then we get more workers," Tenim replied.

"And the food?"

"They can share with the others," Tenim said.

"D'gan barely provides enough," Tarik protested. "If we halve that, the workers will die."

"I don't believe I care," Tenim told him. "How soon can you have your first shipment?"

"Shipment?"

"My dray carries two tonnes," Tenim informed him. "When should I bring it by?"

"But—the workers!" Tarik protested.

"Surely D'gan doesn't collect every day," Tenim said in a tone that was almost reasonable. "I'm sure you could spare some firestone before I bring you additional help. Anyway," he added with a shrug, "I'll need some money to help in acquiring your additional aid. Shall we say in two days' time?"

At those words, Tarik's mind began to work furiously. How long had Tenim been working on his plan? How long had he been watching Tarik's camp? Did he know that D'gan came for firestone no more than twice in a sevenday?

Another thought caused Tarik to ask, "How can you get a dray here? There's no road."

When Tenim didn't answer, Tarik added, "Where did you get a dray?"

Tenim smiled, touching the side of his nose. "Don't ask questions unless you're willing to live with the answer."

Tarik shuddered unwillingly and remained silent.

"I'll see you in two days," Tenim said and, turning on his heel, headed toward the door.

"Wait!" Tarik called out, ignoring the pain of his raw throat. Tenim paused but did not turn back as Tarik said, "For a tonne a day, I'll need eight strong men."

Tenim waved a hand in mocking acknowledgment and disappeared into the night.

Tarik spent the day alternately flogging his workers mercilessly for extra firestone and hoping that his encounter with Tenim had merely been a nightmare. By nightfall the workers had managed to produce only an extra three hundredweight. The next day was no better. Darkness found Tarik nervously pacing in his tent, his dinner uneaten. Two workers were in the stockades, their parched and swollen tongues lolling in their heads, as a lesson to the others.

A loud noise caused Tarik to jump as something was thrown in his tent. He dived out the door, intent on catching the miscreant, only to find his legs taken out from underneath him. He fell heavily, the breath knocked out of him. A hand covered his mouth. Tarik's eyes found its owner.

"Hello," Tenim told him softly, eyes gleaming in the dark. "Is everything ready?"

Tarik nodded.

"Good," Tenim said, releasing his grip and stepping back from Tarik. He gestured expansively in the dark. "My dray is on the far side of that hill, next to your firestone."

"We can't move two tonnes that far by ourselves," Tarik protested.

Tenim smiled a big toothy smile at him. "I promised you I would bring help."

Tenim's "help" was a disheveled crew of young teens and children.

"They won't last long," Tarik complained as he bullied the new arrivals into hauling the heavy sacks of firestone into the dray.

Tenim smiled at him. "Then I'll get more."

"Get 'em older," Tarik snapped. Instantly he regretted it: Tenim's fist landed at the point of his jaw and sent him flying.

"*I* give the orders, old man," Tenim said to Tarik's sprawled form. He gestured for Tarik to get up. Rubbing his jaw, Tarik rose again.

"Hurry them up," Tenim told him. "I'll want to leave before the second moon rises."

Tarik's angry protest died stillborn as he caught the

deadly look in Tenim's eyes. Instead, he swallowed hard and nodded swiftly.

Two hours later, Tenim rumbled out of sight in the fully loaded workdray, leaving his ten recruits in Tarik's care.

By the end of a sevenday, frantic in his efforts to meet both D'gan's and Tenim's unreasonable demands, Tarik was a hollow-eyed wreck of a man.

"Your workers are slacking off," D'gan complained as he surveyed the worksite. "Aren't they getting enough sleep?"

"It's their nerves, my lord," Tarik told him. "They are afraid of an explosion."

"Hmph," D'gan grunted in response to the explanation. He waved toward the small group of new hands he'd found. "Perhaps these six will help."

Tarik scanned the group with little hope. He spotted one body flopped on the ground and pointed. "I'm not sure he'll last all that long, my lord."

"We spotted him on our way here," D'gan said dismissively. "He was extra. Use him as you wish."

Spotted him? Tarik walked over to the unconscious form, half hoping and half fearing that it was Tenim. Instead it was a much smaller teen. Tarik sighed deeply and then, to cover his reaction, asked, "Where was he when you found him?"

D'gan glowered at him until Tarik recognized his gaffe and corrected himself, saying, "I mean, where was he when you found him, my lord?"

"One of my riders found him near a river not far from here," D'gan said. "It looks like he'd tangled with something or someone a while back." He nudged the slumped body reflectively with his boot, adding, "He's got deep scars that are healed and signs of broken bones."

"Did he not say where he was from?" Tarik asked,

careful not to put the tone of his real question—"Are you sure he was Shunned?"—into his voice.

"He doesn't talk," D'gan replied. "We think he'll recover. And if not, well, he'll still be able to work for you."

For a little while, Tarik thought to himself grimly. His eyes strayed to a line of mounds on the other side of his valley, particularly the three fresh mounds of the youngsters who'd died the previous night.

"Can we get more provisions to care for him, my lord?"

D'gan sneered at him. "More provisions? You are too wasteful as it is."

"I was just thinking," Tarik persisted, "that it would be wasteful to have to spend time burying the lad when with a few more supplies we could get some work out of him."

"Mmm, you've a point," D'gan admitted. With a wave of his hand he tossed the matter aside. "Give my wingman your requirements and we'll see."

Tarik took D'gan's words for a dismissal and was relieved to deal with D'gan's second, a reasonable man who asked few questions.

Still, it was a distraction having to remember every jot and tittle needed to run the mines; he made a note to himself to find someone to act as scribe.

It was a sevenday before the injured lad recovered. He still couldn't speak, but Tarik was pleased to discover that the lad could write and immediately set him to work compiling the lists of supplies needed to run the mines.

The extra help was not enough to relieve Tarik's worries. D'gan's constant demands and Tenim's nocturnal visits kept him jittery and on edge.

"Who's this?" Tenim asked when he spotted the silent lad keeping pace beside Tarik.

"Someone the dragonmen dumped on me," Tarik replied with a shrug. "He helps me manage supplies."

Tenim peered at the lad for a moment longer in the dark night, then ignored him, turning back to Tarik. "Why not put him in the mines with the others?"

"Because between you and D'gan, I'm managing over thirty men—" There was a note of pride in his voice. "—and I need help with the records."

"Suit yourself," Tenim said. "But you'd better be shorting D'gan this one's share of the firestone, not me."

"The lad's saved me so much time, I'm thinking of opening another shaft."

"Another shaft?" Tenim asked, looking askance. "I wouldn't do that."

"I'll need to if I'm to meet your demands."

"If you do, then D'gan will get suspicious."

"So what am I supposed to do?" Tarik protested angrily. "There are so many working now that I'm afraid they'll trip over each other and cause an explosion. And you know what *that* would mean."

Tenim cocked his head thoughtfully. It was a moment before he replied, "Yes, that would be a tragedy wouldn't it?

"Do you know," he went on, his eyes glinting in the dark, "I think you should have four tonnes of firestone ready for me when I get back."

"Four tonnes?" Tarik repeated in amazement. He spluttered, "But—but—"

"I have to guard my investment," Tenim told him calmly. "It's important that I have a reserve in case something happens to my stockpile."

"Stockpile? I thought you had a buyer."

"Several," Tenim lied cheerfully. "Which is why I have a stockpile." He nodded curtly to Tarik, saying, "So. Four tonnes in two days' time." With that, he turned away, ignoring all of the inarticulate noises coming from Tarik.

It was easy for Tenim to do so because he was busily plotting. How much would he get if there was *no* supply of fresh firestone? How much would his stockpile be worth then?

It had surprised him to discover how difficult it was to find a buyer for his firestone, given how all the other Weyrs had complained about D'gan's stinginess. Tenim had been convinced that it would be easy, and profitable, to sell firestone, so he was much surprised to discover that neither was the case. In fact, Tenim had considered abandoning the effort altogether and switching to a different venture. But now . . .

Tenim returned to his calculations. How much *could* he get for a hundredweight of firestone?

"Firestone?" Sidar repeated with a horrified look on his face. "You've got firestone?"

Tenim didn't move a muscle. He'd come to Sidar after exhausting all his other resources. The man was known to cheat, steal, and murder for his profit—methods Tenim preferred to reserve to himself—but when he paid, he paid well.

"Where do you store it?" Sidar asked, looking around the room carefully. "The stuff explodes with the merest contact with water."

"Like this?" Tenim asked, throwing a small pebble into one of the cauldrons hanging over the hearth. There was a small hiss, followed by a bluish flare.

"Shells, are you mad?" Sidar asked, jumping to his feet. "If the dragonriders catch you, you'll be Shunned for certain."

"So will you," Tenim said in bored tones. "In fact, one must wonder how you've done so well as to avoid it so far."

"Indeed, particularly when one considers the full implications," Sidar agreed, his lips twisted into a small smile as he countered Tenim's implied threat.

Tenim waved aside the issue, saying, "The question remains—how much will you pay?"

"Pay?" Sidar asked incredulously. "For something that might explode at any moment? Are you mad?"

"No," Tenim said. "It's not just that firestone bursts into flame so easily—it's that firestone's the only thing that dragons can use to flame Thread."

"They can always get more," Sidar replied sourly.

"And what if they couldn't get more?" Tenim asked. "What would firestone be worth then?"

"All Pern depends upon the dragons," Sidar replied. His tone made it clear that Tenim had overstepped his bounds.

Tenim shrugged. "Only when Thread is in the sky," he replied, and glanced up to the ceiling. "The Red Star is still a long way off."

"All the more reason for the dragons to train now," Sidar replied. He rose, indicating that the discussion was at an end. "No, your best bet is to return those goods whence they came and get far away before—"

"Before what?" Tenim interjected, his arm twitching slightly in the dim light. Suddenly he had a dagger in his hand. He toyed with it and glanced up innocently at Sidar asking, "Would there be a problem?"

"Leave," Sidar growled, undisturbed by Tenim's sudden display of a weapon. "Leave before you find yourself as lifeless as your wares."

"It was Tenim," Halla declared as she stood up from her examination of the footprints surrounding the tracks of the stolen workdray. They were at a trader camp just north of Keogh, a smaller hold to the southwest of Crom.

"Are you sure?" Veran asked.

"He taught me how to track," Halla told him.

"Did he teach you how to steal, too?"

"He tried," Halla said. "I didn't like it much." She cast her gaze in the direction of the tracks. "It looks like he was heading due north."

"We didn't find anything that way," Veran told her.

"He would have found a way to hide the tracks," Halla said.

"There are no roads in that direction; he couldn't get far."

Halla nodded to indicate that she heard him, but her thoughts were elsewhere. Why would Tenim steal a workdray? She could understand his desire to take one of the brightly colored domicile drays for himself or his profit, but what would he need a workdray for?

"—that workdray could only haul two tonnes at best," Veran was saying. "We'll absorb the loss. It won't hurt as much as if he'd taken a larger one, and it wasn't even loaded."

"Not loaded?" Halla repeated bemusedly.

"In that respect we were lucky; there was a larger one right next to it, fully loaded with Cromcoal."

What would Tenim want to haul away, if not Cromcoal? Halla wondered. What could be more valuable than that?

"Could I get some supplies?" Halla asked, turning back from her inspection of the distant trail after being certain to memorize sufficient landmarks.

"Supplies?" Veran asked. "What are you going to do?"

"I think I'll see what Tenim is doing," Halla told him.

Veran looked dubious. "That doesn't sound much like what I heard Lord Fenner ask of you."

"How will the traders react when the word gets around that someone like Tenim has stolen one of your drays?"

"Word's already gotten around," Veran confessed. Sheepishly he added, "And we traders are none too happy about it."

"So how will the traders feel when they hear that the dray was tracked down by someone else like Tenim and returned to its rightful owners?"

Veran gave her a long, thoughtful look. "Are you sure you've only twelve Turns?"

Halla shrugged. "That's what I've been told," she said. "I'm not certain."

"Not certain," Veran muttered to himself. "That's not right."

Halla nodded, saying, "That's what Lord Fenner said, too."

"He's a good man, Lord Fenner," Veran said by way of agreement. He looked down at Halla and frowned. "Are you sure you'll be able to track him?"

"Yes," she said.

"And what if he finds you?"

"He won't," Hall declared, trying to sound calm. "I'm a better tracker."

Veran looked at her a long time before responding, with a sigh, "I just hope you're a better tracker than you are a liar."

Halla smiled up at him and patted his arm. "I am, honestly." She paused a moment, then asked, "So, can I get those supplies?"

"You want to leave now?"

"Soonest is best," Halla said. She gestured to the trail. "The trail's days old; I can't wait—it might get wiped out."

Veran shook his head reluctantly. "Maybe you'd better reconsider. There's been rain since that dray was stolen; there probably aren't any tracks."

"I've got to try," Halla replied.

* * *

"It was a good idea of yours, my lord, to send the extra supplies," Tarik told D'gan when next they met, knowing full well that it had been the other way around but now recognizing the need to flatter the Weyrleader. He put an arm around his aide's shoulder. "This one has turned out to be a real timesaver when it comes to toting up tallies."

"Has he?" D'gan drawled in icy tones. "And here I'd hoped to see him get more firestone to protect Pern."

Tarik blanched. "Well, my lord, in a way he has. By freeing me up to work more on mining chores than on numbers, I've been able to up our output."

"Really?" D'gan turned away from the busy mine shaft to the firestone dump opposite it where weyrlings were carefully loading up sacks full of firestone and disappearing *between*. "I could scarcely believe that from the amount of firestone you're storing."

"We need more bags," Tarik told him. Beside him the silent youth gave him an odd look, which vanished before either Tarik or D'gan could comment upon it.

"More bags?" D'gan repeated. "We brought in more than enough bags."

"Well, some of them have ripped," Tarik told him nervously.

"Have someone repair them," D'gan ordered. He waved a hand at the silent youth. "Him, for example."

Tarik's mouth worked up a protest, but under D'gan's glare, he never voiced it, instead bobbing his head obediently.

"Seeing as you're doing so much better," D'gan continued, "I think we should expect more firestone from this mine."

He looked around appraisingly. "You've done well," the dragonrider admitted. "I think you'll have no problem producing another tonne before we next arrive."

Tarik's face went white. Feebly, he stammered, "My lord?"

D'gan nodded firmly. "Yes, I think that will do nicely." He turned to look Tarik in the eye. "My men need a good full Weyr training, so we'll have the extra sacks for you."

"Yes, my lord," was all Tarik could say in response. Irritably he waved at the teen standing at his side. "You, go start fixing those torn firestone sacks."

"And be sure to do a good job," D'gan added.

The youth gave Tarik an inscrutable look, then nodded, handed Tarik his slates, and headed toward the shed where the firestone sacks were stored.

Neither D'gan nor Tarik paid the youth any attention while the firestone was being ferried away. D'gan turned down Tarik's feeble offer of refreshment with a sneering, "We send you the swill that's deemed unfit for dragonriders. Why do you think I'd want some now?"

Finally the last of the sacks were gone and D'gan took his leave, allowing an exhausted Tarik a few hours of respite. Irritably he sought out the silent boy and thrust a stack of new slates at him. "If you didn't keep count of what the dragonriders took, I'll tan your hide."

The silent youth nodded and quickly made new marks on the slates he'd been handed. Disgusted at the lad's diligence, Tarik cuffed his head—"Just to keep you on your tocs."

To his surprise, the blow rocked the small youth. Slates fell everywhere—some shattered.

"Now you've done it," Tarik growled as the lad tried desperately to collect all the slates. "If you don't have this fixed by dusk, you'll spend the night in the stocks, do you hear me?"

With a sullen look, the boy nodded and scampered off toward his work tent.

Alone for a moment, Tarik heaved a deep sigh. He looked around him: The once green valley was now a dry, dirty bowl dotted only with stone sheds, tents, and tracks for the carts—all his.

A screech from the sky brought Tarik's attention back from his musings. He looked up and picked out a black dot moving swiftly in the dark sky above him. Tenim was on his way. It was time to rouse the night crew.

Wearily he turned and trudged off to the secret meeting place. He was halfway there before he paused, swearing, and turned back. He'd forgotten his scribe!

Tarik stood torn between being late and doing without the lad's handy services, before finally muttering, "I don't need him."

He failed to notice a small figure lurking in the shadows beside him. As Tarik turned back to his trail, the figure silently followed him.

"You're late," Tenim snarled when Tarik arrived. He looked around. "Where's your shadow?"

"Huh?" Tarik muttered. "Oh, the lad!" he exclaimed when enlightenment dawned. Hastily, he lied, "In the stocks."

"Good," Tenim said. "I never liked him. You should consider keeping him there—he knows too much."

"He's useful," Tarik protested. "He saves me a lot of work."

"He could tell D'gan all about us," Tenim responded, "and all you worry about is your comfort."

"He won't talk," Tarik replied. "Shells, he *can't* talk."

"Can't talk?" Tenim asked, cocking his head in sudden interest.

"Not a sound," Tarik said. "At first I thought it was from whatever hurt him. Now, I'm not so sure."

Tenim grew quite still as his thoughts outpaced him. Could this be the egg carrier come back to life?

"No matter," he said aloud. He would merely kill the boy again, along with everyone else. Yes, that would work. Tidily. He turned to Tarik, another dead man, and said, "Have you got my firestone?"

"*Our* firestone," Tarik corrected. "Of course."

"Then what are you waiting for?" Tenim replied. He pointed into the shadows. Tarik could just barely make out the outline of a workdray, a patch of darkness in the shadows. "Get your lads to fill it up."

Tarik nodded. With a whistle, he roused the children Tenim had provided. He unhitched the whip he kept looped off his belt and gave it a loud crack. Shadows shuffled out around them. Suddenly the dim light of a glow could be seen shining eerily in the night like a dragon's giant eye.

"Bring the dray over and start loading," Tarik called. He turned back to Tenim. "They'll be no use for any other work tonight."

"No use, why?" Tenim asked. He pointed to Tarik's whip. "Can't you use that?"

"Not in the mines," Tarik replied. A pair of youths passed by grunting as they hauled a full firestone sack between them. "It might make sparks."

"And sparks are bad?"

"Of course," Tarik said. "In fact, there's so much gas building up that we'll have to get more pumps soon or risk an explosion." He frowned, adding, "We've had a few close calls already; workers have been passing out from the fumes, and we've had to wait until we can fan in more fresh air."

Tenim said nothing in response, preferring to watch the dray's loading. The conversation died off until the dray was loaded and the workbeasts, gaunt old things, were hitched up.

"I'll see you soon," Tenim told Tarik.

"You'll not need more firestone?" Tarik asked in surprise.

"No," Tenim told him. "I think you've done enough."

A look of relief, almost gratitude, crossed Tarik's face, plainly visible in the light of Pern's two moons. Then relief was replaced by suspicion. "When will you be back?"

"Soon," Tenim repeated, flicking the reins to urge the workbeasts on. As the dray moved off, Tarik resignedly turned back to the work of the dawning day.

When he arrived back at the camp, he banged on the work tent where he'd last seen his scribe.

"Boy! Wake up, boy! It's time for work," he shouted, determined that as soon as he had everyone working hard enough, he would allow himself a well-deserved rest.

When, after several moments, the boy did not stir, Tarik stuck his head inside the tent, shouting, "Boy, you'd best hope—" But the tent was empty.

Tarik's swearing was enough to rouse the rest of the camp.

The boy, who had been following Tarik earlier in the evening, watched Tenim's departure carefully, noting the direction the young man took. He was about to return to the camp when he noticed that Tenim had stopped. Why?

Curious, he silently moved toward the workdray. He stopped abruptly when he spotted a figure walking back toward him. Tenim. He was carrying something on his arm.

"Remember how I taught you, Grief." Tenim's voice drifted clearly on the early morning air. "The water buckets."

They were on the hill overlooking the firestone camp

and the dam that had been one of Tarik's earliest projects. Tenim stepped closer. The boy recognized the bird on his arm and the partly filled firestone sack hanging from his shoulder.

The boy started running, but he was already too late. In a moment, the falcon was in the sky, zooming down the valley to the carefully placed table outside the mine shaft with its half-full buckets of drinking water. It would take nothing for the falcon to jostle the buckets, tip them over, and have their contents seep into the mine.

But that was only part of Tenim's plan. The second part became apparent when he started lobbing rocks of firestone at the base of the dam. At first they merely sizzled, but soon the air was full of flame.

The boy slammed into Tenim, knocking him off his feet, but the older youth was larger and stronger. Tenim recovered quickly, lashing out with balled fists. Still the boy persisted, even as the dam grew weaker from Tenim's earlier firestone bombings. Taking a moment, Tenim threw the rest of the firestone sack into the water now streaming from the dam and then turned back to his opponent.

"How many times do I have to kill you?" he asked, his fists slamming into the boy's stomach.

Behind him, the firestone exploded and Tenim heard the sudden rush of water. The dam had burst.

The boy stood rooted for one horrified moment as a wave of water rushed down the hillside, heading straight for the firestone dump. His distraction lasted long enough for Tenim to land the boy a knockout blow.

Tenim stared down at the unconscious boy and twitched to release his hidden knife. Two explosions, nearly simultaneous, rocked the morning air and he turned around in time to catch sight of the fireball rising where the firestone dump had been. From the mine entrance came a huge gout of flame and the more distant rumble of an explosion. A worried look crossed his face as he scanned the skies, to be relieved when he spotted the small form of his falcon racing back toward him.

He slid his knife into his belt and raised his arm for the falcon. Grief landed, and he quickly tied her jesses around his arm and placed her hood on her head. Only then did he look back down at the sprawled boy, a considering look on his face.

"I think I'll leave you," Tenim said finally. "That way, they'll think you did it."

With that, he strode off, firm in the belief that he had just made himself the richest, most powerful man on Pern.

The low rumble woke Halla. She jumped out of her sleeping roll in time to spot a brilliant light in the distance. She was only kilometers away.

"Firestone," Halla declared. She'd taken to talking to herself, having not realized how much she appreciated the comforting chatter of the children who had always been in her care. "It has to be."

Now she knew why Tenim had stolen an empty workdray: to carry firestone. Had he been mining by himself? No, that didn't make sense. And hadn't Veran told her that D'gan was getting firestone from some unknown place? Judging by the sound she'd heard, that place was no more.

She broke her camp, hoisted her pack, and set off in the direction of the noise, determined to search for survivors.

Pellar woke slowly and kept his eyes closed, listening for a long while. In the distance he heard the cries of the camp's survivors. Closer, he only heard the sounds of morning. He kept his eyes closed while he gingerly tested each of his limbs. Satisfied that this time nothing was broken, he carefully sat up, wincing as the movement strained the bruise on his jaw.

"How many times do I have to kill you?" The question echoed again in his mind as his memories flooded back.

He remembered fighting the icy stream, sliding backward over a huge fall, and waking up much later, leg and arm broken, his head resting on the stream bank. Shivering with cold, he'd found the strength to pull himself out of the water before he'd collapsed again in exhaustion.

How long he'd stayed there on the edge of death, Pellar couldn't recall. He'd survived on worms, trundlebugs, insects, whatever he could stuff into his mouth.

Once he'd fought off a wild dog determined to have him for dinner, another time he'd survived a wherry's aerial attack by fending it off with fallen branches.

But it was his memories of Mikal's teachings that finally healed him, although it took a terribly long time. He'd sought out the healing rocks from the streambed, looking for quartz above all. Carefully, he'd placed the crystals as he'd been trained by Mikal, aligning their vibrations to help his healing.

As soon as he could, he'd found stringy runners and shorter branches to fashion a splint for his arm and then for his leg. He'd just barely survived winter, huddled in a cave and eating raw fish. When spring came, he set traps, and—when they were full—he ate well. Slowly, his strength returned.

But he could remember only flashes of his past.

When the dragonriders had discovered him, he was initially glad, thinking he'd found aid. But they'd dropped him off here and the cold of *between* had helped settle an irritating cold deep in his chest. It had taken several days of rest before he'd recovered.

He remembered being irritated when he first met Tarik, although he had to feel gratitude for the other's care of him. And he'd felt insanely angry when he'd first seen Tenim, and only caution had prevented him from attacking the larger youth at that time.

But it was only at the sight of the falcon that Pellar had remembered everything. The falcon that had killed Chitter. Pellar's face clouded in memory. Chitter had saved his life.

For what? Pellar wondered bitterly, feeling well enough to stand and survey the wreckage of the valley below. His eyes strayed back to the green dale in which he was standing. There—a leaf good for burns. There— a leaf to reduce pain. He didn't spot any numbweed.

As swiftly as his sore body would move, Pellar started harvesting healing leaves and roots.

Provisioned, he set off at a trot to the camp. As he grew closer he saw, to his horror, that some of the injured were badly burned. Some would not survive the day. He had no fellis juice to ease their pain. Most of the survivors were either lying on the ground in exhaustion, or walking around listlessly. He needed more help.

Could he still speak to dragons?

Hurth, he ventured, *I need help*.

The response was immediate, worried, and full of that special draconic warmth. *Where are you?*

Pellar scanned the valley and closed his eyes, building the image in his mind.

We come, Hurth said.

The immediate response was a tonic to Pellar and he lengthened his stride. He was barely at the first of the tents when the sky above him filled with dragons.

He waved frantically at the large bronze he knew to be Hurth.

"Pellar!" D'vin shouted from his perch atop Hurth's neck, his face alight with joy. "We'd given you up for dead!" He paused and surveyed the scene around him. "What happened?"

D'vin jumped down from Hurth's neck and then turned back to help down the group of weyrfolk that had ridden with him.

Pellar waved his hands and groped around his neck to show D'vin that he had nothing to write with. He turned, holding one hand out to highlight the scene surrounding them, but already it had changed as weyrfolk and dragonriders bustled about, providing aid to the burned and dazed survivors.

"Does anyone have a slate?" D'vin shouted over the growing din. A young woman dressed in riding gear raced over to him, her long black hair highlighted by one white streak.

"Thank you, Sonia," D'vin told her with a smile that went to his eyes. She smiled back at him, turned, and waved good-bye over her shoulder as she sped off in search of more work. D'vin handed Pellar the slate and waited patiently while the boy wrote his message. When he was done, he handed the slate to D'vin who read, "Tenim. Destroyed the mine. Stealing firestone."

"He's stealing firestone?" D'vin asked in amazement. "What for?"

"To sell," Pellar wrote in response.

"Sell?" D'vin repeated in surprise. He shook off the question, asking instead, "Was this D'gan's mine?"

When Pellar nodded, D'vin made a face. "I'll have to let him know." He gestured toward a green dragon hovering high over the valley. "Fortunately, P'lel says we're not too far from our borders."

Pellar gestured for the slate and wrote hastily, "I should go; D'gan's men brought me here, put me to work."

"He's been putting men in the mines?" D'vin asked, brows furrowing angrily.

Pellar nodded in confirmation and wrote, "Tenim brought him children to work a second shift."

"Children!" D'vin exclaimed in shock, adding thoughtfully, "Not that you're all that much older."

The sky grew thick once more with dragons.

"That'll be D'gan," D'vin judged, looking up at the arriving dragons. He looked back to Pellar. "I think you'd best leave until I can calm him down."

Pellar nodded and strode off, heading toward the ruined dam. A new resolution had entered his thoughts: Rather than avoid D'gan, he would track Tenim.

Halla arrived at the outskirts of the valley in time to see a second group of dragonriders appear. She stared at them for a long time, lost in their beauty, before she brought her attention back to the goings-on in the valley. Dragonriders and weyrfolk were attending the injured. In the center of it all, Telgar's Weyrleader was talking to a dragonrider wearing High Reaches colors. With a start, Halla recognized the High Reaches rider as the one she'd met at the Gather.

Carefully, she made her way down the valley, hoping to pick up on the conversation without being noticed.

She need not have bothered. D'gan was shouting so loudly that Halla could easily hear his every word from two dragonlengths away.

"*My* mine!" D'gan shouted. "My workers! I've no stomach for High Reaches poaching them."

"We came to their aid," D'vin replied, his voice firm and not as loud. Halla thought that for all his deferential stance, the High Reaches rider was very angry and only just holding on to his temper. "And I informed you as soon as I could."

"You did, did you?" D'gan yelled in response. "Not

before you carted off a load of firestone, though. I would have never thought that I'd see the day when one Weyr stole from another—"

"My lord," D'vin interrupted curtly. "We are dragon-men. We came to offer aid, not to steal." He paused as he considered D'gan's words. "And why would we cart off firestone when we can fly it off?"

"I don't know," D'gan declared petulantly. "All I know is that there are tracks leading off in the direction of your lands."

D'vin was silent for a moment—communing with his dragon, Halla guessed. "My dragon has found the tracks you mentioned. We shall investigate."

"*You* will investigate?" D'gan roared in response. "This happened on Telgar land—*we'll* investigate."

"As the dray is now in High Reaches territory, tracking it becomes our problem," D'vin replied. He held up a placating hand to prevent D'gan's next outburst. "However, we'd be delighted to accept your offer of help."

D'gan spluttered for a moment before saying, "Fine! You find them."

D'vin nodded curtly. After a moment, D'gan said, "Well, why aren't you going?"

D'vin looked at him in surprise. "Your miners still need aid."

"Leave them," D'gan said. "That's Telgar business, and we'll handle it."

D'vin's reluctance was obvious to D'gan, who ignored the fact that he had brought none of his weyr-folk, and that most of his riders were still hovering over the valley on their dragons.

"I said we'll handle it," the Telgar Weyrleader repeated, tapping his fingers testily against his riding helmet. "You may leave now, Wingleader."

D'vin bit back a bitter response and settled for bringing himself erect and bowing to D'gan. "Weyrleader."

D'gan nodded back and waved D'vin away.

The High Reaches folk were slow to leave their charges, their concern visible on their faces, but in short order they were arrayed once more behind the dragonriders who had brought them. The dragons leapt aloft, formed the wing, and vanished *between*.

Halla was already heading away from the valley by the time the High Reaches weyrfolk departed. She'd learned what she needed to know. As she turned north and west, scanning for the heavily loaded workdray's tracks, she reflected that she could leave Tenim to the dragonriders, that this was not what Lord Fenner had asked her to do, and that Tenim was much larger and more dangerous than she. But she would find him. A cry from one of the injured behind her strengthened her resolve. She lengthened her stride.

To flame the skies
Your dragon must chew
A hundredweight
Or more for you.

Chapter Eight

"So D'GAN'S MINE was destroyed," B'ralar said, looking up from his position at the head of the Council Room. "And he complained when you arrived with aid?"

"Yes," D'vin said. He was still surprised at the speed of events since the destruction of firestone mine #9.

The Weyrleader chuckled. "And all the while he'd been telling us he had no more firestone."

D'vin smiled. "We haven't been too frank with him, either."

B'ralar grinned and nodded. "It seems just as well now," he said. "And it seemed a better idea when we didn't know how your miners would perform."

"Not as well as D'gan's men," D'vin observed. "We'll need a lot more trained men before we start to see a tonne a day."

"They got that much?" B'ralar asked, sounding impressed.

"As near as I can tell," D'vin replied. "I talked with Toldur and Cristov about it."

B'ralar gave D'vin an inquisitive look.

"They said that it was possible to mine that much in a day, but they were concerned that it would require a lot of risks."

"Hmm," B'ralar said. He looked at his wingleaders. "So High Reaches is now the only Weyr that has a firestone mine on its lands." He snorted. "Imagine how D'gan'll feel when he finds out."

The wingleaders grinned.

"I'm worried about this Tenim," D'vin said. "He seems a dangerous character, and he's willing to use firestone in a way we've never considered."

"We should catch him as soon as possible," B'ralar agreed.

"What do we do then?" D'vin asked, his voice tinged by the memories of the burned and injured miners. Worse, more than half of the miners had perished—including Tarik.

B'ralar pursed his lips in thought for a moment. "Let's capture him first, then we'll decide."

The others nodded in assent, and B'ralar assigned his patrols. The meeting broke up, and the wingleaders marched out briskly to issue their orders.

"D'vin, wait a moment," B'ralar called as D'vin rose to leave.

D'vin turned back and looked at the elderly Weyrleader expectantly.

"It's not enough," B'ralar said slowly, "for a Weyrleader to fight against Thread. A Weyrleader needs to chart a course Turns ahead, yet be prepared for any eventuality."

"For which I am glad that I'm not a Weyrleader," D'vin replied with a grin.

"One thing a good Weyrleader does is keep a close eye on all potential Weyrleaders," B'ralar said. "For the good of the Weyr."

D'vin shook his head. "Weyrleader, I wish you a long and happy life."

B'ralar laughed. "I accept and will certainly aim for it." He grew more somber. "But my days are numbered just as any other man's." He caught D'vin's eyes and held them. "Don't forget what I said, and don't do anything you might come to regret later."

D'vin bowed his head in acknowledgment. Then, with an inquiring look, he asked if he could leave. B'ralar waved him away, shaking his head at the waywardness of youth.

Toldur and Cristov were surprised when D'vin arrived at their camp, and grim when he explained his purpose.

"Well, we're safe enough here," Toldur declared after a moment's thought. "We've well water, and our firestone is stored in a well-built stone shed."

"He could still destroy the mine," Cristov objected. The news of his father's real death after all the months he'd spent thinking that Tarik was already dead was something he hadn't yet fully absorbed, and he was determined to bury himself in his work to avoid the issue for as long as he could.

"Only if there's no one guarding it," Toldur said.

"We should consider starting another mine," Cristov said. "Maybe training some others to do the work so we can mine more firestone."

Toldur shook his head. "I can't imagine who would volunteer, especially after news of Tarik's mine gets out."

"But how will the dragonriders train?" Cristov demanded, gesturing to D'vin and his riders. "And if they don't train, what will happen when the Red Star returns?"

"Oh," D'vin said demurely, "I think the dragons might enjoy a short break from firestone." Behind him, Hurth rumbled approvingly. He turned back to the mine. "How are you doing?"

"Well enough," Toldur said. "But Cristov's right:

Two people can only mine so much in a day, even with all the help your weyrfolk are providing."

Cristov looked chagrined and mumbled something about "sorry."

"You've no need to apologize," D'vin replied fiercely. "You and Toldur have done excellent work. If more miners would—"

Cristov coughed and Toldur gave the dragonrider a pained look.

"What?" D'vin asked.

Toldur squared his shoulders before replying, "We sent messages to Masterminer Britell asking for more miners."

"Did you? That's excellent."

Toldur shook his head. "The Masterminer said that there were no takers."

"And that was *before* this news about the other mine," Cristov added.

"And," Toldur said, "before you ask, dragonrider, none of your weyrfolk have volunteered either."

D'vin nodded and propped his chin in his hand, resting one arm on top of the other across his chest.

"We'll think of something," he declared finally.

"They can start at mine number ten," D'gan declared. "If that doesn't work, they can start at old mine number nine."

"Weyrleader, none of the survivors who've remained are fit to stand, let alone work," healer K'rem told him.

D'gan shot a venomous look at L'rat, the wingleader charged with guarding the camp. "Have you found any of them yet?"

Miserably, L'rat shook his head. "No, Weyrleader. Our riders have spread out all over and have had no luck so far."

D'gan fumed. "If we hadn't spent so much effort on

the injured, we could have guarded the able well enough to keep them from running away."

"I don't think they would have worked even under pain of firestoning," L'rat said, spreading his hands in surrender.

"Well, you let them get away so we'll never know, will we?" D'gan retorted scathingly. He waved a hand at L'rat. "You lost them, you'll find their replacements. We'll need two dozen to start with."

"But my lord, the holders say that there are no Shunned left in any hold," L'rat protested.

"Find some," D'gan ordered. "*Make* some. Goodness knows those useless holders are always up to something."

L'rat drew breath to protest but D'gan startled him into silence, shouting, "Well, what are you standing about for? Go get more workers!"

L'rat nodded reluctantly, cast a pleading glance at the Weyr healer, who refused to meet his eyes and departed after sketching a quick bow to D'gan.

"We *have* to have firestone," D'gan said to himself. He looked up at K'rem for support. "Without it, all Pern is doomed."

"Yes, my lord," K'rem agreed, "but I can't help wondering if there isn't an easier way to get it."

The pounding that woke Sidar up was more welcome than the figure he found standing in his doorway.

"Are you insane?" he hissed angrily. "All Pern is looking for you!"

Tenim smiled and forced his way past the other man, heading to the hearth to warm his hands. "And how much of Pern is looking for firestone?" he asked nonchalantly.

"Firestone?" Sidar exclaimed incredulously. "They're getting enough from the mine at High Reaches."

Tenim was glad he had his back to Sidar, for he could feel his face drain of all color. "High Reaches?"

"Yes, you fool," Sidar snapped back. "Tarik's brat has been mining up there ever since that last Gather."

"Really?" Tenim asked, turning to face Sidar, his features once more composed and calm.

"Really," Sidar said. He grabbed Tenim by the collar and pulled him off his stool, shoving him toward the door. "Now get out, you're no longer welcome here."

Tenim turned back to face the older man. "Not welcome?" he asked, looking crestfallen. "After all we've done?"

"Come back and my heavies will deal with you," Sidar promised.

"I wouldn't want that," Tenim said agreeably. He slung his pack off his shoulder and fished in it for something. "Seeing as you've been such a good friend, I've got something for you. Call it a going-away gift." He looked around and spotted a jug. "In return all I want is some water."

Sidar eyed him warily and backed away until he saw what Tenim had pulled out—a rock.

"It's just a rock," Sidar said. "Why should I trade water for that?"

Tenim threw the rock at him and the older man caught it reflexively. Tenim stepped over to the jug and filled a mug.

"No ordinary rock," Tenim responded smoothly. "That's firestone."

Sidar eyed him warily and then the rock speculatively. "It's not worth my water," he growled. "You'd best leave."

"It's quite valuable," Tenim continued in the same smooth tone.

Sidar snorted derisively.

"You don't like my gift?" Tenim asked, sounding sad.

"Neither it nor you," Sidar replied. "Now get out."

"Ah, but that's a special rock," Tenim said, smiling. He pretended to sip from his mug and made a face. "Certainly worth more than this water."

He threw the water at Sidar who grunted in surprise.

"And quite deadly," Tenim added, stepping back as Sidar gave a strangled cry and lurched away from him. Tenim continued on as if nothing were happening, completely ignoring Sidar's frantic movements. "It seems that if the gas doesn't explode outright, it burns the lungs and the air in them. Death is quick, if painful."

Tenim watched as Sidar's desperate movements became more and more feeble and finally stopped. Shaking his head, he turned to go, only to turn back again for one final admonition. "You really should have bought when you had the chance."

Back outside, Tenim climbed back aboard his workdray and drove it around into the shed behind Sidar's cothold. He unhitched the beasts, put them in good stalls, fed and watered them, all the while whistling to himself and examining the runnerbeasts across the stables. Once done, he selected the best beast, saddled it, added his bedroll, travel pack, and falcon's hutch, and rode out into the night heading west, toward High Reaches Weyr.

Halla swore when she lost Tenim's tracks in Keogh. She arrived three days behind him, late enough that the body of the holder had been found. Halla herself had discovered the missing workdray and its deadly load of firestone, but she left before D'gan had arrived to supervise its unloading.

Now Tenim had a horse and a three-day lead.

Halla wondered about the other set of tracks she'd spotted on the way. Why had they continued west even after Tenim had veered south? Still, she had her mission, and the mission Lord Fenner had given her. So far her hopes of finding any of the Shunned had proven just as false as her hopes of bringing Tenim to justice.

"So what am I going to do now?" Halla asked herself. West, she decided. At the edge of town she found a trader caravan that agreed to take her along the moment she identified herself as Tarri's friend.

"Tarri's report said good things about you," their leader had told her, gesturing to her fire-lizard as her source of news.

They camped halfway up the High Reaches mountains that night. Well bundled against the cold, Halla joined the caravanners around a large fire and listened as they talked.

"So what are the odds for that firestone mine?" one of them asked.

"No better than the one D'gan had," another answered.

"But I hear they've got miners working it," the first one said.

The other snorted a laugh. "At least until they make their first mistake."

The group joined him in a bitter laugh.

"And then what? What happens when there's no one to mine more firestone?"

"There'll always be someone to mine firestone, as long as there's the Shunned."

"I hear," the first one said, dropping his voice, "that D'gan's taking even those who aren't to start a new mine."

"You don't say?"

"What a terrible thing to do!"

"They say that half the miners at the old mine were burned in that explosion."

"I heard that one of the Shunned did it on purpose."

"Could you blame them, working like that?"

"Shouldn't get Shunned if they didn't want to work like that," another grumbled.

Halla fought an impulse to finger her forehead.

"Not everyone gets a choice."

"How's that? Isn't it justice that they do?"

"Justice is different from Lord Holder to Lord Holder."

A chorus of assents passed around the campfire. After a while the conversation moved on to other topics and Halla drifted off to sleep, but not before she asked, "Does anyone know where this other mine is?"

The oldsters exchanged thoughtful glances before one replied, "High up in the mountains, near High Reaches. They say only dragons can get there."

Pellar crossed the mountains as quickly as he could. He made good time and found a boat heading downriver at the first decent-sized hold. For keeping watch, he got a free ride. But first he had to show his forehead to prove he wasn't Shunned.

"Not that I'd do it," the boatman explained, "but there's word that Telgar will pay a bounty for a Shunned man."

Pellar looked at the man politely, encouraging him to continue conspiratorially, "I hear that Weyrleader D'gan himself ordered it. He's all put out that High Reaches has their own mine. I guess he figures he's the only one who deserves a monopoly on firestone."

Aside from that, the man spoke as little as Pellar, having gone silent after asking exasperatedly, "Why can't you talk, boy?"

Pellar had pulled down the collar of his tunic and mimicked someone trying to strangle him, which had been enough.

They parted ways at the river's fork, the man heading

farther downstream, and Pellar deciding to see if he could get to High Reaches Weyr.

What he discovered after a grueling day's walk was that the mountains surrounding High Reaches were cold, barren, and inhospitable. A storm dashed his final hopes of arriving at the Weyr to surprise D'vin and left him fearing instead for his very survival.

Hurth, Pellar called, finally admitting defeat.

The storm was so bad that the best D'vin could do was drop down a parcel which, though brightly colored, Pellar took over an hour to locate. Inside was cold bread and jam. He found a place to shelter for the night and ate, savoring every bite.

"You should have bespoken Hurth before you tried anything so foolish," D'vin scolded him the next day when the weather had turned sunny once again.

Pellar nodded in rueful agreement.

"So what were you doing here?" D'vin asked. Pellar explained about Tenim and his concerns about the new firestone mine.

"I agree, we're worried too," D'vin said. "So is Master Zist, who, by the way, sends his warmest regards and demands that you don't get yourself killed again."

Pellar winced. He fished out a note he'd written days earlier on the trail and passed it over to D'vin.

D'vin took one look at the top of it and folded it up. "I'll see that it gets sent to Zist tonight."

Pellar smiled in thanks.

"So what are we going to do with you?"

Pellar had already written his answer to that question, so he merely passed his slate over. "Take me to the mines. I'll guard."

D'vin shook his head. "We've guards enough already," he said. "I think you should go back to Master Zist."

Pellar shook his head and gently pulled back his slate, writing on it, "I can track."

D'vin considered the suggestion carefully before shaking his head. "I'll have to ask the Weyrleader and Zist."

Pellar shook his head again, his expression grim and determined. He wrote, "For Chitter. I have to do this."

When he passed the slate back, he locked his tear-rimmed eyes with D'vin's until the young wingleader nodded.

Smiling sadly, Pellar withdrew his slate once more and wrote, "Keep it a secret, my guarding."

D'vin mulled that over for a long time. "Very well," he agreed at last. He pointed a finger at Pellar. "But I want your promise that you'll call Hurth for help if you spot anything suspicious. It's only that you're so good at calling Hurth for help, that I'm agreeing."

Pellar nodded and wrote on his slate. "Part of my plan."

"Part of your devious plan," D'vin agreed, shaking his head ruefully. "I just hope that neither of us regrets this."

Tenim didn't know whether he wanted to swear or laugh when he found the High Reaches firestone mine. There was Tarik's brat digging firestone along with one of the other miners from Natalon's camp. Why, this was perfect! He'd get revenge for all the things the miners had done wrong to him, *and* he'd have the honor of exterminating Tarik's brat! On the other hand, it infuriated him to see how well Cristov and the other man worked and how much firestone they brought up with each load. Worse, they were obviously being treated like Lord Holders—a warm stone house in which to sleep, pumps built by Mastersmiths, rails laid by the weyrfolk themselves—they were too well dressed to be

anything else, and a dump where they had to do none
of the tedious sacking.

What made him want to swear the most—and laugh
the most—was the way the mine was guarded day and
night. In the two days and nights he'd been watching,
Tenim had never seen the mine unguarded, but the
guards were all old men and scrawny women, no match
for him. The dragonriders were too complacent, Tenim
decided. For which they would pay—and then pay him
handsomely.

Because for all their guards and their careful planning,
the dragonriders were mistaken if they believed they
could protect their precious mine from him. He had a
plan. And he would execute it just after the miners went
down for their first shift. And then even *dragonriders*
would listen to him.

Pellar refused to be angry with himself for not finding
Tenim's trail sooner; clearly, Tenim had gotten better at
disguising his trail than when Pellar had last encountered him. His discovery had been made more difficult
by the decision to move only at night. But at night
Tenim's falcon was sleeping; Pellar would only have to
evade one pair of eyes, and those eyes tired from their
own full day of surveillance.

It was clear that Tenim had arrived some days before,
and that once he'd arrived, he had moved very little, going only from his resting place to his observation spot
and back again, making it all that much harder to spot
his trail.

In fact, Pellar would have never spotted it if he hadn't
decided that Tenim's intention was to attack Cristov's
mine. Guided by that idea, Pellar had spied out the best
locations from which to observe and launch an assault.

What he hadn't figured out was how Tenim hoped to
succeed in any single-handed attack. But then, he didn't

plan to find out. All he needed was for Tenim to move, and Pellar would have him.

What Pellar didn't count on was the falcon, Grief.

The first sign of the attack came in the predawn when a commotion arose from beyond the clearing, back where the watch-dragon was posted. The dragon cried first in startlement, then in pain as the falcon dived repeatedly, beak and talons raking dragon hide, despite the desperate efforts of his rider to protect him.

The commotion woke the weyrfolk in the house, who all rushed over to see what had happened.

"Stay there!" the older guard shouted to the youngster on duty with him. "I'll see what's happening."

Toldur and Cristov emerged and exchanged words with one of the weyrfolk. "You go!" Toldur urged them. "We'll watch the mine."

Pellar watched them enter, still wondering what Tenim hoped to gain from assaulting a dragon.

It was then that the second part of Grief's attack began. Pellar had only time to catch a fleeting spot of darkness falling from the early morning sky before he realized what was happening. By the time he'd jumped up from his cover, the guard was already down on the ground, his hands covering his clawed and bloody face.

Pellar raced toward the mine entrance but before he was halfway across, a large object was lobbed from Tenim's lair toward the mine entrance.

Hurth, help! Pellar shouted at the same time as another voice shouted, "Help!"

For one brief moment, Pellar thought perhaps the words were his own, that in his panic he'd found his voice. And then Pellar realized that the voice wasn't his own. In that brief instant, Grief reacted—dropping from the sky with a raucous cry toward the back of Pellar's head.

But Pellar was ready. He twirled around, pulling his

knife from his belt and knelt, holding the knife above him.

With a hideous shriek the diving falcon impaled itself on the knife, showering Pellar with blood and feathers.

"You!" Tenim cried in fury, bursting from his cover. As Pellar turned to face him, a roar exploded behind him and he felt a gout of flame. Immediately, Pellar turned back and raced toward the mine entrance, ignoring the deadly peril at his back and the fire in front of him.

He reached inside the mine, groped, and found a hand. He pulled, but the body wouldn't budge; then, suddenly, as if pushed, the body lurched forward. Pellar pulled the body to one side and was about to go back for the other miner when another, larger explosion rocked the mine and shook him off his feet.

Rough hands grabbed at him as he tried to stand up again, and he turned to see the irate, bloody, and burnt face of Tenim above him. Pellar had no idea where his knife was. Tenim's, however, was right in front of him.

"Catch!" a voice shouted from behind him. Pellar swiveled, and reaching up in one fluid movement, grabbed a knife out of the air and pivoted back to face Tenim.

"You killed my bird!" Tenim shouted over the roar of the explosion, lunging down to bury his knife in Pellar.

The blow didn't connect. Instead, Pellar dropped to the ground and thrust up and out with the knife he held, which caught Tenim square in the chest. Tenim lurched, his mouth going wide in surprise, and Pellar quickly pulled his knife out and thrust it up again, higher, into Tenim's throat.

That, he thought hotly, *was for Chitter.*

Pellar slipped to one side as the hot blood erupted and Tenim dropped, dead, on the ground.

It was only then that Pellar turned back around to

seek out his benefactor and see whom he'd managed to rescue.

The sudden movement, coupled with the heat of the explosion and the stress of his exertions, was too much. He collapsed.

Dragonrider, this is true:
Others all look up to you.
Your hard work and bravery
Keep Pern safe and skies Thread-free.

Chapter Nine

"DON'T MOVE," a muffled voice said in kindly tones as Cristov opened his eyes. A cool cloth was placed on the side of his head and neck. "You must remain still for the healing to work."

A face came into his view, a young woman's, with olive eyes set in a face framed by long dark hair made darker still by a single long streak of white flowing from the top of her forehead.

"I'm Sonia," she said. "You're Cristov, and lucky to be alive."

Cristov blinked and tried to sit up. Sonia held him down, telling him imperiously, "I said, don't move."

Cristov obeyed, having neither energy nor inclination, in the light of Sonia's scolding, to consider otherwise.

Where was he? What had happened? He peered around the room, rolling his eyes to the limit of their vision.

Not the mine, obviously, nor his quarters. He caught sight of herbs in jars and sniffed—he was in a healer's room.

"If you don't move, the healer said there's a good chance you'll have no lasting pain from the burn," Sonia cautioned him.

Burn? Cristov remembered, closing his eyes in a wince. He and Toldur—he snapped his eyes open, hoping to convey his question by look alone.

"Best get some rest," Sonia said. "It'll be three sevendays, maybe a full month, before you're back on your feet." She could not quite suppress a grimace as she added, "Firestone leaves nasty burns.

"If the pain gets too great," she continued, "you're to have some fellis juice."

Firestone? The mine? Cristov remembered sudden searing heat, cries of surprise and pain and someone tugging on him—Toldur? What had happened?

Slowly he drifted off to sleep, distracted occasionally as Sonia gently bathed his wound.

His last thought on the very edge of a troubled sleep was a startled realization that Sonia was bathing the whole side of his head, not touching about his car. What had happened to his ear?

"What will happen now?" The question startled D'vin, who had been expecting Toldur's mate to burst into distraught tears and crumple into a trembling wretch at the sight of the burned-out mine and her mate's tomb.

"No one will disturb this site," he told her reassuringly.

Alarra shook her head, indicating that he had mistaken her. "What about the dragons and firestone?"

D'vin shook his head and spread his hands. "This site has been destroyed—"

"So we find another."

"That's what we intend," D'vin agreed with a firm nod, his eyes rapidly reevaluating this mate of Toldur's.

Alarra correctly interpreted his look and bowed her head slightly to him in acknowledgment. "I'm the mate of a miner, dragonrider; we share our burdens," she told him. A smile twisted across her lips fleetingly. "If I'd been the stronger, Toldur would have had me in the mines."

D'vin was surprised and it showed.

"He was a special man," Alarra said.

"And a special man needs a special woman," a voice observed from the distance. Alarra and D'vin turned to see Sonia approaching them, her long hair braided into a tight ponytail. Sonia extended a hand to Alarra. "You must be Toldur's mate."

Alarra nodded. "So, dragonlady, what needs to be done?"

Sonia shook her head and laughed. "I'm not a dragonrider, merely weyrfolk. I help my father, who is the Weyr's healer."

"Cristov?" Alarra asked.

"He lives," Sonia told her. "He is badly burned on his neck and the left side of his head." She took a deep breath and added, "He thinks that Toldur must have shoved him down when the blast came and sheltered him with his body."

Alarra gasped, and she bit her lip harshly before responding in a choked voice, "He would—he loved that boy like he was his own."

She drew a deep breath and straightened up, gazing firmly at D'vin. "My lord, as Toldur's mate I stand ready to serve in his place. When shall I begin?"

D'vin could think of no answer and turned entreatingly to Sonia, who said, "First I think we need to consider our options." She gestured toward the waiting dragons. "Perhaps this is best discussed at the Weyr."

"No sign? No sign?" D'gan emphasized his irritation by pounding on the Council table. He jumped to his feet and leaned on his arms, shouting at his assembled wingleaders. "What do you mean, no sign?"

"They've dug at five different sites and found nothing," K'rem said.

"And those twelve Shunned died in that cave-in," another wingleader added.

D'gan purpled, ready to blast his wingleaders into action once again, but stopped, letting his breath out in a sigh. He glanced at each wingleader in turn as he said in a hard voice, "Without firestone the dragons cannot flame. Without flame, Thread will burrow. When enough Thread burrows, it will suck all the life out of Pern. We . . . *must* . . . have . . . firestone."

"The Masterminer—"

"Knows nothing," D'gan growled at the unknown wingleader. "We'll just have to find more of the Shunned—"

"What if there aren't more?" K'rem asked worriedly.

"Find some," D'gan said. "There are always those who should be Shunned." He pushed off the table with his arms and stood. "Dragonriders need firestone to serve Pern. We shall get it."

"D'gan is looking for more miners," Zist commented sourly to Murenny as they paused in their discussion to listen to the drums.

Murenny snorted derisively. "I can never figure out how his Kaloth ever caught Lina's queen." With a shake of his head, he added, "They say that the mating flight chooses the best Weyrleader, but . . ."

"Well," Zist said, "you know how it was. D'gan was the strongest rider from Igen, and it seemed the right thing that the two Weyrs should merge bronze and gold."

Murenny gave him a reproachful look. "That's *my* theory you're poaching."

"It seems to be the only one that fits," Zist said with a shrug. He glanced at the sandglass that he had turned over just moments ago and then thoughtfully back to the Masterharper. Perhaps he would lose the bet after all.

But no! A rush of feet and a hasty knock announced the arrival of the Harper Hall's newest apprentice.

Zist allowed himself a small smile as he exchanged looks with Murenny, who shrugged and cautioned, "You don't know it's him." Zist merely smiled wider as the Masterharper called, "Enter."

"Sir," Kindan began breathlessly, his sides heaving from his mad dash to the Masterharper's quarters. "Is it true?"

Zist allowed himself one moment of triumph before he turned to Kindan and asked, "Is what true?"

"Toldur and Cristov," Kindan replied, gasping for breath. "And the mine at High Reaches."

"It is true," Murenny replied, shaking his head sadly. "Our reports are that the mine was completely destroyed."

"And Cristov?"

"You heard the reports," Zist said, his tone mildly disapproving as he wondered if Kindan had come to gloat over Cristov's tragedy. But the lad's next words relieved him, as Kindan asked, "What can I do to help?"

"You can learn everything there is about mining firestone," Murenny said, catching Kindan's attention. He gestured down to the Archives Hall. "You'll start there and then—if necessary—go through the Masterminer's records, the records at Telgar, and wherever else you can find any reference to firestone."

Kindan's eyes bulged and his mouth hung open in shock. But only for a moment. Then he closed his mouth and nodded, saying, "I'll get started right away."

"You can look now," the Weyr healer told Cristov. It had been nearly a full month before the healer had pronounced Cristov properly healed. He placed a small mirror in Cristov's right hand.

The face that peered back at him was his own, Cristov saw with relief. But then he turned his head to the side and saw the horrid mottled flesh that lined the left side of his head where hair and ear should have been, the burn mark where the exploding firestone had seared his flesh completely away.

"Scars like that make a dragonrider look distinguished," D'vin declared as he entered the room. Sonia looked up and flashed him a smile, which the dragonrider returned enthusiastically.

Cristov turned his scarred head to Sonia and asked, "Do you think so?"

"No," Sonia admitted. "But I look at the heart of a man, not his face."

"Anyway, I'm not a dragonrider," Cristov said to no one in particular.

D'vin ignored the comment, turning instead to the healer. "Is he fit?"

"Fit enough."

D'vin nodded at the assurance and turned back to Cristov. "Why don't you come for a stroll with me? I'd like to show you what you gave so much for."

Reluctantly, Cristov rose and followed the bronze rider.

D'vin turned back at the entrance and said, "You might want to come, too, Sonia."

Sonia gave him a look that Cristov couldn't read, exchanged an inquiring look with her father, who nodded in assent, and joined them, her eyes gleaming.

Cristov found as he walked that the left side of his neck felt tight, awkward.

"It will take a while for the skin to stretch out," Sonia commented from behind him, grabbing his hand as he reached to touch the scarred surface. "It's best not to irritate it. Father will give you a salve to help the skin stretch more."

As they exited the tunnels into the great Bowl of the Weyr, he noticed with annoyance that it hurt the left side of his neck to squint against the light, and he felt a twinge as he lifted his head upward. But the sight before him drove such minor aches completely away from his thoughts.

Dragons!

Golds, bronzes, browns, blues, greens, all soared in a graceful pattern over the top of the bowl, striping the ground below with wing-shadows.

An older man detached himself from a group of drag-onriders who were also watching their friends' aerial antics.

"They're honoring you," the man said, giving Cristov a slight nod.

Cristov could only nod back, still transfixed by the sights above him. So many dragons! Twisting, spinning, pirouetting, climbing, diving—it was almost as though a rainbow had taken flight.

For a moment, Cristov imagined himself on the back of one of those dragons, soaring up and diving down with delight. He could almost feel it.

Almost. "They're beautiful."

"They are indeed," the man agreed. Cristov tore his gaze away from the aerial antics and looked at the man who had spoken. His hair was gray and his face griz-zled, his body seemed shrunken, tired, but he bore him-self with an air that commanded respect. Cristov's eyes widened as he took in the rank knots on the man's shoulder.

"Weyrleader," Cristov breathed. He shook himself, angry at the pain on the left side of his neck. "I meant no disrespect."

"None was taken," High Reaches's Weyrleader told

him with a smile. He held out his hand and Cristov took it. "I am B'ralar."

"Weyrleader B'ralar," Cristov said, bowing deeply. "Thank you for your kindness."

B'ralar gestured for Cristov to straighten up and waved aside his thanks, saying, "It's we who should be honoring and thanking you."

Cristov was so surprised that B'ralar chuckled. "Why, it's because of you that we had any firestone at all."

"But the mine's ruined!" Cristov cried. "And Telgar has no mine, either." Cristov stopped for a moment as he absorbed the full impact of his words, then squared his shoulders, looked up into B'ralar's eyes, and said, "I'm ready to start again, Weyrleader."

B'ralar looked into Cristov's eyes for a long while before responding, "I see that you are. But, I think it would be best if you were to wait here with us awhile longer." When Cristov made to protest, B'ralar raised a hand. "We have enough firestone—thanks to you—to keep us for a month, if necessary."

The Weyrleader waved his hand to indicate the entire Weyr. "In the meantime, we would like to offer you our hospitality as thanks for all you've done."

Cristov still looked ready to argue. B'ralar smiled at him again. "Please," he said, "we owe you."

"But—"

"Come see the Hatching Grounds," D'vin interrupted, laying a firm hand on Cristov's right shoulder. "There are twenty-three eggs near to hatching."

"Yes, do!" B'ralar agreed, waving him away.

Cristov had only a few moments to notice High Reaches's lofty seven spires, the uneven peaks that gave the Weyr its name, before he found his eyes adjusting to a darker indoors, the tunnel to the Hatching Grounds.

Sonia, who had paused to chat with some weyrfolk, eagerly rejoined them.

"Garirth is bathing," Sonia said as she joined them. "I'll take a chance to check out that egg."

D'vin chuckled. "You've no need, now that your father confirmed that it's safe." To Cristov he explained, "We thought one of the eggs had a crack in it, but it turns out it's just a strange marking."

"My egg," Sonia declared, fingering the white streak in her hair. D'vin didn't laugh. In a softer voice, she added, "Maybe Garirth's last queen."

"You don't know that," D'vin said.

"Jessala's not been well these past two Turns," Sonia said. "And Garirth's mating flight was short and low."

"Garirth's strong."

"Her strength is as much as her rider's," Sonia replied, shaking her head.

They continued on through the tunnel into the Hatching Grounds in silence.

Instead of darkening further, the way slowly brightened. Cristov gasped. The Hatching Grounds were as well lit as the Weyr Bowl outside.

"There are mirrors guiding the light into the Hatching Grounds," D'vin explained, seeing Cristov's expression. He shook his head at memories of his youth. "Made of some sort of metal. The weyrlings are assigned to polish them when it's dark."

"Some more than others," Sonia quipped, glancing slyly at D'vin.

D'vin acknowledged her gibe with a wave of his hand, confessing to Cristov, "The Weyrlingmaster had it in for me."

Sonia snorted derisively, but said no more, her levity fading as she caught sight of the far end of the Hatching Grounds.

"There are only twenty-three," D'vin said apologetically. "There'd be more if Garirth were younger."

Eggs as high as Cristov's chest were sheltered together

in an array of mottled brilliance—bluish, greenish, brown, soft brown, the eggs were swirls of color that confused the eye.

Sonia loped away, intent on one egg set slightly apart from the others.

"She's hoping it's a gold," D'vin told Cristov in a low voice, "but the queen usually rolls queen eggs aside. Sonia says that it's a sign that Garirth is weak that she couldn't roll the egg very far away."

Cristov nodded, thinking that was the polite thing to do.

"If it's not a queen egg," D'vin continued, "and Garirth dies, then we'll be queenless, like Igen."

"Would High Reaches band with Telgar?" Cristov asked worriedly.

D'vin laughed, shaking his head. "I doubt that would be Weyrleader B'ralar's first choice," he said. "No, I imagine we'd barter for a queen egg." His face grew grim as he added, "Doubtless *that* egg would come from Telgar and we'd be beholden."

Cristov gave him a questioning look.

"We'd be beholden," D'vin explained, "to open our mating flight to the bronzes of Telgar."

"So you hope that's a gold egg, then," Cristov surmised.

"I do," D'vin agreed. He pointed to the other eggs, turning away from Sonia, who was carefully inspecting the odd striations in the larger egg. "Why don't you look at the others while you're here?"

Cristov looked at the eggs and back at D'vin in alarm. Sonia turned from her egg and said to Cristov, "Go on, when will you have another chance?"

"But—" Cristov's protests were so many and varied that he couldn't pick a first one.

"Everyone does it," Sonia said. "And you've earned the right."

Is that what the Weyrleader had meant? Cristov asked himself. He turned his gaze back longingly to the eggs lying less than a dragonlength away. The light played upon them like they were jewels beyond imagining. Without realizing it, he stretched a hand out as if to grasp one—but they were well out of his reach.

"You'll have to get much closer than that," D'vin said humorously. Just as he gestured for Cristov to move closer, a loud bellow sounded from in the Bowl.

"That's Garirth," Sonia said with an edge of nervousness in her voice. "She's on her way back."

D'vin sighed and said regretfully to Cristov, "We'd best leave. We can come back another day."

"It's not like you're going anywhere soon, after all," Sonia said.

Cristov gave her a questioning look, which she referred by a jerk of her head to D'vin, who sighed before responding slowly, "One man by himself, what could he do?"

Cristov felt himself flush with angered pride as he answered, "I could do my duty, dragonrider."

Sonia made a rude noise, surprising Cristov. "By yourself, you'd die, and neither I nor my father are willing to let you," she told him. She glanced at D'vin, who nodded, saying, "You're the only one alive on Pern who's mined firestone. It'd be foolish to let you go before you could at least teach what you know to others."

"I don't see how the Weyrs could have survived with the beastly stuff for all these hundreds of Turns," Sonia said with a shake of her head.

D'vin indicated a side passage off the main tunnel to the Hatching Grounds, which they took just as Garirth's lumbering form blocked the light from the Weyr Bowl.

"I agree," he said. He looked curiously at Cristov. "Hurth hates the stuff."

"Fire-lizards won't eat it," Sonia added. "I tried."

"But it was the same as you gave us," Cristov protested defensively.

"It was," D'vin agreed. "And all that Hurth's ever eaten for flame. The flames are hot and quick, but—"

"Maybe the Harper Hall will know more," Sonia said. Cristov gave her a questioning look. "B'ralar sent to the Harper Hall for more information on firestone mining."

"They assigned their best lad to the job," D'vin added.

With a growing sense of surprise and dismay, Cristov guessed the answer to his own unspoken question. "Kindan?"

"Yes," D'vin said with a curt nod of his head. "That's the lad. Do you know him?"

Cristov could only nod wearily. And then the humor of the situation dawned on him: Kindan was working for *him*!

"I'm going to go blind and it'll be all your fault," Kelsa complained as she pored over yet another moldy Record stored deep in the bowels of the Harper Hall.

"Nuella's blind and she's got a watch-wher," Kindan replied affably, feeling no less scratch-eyed and irritable than Kelsa but refusing to admit it.

"These Records are *useless*," Kelsa growled. "Who wants to know who was married to whom?"

"It's important for lineage," Kindan replied.

"Why did you have to pick me to help?" Kelsa moaned.

"You're good at spotting things," Kindan replied.

"I'm better at writing songs." Angrily, Kelsa grabbed a Record. "I can barely read this one."

"Be careful then," Kindan said. He waved a hand at

the neat stack of Records in front of him. "These are easier to read, but they make no sense."

"What do you mean?" Kelsa asked, glancing from her stack to Kindan's. She'd ceded him the oldest Records in the belief that they'd be the hardest to read and was now regretting her choice.

"Well," he said, holding up the sheet he was currently reading as an example, "this one's all on about how they first discovered firestone."

Kelsa leaned toward him, eyes wide. "That should be great, Kindan."

Kindan shook his head. "It says that they spotted fire-lizards flaming and tracked it down to firestone on the beaches."

Kelsa made a face. "Fire-lizards don't flame."

Kindan nodded. "And wouldn't firestone just burn up when the tide covered it?"

Kelsa nodded. "You're right, that's cracked." She moved closer, peering at the Record in his hand. "Maybe this is some child's story that they preserved. You know, proud parents and all that."

Blearily remembering that Kindan had no parents to be proud of him, Kelsa held out her hand, gesturing for the Record by way of diversion.

With a shake of his head, Kindan passed the sheet to Kelsa.

"You know," he mused while she read the paper, "it must have been very odd the way the colonists discovered firestone. I mean, it's buried under a certain sort of rock and all."

Kelsa bent closer to the Record. "I wish we had better light," she murmured, bringing her glow closer. "Glows just aren't bright enough to read with."

"We could wait until day," Kindan suggested jokingly.

Kelsa glared at him. "I can just imagine how the Masterharper would react to *that* decision."

"I suppose we could use a candle," Kindan said.

"Are you mad?" Kelsa squeaked, gesturing around at the stacks of Records. "They'd *burn*, Kindan."

"Only if you put them near the flame," he retorted. He waved aside any further argument and gestured to the Record in Kelsa's hands. "What do you think?"

"The print's too small and fine to be a child's," she declared after a moment. She pointed at the text. "And the phrasing doesn't sound like one either: 'The small winged creatures dubbed fire-lizards were observed to chew a particular rock scattered along the shoreline and then emit flame to defend themselves against Thread. It was later determined that the rock was phosphine-bearing.' " She looked up at Kindan. "That sounds like Master Zist when he's teaching."

But Kindan wasn't looking at her. He was staring off into space.

"Kindan?" Kelsa muttered, snapping her fingers under his nose. "You're not asleep, are you?"

Kindan batted her fingers away and focused back on her. "Kelsa," he asked slowly, "have you ever wondered why they're called 'fire-lizards'?"

Kelsa looked from Kindan to the Record she held in her hands and then back again, frowning thoughtfully.

"I think we should wake the Masterharper," Kindan said.

"It's the middle of the night," Kelsa protested. Apprentices who were foolish enough to wake the Masterharper anytime, let alone the middle of the night, often found themselves regretting their mistake for a very long time.

Kindan nodded. "It is here," he said. "But when will it be dawn at Telgar?"

Kelsa was tired and it took her a moment to think

through to his meaning. Dawn would come earlier at eastern Telgar than the westerly Harper Hall. And when dawn came, some would be working the mines. Some would possibly even be digging new firestone mines.

"Let's run," Kelsa said.

Harper learn,
Harper read.
Harper help
Those in need.

Chapter Ten

"IF I DON'T GET those herbs, she'll die," Moran repeated, glaring at Jaythen and Arella. Since his arrival, their acceptance of him had been conditional at best, hostile at worst. But they could not hope to match his skills as harper and healer. Now Aleesa lay before them, burning with fever.

Moran quickly determined that the self-styled Whermaster was more than a little crazed by a long life of trauma, not eased any by her association with watch-whers. But somehow he and Aleesa had found and kindled a strange sort of respect, bordering on friendship.

Perhaps he recognized a kindred spirit, tormented by past decisions and indecisions, torn between high ideals and petty indulgences. Or perhaps it was Aleesk, with her strange looks and quiet presence. He learned quickly enough that Aleesk was the last gold watchwher, and that Master Zist and even the dragonriders found the creatures valuable. After so many Turns spent fruitlessly striving to find an answer for the Shunned, or hope for their children, Moran found the issue of the watch-whers and their handlers to be a much easier burden, and he was in need of a rest.

"I don't trust you, 'harper,'" Jaythen said. "How do I know you won't betray us?"

"How do I know you'll return in time?" Arella asked, her face tear-stained from worry and haggard from hours of caring for her ailing mother.

"You don't," Moran said in reply to both of them. "But I can guarantee that the longer before I return, the less likely she'll live."

Arella looked away and bowed her head. Jaythen held Moran's eyes for moments more before dropping his arms and growling, "Go then." He took a deep breath. "But if you don't come back, I'll hunt you down and kill you."

Moran laughed. "You and Tenim both," he said. He gestured beyond them to the crevice where the watch-wher was sleeping restlessly and said to Arella, "If I don't come back in time, can you save Aleesk?"

Arella shook her head. "Not with a watch-wher of my own," she told him. "If you don't save my mother, we'll lose the last gold watch-wher on Pern."

Moran winced as he rose to his feet. "Then I'd best hurry," he said, striding quickly toward the light of the brightening day.

"How long will you be?" Jaythen called after him.

"Three days if I'm lucky," Moran called back.

"Be quick," Arella called after him.

"Be lucky," Jaythen growled ominously.

Moran shouldered his pack at the cave's entrance and strode quickly away.

He made good time the first day, better than he'd hoped. He knew that a lot of that was due to his new environment; the short rations of the wherhold and the work that Jaythen and Aleesa had demanded of him had forced him to grow stronger and leaner.

He woke early the next day, sore. It took him longer than he would have liked to get moving and he found it hard to keep the same pace he'd set the day before. The ground between the wherhold and Keogh was rough and barren. Moran chose his path with care; any fall here might well be fatal, even if he only broke a leg.

His concentration on his path was his undoing. He didn't notice the dragon above him until its shadow fell over him.

For a moment he froze in panic. What if D'gan found out about Aleesa? What could he do? He thought frantically, desperate for a plan. Finally, a slow grin spread across his face.

He looked up and waved at the descending dragon and rider. His waving grew more frantic and he smiled and bellowed, "Over here! Over here!"

When the dragonrider dismounted, Moran ran over to him. "By the First Egg, I'm glad you found me," Moran declared. "I was afraid I was dead for certain."

"What are you doing out here?" the dragonrider demanded, glancing around the barren terrain.

"I ran away," Moran said, waving behind him. "The Shunned were after me and I ran away. They caught me sleeping and it was all I could do to get away with my pack."

"Shunned, you say?" the dragonrider repeated. "How do you know they were Shunned?"

"Who else would be out here attacking the unwary in the middle of the night?"

"What were you doing out here?"

"I was heading to Keogh," Moran replied. "I need to get some medicines."

"Medicines?"

"Yes, I've left a sick mother behind at a cothold a ways back," Moran said, gesturing generally far north of Aleesa's camp, "and I need to get her feverfew or she'll die."

"Feverfew," the dragonrider murmured, then looked intently at Moran. "How do you know medicines?"

"I am a harper," Moran said, bowing low. "Moran, journeyman to Master Zist."

"K'lur," the dragonrider replied shortly. "I thought that Jofri was Zist's journeyman."

"A harper may have more than one journeyman," Moran temporized quickly, hoping that his surprise at K'lur's news hadn't shown on his face.

"Well," K'lur gestured impatiently toward his green dragon, "come along. I can get you where you're going faster than your legs."

"Thank you, green rider," Moran responded gratefully.

K'lur's response was a rough grunt that left Moran feeling uneasy until they were airborne and the dragon went *between*.

Moran's unease exploded into surprised outrage when they burst out from *between*. "This is Crom Hold!"

"Yes," K'lur agreed. "Lord Fenner must judge you. If, as I suspect, he knows nothing of you or worse, then you'll be Shunned and sent to the mines."

Moran was too stunned by this change in plan even to speak as they descended to the entrance to Crom Hold. Even if he could get the feverfew, he was now more than five days' journey from Aleesa. She would die—and then what would happen to the last queen watch-wher of Pern?

At K'lur's commanding gesture, Crom Hold guards formed up on Moran's flanks to prevent his escape and his walk assumed the nature of a march—a march of doom.

The great Hold doors opened and Moran found himself admitted to the Hold's Great Hall.

Moran had seen Lord Fenner several times from a safe distance but he'd never been introduced. He could hope that no one he'd cheated out of their marks had reported a good likeness of him to the Lord Holder. He did not want to be Shunned and turned over to K'lur and the firestone mines.

As he marched up the length of the Great Hall to the dais on which Lord Fenner sat, Moran noticed several people—even children—watching from tables placed alongside the walls. One of the children pointed at him with wide, surprised eyes. Moran paused, stunned. "Fethir?" Another child appeared familiar. "Marta?"

Rage, sudden and immense, filled Moran. He shook off his guards and raced to the end of the hall. "What are you doing with them?" He demanded at the top of his lungs. "Are you sending children into the mines?"

He looked around feverishly, recognizing the children he'd left with—"Where's Halla? What have you done with her?"

The guards caught up with him and wrestled him to the ground before he could assault Lord Fenner. Moran fought back as hard as he could, only to have more guards descend upon him. Even so he fought. *Must save them!*

K'lur stunned him with a two-handed blow to the back of the neck. Moran slumped over, and his lips split against the hard stone floor.

"What justice is this?" he asked through bloody lips, lifting his face up enough to catch a glimpse of the Lord Holder's boots. "What justice is it to send children to the mines?"

"Not mine," Lord Fenner answered from above Moran. At a gesture, the guards stepped back but retained wary holds upon the battered harper.

Moran straightened enough to meet Fenner's eyes. "Where's Halla then? I left these children in her care."

"She went off after Tenim," Fenner said, meeting Moran's gaze squarely.

"Are you mad? He'll kill her!"

Fenner shook his head. "It was not my idea," he said, glancing for just a moment at K'lur. "I'd sent her on a different task. But the traders told me that she changed *her course."

Moran realized that he was missing something and gathered that Fenner was guarding his tongue, but he couldn't understand why.

"You must send someone to get her," Moran said desperately. "She's not safe with him out there."

"Who is Tenim?" K'lur demanded from behind him.

"He was my ward, until he turned thief and worse," Moran said, not quite telling all the truth.

"Thief and murderer," Fenner said. Moran tried to cover his surprise—and his fear. "He was implicated in the death of one Sidar of Keogh."

"Someone used firestone," K'lur growled from behind Moran.

"He was burned?" Moran asked queasily.

"No," K'lur said. "Sometimes firestone gas won't burn; breathing it alone kills."

"What were you doing with the Shunned?" Fenner asked.

"Isn't it enough that he was consorting with them?" K'lur said. He failed to notice the irritated look on the face of Crom's Lord Holder as he continued, "D'gan will want him in the mines. The dragons need firestone."

"I was ordered," Moran replied to Fenner.

"By whom?"

"My master, Harper Zist," Moran said.

Fenner was silent for a moment. When he spoke again, it was to K'lur. "Dragonrider, I will have to investigate this," Fenner told him solemnly. "It will take no more than a day to get word to the Harper Hall."

"When you do, please send word that Master Aleesa needs feverfew and a healer," Moran begged.

Fenner gazed for a long moment at the green rider before asking frostily, "You took this man from the sick?"

"He was wandering alone," K'lur said. "He claimed he was going to Keogh, but I didn't believe him."

"Dragonrider," Fenner began and paused, putting a smile on his face, "I thank you for your kindnesses and for bringing this man to my attention. I will, of course, deal with any punishments necessary in my capacity as Lord Holder."

K'lur recognized Fenner's words as a dismissal. "But D'gan wants more workers," he protested, easily imagining his Weyrleader's fury when he returned empty-handed.

"So he has repeatedly told me," Fenner replied. "But there are only so many holders whose behavior warrants being Shunned."

K'lur looked like he wanted to argue the point but could think of nothing to say. With a curt nod, he turned on his heel and strode out of the Great Hall.

"That wasn't courteous, was it?" a young voice asked curiously as the great doors slammed shut.

At a gesture from Fenner, the guards stood completely away from Moran.

"Grab him a chair, child," Fenner replied. "And no, it wasn't." To Moran he said, "The dragonriders of Telgar seem short of courtesy since they integrated with the Igen riders."

The young girl, whom Moran didn't recognize, pushed a padded stool noisily to him. Moran stumbled upright enough to sit on it gratefully.

"Thank you," he said absently.

"You're welcome," the girl replied. "Marta, get a washcloth and some water, please."

Moran heard but didn't see the patter of Marta's feet as she raced off on her errand. Painfully he raised his head so that his eyes met Lord Fenner's.

"Please, my lord, could you send that message now?" Moran asked softly. "More than one life depends upon it."

"I can," Fenner said, "but I wonder if you recall that the Harper Hall is farther from Keogh than we are."

Moran nodded wearily. "Help will have to come a-dragonback if it's to be in time."

"You'll get no help from Telgar," the young girl snorted derisively.

"Nerra, that's no way to talk," Fenner said reprovingly. "We are beholden to Telgar Weyr."

"Yes, Father," Nerra said in a tone that showed she accepted the fact but didn't necessarily like it.

"The Harper Hall could ask for help from Fort Weyr or Benden," Moran said. He examined Fenner's face carefully, seeking to determine the nature of his character. He had heard that Fenner was a shrewd, cautious man who was not above sharp dealing. This man didn't seem to match the description. Moran's own judgment was suspect, he knew, for he had clearly misjudged Tenim. Still . . .

"The other life is a watch-wher," Moran said, watching Fenner's eyes for any reaction. Lord Fenner nodded and leaned forward in his chair. "She is the last gold watch-wher on Pern."

"I see," Fenner said, nodding. He glanced up and waved imperiously to his daughter. His words were clipped and fast, urgent. "Nerra, run to the drum tower. Do you know what to say?"

"Of course," Nerra replied, racing away. "Shall I use the emergency signal two or three times?"

"Three," Fenner called after her. Without pausing,

Nerra acknowledged him with a wave of her hand and was gone.

"Thank you," Moran said with feeling. The emergency signal was repeated three times only in a Pern-wide emergency.

"We'll see if you still feel that way later," Fenner said. He gave Moran a sour look. "Your name came up not too long ago, as I recall."

Moran raised an eyebrow. "My lord?"

"Yes, a poor man named Nikal swore a complaint on you," Fenner said. "Said he'd paid you for a month's Cromcoal and never got it." Fenner paused, watching Moran's face carefully. "When he told me that you'd claimed to be one of my harpers, I felt obliged to fill his lack."

"I had hoped—" Moran began but Fenner cut him off with a raised hand.

"The issue will be between you and the Masterharper," Fenner told him. "For which you should be grateful; I've Shunned men for stealing."

"It was for the children," Moran explained.

"You should have come to me," Fenner replied.

Moran shook his head, confused, and momentarily lost for words. He licked his lips and winced. "They were Shunned."

Marta came back at that moment with a wet washcloth. Fenner smiled at the child and directed her toward Moran. She handed him the washcloth and darted away, an action that spoke of no great affection for the harper. Fenner's frown was unseen by Moran, who was busy wiping the blood off his face.

When Moran had finished cleaning himself up, Lord Fenner said, "I think there will be some time before we get a response. Why don't you rest for a while?"

"Thank you, lord," Moran said, rising slowly to his

feet. Upright, he was surprised to find himself swaying with shock and fatigue. "I could use it."

"Kindan, Kindan," a voice shouted urgently in his ear. "They're calling for you."

Blearily Kindan opened his eyes to find Kelsa hovering over him, shaking him into wakefulness.

"Didn't you hear the drums?" Kelsa continued.

Kindan shook his head. He had been up through the night and well into the next day before he and Kelsa had been dismissed by an ecstatic Zist to catch what sleep they could. Judging by the light from Kelsa's glow, it was still dark out.

"News from Crom," Kelsa told him. "A triple emergency, help for Master Aleesa."

Kindan was on his feet so fast that Kelsa had to jerk her head back.

"Master Aleesa?" he cried. "What's wrong?"

"She's ill."

"They'll want me," Kindan said, fumbling for the door.

On his second attempt, Kelsa pushed him aside. "Let me," she said. As he stumbled out the door, she grabbed him, saying, "Maybe I'd better come along."

Kindan nodded a quick thanks. It was moments before the thought struck him that Kelsa usually did everything she could to avoid the attention of the Masterharper.

When they arrived at the Masterharper's quarters, Kelsa reverted to form and thrust Kindan inside before she could be noticed.

Kindan was not surprised to see that Master Zist was already there, but he *was* surprised to see another older person in the room.

If Zist was old, and Murenny older, this man was ancient.

His hair was completely white and thinning. Bright, light blue eyes stared out of a face that was lined with creases: crow's feet at the edges of the eyes, and pain lines around the mouth.

"Mikal?" Kindan guessed, surprised that the Harper Hall's famous recluse had deigned to emerge from his crystal cave. Mikal, once dragonrider M'kal, had made a place for himself in a cavern, shunning the more boisterous atmosphere of the Harper Hall itself. The ex-dragonrider had devoted himself to the study of healing and had become a master in his own right, developing his own brand of healing arts, which relied mostly on crystals, physical exercises, and meditation. His techniques were unique to the Harper Hall. Many otherwise incurable injuries had been overcome with his practices.

"Yes."

"You're late," Master Zist said, motioning for Kindan to grab a seat. "I was expecting you minutes ago."

Kindan took the indicated seat and apologized. "I was tired."

"Hmph! Tired while we old men keep longer hours than you?" Murenny snorted.

"He knows this Aleesa?" Mikal asked, gesturing to Kindan.

"Not well, my lord," Kindan answered quickly. "I met her once, Turns back, when I got my watch-wher egg."

"I have just been informed about the watch-whers," Mikal said, shaking his head. A strange, pained look flashed across his face as he added, "I hadn't really thought about them much."

"According to Moran's message, Aleesa's queen is the last of the gold watch-whers," Zist said. His tone suggested that he was continuing a discussion that had begun before Kindan's arrival. "If she dies—"

Mikal ignored him, turning to Kindan. "Zist tells me that you broke bonds with your watch-wher."

Kindan took a moment to process the ex-dragonrider's words before he nodded. "It was an emergency. Unless she let Nuella bond with her, the miners would have died."

Mikal nodded as he absorbed Kindan's response. "So, wouldn't it be possible for the queen to bond with someone else?"

Kindan shrugged. "Maybe."

"So you're saying you won't go?" Murenny pressed. "Because the queen might re-bond?"

"No, I'll go," Mikal replied. He nodded to Kindan, "He comes, too."

It took the cold of *between* to rouse Kindan out of his fatigue-induced haze, but what really woke him up was the dragon's dizzying descent in full darkness.

"I'll wait here," the dragonrider told them after they alighted. Kindan guessed that the rider's behavior was more in deference to Mikal than for any concern for the wherholders. "The watch-wher knows you're coming," he added with a hint of humor in his voice.

"Why the laugh?" Mikal asked.

"The watch-wher was surprised that a dragon could make a night flight," the rider replied, chuckling.

"They see in the dark," Kindan said.

"So do dragons," the rider replied with pride in his voice.

"Well, I don't see well," Mikal said, grabbing Kindan's shoulder. "I hope you see better, miner's son."

"The last time I was here was in daylight," Kindan said defensively.

He need not have worried, for his night vision was good and he quickly found a way into the wherhold.

"Which one of you is the healer?" The woman's voice startled them.

"I have some understanding of the art," Mikal replied. "The lad carries supplies."

A man's voice spoke out from a different location—behind them. "Where's Moran?"

"Crom," Kindan replied. "He was intercepted by a Telgar rider and brought before Lord Fenner for judgment."

"He sent word to the Harper Hall," Mikal added, "and Master Murenny asked me to come."

"What about the boy?" the man asked suspiciously.

"I was once bonded to a watch-wher," Kindan said.

"Once?" the woman snorted derisively. "How'd you lose it?"

"Kisk bonded with Nuella and is now Nuelsk," Kindan replied, surprised at the anger in his response.

No words were spoken but Kindan felt the atmosphere change from dangerous suspicion to cautious respect.

"If you don't want us here, we'll leave," Mikal said, turning around.

"Wait!" the woman called desperately. A dim light suddenly emerged in front of them. "Follow the glow."

In short order they found themselves being led through a set of canvas doors into a room lit dimly by red coals. The woman holding the glows handed them off to another woman.

"I'm Arella," the woman said. "Aleesa is my mother."

The rustle of canvas behind them caused them to turn; a hard-faced man entered, his hand on the pommel of his dirk. Mikal stared at him for a long moment before the man removed his hand from his weapon and, instead, held it out in greeting. "I'm Jaythen."

Mikal shook it quickly, then turned back to Arella. "Where's your mother?" he asked, gesturing with a hand for Kindan to give him the pack of supplies.

"In there," Arella said. Her eyes roved over the older man's face seeking some sign of his skill. "You arrived quickly enough," she said. "Moran said she'd be all right for a number of days."

"He might be right," Mikal said noncommittally. Gesturing politely for Arella to proceed him, he followed her into another chamber, muttering, "This is nice rock; I can feel the crystals in it."

Kindan, relieved of his pack, turned slowly around the room, spotted a familiar crevice, and asked Jaythen, "Is that where Aleesk lives?"

Jaythen's eyes narrowed in an instant of surprise, which he covered immediately with a derisive snort. "You don't know much about watch-whers if you don't know she's out hunting; it's night."

"My watch-wher was a green; one of Aleesk's," Kindan said. He made a cheerful sound of greeting toward the crevice, so reminiscent of the noise he'd made over four Turns ago that he felt a moment of regretful memories.

Aleesk's response from the crevice was no shock to Kindan, who merely turned back to Jaythen, saying, "I'd like to see her—she sounds worried."

Jaythen looked at the young man with renewed interest mingled with respect. Kindan turned back toward the crevice. Jaythen's hand on his shoulder startled him. The man spoke softly in his ear, saying, "Do you know what will happen if Aleesa dies?"

Kindan turned his head back to meet Jaythen's eyes. "I do," he said. "It's hoped that I could bond with her."

Jaythen nodded slowly. "Maybe you could," he said after a moment. His expression softened and he added, "I hope it doesn't come to that."

"So do I," Kindan agreed fervently. "This is something I think Nuella would be much better at."

He turned his head back, squared his shoulders, and walked into the watch-wher's lair.

Much later, Kindan was awoken by steps and a voice calling in awe, "She's a real queen."

It was Mikal. Kindan looked up from where he lay near the queen watch-wher and felt tentatively with his thoughts—had Aleesa passed on in the night? Was Aleesk now bonded to him?

"She is all right," Mikal assured Kindan. "Moran was right to send for feverfew and wiser to ask for help. He didn't understand some of the subtler issues."

Kindan nodded. Until the other day, he'd known nothing of Zist's missing journeyman but he knew much of Mikal and the ex-dragonrider's renowned abilities as a healer.

Mikal looked around the dimly lit chamber with interest, turning this way and that, reverently feeling the rock walls.

"There is good rock here," he announced. He turned back to Kindan. "I will stay here. The rock is good, and the watch-whers are pleasant company."

Kindan was startled; he'd thought that Mikal would always be a fixture of the Harper Hall. But Mikal was lured by rocks and crystals and—

"Do you know of a different firestone?" he blurted suddenly.

"A different firestone?" Mikal repeated blankly. "Why do you think there is a different firestone?"

"Because the records speak of fire-lizards chewing it on the shore of the Southern Continent," Kindan told him. He wondered why neither he, nor Master Zist, nor even the Masterharper himself hadn't thought of asking the ex-dragonrider.

In an instant he knew why.

Mikal sank against the floor, his legs suddenly weak.

Kindan moved to help but the old man waved him away. Feebly, he explained, "My dragon died from a firestone explosion." He searched Kindan's face. "Are you saying that there is a safer firestone?"

"Maybe it was all used up," Kindan said in a vain effort to ease the pain so evident in Mikal's eyes. He had heard of the bond between dragon and rider, but he'd never thought it was *so* strong that tens of Turns later the loss would still cause so great a pain. This was nothing like the feeling he'd had when his watch-wher had bonded with Nuella.

Mikal's look demanded more.

"The Records said that fire-lizards ate firestone on the shore," Kindan said again.

Mikal shook his head in disbelief. "The sea air alone would destroy the firestone, to say nothing of sea spray and the tide."

"That was my thought," Kindan said. "But why were they called fire-lizards? They won't eat firestone."

"They won't?" Mikal repeated faintly in surprise. His brow knotted in thought. "If there was a different firestone, then you'd know because a fire-lizard would eat it. Look for the stones that fire-lizards eat."

"Fire-lizards are hard to find," Kindan said. "There are a few at the Harper Hall. Fort's Lord has a new clutch."

"Pellar had a fire-lizard," Mikal said. "Send for him."

"Pellar?" Kindan said. He shook his head. "We don't know where he is."

Mikal shook his head. "Finding fire-lizards is easy enough, it's finding this firestone of yours that will be hard, if it exists."

"Maybe they couldn't find it in the north," Kindan suggested.

"Maybe," Mikal agreed dubiously. Then he brightened. "But you know where it was, so you could go there."

"Go to the Southern Continent?" Kindan asked warily. Everyone knew that the Southern Continent was unsafe: That was why the colonists had moved to the northern continent nearly five hundred Turns ago. He mulled over the thought. "Perhaps we could go just to find a sample."

"Wouldn't the Masterminer be able to tell you where to find this firestone here, once you had a sample for him?" Mikal asked.

"I don't know," Kindan said, then shrugged in apology for contradicting the old man. "It's just that the records seem to show that firestone mining has been dangerous for several hundred Turns. If there was a safer firestone, we'd be mining it."

"Unless the only ones who could tell had died," Mikal said.

"It would have been an accident, most likely," Kindan said. "Perhaps they discovered a vein of our firestone and it blew up before they realized their mistake."

Mikal mulled the suggestion over. "Perhaps."

Kindan was intrigued with the notion. "If they didn't know about our type of firestone, they'd never know their peril."

"And if the fire-lizards' firestone was impervious to water, they might have dowsed the new firestone with water without realizing the danger," Mikal said.

Kindan had a horrific image of miners using water to clean a wall of rock only to have it explode in a sheet of flame, extinguishing them in a terrifying instant.

"But why wouldn't the next miners have simply gotten a new sample from one of the Weyrs?" Kindan wondered.

Mikal shook his head. "We'll never know.

"And we'll never know if there is such a firestone until someone gets a sample from the Southern Continent." He pushed himself upright and turned determinedly toward the entrance. "We must talk with the dragonrider."

In your Hold you are secure
from perils that the dragons endure.
'Tis your duty, 'tis their due
You give to them, they shelter you.

Chapter Eleven

CRISTOV HAD NEVER FELT more uncomfortable in his life. He was in a meeting with the Weyrleader of High Reaches Weyr and all his wingleaders: the Masterharper of Pern; Master Zist; a grizzled old healer named Mikal who was treated with awe by the dragonriders; Toldur's widow, Alarra; and Kindan. The grouping of so many august personages had been so frightening that Sonia had avoided it, which only increased Cristov's own sense of alarm.

Of all them, Kindan made him feel most uncomfortable. However he tried, Kindan could not quite keep his eyes from Cristov's injuries. If he hadn't been so obviously understanding and sympathetic, Cristov might have hit him.

If Kindan had just looked a bit smug, Cristov probably would have. But Kindan looked even more apprehensive than Cristov felt.

"So you want us to go to the Southern Continent, from which our ancestors fled, to search for a firestone that fire-lizards will chew?" B'ralar asked, summarizing Kindan's report.

Kindan flushed and nodded. "Yes, sir—I mean, my lord," he said in a small voice.

"I think he's right," Mikal said. "For myself, I shudder to think how many have suffered needlessly if this is so."

"But what if this firestone is only good for fire-lizards?" one of the wingleaders protested. "What then?"

"The only way to know is for a dragon to test it," another observed.

"I'll do it," D'vin declared. "Hurth is willing."

B'ralar pursed his lips. "We don't have that many bronzes."

D'vin pointed at Cristov. "And we've even fewer miners."

B'ralar glanced at Cristov and Alarra sitting beside him, sighed, and nodded in agreement. "Very well," he said. "I approve this journey."

"You know," Murenny said thoughtfully, "even if we find this new firestone here in the north, who's going to mine it?"

"I'll mine it," Cristov declared.

B'ralar gave him a troubled look. "There's a Hatching soon; you should stay here."

For a moment Cristov's eyes lit with joy. The Weyrleader was offering him a chance to Impress a dragon!

"I'll go," Alarra said. "I owe it to Toldur's memory."

Cristov nodded. "I'll go," he said. He met the Weyrleader's startled look. "I owe it to Toldur, and I owe it for my father."

"Even that won't be enough, just the two of you," Kindan objected, somewhat surprised by his own jealous reaction to B'ralar's implied offer to Cristov. "You need a shift of ten to do any serious work."

"That's for *coal*," Cristov corrected.

"Rock's rock," Kindan replied, standing his ground. "There's only so much a person can mine in a day."

"The weyrfolk helped," Cristov responded.

"But will they be able when Thread falls?" Zist wondered. He glanced at B'ralar, who returned his glance with a troubled look.

"We could use the Shunned," Mikal suggested. In response to the others' muted reactions, he added, "Offer them an amnesty for a Turn's worth of work."

Murenny shook his head regretfully. "A good suggestion, but Telgar's been putting the Shunned to work in the mines for Turns—they know it's death to work firestone."

"Someone would have to tell them otherwise, then," Mikal suggested. "If they knew the firestone wouldn't explode, I'd bet they'd come in droves."

Zist gave him a thoughtful look and then said to Murenny, "It might be the solution to our problem."

Murenny nodded and, in response to B'ralar's questioning look, explained, "Master Zist and I have been concerned with the issue of the Shunned and what will happen with them during the Fall."

"They'd be protected like anyone else on Pern," B'ralar said immediately.

"But they've no holds, no place to grow crops," Zist pointed out. "Such people will be desperate."

"We sent Journeyman Moran out to make contact with them, Turns ago," the Masterharper added, shaking his head sadly.

"Perhaps Moran would be willing to continue his mission," Zist suggested to Murenny. He looked up at the Weyrleader. "Would it be possible for me to get to Crom on Harper business?"

"P'lel could take you," D'vin offered. "I'm sure his Telenth would oblige."

Halla tracked Pellar down at last, ready to pummel him for departing their hidden camp without leaving her the slightest message. It had taken her over an hour to find the first sign of his trail and another two to find him. She was hungry, hot, irritated, and—she hated to admit it—relieved at finding him.

Her relief gave way to surprise as she took in his position. He was kneeling. Was he sick? It had taken all her strength to pull him away to safety that day, so many sevendays ago. When she had found enough energy to go back for the other boy, she discovered that he was gone, as was Tenim's body.

"Dragonriders," Pellar had later written in explanation. But by then days had passed, and Halla had spent sleepless nights wondering if the blast had made Pellar addled. It had taken several more days before she recognized his strange gestures as attempts to write, and then she'd spent a fruitless day searching for something he could use, only to find, on her return to their camp, that Pellar had cleared a patch of ground and had used a stick to write, "I'm not addled. Remember, I can't speak."

Halla's relief had been so great that she had cried for the first time since she'd been with Lord Fenner of Crom. She was surprised and grateful when Pellar wrapped his arms around her and held her tight while she cried out all the fears and horrors of the past weeks. But she also felt a bit uneasy; with Lord Fenner, Halla had felt that she'd been with someone like the father she'd never known, but with Pellar she felt more like she'd come *home*—and it scared her.

They'd had to change camps and hide when they discovered that the firestone mine had attracted several groups of the Shunned, who looted the wrecked mine and outbuildings for whatever they could find. Halla had refused to allow Pellar to contact the dragonriders, protesting, "They'll capture them and put them to work in firestone mines!"

Nothing Pellar wrote could persuade her otherwise,

and they spent several days angrily apart, not communicating beyond the barest necessary for survival.

The Shunned had fled when the dragons returned. But the dragonriders had stayed only briefly and were gone before Halla and Pellar could resolve yet another argument over whether to contact them.

And now the last of the food Halla had was gone; they would have to move camp soon, as the local game was now too wary of their traps, and Pellar was here kneeling in the grass.

He turned at the sound of her approach—which irritated Halla no end as she could have sworn that no one could hear her—and grinned, holding up something cupped in his hands.

It was yellow. No, *they* were yellow.

"Yellowtops!" Halla exclaimed in surprise. Then she remembered her worried hours of searching and shouted at him, "You went looking for yellowtops?"

Pellar nodded, his grin slipping into a smaller smile. He stood up and handed her one, gesturing for her to follow him. Halla raised an eyebrow at him but shrugged and waited for him to lead the way.

They walked in silence, which grew more companionable with every step. Pellar was clearly excited about something, and his excitement was infectious. What was he going to do with yellowtops?

The question had just turned over in Halla's mind when they topped a rise and she knew what he was going to do. She lengthened her stride and caught up with him, pulling him to a stop. Pellar's eyes met hers just as Halla leaned up and kissed him.

"It was you!" she said. "You were the one." ·

Pellar nodded. She kissed him again and grabbed his hand, dragging him after her as they made their way down the rise to the neat graves set in the dale below.

Wordlessly they stopped and knelt in front of the

mounds. After a moment they leaned forward and carefully placed the small yellowtops on each grave.

One was Toldur's, one was Tenim's, but Halla could not tell which was which. Nor did she care; in her mind, the dead were clear of all debts.

Zist was surprised at the sight of Moran. His memories of the man were over a dozen Turns old, but he hadn't expected to find the young man he'd sent on a perilous journey changed into such an old, worried person.

"Master Zist, I'm sorry," Moran said, bowing deeply. "I've failed you and the Masterharper."

Zist waved his apology aside. "Not your fault, boy. The job was bigger than you."

"Then why have you let Lord Fenner send a mere girl on the same mission?" Moran demanded hotly, meeting Zist's eyes squarely.

Zist raised an eyebrow and turned an inquiring look to Lord Fenner, who had the grace to look embarrassed. Behind him, however, a girl who bore a remarkable resemblance to Crom's Lord merely snorted in annoyance.

"Father was absolutely right to send Halla," the girl declared. "She's a girl, after all."

"Nerra, hush!" Fenner said quellingly. Nerra took an involuntary step backward before she caught herself, huffed, and defiantly regained her previous position.

"I will not," she said. "You were right to send Halla—she was a much better choice to deal with the Shunned."

"She was so small," Moran objected.

"Exactly!" Nerra said, pouncing upon his words. "No threat to anyone and quick on her feet, as well as her wits."

"So where is she?" Moran demanded.

Nerra's exultant look collapsed, and she was reduced to murmuring, "They didn't find her body at the firestone mine."

"The dragonriders could search for her," Zist suggested.

"Not Telgar," Nerra declared. "They'd take her to the mines." She pointed at Moran. "They were all ready to take *him* to the mines except that Father refused." She sniffed. "At least D'gan still recognizes the rights of the Lord Holder, if nothing else."

"Nerra, that's no way to talk about our Weyrleader," Fenner said, but it was clear to Zist that his heart wasn't in it. Nor could the harper blame him; he'd seen enough of D'gan's imperiousness firsthand. Dragonrider or not, the man bore his rank and responsibilities poorly.

"What did you ask this girl to do?" Zist asked Fenner.

"I asked her to track down the Shunned in hopes of opening communications with them," Fenner said.

"That's what Master Zist asked of me!" Moran exclaimed.

Nerra looked ready to say something acerbic, but was quelled by a look from her father.

"The traders had taken her under their protection," Fenner explained. "They agreed to lend her aid and support."

"And if she'd contacted the Shunned, what then?" Zist asked, curious to see if Crom's Lord Holder had come up with a solution to the knotty problem of Pern's dispossessed.

"Arrangements could be made," Fenner said. He met Zist's eyes squarely. "Some of those are doubtless people I've Shunned myself. But the Red Star grows larger and Thread will return. And when it does, what then will people with nothing to lose not do in order to survive?"

Zist nodded. "That was a question the Masterharper and I considered many Turns ago." He glanced at Moran. "Our plan miscarried, however."

"The only plan that seems to be working is D'gan's," Fenner admitted ruefully. "Round them up and force them to mine firestone."

"Perhaps not force," Zist said, "but encourage." To Lord Fenner he explained, "We've just discovered Records that indicate there might be two types of firestone." He went on to describe the meeting at High Reaches Weyr and the conclusions that Mikal, Kindan, and Cristov had reached.

"So they are going to the Southern Continent?" Fenner asked in surprise.

"Only the shore," Zist said in reassurance. "To see if they can find any of this fire-lizard firestone."

"A firestone that doesn't explode in water," Moran muttered to himself. He looked up at Zist. "What do the Shunned have to do with this?"

"This new firestone wouldn't be deadly to mine," Zist explained. "And all Pern will need it soon. If they could be convinced to mine it, their place and their protection would be assured directly by the Weyrs."

"That *could* work," Moran agreed, stroking his chin thoughtfully. He looked up again to Master Zist. "Master, I'd like to offer my services. I will make contact with the Shunned."

"And find Halla while you're at it," Nerra demanded.

"And find Halla," Moran agreed, turning to sketch a short bow in the girl's direction.

"Perhaps P'lel will drop you somewhere along our way," Zist said, turning to the green rider who had silently watched the entire exchange.

"For a firestone that doesn't explode, I will do anything," P'lel agreed fervently.

* * *

The Southern Continent!

Cristov couldn't believe his luck as he sat perched atop Hurth's huge neck and peered cautiously down at the headland below. Beside them, blue Talith struggled to keep up with the huge bronze dragon's easy turn of speed.

It had startled Cristov for a moment to think that dragonriders couldn't just *go* to the Southern Continent.

"We need someone who's been there before," D'vin had explained when they first set out. "Perhaps someone in Ista will know."

Weyrleader C'rion greeted them courteously enough when they arrived in Ista Weyr's Bowl.

"What do you want with the Southern Continent, D'vin?" he asked when D'vin presented their request.

"Firestone," D'vin said immediately. He recounted the meeting at High Reaches and the conclusion reached by Kindan, Cristov, and Mikal.

C'rion looked skeptical until D'vin added, "Mikal was a dragonrider many turns back."

"Firestone accident?" C'rion asked.

D'vin nodded.

"There have been so many of those," C'rion said. He looked at Cristov. "And you say there's a firestone that doesn't burn in water?"

"The fire-lizards got their name for some reason," Cristov pointed out.

"And B'ralar approves this?" C'rion asked, rubbing his chin thoughtfully. "Well, he's a cautious one. If he says so, then I'm up for it."

"Do you know someone who could guide us?" D'vin asked.

C'rion heaved a sigh before replying. "You know that the Southern Continent is banned," he said. When

D'vin nodded in agreement, he continued, "There's good reason for it, I'm sure. But I've one blue rider who won't listen to reason and just flies off by himself now and again. When he comes back, he's always got these most amazing fruits of the largest size."

"He goes to Southern?" D'vin asked.

"I've never asked," C'rion replied drolly, his eyes lit with amusement. "But perhaps he can guide you."

And so, without actually saying it aloud, D'vin managed to get J'trel to agree to give him the coordinates, provided he could come along.

"I suspect he wants an official reason to know where the Southern Continent is," D'vin confided with a grin to Cristov as they rose out of Ista Bowl and took station beside the wiry blue dragon.

And now here they were.

D'vin gestured to the beaches beyond the headland, indicating that they should land there.

The sun was warm and the sand hot as they jumped down and looked around.

At some unspoken word from Hurth, D'vin laughed and told his dragon, "Yes, go play! But be ready when I call."

With a huge cooling breeze from his wings, Hurth leapt into the air. Soon he and J'trel's Talith were cavorting in and out of the warm southern water.

"Any sign of your rocks, Cristov?" J'trel asked as he strode up to them.

Cristov looked dismayed to hear the fire-lizards' firestone referred to as "your rocks." He wondered how the dragonriders would react if none were found.

"Are there any fire-lizards around?" he asked hopefully. "Maybe we could find the rocks they like."

After an hour, D'vin suggested they try further south. The dragons returned from their water play quickly enough, though neither Cristov nor D'vin were quite happy to be riding a wet dragon.

"We won't go *between*," D'vin said reassuringly to Cristov, "but fly straight. Call out if you see anything."

They checked out two more beaches, but there was no sign of any rocks worthy of consideration.

"Let's rest a bit, and continue later," D'vin suggested as they trudged in the hot sand.

"Good idea," J'trel agreed readily. "I know where to get some fruit—" His face fell as D'vin smiled knowingly at him, but he recovered quickly, adding, "It's the best fruit you'll ever taste."

"I'm sure of it," D'vin said. He waved J'trel off and called Hurth in from the sea. The dragon curled up comfortably in the sand, tired from his exertions.

J'trel returned shortly, his sack full of large, orange-mottled fruits, which he shared with the other two. Cristov waited until D'vin had bitten into one—manners, he would have said if challenged—but when the Weyrleader's face lit with appreciation, Cristov's restraint vanished.

"They're great!" he exclaimed as soon as he swallowed his first bite. He'd never tasted anything like it. He could completely understand why J'trel had ignored all prohibitions to search out this fruit.

Silence descended as the three ate heartily. The silence continued as the sun reached its highest point and bore down on them relentlessly. Fortunately, Hurth agreeably stretched a wing out over D'vin and Cristov, providing them with shade. J'trel sought the company and protection of his smaller Talith.

Soon all three humans and two dragons were asleep, lulled by their full stomachs, exertions, and the hot noon sun.

Cristov woke with a start, angry with himself for nodding off. He tried to get up but discovered he was

trapped by D'vin's arm across his chest. D'vin silenced
him with a look, and then, deliberately, turned his head
slowly forward, away from Cristov. Cristov followed
his gaze . . .

Fire-lizards.

He tracked them with his eyes, picking out prominent
landmarks so that he would know exactly where they
had been. There was a little queen and several bronzes.
A mating flight? No, there were blues, greens, and
browns, as well.

Idly, Cristov wondered whether a fire-lizard could
help in the mines.

One of the bronzes had noticed them. It flew toward
them and then, with a chirp of surprise, blinked *be-*
tween. Immediately, the rest of the fire-lizards vanished.

D'vin chuckled. "Hurth tells me that the bronze
couldn't believe he was looking at a relative that was so
big."

D'vin released Cristov and the two got up. J'trel
joined them, his eyes alight. "Such antics! Did you get a
good fix on their location?"

"Not far from that promontory," Cristov replied,
pointing. "Maybe five or six hundred meters away."

"It's a pity they weren't flaming," J'trel said.

"It's possible that they won't be looking for firestone
until the first Threadfall," D'vin remarked, with a sideways glance at Cristov.

Cristov groaned and his shoulders slumped. "I hadn't
thought of that!"

"Nor had anyone else," D'vin told him reassuringly.
"Still, we can look." He cocked an eyebrow at J'trel. "Is
your Talith up to chewing strange rocks?"

"Certainly," the blue rider replied after a moment's
silent communication with his dragon.

"It's a pity we forgot to bring a shovel," D'vin remarked as they started toward the promontory. Behind

him, Hurth grumbled and leapt into the air, arriving at the site before them. A shower of flying sand flew into the air as the great dragon began to dig. "Sorry, Hurth, I'd forgotten we didn't need one," D'vin apologized with a smile.

"For a fire-lizard, the stones would have to be about this big, wouldn't they?" J'trel asked Cristov, making a shape about half the size of his fist.

"I suppose," Cristov agreed judiciously. He looked around. "And they wouldn't bother with the larger rocks, so if we found any place where there were lots of larger rocks of the same type and no smaller ones—"

"Like these?" D'vin asked, holding up a rock the size of his fist.

Cristov beckoned, and D'vin tossed the rock to him. The young miner examined it for a moment; started to toss it aside, then changed his mind and tossed it to J'trel. "That's too heavy for firestone; it should be lighter."

Cristov spied some rocks not far from Hurth's new hole. He walked over and picked one of them up.

"This is more like it," he said, hefting the rock judiciously.

"It looks like sandstone," D'vin said, picking up another one from the pile.

Cristov nodded and threw his rock down hard on a larger rock. His specimen cracked, revealing a blue-green crystal.

"Is that firestone?" D'vin asked.

"It could be," Cristov replied.

"There's only one way to find out," J'trel said, picking up the other half of Cristov's specimen. "Talith, if you'd be so kind?"

The blue dragon opened its mouth and J'trel threw the rock into it. Shortly there came the grinding sound of a dragon chewing and then Talith swallowed, visibly and audibly.

"Now, we wait," J'trel said. The three found it impossible to wait patiently. Cristov found himself examining the promontory for more signs of sandstone or blue-green rock; D'vin found more of the sandstone rocks and started cracking them, throwing the ones that were pure sandstone into one pile and the ones with hints of the blue-green rock into another pile; J'trel merely spent his time nervously pacing in front of his dragon.

"So how do you feel?" J'trel asked out loud. "Does it feel like firestone?" Before he could get a response, he jumped away, arms outstretched, crying, "Stand back!"

Talith opened his mouth and burped. A tiny flicker of flame erupted.

"That took longer than regular firestone," D'vin said.

"Talith says that it didn't burn, and he'd like to try some more," J'trel reported, gathering up some of the rocks that D'vin had sorted and feeding them to his dragon. D'vin started doing the same with Hurth.

In a few short moments, both dragons produced a decent flame, and both pronounced it much less stressful than the firestone they were used to.

"Does it look like they can sustain flame longer?" D'vin asked J'trel.

"Yes, it seems like this firestone produces the fire gas more slowly," J'trel agreed. He looked up at Talith again. "Is that how it feels to you?"

Cristov understood Talith's response merely from the blue's emphatic nod. He picked up a specimen and walked with it to the sea.

"Cristov, what are you doing?" D'vin asked, his voice tinged with equal parts curiosity and alarm.

Cristov threw his rock, with its exposed blue-green

crystal, into the surf and watched carefully. Nothing. No explosion, no puff of gas, nothing.

"I just wanted to be sure," he said, turning around and walking back to the others. He picked up several specimens and stuffed them into his pouch. "This firestone doesn't explode on contact with water."

"There must be something extra in the dragons' stomachs to make the flame," D'vin suggested, hefting a rock in his palm. "If this were the old firestone, the sweat from my palms alone would produce some gas."

"If this were the old firestone, all the sea air would have combusted it long ago," Cristov remarked.

"Well, now that we've got the right firestone, what do we do next?" J'trel asked.

"We find it in the north, if we can, and mine it," Cristov replied. He turned to D'vin. "I'd like to start immediately."

"If not sooner," D'vin agreed, looking very thoughtfully at his sample. It was a long moment before Cristov's agitated movements attracted D'vin's attention. The dragonrider smiled at him but did not apologize, merely gesturing for Cristov to mount Hurth.

"I do *not* understand," Halla cried to Pellar in exasperation.

Pellar started to write again, but Halla pulled the stick out of his hand and snapped it in two, throwing it to the ground.

"Our traps are here, our food is here—why do you want to go north?"

Pellar sighed and picked up the thicker piece of his broken stick. Bending down, he wrote, "Dragonriders."

"That's what you said before!" Halla exclaimed, her frustration evident. "We can avoid them. The woods are too thick for them to land, and we can hide." She looked up entreatingly into Pellar's eyes. "We're safe here," she said in a small voice. "We don't have to run anymore."

Pellar nodded, but still he smoothed out the patch of dirt he'd written on and bent down to write again. "We help."

"Help?" Halla repeated. "We don't need help, we can get along just fine on our own."

"Thread," Pellar wrote in response.

"Thread won't come for Turns, you said so," Halla replied irritably. What was wrong with him?

Pellar wrote the word "fight" just above "Thread."

"Fight Thread?" Halla shook her head. "Why should we worry about that? That's dragonriders' work!"

Pellar nodded, then wrote another word above "fight." The word was "firestone."

"Firestone fight Thread," Halla repeated. She paused to digest the meaning. "The dragonriders need firestone to fight Thread and you want to help them?"

Pellar nodded, smiling.

Halla shrieked at him, "You'll get killed!"

He shook his head.

"Then you'll get burned just like your friend," she said. She pushed him away from her, tears streaming down her face.

"Go on then, get killed. See if I care," she cried, and ran away from him into the dense underbrush. She didn't go far and crumpled into a small heap when she failed to hear Pellar coming after her.

I don't need him, she thought. I can survive on my own.

After a moment she asked herself, then why do I hurt so much?

Pellar sat in silent thought for a long time after Halla had run off. Then, with a sigh, he stood and walked off purposefully in the opposite direction.

*   *   *

"There!" Moran pointed below them as they flew over the vast barren country north of Keogh.

Zist peered down, following his arm, and saw faint marks on the dusty ground below.

"It could be traders," he said.

"This far north?" Moran asked, shaking his head. To P'lel he said, "Put me down somewhere in front of them."

Moments later, they were on the ground and Moran was hefting his pack onto his back.

"You'll stay in touch?" Zist asked.

Moran nodded. "I will."

"And be careful?" Zist asked.

"More than last time."

"If I don't hear from you in a month . . ."

"You'll hear from me," Moran promised, turning toward the oncoming wagon. "Probably sooner than that!"

Halla awoke, angry with herself for having fallen asleep and cold from the chilly, late afternoon breeze. She peered blearily around for Pellar and then remembered their last conversation and how she'd pushed him away.

People always leave, she thought bitterly. Why should Pellar be any different?

Something caught her eye, fanned by the breeze. Halla turned her attention to it, then pounced on it eagerly.

It was a pair of yellowtops, their stalks twined together. Halla picked them up and held them gingerly in her hands, impressed at how deftly Pellar had woven them together. A smile wobbled on her lips.

In the distance she saw another bright bundle. Intrigued, she went toward it and discovered another pair of yellowtops. She picked them up, too, just as she noticed a third pair. A trail.

Halla's earlier thought echoed: People always leave. But no one had ever left her a trail.

It was dark by the time Halla caught up with him. She would have missed the last bundle of yellowtops if Pellar's trail hadn't continued unerringly north.

He was camped in the open, which surprised Halla. Clearly he wasn't worried about intruders, but his lack of precaution increased the danger of attack from night animals. Pellar slept like someone who was under a nighttime watch.

Who?

The answer brought a smile to her lips: her. She dropped her armload of yellowtops on the ground beside him—she stuffed them into her pack where they would create a great pillow—and lowered herself to the ground, dropping her pack under her head. She lifted his blanket. Pellar shivered in the night air until she bunched herself up, scooched against him, and lowered the blanket. For a moment, Pellar was awake. He wrapped an arm possessively over her, drawing her tight against his stomach; then he fell asleep once more.

Though her back was against him she knew he was smiling. She smiled, too, and closed her eyes peacefully, a feeling she hadn't felt in Turns overflowing in her heart. She had only one name for it: home.

Cristov was depressed. They'd been searching the shoreline of High Reaches for three days and they'd nothing to show for it but a nasty collection of cuts, bruises, and sore muscles. Except, now, Alarra had broken her leg as she ran from a rockslide they'd caused with their digging.

She'd been quickly evacuated to the Weyr, where the

healer had set her leg and ordered her to rest until the bone knitted together once more—at least six sevendays.

Cristov had insisted on continuing the search, and D'vin, after consulting with B'ralar, had reluctantly returned Cristov to the mountains south and east of their previous location.

"Hurth will be listening if you need help," D'vin told him. "Otherwise, I'll send someone by next sevenday."

When Cristov looked curious, wondering why D'vin hadn't promised to return himself, the wingleader said, "The Hatching will be any day now. Seeing as we want to present as many suitable candidates as possible, I'll be riding in Search."

Cristov promised himself that he would not call the bronze dragon except to announce success.

On the first day he had no luck at all. He wasn't sure if his technique was right anyway: He would stop at a spot that caught his fancy, usually a place where the rock had been bared already, and dig around it, looking for signs of sandstone in the layers. If he found any, he'd dig around, looking for loose rock; failing that, he'd use his pick to break some rock free.

He worked for no more than an hour and then moved northward again, looking for a new spot. In this way he covered two kilometers and had made five excavations by nightfall.

The next day, though sore, he repeated this method. He was pretty certain that he'd found a vein of sandstone, but he couldn't be sure—he'd never learned this sort of minecraft from his father, or even from Toldur.

On the third day, Cristov changed his tactics, deciding to dig deep into the sandstone vein he'd located the night before.

It was a hot day and Cristov was all the hotter, digging into the moist cliff in front of him. He liked sandstone because it was soft; he disliked it because it was crumbly—not a good supporting material. He had dislodged a fair amount of the soft stone and was making amazing progress digging into the side of the mountain when it happened: From one blow to the next, the whole nature of the vein changed, and instead of a trickle of loose rock, Cristov suddenly found himself facing a flow, then a rush, and finally a torrent of sandstone that threw him backward and engulfed him.

For the past two days Pellar had been traveling due north, and Halla had followed. They were tired, irritable, and hungry, but they were together, and Halla found that Pellar's mute companionship more than made up for his annoying determination.

Thirst, however, was something neither could ignore, and so they were drinking at a stream when Halla heard it: a distant rumble that quickly died away. A glance at Pellar confirmed that he'd heard it, too.

"Come on!" Halla shouted, racing off in the direction of the sound.

When they reached a clearing, they spotted a cloud of dust rising about a kilometer north of them. Wordlessly they broke into a steady, ground-eating trot.

Pellar lengthened his stride, his long legs quickly widening the gap.

"Go on," Halla called, waving him onward. "I'll catch up."

When Halla arrived at the site, she found Pellar inspecting the remains of a mine. She quickly toured the immediate area and found a campsite. The footprints around it belonged to one person, someone bigger than her but not by all that much. She returned to Pellar and the disaster.

"Only one person," she told him between ragged

breaths. She knelt over, filling her lungs with cooler air and forcing herself to take slow deep breaths.

Pellar nodded and began to pull armloads of the rocks away.

"You think he's there?" Halla asked as soon as she'd recovered. She stepped up opposite him and began to throw stones away. She stopped when she caught sight of something shiny among the coarse, red rock. Thinking it was odd, she quickly pocketed it, then returned to her work.

A little while later, Pellar encountered hair. He rapped two rocks together to get Halla's attention and pointed. Wordlessly she came around to where he was and began to help.

In moments they uncovered a head.

"I *know* him!" Halla cried. "That's Cristov."

Pellar nodded and bent over the face, clearing the smallest dirt away. He pressed his ear close to Cristov's mouth and then looked up at Halla, alarmed. Then, to her surprise, he leaned over again and parted Cristov's lips, put his own mouth over Cristov's and blew a death breath.

"Pellar!" Halla exclaimed disgustedly. "Eww."

Pellar paid her no attention, looking instead at Cristov. He repeated the movement. This time Cristov coughed and sputtered.

"Stay still!" Halla ordered. "You're in a landslide."

Quickly Pellar and Halla dug Cristov's chest out from under the loose rock. It took more effort and more care to extract his legs.

Finally, Pellar motioned for Halla to stand back and gestured that he would pull Cristov out.

"No, I won't," she declared firmly, eyeing the rocks above them. "We'll do this together."

Pellar pursed his lips angrily in response, and Halla stuck her hands on her hips and glared in return. Pellar gave her one last angry look, sighed, shook his head regretfully, and gestured for her to come help.

Together, slowly, they pulled Cristov out from the landslide. When he was far enough out, Halla moved to his legs and picked them up. Cristov groaned painfully.

"I'm sorry," Halla told him, "but we've got to get you away from here."

"My rock," Cristov cried through clenched teeth.

"Shh," Halla told him soothingly. "We can find you plenty of rocks."

Cristov was in too much pain to argue. They went about twenty meters before Pellar gestured to Halla to set the boy back down.

"I'll get some water," Halla said, moving quickly to the campsite.

Pellar was kneeling beside Cristov when she returned.

"Am I dead?" Cristov asked Halla.

"No," Halla replied testily.

"But *he's* dead," Cristov said, pointing to Pellar.

Halla shook her head and opened the flask. "Here, drink this." When Cristov complied, spluttering a bit on the water, she looked at him and said, "There, do you think dead people cough when drinking?"

Cristov thought for a moment and shook his head. He winced at the movement. Pellar laid a hand on his head and glanced up to Halla, shaking his own head.

"Pellar says that you shouldn't move your head," Halla told him, her tone implying that she expected that Cristov had already figured that out himself.

"You can talk to him?" Cristov asked in wonder.

Halla shook her head. "No, but it's easy to guess what he means."

Pellar shot her a penetrating look and broke into a huge grin.

"My rock," Cristov said. "We must find it."

"There are plenty of rocks," Halla repeated soothingly. "We can look when you're better."

"No, we've got to find it," Cristov responded, his face twisted in irritation. "If not, we'll have to go back to the Southern Continent to get another."

"What sort of rock is it?" Halla asked in surprise. "And what were you doing on the Southern Continent?"

"Looking for firestone," Cristov explained.

"But you've found it already," Halla said. Her brows drew close. "You weren't hoping to find it in that sandstone, were you?"

"Yes," Cristov said. "That's where we found it before."

"Sandstone?" Halla repeated dubiously. "But firestone explodes in water."

"Not this firestone," Cristov replied. "It doesn't burn in water. It's what the fire-lizards eat, and they find it on the shore in the Southern Continent." He frowned. "I've got to find that sample."

"What's it look like?" Halla asked.

"It's a blue-green crystal," Cristov told her. "There's usually some sandstone around it."

Halla fished in her pocket. "Like this?"

"That's it!" Cristov cried, reaching for it. Halla gave it to him readily.

"But there's loads up there," she said, waving her hand back up toward the landslide. "That was just the smallest piece."

Cristov's eyes widened and he looked at Pellar for confirmation. The young harper nodded. A mixture of joy, relief, and impatience crossed Cristov's face.

"We've got to tell the Weyr," he exclaimed. Of Halla he demanded, "How much was there? How quickly can we get it?"

Pellar shook his head and pointed at Cristov's legs.

Halla guessed his meaning and said, "We've got to take care of you first."

"No," Cristov cried, "we've got to tell the Weyrs! Until we prove this is the right firestone and there's enough, they'll still try to mine the old firestone."

Pellar and Halla exchanged worried looks.

"All we have to do is find the blue-green rock?" Halla asked, an idea forming in her mind.

"Yes," Cristov agreed.

Halla gave Pellar a questioning look; he nodded.

"We'll do it," Halla said.

"Any luck?" B'ralar called as D'vin strode into the Kitchen Caverns.

D'vin pulled a face, shaking his head while filling a mug with *klah* from the kettle left on the warming stove. "Nothing in Tillek," he said. "I tried Hold Balen as well, but found no likely lads there, either."

"We've twenty-three eggs and only nineteen solid candidates," B'ralar said, frowning.

"Perhaps B'neil will have better luck," D'vin suggested.

B'ralar made a sour face. "His Danenth is nowhere near as good as Hurth at spotting candidates," he said. "I don't think there will be more than two sevendays before the Hatching."

"I can go out again, if you'd like," D'vin suggested. He started to say more but stopped, clearly listening to his dragon. When he spoke again, he was already moving, dropping the mug of *klah* on the nearest table. "Pellar's found Cristov. Cristov's injured."

"Go," B'ralar said, waving him off. "I'll let Sonia know."

D'vin waved acknowledgment as Hurth descended from his perch to retrieve his rider.

* * *

"No broken bones this time, either," Sonia said to Cristov when he woke the next morning to find himself tucked once again in the High Reaches Weyr infirmary. She smiled at him. "I think you do this just to spend time with me."

Sonia's hand descended on his chest as soon as Cristov tried to sit up. "And again, you're trying to move too early," she added with a sigh. She shook her head at him. "You're going to rest for a while."

"How long?" Cristov demanded petulantly. "I found the firestone—we've got to mine it."

"I know," Sonia replied, smiling. "Everyone's talking about it. Alarra was furious that you'd found it before she could get back out again."

"I still am," Alarra snarled from a bed just out of Cristov's sight in another alcove of the infirmary.

"You'll be on your feet soon enough," Sonia assured her. "And, if you're good, we'll give you crutches in another sevenday." Cristov looked startled, so Sonia explained, "We had to take her crutches away because she was doing too much on her feet." She shook her head wonderingly. "What is it about you miners? It's not as though you don't have time."

"But we don't," Cristov protested, his words cutting across a similar protest from Alarra. "A Weyr needs forty tonnes of firestone a week when fighting Thread."

Sonia shrugged.

"This new firestone isn't as dangerous as the old firestone," Cristov continued in response. "We could mine it now and build a stockpile."

"And have it ready before Threadfall?" Sonia asked.

"Maybe even have some in reserve," Alarra called.

"But we need to start *now*," Cristov groaned, leaning back in his bed.

"I think you're going to be a worse patient than you were the last time," Sonia muttered ruefully.

As the days passed, Sonia discovered that her prediction was more than accurate. S'son, her father and the Weyr's Healer, would steel himself every day to enter the infirmary and deal with the two impatient miners.

"*You* can go tomorrow," S'son told Cristov the evening of his third day at the Weyr, "provided you agree to do no work."

"What's the point then?" Cristov demanded.

"You can supervise," Sonia told him.

"There's no one to supervise," Cristov snapped.

Sonia merely smiled and rose from her place beside him. "In that case, you can wait until you're healed," she said. As she stood in the doorway, she called over her shoulder, "What should I say to D'vin?"

Cristov schooled the sour look from his face. "Please tell him that I'd like to go back at first light."

"Are you sure?" Sonia asked. "There's a Hatching soon. You don't want to miss that."

"What's the use of a dragon if it can't flame?" Cristov demanded, shaking his head irritably. "I'll do my duty and mine firestone."

Sonia turned back to face Cristov, eyeing him cryptically and saying, "There are other ways to serve Pern, you know."

Cristov grimaced. "This is the one I know." He remembered his father's sour comment from Turns back. "It's what I'm fit for."

The look Sonia gave him was pitying. "If you say so."

"There've been some changes since you were last here," D'vin warned as they descended through the morning mist.

Cristov couldn't imagine that Pellar and Halla could have done all that much in the four days he'd been gone, however hardworking and dedicated the two seemed to be.

The mist thickened into fog as they settled into the valley. Cristov was surprised that Hurth could find the ground, let alone a safe place to land, but the dragon landed without even a bump.

"I can't stay," D'vin apologized. "We've more eggs on the Hatching Grounds than candidates, so I'm still on Search."

"Good luck," Cristov said. D'vin gave him an odd look and started to say something, but shook his head and said instead, "Good luck to you, as well."

Cristov was alone in the foggy valley, the sun a dim dot just above the horizon. He stopped to get his bearings, then started in surprise as he heard noises in the distance. The creak of a loaded cart on rails, the distant sound of bellows, the even fainter but unmistakable noise of picks against rock—the whole valley was filled with the noise of work.

"Cristov?" a voice called from the fog. A small figure resolved from the shadows. It was Halla. She smiled when she saw him. "Pellar says you're not to work," she warned him. "But we need you—"

"I'm sure I can do something," Cristov told her.

"Not to work," Halla said, shaking her head. "We need your advice."

Cristov cocked his head in inquiry. Halla sighed and grabbed his hand, dragging him after her and saying over her shoulder, "It's best if we show you. Come on up to the mines."

"Mine," Cristov corrected. "Unless you've got more than one, it's just a mine."

"Mines," Halla replied testily. "And we've got three."

Cristov was dumbstruck. "Three? Why did you start three?"

"Well, it seemed pointless not to put everyone to work," Halla told him.

"Everyone?" Cristov repeated blankly. He squinted,

trying to see through the fog. He could see Halla clearly now and make out the color of her clothes. They were new and looked freshly washed. He wondered how she'd found the time to wash her clothes. Everyone? "How many people are here?"

"I don't know," Halla said. "Ask Pellar. I think he's trying to keep count."

"Trying?"

"Well, the numbers keep changing," Halla explained. "I think another wagon came in during the night. And we've got some farmers further up the valley. They're really thrilled with the soil—they say it'll be great for crops."

"Crops?" Cristov repeated dully. Farmers?

"Pellar!" Halla shouted. "Pellar, Cristov's here!" She turned back to Cristov. "Mind your head."

Cristov caught a glimpse of a dark space in front of him and instinctively ducked. They were in a mine.

"Watch out for the rails," Halla cautioned. "There should be some glows here," she muttered. "I'll have to talk to Spennal." She raised her voice again to shout, "Spennal! Spennal, where are the glows, you dimwit?"

A glow approached them, illuminating an older man.

"Sorry, Halla, I was just down with Pellar," the old man, Spennal, said. "I'll get more glows now," he said, handing her his glow basket.

"It's all right, just bring us to Pellar," Halla said.

"Certainly," Spennal replied. He glanced at Cristov and his eyes widened. "Is this him?"

"This is Cristov," Halla said. She turned to Cristov and whispered, "Everyone's excited that you're here."

"Why?" Cristov whispered back.

Halla's response was a bit embarrassed. "Well, Pellar and I might have bragged about you a bit," she confessed. "But you're the one who found firestone that doesn't burn."

"So?"

"You saved them," Halla explained, still in a whisper. "When word got out, they came from all over."

"Miners?"

"No," Halla said, "the Shunned." She took in Cristov's stunned expression. "They can work here without shame and without fear. This is their hold."

"Their hold?" Cristov repeated in surprise. A hold for the Shunned—how was that possible?

"If they work," Halla said. "If they don't, they can leave. We feed their children, but if the adults don't work, they don't eat and they don't stay."

"Three mines?" Cristov said, repeating Halla's earlier statement.

"Yes," Halla replied, looking at Cristov as though wondering if he were all right. She glanced ahead. "Here's Pellar."

The mute harper waved and smiled at Cristov, beckoning him forward to look at a drawing he'd made on a huge slate.

"What is it?" Cristov asked, splitting his question between Pellar and Halla.

"It's a map of the mines," Halla explained. Somehow Pellar had found several colors. She pointed out the various sections. "Red is where we've found the greatest concentrations; white is where we're planning on going. Pellar wants to know if you have any suggestions."

Cristov bent over the map, wishing the light were brighter. Halla must have sensed it, for she lifted her glows higher and closer to the map. He peered at the map for a long while, confessing, "I've never seen anything like it before." He glanced up at Pellar, who looked nervous until Cristov told him, "It's perfect."

He pointed to several areas, particularly the red spots. "It looks like there's a vein running through the mountains and all three mines pierce it," he said after a moment. He frowned over Pellar's white lines and looked around for something to write with. Pellar handed him some white chalk and a bit of cloth for an eraser. Cristov declined the use of the eraser. "I don't want to change anything just yet," he said, drawing a number of dotted lines. "I'm thinking," he explained as he drew, "that perhaps the vein runs north-south through the mountains. If that's so, you could mine here and here to meet the center mine."

"Pellar was afraid of cave-ins," Halla said.

Cristov glanced up and inspected the beams and woodwork over them. "Not if your people keep shoring the roof up like *that*," he said, grinning. He said to Pellar, "You're right to be worried about the sandstone—it's very soft and not good at holding weight. Shore up everything and you'll do fine." He looked around. "Just how big is the vein, anyway?"

Halla smiled. "It's as big as this shaft. We're getting over a tonne a shift from each mine."

Cristov whistled in surprise.

"You said we need forty tonnes every sevenday for one Weyr," Halla said, looking grim. "We can only get about twenty-one tonnes right now."

"But now we know what to look for," Cristov replied. "We can find more mines, maybe one for each Weyr."

A disturbance from the mine entrance distracted them. Spennal called out, "D'vin is here."

"What does he want?" Halla asked in wonder. Pellar shrugged, carefully took the large slate now marked with Cristov's dotted suggestions, and hung it back up on the wall before gesturing that the others should precede him.

"Some of the Shunned were telling me that holder children don't start working until they've twelve Turns or more," Halla remarked as they walked toward the shaft entrance.

"That's silly," Cristov said. "What would they do with all their free time?"

"I don't know," Halla said. "The youngsters here all work." She gestured toward the camp outside. "They want to learn a craft before they marry and, by twelve, they're already courting."

Pellar handed Halla a slate he'd been writing on and she read, "Harpers don't marry until they're older." She glanced back at Pellar. "What's older?"

"Sixteen?" Cristov guessed, glancing to Pellar for confirmation. Pellar made a "go higher" gesture with his free hand. "Eighteen?" When Pellar nodded, Cristov exclaimed in surprise, "Miners are lucky to live thirty Turns. We usually mate much earlier."

They came to the mine's entrance and squinted: The sun had broken through and was bathing the valley in bright morning sunlight. A gentle breeze had moved the last of the morning's mist away, wafting fragrant smells through the valley.

Cristov grunted in surprise at the vista exposed before him. There were tents, wagons, and some small houses sprouting up all over the valley. Three paved roads led up to the hills, one running right up to this mine, the other two to the other mine entrances.

"All this in four days?" he asked in amazement.

"They were hungry," Halla said. At Cristov's look, she explained, "They had to work to get fed. And Moran brought in a whole group when he came in two days ago."

"Halla, there's another wagon coming in," a woman called up to them.

"You know what to do, Lorra," Halla called back. "See what they can do, find out why they're here, and

what they'll do. Make sure that Harper Moran knows
about them, too."

"Where should I put them?" Lorra called back.

"Find out what's up and then decide," Halla called
back, glancing at Pellar for confirmation. Pellar smiled
and nodded at her decision.

Cristov looked at Halla with renewed interest. It
seemed that everyone in the camp looked to her for
guidance. He guessed that some of that was due to her
nature, some of it due to her position as Pellar's
"voice," but he couldn't quite imagine what else would
be required to get adults to accept directions from a girl
who was just coming into womanhood.

"It wouldn't have worked out this way if it hadn't
been for Pellar's ability to talk with dragons," Halla explained. Cristov's confusion must have been evident for
she explained, "Even the Shunned are wary of the dragons. Having a wing show up whenever Pellar needed it
was enough to convince even the hardest heads to listen
to reason. And Harper Moran sent them all here." She
made a face and then grinned. "We keep an eye on his
drink, and he teaches the little ones their Ballads—
respect for dragonriders and dragonkind."

The reference to dragons reminded Cristov that they
had left the mine to see D'vin. He scanned the valley below and picked out the bronze dragon easily. D'vin was
much closer to them, moving purposefully.

A group of miners noticed the dragonrider and then
noticed Cristov, Pellar, and Halla. The miners paused
on their way to the mines, curiously, some pointing at
Cristov, others at D'vin.

"Pellar," D'vin called when he was close enough to be
heard. "There's a Hatching."

"A Hatching?" Halla cried delightedly. "Pellar, did
you arrange for us to—" The look on his face cut her
off. "What's wrong?"

"Not going," Pellar wrote quickly, holding it up to her and then to D'vin as he joined the group.

"You can talk to dragons," D'vin said. "We're short just one candidate."

Pellar shook his head again and pointed firmly to the ground.

"But if there's not enough candidates for the hatchlings," D'vin said, his voice full of despair, "then—"

"What will happen?" Cristov asked. Halla glanced between them, her face betraying a wide range of emotions. Pellar gave Halla a horrified look, and she knew.

"The hatchling will die," she said.

"It will go *between* forever," D'vin confirmed.

Pellar frowned, torn. D'vin caught the way he looked around: at the valley, at Halla, at the mines, at Halla, at Cristov, at Halla, and finally at some distant vision only he could see. When he caught D'vin's eyes again, the wingleader knew Pellar's decision. For whatever reasons, and Halla was bound at the center of them, Pellar felt obligated to stay.

"Who else could go?" Halla asked D'vin, flicking her eyes toward Cristov.

Cristov caught the look and held up his hands, protesting, "Not me, I don't deserve the honor."

"Why don't you let the hatchlings decide?" D'vin suggested.

"But there's work to do here," Cristov protested.

"We'll do it," Halla assured him, jerking her head toward Pellar, who nodded emphatically in agreement. "You've shown us how."

"But—"

"Go on," Halla said, jerking her head toward the dragon in the distance.

Cristov's eyes widened. He looked longingly toward the dragon and then back to Halla.

"Are you afraid, then?" she taunted. She grabbed him

and turned him toward the dragon. "There's your future. Go on, Impress! Impress a bronze for us all and show them at High Reaches. Show them what to expect from Fire Hold."

She gave him one final push and turned away, walking back to the waiting crowd of miners.

Head held high, Cristov walked to his future.

Dragon's fire way up high,
Light the way, protect the sky.
Dragon's flame, burning bright,
Char away the Thread mid-flight.

Epilogue

As C'TOV CIRCLED DOWN, he was surprised by how much Fire Hold had changed in the three Turns since his Impression of bronze Sereth.

He was not surprised to see Halla standing in the center of all the activity, but he was surprised at how tall and graceful she had grown. She raised a hand as soon as she identified him and then was jumping up and down, waving both hands frantically to catch his attention.

C'tov smiled. *Ready?*

Ready, Sereth agreed. The bronze dived and then flipped wingtip over wingtip, rolling around in the air so that the world was one moment below, next moment beside, next moment above, beside again and, finally, properly below. A surge of elation spread through dragon and rider while beneath them erupted noises first of fear, then of amazement and outright pandemonium.

I think they know we're here, C'tov said with a huge grin. He asked Sereth to land in the clearing.

Halla had grown into a great beauty; for a moment C'tov's heart faltered and he wondered whether it had been a mistake to return, particularly on this festive day. The moment lasted only as long as it took Halla to race across the distance and grab him in her arms tightly.

"You came, oh, we'd hoped you'd come!" she roared into his good ear, her exuberance complete and unfeigned.

Just as C'tov thought he might recover, another figure thundered into him and grabbed both him *and* Halla into a huge bear hug.

Pellar? C'tov thought to himself in amazement. C'tov had never imagined that Pellar could grow so tall and broad. Indeed, the bronze rider felt nearly dwarfed by the other.

The two fireminers pulled back as one and in that instant, C'tov lost any misgivings he'd had at coming back. Pellar's gentle movements were complemented and amplified by the exuberant but indefinably graceful movements of Halla.

Just as he, C'tov, was forever bonded with Sereth, so were Pellar and Halla bonded to each other. They moved, C'tov decided, like parts of the same body, with a respect and strength that flowed between them.

"I'm glad I came," he replied, and he realized that he truly was. He took a moment to grab Pellar and pull him into a deep hug, putting into his motion all the gratitude he felt for the other's selflessness Turns gone by. Strengthened by the warm embrace, he pushed Pellar away and stared deep in his eyes. Then he turned to Halla. "Would you let us talk alone for a moment?"

Halla raised a hand toward Pellar, who nodded in response. Halla cocked her head at both of them. "Only for a moment, no longer," she declared and raced back to the other miners of the hold.

Pellar followed her prancing movement with his eyes until she was lost in the throng, then politely turned his attention back to C'tov.

C'tov turned to Sereth, unable to keep the joy of Impression from brightening his face. He turned back to Pellar again, looking serious.

"You could have had him, you know," he said softly. "I'm sure you would have got a bronze."

Pellar met his friend's eyes and nodded slowly, glancing only briefly at the beautiful bronze dragon.

"Why?" C'tov asked, his face full of honest inquiry.

Pellar pulled something from his tunic and handed it to C'tov. It was a tiny yellow flower. He reached into another pocket and pulled out a second yellow flower. Beckoning politely to C'tov to hand the first flower back, Pellar gently took the two flowers and wound them together by the stems. He handed the paired flowers back to C'tov.

C'tov looked at them and then at Pellar. "I don't understand."

Pellar pointed to the flowers and then to C'tov and Sereth. Then Pellar pointed to the flowers again and to himself and off to where Halla had vanished.

"You are bound to Halla like I am to Sereth?" C'tov guessed. "I'd say that everyone sees that," he added with a laugh.

Pellar waggled a hand in response: not quite. He turned away from C'tov and gestured far off in the distance. C'tov followed his gesture and spotted a meadow full of yellow flowers, the same as those Pellar had produced.

The flowers are on mounds, Sereth, with his greater eyesight, informed him.

"Graves?" C'tov asked Pellar. "Halla was the one who put the flowers on the graves?"

Pellar smiled and nodded.

"But you could have still Impressed and brought Halla to the Weyr," C'tov protested. He wouldn't have traded his bond with Sereth for anything, but he couldn't help feel that the chance should have been Pellar's instead.

Pellar turned back to C'tov and nodded, his lips pursed in acknowledgment.

"So why didn't you?"

Pellar pointed to the two twined flowers in his hand. He crumpled them up and then pointed to the graves in the distance.

"If you and Halla weren't here, then no one would tend the graves?" C'tov guessed.

Pellar nodded, then held up a hand—there was more. He raised both hands and made the gesture of pushing away, turning in a great circle.

"And no one would care for the Shunned," C'tov guessed.

Pellar nodded.

"That still doesn't seem enough to exchange for a dragon," C'tov said.

Pellar held up a hand again for patience, then raised the other and grabbed them together, going down on one knee—pleading.

"Whatever you want," C'tov told him fervently. "Always and forever."

Pellar shook his head and held up just a finger—only once.

"Anytime," C'tov corrected him firmly. "Ask away."

Pellar looked very nervous, which surprised C'tov. For a moment the bronze rider wondered if he had promised more than he could deliver, then the moment passed as he resolved that he would meet any request Pellar placed on him.

Pellar pointed, hesitantly to his head, and then to Sereth's great head.

C'tov grasped the request instantly. *Sereth, what does Pellar want to say to me?*

C'tov waited, trying to control his anxiousness, as he

felt his dragon communicating with another. It was an odd feeling, and C'tov forced any jealousy out of his mind. After all, he could talk with Sereth anytime.

Pellar, and C'tov was surprised by the warmth of his dragon's tone when referring to the mute harper, *says that Halla is his voice; that he is her song; and only together can they make music.* The dragon paused for a moment. *The music they make is compassion, and their song is for all Pern.*

Keep reading for an excerpt from

Dragon Harper,

a brand-new Dragonriders of Pern novel from
Anne McCaffrey and Todd McCaffrey

Available in hardcover at bookstores everywhere
Published by Del Rey Books

White robe, high hopes
Hatching Grounds, tight throats
Sands heat, eggs move
Shells crack, hearts prove.

"PUT THIS ON," D'vin said to Cristov as they rushed to the Hatching Grounds. The white robe was the traditional garb for candidates, as every child on Pern knew from the Teaching Ballads.

Cristov suddenly realized that his heart was racing, his throat dry. In not much longer than it took D'vin's bronze dragon to go *between*—no more time than it took to cough three times—Cristov went from being a miner recovering from an injury to being a candidate for a Hatching.

This can't be happening, he thought. It should have been Pellar.

Pellar was the mute Harper who had rescued Cristov when his mine had collapsed, had saved Cristov when Tenim had purposely exploded the old firestone mine, and who had had a fire-lizard before Tenim's hunting bird had killed it—and had nearly killed Pellar, as well.

Pellar deserved to be a candidate . . . but Pellar had insisted upon remaining at the newly named Fire Hold to help the young holdless girl, Halla, manage the Shunned of Pern to redeem their honor by mining the firestone of Pern.

"Cristov!" The voice, close by his ear, startled him. "You're here! Excellent!"

Cristov's eyes widened as he recognized Kindan. Turns back, he and Kindan had been enemies. Back then, Cristov had despised watch-whers, just as he'd been taught by his father. Kindan's father had been a wherhandler, a person bonded to the ugly night-loving creatures who were only distant cousins to the great dragons that protected Pern. Infected by his father's attitudes, Cristov had despised Kindan, and they'd fought many times as youngsters. In the end, however, Cristov had realized that it was Kindan who had been right and his father who had been wrong—and Cristov had found himself, at an early age, making a grown man's choice and doing what was right instead of what was expected. He'd even come to regard the ugly watch-whers with respect bordering on awe. And now he greeted Kindan with a huge grin.

Kindan saw the robe clasped in Cristov's hand and his eyebrows rose. He held up his hand and showed Cristov that he, too, had the white robe of a candidate.

"Great, we can go together," he said to Cristov, as he pulled his robe over his head and tied it with the white belt.

"I thought you wanted to be a harper," Cristov said in surprise.

"Harpers can be dragonriders, too," Kindan replied with a big grin.

"You'll be certain to Impress, after your watch-wher," Cristov said. "Probably a bronze, too!"

Kindan shook his head. "I'll just be happy to Impress," he replied. "I'll leave the bronzes to you."

"Cristov, Kindan, hurry!"

They both turned and saw Sonia, the healer's daughter, also dressed in white robes. "Oh, I do hope that egg's a queen!"

Cristov knew that Sonia had been eyeing the funnily-marked egg on the Hatching Ground for some time.

Traditionally, though, the queen dragon would carefully push aside any queen eggs, and Jessala's Garirth hadn't done so.

In fact, the egg looked so odd that the Weyr's healer, Sonia's father S'son, had been asked to examine it to be sure it was whole.

Garirth was so old that her gold hide was a mere pale yellow, and Jessala, her rider, was so pained with age that she rarely moved from her quarters. It was entirely possible that age had caused this egg to have come out *wrong* somehow. But S'son had declared it fine.

D'vin gestured for them to go forward, saying, "I'll watch from the stands!"

Together the three moved to join the other candidates on the Hatching Grounds.

There were only twenty-three eggs on the Grounds. Cristov had learned that traditionally a queen would lay as few as thirty and as many as forty or more eggs. That Garirth had lain so few was a further indication of her extreme age.

Sonia, who had been examining the other candidates carefully, groaned. "There aren't enough candidates! There are only twenty boys and twenty-two eggs. And there are no other girls, either."

A rush of cold air from dragon wings startled them and they turned to see a smattering of boys and girls rush forward, dressed in white robes.

"Those are Benden colors," Sonia said, pointing to a dragonrider waving in the distance. "B'ralar must have sent for them."

"It's M'tal!" Kindan exclaimed, waving excitedly to the Benden Weyrleader. M'tal waved back and gave him a thumbs-up for good luck.

"What if one of the Benden girls Impresses the queen?" Cristov asked.

"She'll stay here," Sonia said. "But I wouldn't be surprised if she found herself Weyrwoman at the moment of Hatching." She cast a worried look at Garirth, whose head lolled listlessly on the ground beyond them. "I think Garirth and Jessala are only waiting for the hatchlings before they go *between* forever; they're both so tired with age."

The humming noise of the dragons rose louder. Cristov felt the sound in his very bones, reverberating. The noise was so loud it should have been deafening, yet Cristov felt no fear.

"Over here!" Sonia called to the other girls, waving toward the strange egg. They gave her a surprised look before joining her. To herself she muttered, "Whew! I was afraid the queen wouldn't have a decent choice!"

"We're supposed to be over there," Kindan said to Cristov, gesturing to the other boys clustered in the distance.

"I shouldn't be here," Cristov said. "I'm a miner."

Kindan shook his head and told him feelingly, "More than anyone you should be here, Cristov. You earned the right and you were Searched."

Cristov started to explain that D'vin had come for Pellar, not him, but Kindan shushed him. "Look!"

Cristov saw that the eggs were now rocking from side to side. One of them had a crack in it, then another, then a third. Cristov thought like a miner, imagining the blows required to break the shell. But suddenly he squinted, perplexed—the shells were cracking far more than he thought natural. He'd rapped one of the shells himself on the Hatching Grounds, and he'd held an old bit of shell in his hands, so he knew its strength.

And yet now the shells were shattering rapidly, and, strangely, Cristov started to get the feel for which shell would crack next. Something about the dragons' humming. It was as if their humming was helping the hatchlings. As if, Cristov realized suddenly, the dragons' humming resonated with the shells themselves.

The dragons' pitch increased just before one hatchling broke his shell in half and burst forth. Cristov started to take a nervous step backward but found Kindan's hand on his arm.

"They're scared," Kindan said. "They're just little and they're frightened."

Cristov could see that it was true. Even though the brown hatchling towered over Cristov, he could see that it was frightened. It creeled sharply as it searched among the Candidates and then—it found its mate. Cristov saw the look of glowing astonishment on the youngster's face, the look of fear breaking into a huge grin as boy and dragon were united in a bond that only death could break.

"You are the most beautiful dragon on all Pern, Finderth," the youngster cried aloud as he grabbed the wobbly brown dragonet in a great hug.

Kindan waved at the boy, calling, "Well done, Jander!" Then he blushed and corrected himself: "I mean, J'der."

But not everything went well. Some of the Benden lads were too frightened and didn't move out of the way of a creeling green. One youth was brutally trampled and tossed aside by the green's awkward stumbling to lie in a bloody heap nearly a dragonlength away.

"Look out!" Kindan called, prodding Cristov as a baby bronze came their way, searching among the candidates for its mate. It tore past them and then stopped, crying piteously.

Cristov remembered what D'vin had said would happen if there was no candidate for a hatchling: *It will go between forever.*

"Come on," he said, tugging at Kindan. They couldn't let the bronze hatchling get away. But Kindan was gazing across the Hatching Ground, saying, "Look, Sonia's egg is hatching!"

Urgently, Cristov sidestepped around Kindan and raced up to the forlorn bronze. He grabbed its tail and yanked. "Back here," he shouted desperately. "We're back here!"

There you are! a voice said suddenly. The dragon's whirling eyes were looking right at him. *I've been looking for you.*

"It's a queen," Kindan shouted over his shoulder, unaware of the drama that was unfolding behind him. "And it looks—yes, Sonia has Impressed the queen. Cristov—" And then Kindan finally turned to look over his shoulder.

The grin on his face slipped as his mind was flooded with memories of Kisk, the green watch-wher he had once shared a bond with. He swallowed hard and squared his shoulders. I gave her up, he reminded himself, wondering if perhaps that rendered him undesirable to the hatchlings.

Briefly he recalled Nuella's brilliant smile as Kindan encouraged her to ride the watch-wher *between* to the cave-in that had trapped her father, brother, and eight other miners. Only blind Nuella could have visualized the image needed to guide the heat-seeing watch-wher safely. So giving Kisk to her had been a good decision, everyone had agreed. And it meant that Kindan wasn't trapped forever in the mines with a watch-wher. He was free to become a harper, maybe even a dragonrider . . . but not this time. He shook himself out of his reverie.

"C'tov?" he asked, using the honorific contraction for the first time. "What's your dragon's name?"

The other lad's eyes shone with a brilliance that Kindan had never seen before.

"My dragon?" Cristov repeated in surprise. He turned to the bronze hatchling in silent communion. "His name is Sereth."

"Congratulations, dragonrider," Kindan said firmly, reaching forward to slap C'tov on the shoulder.

A hideous sound erupted behind them and they all turned. Garirth was upright, her multifaceted eyes whirling in a frantic red. She let out one more despairing wail and then was gone forever, *between*.

Kindan bowed his head. Jessala was no more, or her dragon wouldn't have departed so dramatically. The two had survived long enough to see the hatchlings Impressed. Whether it was the joy or the burden of extreme age that finally overwhelmed the queen's rider did not matter—the Weyrwoman of High Reaches Weyr was dead. When he raised his head again, he turned to Sonia and her young queen dragon. Sonia was now the Weyrwoman.

All the eggs had hatched. There were none left for him.

"Forgive me, C'tov," Kindan said, bowing to his friend, "but I think I'd best get my gear. There will be much harpering tonight, and Master Murenny will want to be informed of the news."

C'tov nodded absently, his attention focused exclusively on the most amazing, marvelous, and brilliant creature beside him.